Waiting
for
Something Else

Waiting for Something Else

MARTIN CLOUTIER

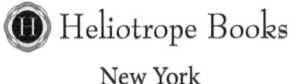 Heliotrope Books

New York

Heliotrope Books LLC
heliotropebooks@gmail.com

ISBN 978-1-956474-62-6
ISBN 978-1-956474-66-3 eBook

Cover design by Isip Xin
Typeset by Naomi Rosenblatt with AJ&J Design

I said to my soul, be still, and wait without hope
For hope would be hope for the wrong thing; wait without love,
For love would be love of the wrong thing; there is yet faith
But the faith and the love and the hope are all in the waiting.
Wait without thought, for you are not ready for thought:
So the darkness shall be the light, and the stillness the dancing.
—T.S. Eliot, *East Coker*

… but had she ever loved in the noblest way, where man and woman, having lost themselves in sex, desire to lose sex itself in comradeship?
—E.M. Forster, *Howard's End*

Prologue: Brooklyn 2006

They came from the neighborhood—the newly rich, the comfortably young, the entrenched urban pioneers. And they came from the city—the trendsetters, jetsetters, the epicurean explorers. The paupers who saved all month, and the pampered with Daddy's credit card. They followed food critics and bloggers—Eaters, Yelpers, Chowhounds of renown—across the potholes of the Brooklyn Bridge and into the capital appreciations of a new millennium. Only six years in and the new century promised gastronomic delights in every ghetto, each abandoned building and empty warehouse just waiting to be repurposed into a vegan bakery or macrobiotic kitchen. Having survived Y2K and 9/11, as well as WMDs and the reelection of GWB, they craved satisfaction from the savory and the sweet.

They came for the white truffle honey, the rabbit saltimbocca, the veal cheeks, the speck. Some came for the cozy brick walls and velvet curtains that on Saturday nights, with the hum of voices and strings of stereo jazz, turned the tiny space into a gently throbbing womb. Others favored the smoky mirrors where they could examine themselves between courses, peeking out between the gold letters of *Biere et Vin*, *Armagnac et Pastis*.

They came for the cheap thrill, the controlled anxiety, the buzz. To see Smith Street—former heroin alley, hijackers' highway, bordered by the Brooklyn House of Detention on one end and the Gowanus Housing Projects on the other, where, in the past, one didn't venture after dark unless for a forty or a fix—now, gentrified, sanitized and whitened: the fixes all consumer, the forties, microbrews. The street once settled with dollar stores,

Latino social clubs and hair braiding salons, presently transformed into Pilates studios and handmade paper shops. The ethnics had gone, but they left behind their merchandise in the form of clothing boutiques and restaurants of every ilk: Thai, Peruvian, Bhutanese, Guyanese, Malaysian, Crustacean. And the restaurant at the top of this food chain, the anchor store in the Smith Street Mall was Bartholomew—a former bail bonds office turned bistro. Named after its owner in the grand tradition of Bouley, Daniel, and Jean-Georges—chefs so exultant they surpassed all apostrophes. Not Bartholomew's place, but his very being. Patrons weren't merely occupying his restaurant, but inside Bartholomew himself—tasting Bartholomew—diners in divine communion with their culinary deity, every peppercorn in the grinder proof of their god's essential goodness.

If they came from Manhattan, they came with expectations. And sometimes the small restaurant with its plain brick façade couldn't fulfill them. There was no coat check, no elongated bar or sexy mixologist, no giant statues, water walls, or crystal chandeliers. Just a frosted glass door with a cursive B. People often walked right by without noticing. Then they would call, irate, and claim they'd been given bad directions. Inside, the room held only twelve tables with plain white cloths and small wooden chairs. A lectern taken from a local high school separated the door from the diners. Its angled surface still showed the carved initials of love struck students: *MB + LV, Crazy Dawg* ♥ *Lil Shorty.*

Even tourists came with expectations. In the early aughts, before the maligned borough had yet reached peak gentrification, before the term gentrification became known simply as Brooklynized, judgments still prevailed: Brooklyn as second rate, below par, provincial; Brooklyn as another way to say New Jersey; Brooklyn as a foreign land that needed to be traversed with a local guide and a language dictionary. Sightseers came with ironic smiles and eyebrows arched: eyes ready to roll at the first elongated vowel, tongues prepared to tsk at the drop of an R. On the lookout for a neck tattoo, a fist pump, a shooting. They anticipated being both charmed and revolted, entertained by the accents and repelled at the velour tracksuits; engaged by the immigrants, yet confused by the nose rings and tribal scarring. That gourmet food could happen in this clusterfuck of beatniks and ethnics was a statement that required investigation before it was thoroughly dismissed.

It was astounding that desire could be so mitigated. That people could give up the great dining rooms of Manhattan. Forgo the comforts of Babbo and Momofuku for the earnest and the plain. But what was desire anyway but the need for something else? The itch that keeps moving as soon as it's scratched. They may have grown up on Hamburger Helper but their palates had been reprogrammed by extra virgin olive oil and artichoke foam.

And between their comings and goings, munchings and nibblings, there may have appeared a small inkling that desire didn't originate in the biggest or most beautiful. Desire might possibly be found in a boxy bistro with rickety chairs; in the blue-veined hand clutching a rubbery penis; in the pendulous breasts swinging over a bloated stomach—desire always found a way.

And so they kept coming. In Prada heels and Puma slides. Wearing both Chanel and Canal Street. Expecting their palates to be transported and their throats galvanized. Hoping that steak au poivre would make their jobs bearable and their husbands less boorish. Believing that duck confit would confer that extra soupçon of happiness. Of comfort. Of mother's love wrapped in seven layers of rendered fat and crispy skin. Yet, for all their frivolity, these places—these gastronomic palaces—did mean something. They meant position and money and the cloying complex feeling of privilege. For to even know about them, to find them in their hole-in-the-wall destinations, to be cognizant of the difference between them and the corner diner counted as some kind of status. And this, on most nights, was enough to quiet the subterranean fears of emptiness and ennui.

1: Poor Bald Duck

Just as every castle has a castellan and every president a chief of staff, Bartholomew had James—the man managing expectations: supervising the staff, organizing the inventory, counting the tips, running the reports, turning complaints into compliments, and negotiating the frenzied mood swings of Bartholomew himself. Having only been in the city for nine months, plucked out of the Midwest like a gangly milkweed and plopped in the Daedalian vahz of this James Beard award-winning restaurant, one might have thought him ill-equipped for the task. Yet, he proved surprisingly adept at his job. A job, which Melissa, Bart's wife, described in his interview as something akin to a peacekeeping soldier. A Midwestern girl herself, she didn't like New York servers, as they came with too much attitude and too little gratitude. She usually hired from out of state, preferably as far from the city as possible.

Though Melissa's bias for alien help may have secured James the job, it was his ability to sacrifice himself on the front lines that sustained it. The balance was fragile: a couple of late arrivals, one overlooked reservation, or a lingering table could decimate his defenses and create a mob at the host stand, their impatient huffs threatening to take over the room. One time, a man told James his bald head made him look like an uncircumcised penis.

Twenty-six years of Buddhism had made him extraordinarily good at defusing anger. No matter how irate the customer, James remained humble. Whether holding out a chair or setting down a menu, he maintained an awareness of his movements and sought to Do No Harm. He greeted every customer with soft eyes and a benign smile. They would come busting through the door with their jagged New York energy only to be walloped by his serene countenance: the deliberate slowness of him contemplating the seating chart, the ease at which he escorted them to their table, one careful step at a time, eyes subtly taking in the gilt of the mirrors, the roughness of the brick, and leaving them just enough time to register the electric tones of Miles Davis or the syncopation of Dave Brubeck on the stereo system. By the time a customer landed at their seat, indicated by James's supple arm embracing the air around it, they would be soothed into a benign stupor.

Given such an environment, it was difficult for customers to complain. And when they did, whether about too much salt in the Saltimbocca, or not enough beef in the Daube de Boeuf, he would remove his oversized glasses and bathe their burning foreheads with his brown doe eyes. *When you have been shot by a poison arrow, it is more important to get the poison out than to retaliate at the shooter.* And the best remedy for poison was to dilute it with loving-kindness. He would imagine them as children, with a child's lack of control. And, as one would do with a child, he'd guide them back to a state of equilibrium. He would bend his tall frame and enfold a thin arm around the back of their chair and radiate empathy: "I'm so sorry." "We'll fix this immediately." Most of the time the complainers just needed to expel their anger, and James was the all-purpose sponge, ready to absorb it all.

Some days it seemed he couldn't dilute the poison fast enough. Still, he took pride in performing the nightly miracle of feeding the pulchritudes—turning money into sustenance for the beautiful people. Give him a hundred dollars and he would give you gastronomic illumination. Though inevitably it was an impure transaction, a zigzagging detour on the road to spiritual enlightenment. Not like dropping a mound of rice into a beggar's bowl, or giving a cup of water to a thirsty monk. The people who came here were not enlightened or even nice. The Buddha said, *Giving food to a hundred bad people is not as good as giving food to a single good person.* So each night James looked for that single good person. The person not here for the hype or to impress his new client or to get laid right after the check was dropped. A person with a kind face, unclouded by striving. He would stand behind the lectern and let the wet hum of sounds wash over him: the shreddings of solids, the sippings of liquids: glass stems pinging, knives scraping plates. He would search the room of masticating mouths and swallowing throats for his good person. And most times he would find them. It might be the quiet woman at a table of ladies arguing over the optimum circumference of a penis. Or a grandfather explaining the French menu to his grandson. Or the hipster with ear plates who was knitting a sweater for his dog in between courses.

Usually, finding his single good person soothed the sting of poison arrows, but tonight, all the diners looked mercenary: the women plumed with spiked and colored locks, the men prickly with aggressive facial hair, their collective eyes dulled from a day staring at screens, skin as blue as fluorescent lights. Tonight, the restaurant was inexplicably overbooked, and people crowded the door claiming to have reservations not listed on the sheet. As more patrons demanded to be seated, his anxiety elevated as if an angry man were trampolining on his stomach. *Holding onto anger is like grasping a red-hot coal with the intent to throw it at someone else; only you are the one who gets burned.*

A woman stood by the door with a cluster of folks waiting for a table. With her helmet of jet-black hair and nicotine-colored skin, she reminded him of his grandma. His dead grandma. Whose funeral he had just returned from, flying back in the wee hours of the morning with barely a chance at sleep before returning to work. Fine lines accordioned her mouth. She gazed about the restaurant as if it were yet another "I Heart Nanna" coffee mug she didn't want. She was with a middle-aged couple in coordinating cargo shorts. He told them they could go to the bar next door, and he would collect them when their table was ready. They carefully escorted her out. Before she left, she waved a bejeweled hand in his direction, either a thank you or a dismissal; he couldn't tell the difference.

Coming back from the funeral in Ann Arbor, with the plane circling the illuminated towers of New York and the gaping hole in the middle of downtown, he'd thought about how easily one light could be extinguished— one room went dark, another lit up. On the moving walkway at JFK, he stood like an object. People bumped and jostled him, their bags snagging his ankles. In this last year, he hadn't spoken much to his grandma. She would have hated Bartholomew. She would have found it overpriced and under-nourishing: *Where's the mashed potatoes? Where's the brisket?* She would have scorned the brick walls and wide plank floors: *Dirt catchers.*

And she wouldn't believe for a second that checkered curtains and smoky mirrors transformed a dingy office space into a Parisian bistro.

As the early birds got up to leave, crumbs twinkling in their beards, stomachs stretching their yoga pants, he smiled and said: good night, bonsoir, bonne nuit. He tried to send out good energy, but all he could picture were the hundred-dollar meals curling through their intestines and coming out in painful discharges. He visualized his mandala and the circles of life and death, but kept returning to his customers on the toilet with pained expressions on their faces and liquefied foie gras spraying from their asses.

"Here you go, James. I made you a little pick-me-up." Sherry handed him a pint glass.

He took a sip. It was half pineapple juice, half vodka. He looked at her and raised his eyebrows, and then stashed the glass underneath the lectern. He didn't condone drinking on the job, but he knew she was trying to comfort him. They'd had a long talk at pre-shift about dead grandmothers— hers had died when she was fourteen—and she seemed sympathetic, perhaps even simpatico.

She gave him a salute and shot back to clear her tables. He watched her stacking the plates in the crook of her arm. Her wide cheeks and blonde braid, which she wore in a circle around her head, lent a wholesome appearance to her solid stance, resembling a rough-and-tumble milkmaid who at any minute might slap you with her pail. She wasn't clearing from the right, and he made a note to mention it later. It was impossible to think that after all these months of working side by side, they were finally becoming close. He hesitated to imagine his dead grandmother as the agent that brought them together, but from every toppled tree new life arises.

James didn't believe in heaven. His grandma had either dissolved into nirvana or was immediately reincarnated into something else: a bumblebee, a bullfrog, the future president of the Anti-Defamation League. She was gone, unreachable, and he could accept that. Life, like death, was about waiting around to become something else. Something you didn't know or want or perhaps even care about. And when you became something else, there was no continuity. The butterfly did not remember the caterpillar. The golden chalice didn't recall the rock that formed it.

It seemed as if he'd been waiting for something to happen his entire adult life. The chance that would allow him to shed his hairy slug-like body and grow wings. He believed coming to New York would facilitate this transformation. Through swimming and yoga, he'd lost forty-five pounds, making him height/weight proportionate for the first time in his adult life. But he still felt the heft of his former body; he continued to rattle around in his cocoon wanting caterpillar things: the salty comfort of nacho cheese, binge-watching *Battlestar Galactica*. He couldn't acknowledge his butterfly desires, yet they were equally compelling. The wisdom of thousands of years of Buddhism warned about the perils of desire and attachment. But still, he could not accept being alone. He could not accept being merely a restaurant manager. No matter how it clashed with his spiritual teachings, he coveted—he yearned—he stretched his hairy antennae into the world, striving to gorge himself on its leafy goodness.

His grandma wouldn't have approved of Sherry. She wore her t-shirts too tight and her mascara too thick. Technically, she was an "older woman," though only by five years, and still eight years younger than his last girlfriend, Tracy, whom his grandma called "the cradle snatcher." She also wouldn't have appreciated Sherry's cussing. After a few drinks, she had the mouth of a sailor, if the sailor had been raised in a whorehouse by a family of rap musicians. The space between her front teeth made her look either stupid or slutty, depending on which school of dental spacing you followed. Blondes, of course, were always suspect. And milky-skinned, blue-eyed ones were especially dubious with Jews. Not that his family practiced Judaism anymore, but his grandma had always hoped if the religion couldn't be carried on, at least the genes might be. Though where a Buddhist in Michigan was supposed to find an eligible Jewess who wanted to convert to the Sevenfold Path was an issue she had never addressed.

He checked the reservation book and noted that if half the diners didn't leave within the next fifteen minutes, the finely oiled machine of his restaurant was going to seize up and cease to function. With a deferential bow, he picked up credit cards from two tables and ran them through the computer.

The main problem with Sherry, aside from the fact that up until today she'd not shown him one iota of interest, was that she already had a live-in boyfriend: Sean—the artist. A temperamental manbaby who careened from crisis to crisis, and required more nurturing than a hothouse orchid infected with root rot. Still. What was he supposed to do with his feelings? Sweep them up like so many broken wine glasses and toss them into the recycling bin of his soul? Hope they someday composted into a great film or epic poem or significant journal entry? He needed some kind of hope. Even if it was a mistake. Daiyu, the sensei at his Zendo in Michigan, used to say: *a mistake was only an opportunity to change.* And he wanted to change. He wanted to change everything about his life. And that too, he understood, was also a mistake.

He gripped the sides of his lectern and watched Roger and Sherry at the cappuccino machine. She was laughing at something he said. The steamer slipped from her hand and she sprayed herself with milk. Roger took Bar-Naps and dabbed at her breasts with disaffected interest, his long fingers tapping out some mechanical rhythm. Gay guys could get away with anything: mean jokes, outrageous clothes, and fondling a girl's breasts without so much as a by-your-leave. Every woman wanted a man as funny, well-groomed and emotionally available as their gay boyfriend. On the evolutionary scale, gays were the new and improved men, and straight guys, Neanderthal lunkheads, soon to be extinct.

A splinter of wood slid underneath his fingernail. Roger didn't deserve to daub those breasts. For him, they were probably no more than fatty lumps stretching out her shirt. Whereas James had spent many a night considering their weight, heft, and malleability, while his hand pumped furiously below the covers. One could say he loved those breasts. Though love was perhaps a ridiculous exaggeration of his feelings; it distorted the depth and selflessness of love. When it came to Sherry, he was experiencing lust, stabbing-at-the-viscera lust. But if he conceived of it as love, if it flourished in his mind as a compassionate and eternal union of non-possessive love, then at some later date it might become so. He had been meditating on transforming his base desires. Sometimes he meditated with an erection sticking straight up from his sweatpants like a weapon waiting to discharge. But already desire was transforming through his chakras, through his solar plexus and into his heart: *breathe in—love, breathe out—lust.*

"Excuse me." An old man with a liver-spotted forehead tapped his shoulder. "We have an eight o'clock reservation. Kraft-Mueller."

James tried to manifest a tenderness for those spots—to think of them as valiant medals of long-standing service in the war of life. "Yes, sir. Welcome to Bartholomew." Another group was pushing in behind the old man and his wife, and he noticed Sherry dropping a check on table six. "Your table should be ready in less than fifteen minutes."

"My reservation was for eight, and I expect to be seated at eight."

"I apologize for the delay. It shouldn't be more than ten to fifteen minutes."

The man leaned on the podium and exhaled a stream of dragon breath. "I'm diabetic and hypoglycemic and can't stand for long periods. I need to be seated immediately."

James retrieved two extra stools and squeezed the couple around the small bar, next to a foursome of gesticulating ladies. He brought a glass of champagne for the man's wife and some orange juice for the man's low blood sugar, but when he put his arm around the back of the man's bar stool, an image came to mind of the geezer choking on his drink, coughing up little dollops of orange pulp.

The other group at the door also claimed to have a reservation not on the books. The only explanation was Melissa. In the early afternoon, before James came in, she took it upon herself to answer the phone. He'd often find reservations scribbled on the backs of envelopes or torn-off magazine pages. Sometimes Melissa would forget altogether and call in when she discovered an odd scrap with a name and date in her pocket. Fortunately, thanks to his meticulous record keeping, this seldom amounted to catastrophe. It was policy at most upscale restaurants to overbook by ten percent anyway. Every night he drew a seating chart with tables in color-coded time signatures, the first turn in blue, the second in red. But now, his seating chart was starting to resemble the chaotic motion of a Jackson Pollock painting as he struggled to fit sixty-some people into a forty-two-seat restaurant.

Roger walked over and slapped a check on the lectern. "Void the oxtails on seventeen."

"Here. I'll give you the manager card."

"It's *your* job." He pointed his fingers in gun formation and marched back through the aisle.

This was not how he imagined life in New York City. This was not how he imagined managing an upscale restaurant. Nine months ago, when he first gave notice at The Lamplighter Grill in Ann Arbor, he envisioned himself escorting movie stars to tables, while waiters imperceptibly bowed as he crossed their path. The captain of a ship was how he used to think of himself. Even Melissa's description of a peacekeeping soldier held the allure that he was protecting his crew from assaults and air strikes. However, he was slowly beginning to realize he was only the swabby, cleaning up the messes and taking orders from everyone on board.

The death of his grandma had sparked an existential crisis: What was he doing with his life? He'd come 613 miles to start a new life, and he was essentially doing the same thing he was doing in Ann Arbor, except with more stress and less disposable income. Everyone was so mean here. How could he ever find a girlfriend, much less a friend?

"James! Help me clear three." Melissa grabbed his elbow and dragged him to the table. Her nails dug into his skin.

As a Buddhist and pacifist, his father abhorred any kind of violence. He had never let James play with toy guns and even censored his television programs. He was nine years old before he saw his first cartoon. At a friend's house, he watched in horror and exhilaration as Elmer Fudd shot the feathers off Daffy Duck. He was jittery for days afterward thinking about that poor bald duck. He had the same jittery feeling now, thinking about Roger's fingers, Melissa's fingernails, and that old man's forehead.

A woman in a cashmere shawl at table eight tapped him on the leg. "Young man, could you find me some salt?" He smiled and nodded—*bullet in the head.*

He tried to calm his breathing and allow the images to pass. Even when kids in school used to make fun of him for being a "fat blubber butt," he never had such violent reactions. He would usually dance and shake his butt, accepting their assessment and compounding their laughter. The pain wasn't as harsh if he inflicted it on himself.

In the kitchen, scraping the plates over the garbage, an image asserted itself: all the diners showered with bullets; heads falling into arugula salads, severed fingers flying into breadbaskets, bodies blown out of chairs and tiny rivulets of blood commingling with the white truffle oil. Not just dead, but cinematically dead—Sam Peckinpah dead. A fork clattered into the sink for emphasis.

"Hey! Who's watching the door?" Bart yelled. When things got busy, he hated people in the kitchen. Always the perfectionist, if he didn't have time to make each dish look flawless, Bart came down hard on himself and even harder on the staff. At six-foot-five, he could get pretty scary. In good moods, he hunched and stooped, making his voice higher-pitched so as not to be threatening. But in bad moods, he straightened his spine and shot black daggers in all directions. Between these two postures, he vacillated. When entering the kitchen, one never knew if one would be greeted by the gangly kid or the scary ogre.

"Get your ass back on the floor," Bart said. "I don't pay you to prance around my kitchen."

Patrons were lined up in front of the restroom; he pushed past them, hearing the distant base of Bart's curses.

"Excuse me?" A young girl with a diamond tennis bracelet waved. "I don't think my fish is quite cooked?"

"Oh, I'm sorry. We'll give it a bit more fire." *Knife in the esophagus, arrow in the heart.*

He couldn't go back to the kitchen now, especially with a refire. Even on quiet nights, Bart hated re-cooking food. As he carried the grilled Branzino in a funeral march to his own funeral, Sherry sped by on her way to pick up entrées. "Sherry? This needs more fire. Table two. Thanks." He plopped the fish in her hands as easily as removing the pin from a grenade and turned toward the door. Just before he passed table two, he heard a crash from the kitchen, sounding very much like a plate hitting the floor.

"I'm sorry, Ma'am." He leaned over Ms. Tennis Bracelet. "It'll be about ten more minutes. The chef is making you another fish." He didn't have time to feel guilty about Sherry; a new crowd had amassed at the door, and Melissa was eyeing the reservation book as if searching for a spell to cast away demons.

"Young man, I'm still waiting for my salt." The cashmere lady stopped him again.

"Of course." *Drawn, quartered, and head on a spike.* He walked over to Max, deeply absorbed in adding the gratuity on a check. "Max, your table five needs salt."

Max gazed back, amazed, as if asked to prove the existence of God, the grey hairs of his buzz cut bristling with indignation. "Kind of busy right now, James." Max was in his fifties, with a deep *basso profundo* voice and a passive bewilderment about life. He frequently misheard someone's order or entered the wrong dish on the computer, but customers forgave him anything because his sonorous voice made him seem like a fallen king.

"Just do it." James took a BarNap and wiped the top of his head. In college, they used to call him Wet Head. His roommate, who had a mop of unruly blond hair, was known as Bed Head.

Up front, the crowd closed in around Melissa.

He ran to the podium and grabbed the book.

"I'm looking for Como and it's not there," she whispered.

He checked the master sheet and did some quick calculations. He told Melissa to drop dessert menus on table twelve.

"I'm sorry." He turned to the Comos. "We'll have a table for you in less than thirty minutes. Our bar is full, but if you care to go next door and have a drink, we'll come and get you when your table is ready. Just bring the receipt and we'll deduct it from your check."

That seemed to appease the Comos, and they left in a chatty clatter.

Sherry then emerged from the kitchen carrying two plates of lobster cocktails. Wisps of hair caught in the corner of her eye and her jaw quivered slightly. The plates wavered; her pale cheeks held a burgeoning redness. Bart had obviously upset her. James had been the cause. He wanted to apologize, but the image of Roger and her laughing at the cappuccino machine kept spooling in his mind: laughing and daubing, laughing and daubing, Roger's long fingers.

He surveyed the dining room: at least three tables were getting ready to pay, Melissa had dropped checks on two more, and Roger was at the computer terminal drinking a bottle of beer. *Broken bottle gouging out eye socket.*

James put a hand over the touchscreen. "You're not supposed to be drinking on the floor."

"And what was that concoction you were imbibing at the podium, I wonder?"

"Even so, I wasn't drinking straight from the bottle."

"Do you want to observe my deep-throating technique?" Roger took the bottle and swallowed down to the label.

He moved to block Roger from the dining room and took the bottle from his hand. James was used to his brand of humor. He perpetually walked around in a cloud of innuendo, raining sexual irony on everyone. Sometimes, Roger would stroke his tie and say, "You know, James, there'll be only eight planets left after I destroy Uranus." Or, when Bart made spaghetti for staff meal, he would catch Max with a mouthful and say, "Hello spaghetti. I want you to meet my balls."

Roger slinked off, and James put a fresh roll of paper in the printer. Max arrived and swiped a credit card through the machine.

"Just so you know, James, I don't appreciate being yelled at on the floor." His cropped gray hair projected like some angry hedgehog. "I'm an adult human person. You're capable of getting salt just as much as I am."

After another hour, the gears of the restaurant machine unclogged, and what had been halting and grinding became humming and smooth. James stood in a bubble of calm with nothing to do. There was a certain letdown after a Saturday night rush, and he panicked, thinking he must have forgotten something. It was bewildering to discover that he wasn't needed, when for the last two hours everyone had been clamoring for his attention. Now, with the energy of the night dissipating, he was stuck again with his wet head and guilty conscience: he needed to apologize to Sherry.

She was back at the cappuccino machine: her delicate elbows fluttering about, tamping the coffee and twisting the handle into place.

"Um, Sherry?" The steamer squealed. She was focusing on her froth, acting all professional. "You know that Melissa wants us to serve on the left and clear from the right?"

"I was never told that."

"Yes. Well. I just thought I should mention it ..."

"No worries."

"It's a fine dining thing. You know, what they do in three-star restaurants."

"I worked in a couple of three-star restaurants, in case you forgot." She ladled out thick spoons of froth. He wished she would spill some on her shirt so he could daub around her breasts.

"That's right," he said. "And about the fish..."

"Next time you want a re-fire—take it to the kitchen yourself." She clanged the spoon on the grill and walked away.

So now it was official: he'd alienated every person on staff. Time to have a smoke.

He sat on the stoop next door and gazed at the sidewalk. Swirls of dirty little galaxies lodged in the cement, and he added to it his own comet of ash. The burning cigarette inched closer to the underside of his wrist; he felt a prickle of heat. The skin was delicate there—defenseless. In his nine months in New York, not only had he failed to find a girlfriend, he'd failed to find a friend. All because he didn't know how to talk to people; every conversation was a mathematical puzzle, posing some question he didn't know how to answer. Sherry was angry. Max hurt. Roger was ... whatever he was, and Bart was sure to blame him for the overbooked reservations. And then there were all those violent images, the aftershocks of which still reverberated in his head.

He tried to self-report his bodily sensations as Daiyu had taught him: shallow breath, racing heart, heat on his face and the back of his knees, moisture in his armpits and crotch, shame, sadness, thoughts about his own inadequacies, still more violent images. Sometimes living in the moment wasn't much fun.

The cigarette started to feel good the closer it came to his skin. Ash blackened his wrist and made curlicue patterns along his arm. Since coming to New York, he'd taken up smoking as a way to relax after work. He allowed himself one cigarette a night and felt totally defiled afterward, always making sure to brush his teeth and wash his hands.

He should have stayed in Michigan instead of rushing back to this war zone, but the funeral with its arcane rituals proved exasperating. His father, through some atavistic tick, had rediscovered Judaism and sought to execute all its pomp and circumstance, like some manic event planner organizing a theme party. Only the theme of this party was death. James found Jewish funeral customs spooky: the lowered chairs and shrouded mirrors, the solemn prayers that his father mumbled to himself, and the proscribed expressions of grief. It only confirmed his belief that Western religions were steeped in misery and retribution. The last Buddhist memorial service he attended featured a five-piece band that played Bee Gees covers and a potluck supper in the backyard with a chocolate fountain.

Much to his father's disappointment, he only stayed for the first day of Shiva. His mother went back to teaching the day after the funeral. His Aunt Barbara agreed to stay for the entire seven days, but only if she could sit on a regular chair and wear her teeth-whitening-strips. The rabbinical texts held no proscriptions on teeth-whitening strips, though James's father voiced strong opposition. He had sent a twenty-page email to the extended family on Jewish funeral rites. As a professor of philosophy at The

University of Michigan, he assumed two things: that everyone shared his enthusiasm about diverse ideologies, and that his textual interpretations were irrefutable.

This sudden concern for Judaism and rabbinical law came as quite a shock to James. A few weeks ago, his family had been committed if casual Mahayana Buddhists, decades-long members of The Society for Compassionate Wisdom. If they were now going to be Jews, he would have to reassess his whole position on pacifism and the P.L.O. When asked, his father replied, "Your grandmother was a Jew. We're burying her as a Jew. We owe her that much."

He couldn't understand it; his grandma wasn't the least bit religious. And his father had long ago embraced Buddhism as an escape from the rigid tenets of organized religion. Was this some kind of mid-life quest for his roots? Was he now going to travel to the Wailing Wall and pray for the Messiah? Get a timeshare in Boca?

James understood the universe was in a constant state of flux, and that people underwent transformations, but couldn't some changes be detrimental? The caterpillar didn't always become a butterfly; sometimes it changed into a moth that flew around light bulbs and got burnt.

His father had discovered Buddhism in his twenties and raised his family according to the teachings of The Eightfold Path. James had never been to a synagogue or atoned on Yom Kippur. On his mother's side, they were lapsed Lutherans. As a child, the only religious events he attended were meditation ceremonies at The Society for Compassionate Wisdom and tribute concerts to Ravi Shankar.

He spent the first day of Shiva with his family—drapes drawn, mirrors covered, the candle of his grandma's spirit blazing on the coffee table between them. James and his dad sat on wooden stools from Costco, the price tags still dangling underneath, while his aunt reclined on the couch, sipping Diet Coke from a straw and reading Entertainment Weekly. Occasionally, she would make some snide comment about Richard Gere or the Dalai Lama, her speech slightly slurred from the teeth-whitening strips. His dad occasionally stopped mouthing a psalm to cast a reproachful glance her way. Sometimes James caught him raising a bushy eyebrow in his direction, as if to say, "When are you going to get serious about your life and become a Jew?"

Some family friends stopped by, but, much to his father's consternation, there was never enough for a minyan. Around Ann Arbor, it would probably have been easier to find ten tree-worshipping druids than ten religious Jews, but by 2p.m., they reached peak Jew with nine adult males, and there was a push to find a tenth. Everyone scrolled through their phones, calling friends and acquaintances. Many discussed going to some of the shops on Washtenaw Avenue and conscripting the dry cleaner with the big nose or the curly-headed boy at Kinko's, but no one could confirm their heritage. In desperation, his father rushed out to enlist the mailman, whom he claimed to have overheard say "oy" one time when dropping a package. Unfortunately, he turned out to be a Jehovah's Witness and took the opportunity to discourse on "the end of times" and bestow on him a copy of The Watch Tower.

James had expected to see his ex-girlfriend Tracy at the funeral or at least the Shiva. They'd dated for nearly two years, until she broke things off after meeting a real estate salesman, who was a real "go-getter." She'd been to his grandma's for dinner, jet-skied with his family at their lake house and was in attendance at Vesak and Thanksgiving. When she didn't show, he violated several Jewish laws by shaving, showering, and changing his shirt, and drove to her place. He inhaled the loamy night air and thought about all his previous drives to Tracy's house, the tires chewing up the pavement, rolling out the promise of sex, every landmark along the way pointed toward procreation: the pink beauty salon with its labial curtains, the bosomy golden arches of McDonald's. Even Tracy's street name hinted at carnal delight, and he couldn't help plumping up as he turned down good ol' Hardon Avenue.

He shuffled around the porch in the new felt slippers his father had bought him—Jews in mourning weren't supposed to wear leather. He worried they were not the most masculine of footwear—felt slippers being just a notch above pajamas with feet. His khaki pants dangled off his hips from the absence of a belt, but he didn't mind; he wanted to flaunt his new slimmer body. His love handles were now merely love knobs. And he could actually feel a millimeter of space between his stomach and his polo shirt. He was going to flaunt his new New York body and show Tracy his victorious self. Her dumping him had provoked his move to New York—a reactive attempt to show her that his go-getterness could go even further. He still harbored a furtive wish that his long absence and improved presence would reawaken in her some feelings, even if those might be jealousy and regret.

As he knocked on her oak-paneled door, he felt like Odysseus returning home from the Trojan Wars. And, like a true conqueror, he had brought with him the spoils: a box of cupcakes from the famous bakery in the West Village. The one featured on TV shows and in magazine articles, where devotees lined up around the block to get their sugar fix. In New York, one might not have the best job or swankiest apartment, but one could easily afford the best cupcake. And this was usually enough to make the city bearable. These red velvet cupcakes would show Tracy that he was living at the center of the world, while she was still stuck in provincial Ann Arbor, where baked goods came in cellophane wrappers with tawdry pictures of pubescent girls named Lil Debbie.

When she answered the door, it quickly became clear that the only feelings being reawakened were ones of annoyance and ennui. She flipped open the screen on her Motorola RAZR while he made his perfunctory speech about being back in town for his grandmother's funeral. She told him she was waiting for her fiancé to come and celebrate her first sale as a real estate broker. Two bombshells that she exploded at his feet before even inviting him in and closing the door.

They had a brief, if awkward, conversation about death and the importance of living to the fullest, in which she said, "We all have to live our truth. I'm living mine now. I hope you can find yours." As if he had somehow stopped the mighty flow of her truth during the course of their relationship.

She went on to dissect the carcass of their relationship, laying out its organs on the stainless steel table of truth, while James stood there mute and somewhat stunned. She related that he was never her type. That his lack of ambition had caused her to question her own goals. And that during their relationship, she'd "acted out" due to frustration and unfulfilled desires.

The Buddha warned that each nugget of truth came with a bushel of suffering, and James didn't know how much more truth he could take. He stopped listening somewhere in the middle of her tirade, while images of Tracy skewered on a spit—burning on a pyre—harikari-ed with her own RAZR—flashed before him. He had no choice but to run out the door before she had finished. He didn't even give her the cupcakes.

In the car, he stuffed the cupcakes in his mouth, one by one, icing dripping down his chin. They tasted like bloody hearts—sugary, bloody hearts filled with rage and regret. By the time he got to the sixth, his brain was buzzing, and his stomach was full.

Driving down the tree-lined streets, he calculated Tracy's and his time together: twenty-one months and seven days. He calculated the time he had been gone: nine months and fourteen days. Total time knowing Tracy: two years, six months. She was only his second girlfriend, and he wondered at what point along this continuum he had stopped being her type. It seemed painfully clear that half of the women he had slept with had failed to find him attractive. Ignoring the stop signs, he sped through the leafy tunneled streets—a bullet in the barrel of a gun aimed at nothing at all.

When he pulled into the driveway, the moon was just visible over the house; hundreds of stars pinpricked the sky. A blue TV light flashed from the guest bedroom where his Aunt Barbara was staying.

Inside, his father was still stuck on his stool. He had put away the Talmud, but in keeping with his newly reclaimed Judaism, he was reading *Tuesdays with Morrie*. Candlelight flickered on the sheets covering the mirrors. James felt his silent rebuke for shaving, showering, and leaving the house during shiva.

He walked down their dark-paneled hall to the kitchen where his mother was hand-washing dishes in the sink.

"Why didn't you tell me Tracy was engaged?" He banged a palm on the counter.

"Is she? I didn't think she stayed with one man long enough."

"We were together for two years."

She chucked the last plate in the dish rack. "You saw each other for two years. Yes."

"I thought you liked Tracy."

"I liked her when you liked her. Now, I don't have to. Here." She threw a towel in his direction. "Help me dry the dishes. It will ease your pain."

"Housework is forbidden. Didn't you get the email?"

"I don't want your Aunt Barbara telling the rest of the family that I keep a dirty house."

He picked up a cloth and started drying. "Is he mad at me?" He nodded toward the living room.

"He's mad at all of us. Himself mostly." She put the last dish on the rack and snatched the towel from James.

"What's wrong with him? We're *not* Jews."

"That's debatable."

"You're not Jewish. And Jewish heritage is passed down through the mother. So I'm not Jewish."

"Yes but Reva was Jewish."

"Grandma never went to temple or had a Seder."

"She stopped all that when your father turned Buddhist. I think that's what's bothering him now."

"Okay. But after all these years, he can't just stick on a kippah and call himself a Jew."

"People change. You could become a Lutheran and start eating the body of Christ." She handed him the last dish.

"What about The Eightfold Path? The Four Noble Truths? Meditation and reincarnation? Do we just forget about those and start separating the milk from the meat?"

"Jamie, I don't want to talk about your father. I want to talk about you. Your life. What are you doing?"

"I'm mourning my grandmother. That's what I'm doing."

"Are you going to grad school?"

"If I'm a Jew, I guess I'd better." He opened the refrigerator and peered inside.

"You said this restaurant job was only temporary, but I don't see you moving forward."

"You mean I'm not on track to be a mathematics professor?"

"Jamie, I don't want you to be like me. You have a gift for math. You can always fall back on that. I thought you might want to study computer engineering. You always enjoyed video games. Or you could use your mathematic skills in actuarial studies or statistics?"

"I told you. I'm going to NYU Film School."

"But what if you don't get in?" She folded the dish towel in half and threaded it through the drawer handle. "Or what if you can't afford it? And if you do get in and manage to afford it, what happens when you graduate? They're not just handing out jobs at Pixar."

"I don't know."

"Look, Jamie. You're in New York. Why not at least get a job in the industry? A key grip or best boy—whatever you call it? My friend, Sandra, at the journalism school knows someone at CNN. She says she can possibly get you a paid internship. That would be a start."

"I'm too old to be an intern."

She took out her basket of vitamin pills and portioned out her dosages for the night. "Listen, Jamie, I don't want to argue with you. I just want you to ... realize your potential."

"And what if my potential is being a restaurant manager?"

"That's fine. Just make sure you're right." She gave him a tight smile and swallowed the handful of pills. "Be nice to your father. He's very upset over Reva's passing." She patted his cheek and walked out.

James picked up the dish towel and finished drying the rest of the dishes. Then, out of guilt, he scrubbed the sink and Brillo-padded the stove. It was possible that restaurant management could be his bliss. Worse things might befall a person. Like not being attractive to the person you love. Like not being desired by anyone at all. Ever.

More people passed in front of him on the street; he studied their shoes. It was difficult to keep shoes clean in New York, and he marveled at all the pristine white sneakers. It seemed like these people knew something about living that he didn't. He stepped on the cigarette and rubbed the ash from his arm.

Inside, the restaurant hummed along without him, and he soldiered through the night, trying to assist Sherry, befriend Max, tolerate Roger, and generally make up for his transgressions. Thirty seconds after the last table had mispronounced their last "bon sewer," Bart stormed out of the kitchen, keys in hand.

"Don't call me for any reason," he said to James, and stalked out the door.

He looked back and saw Max shuffling out of the kitchen as if emerging from an air raid. Bart must've lashed out. He leaned against the wall, arms folded.

"Are you all right, Max?" James said.

"I'm a human being. I deserve better than this." He threw his apron on the bar and walked out the door.

James turned to Sherry. "What happened?"

"Bart went-off on him." She was wiping the bar and her shirt had come slightly unbuttoned; he could see a small bejeweled blemish just above her left breast. She hung the bar rag over the sink and dried her hands. "Something about a customer ordering risotto and Max putting in ravioli."

"That happened over an hour ago. I explained it to Bart."

She checked her face in the bar mirror, daubing a finger in the corner of her eyes to unclump her mascara. "Apparently, Bart still had something to say about it."

James would now have to smooth things over with Max, shower him with praise and convince him not to quit. He wasn't the best waiter, but this was probably the only server job he could find at his age. "Poor Max."

"Poor all of us." She strapped her purse over her shoulder and started out. "I restocked the wines. We're low on the Bogle Pinot Noir."

"Can I talk to you for a minute?"

She walked back and leaned a hip against the bar. This was his big moment. Time to live his truth.

"I'm sorry about before," he said. "With the fish. I should have taken it to the kitchen myself."

"No biggie ."

"I should've known Bart would yell at you. I was caught up in the rush and wasn't thinking. Things don't always come out right with me. Especially now ...." He started to say, after the funeral, but stopped himself. Sherry was looking at him as if he were one of those crippled dogs with their hind legs in a cart. He'd always wondered about those dogs. What happened when they went to the bathroom? Did they just piss and shit all over their cart? He hoped her imagination didn't go that far.

Sherry hitched up her purse and smoothed out the strap. "Don't worry. We're good. I have to get home. Sean has a big show coming up." She gave him a tight smile and before he knew it, she was hurrying out the door and waving goodbye with the back of her hand.

He collected the cash from the register and faced the bills. Of course, Sherry was in a hurry to go home to her artist boyfriend. They would probably fuck on the floor underneath his latest canvas. In the future, he would have to train himself to be professional. He would have to start thinking like a crippled dog.

He printed out the master report and watched the long strip of paper roll out of the machine. His grandmother would have told him to stay away from blondes. Even though, when she was younger, she bleached her hair. "I had Betty Grable's legs and Jane Mansfield's rack." She would bring out her photograph album and show him the undisputed proof. Each page had pictures of her in bathing suits with fluffy skirts, in evening dresses, posing in front of bulbous cars that looked like small tanks. For his seventh birthday, she bought him a Cookie Monster puppet. It started him making puppets of his own—friends for Cookie Monster. Soon he was modeling puppets after family members. He made versions of his grandma, his mother, and even one of his dad. They were mainly constructed from tube socks with magic marker faces, but eventually they became more complicated. His grandmother showed him how to sew simple shift dresses and jackets. Every year for her birthday, he would make a new puppet in her likeness, gradually experimenting in various mediums: fabric, felt, clay, until he discovered the flexibility of paper mâché. She would display the whole collection on top of her console TV, which, when James came over to visit, always gave him a little bubble of pride. Occasionally, during commercial breaks, she'd scowl at the puppets and say, "Why you got to make me so fat? Don't you know artists are supposed to flatter their subjects?"

He folded up the master report and started to laugh. He didn't know why he was laughing—it seemed disrespectful, so he covered his mouth with both hands. The laughter was just on the verge of ending when Roger walked past, carrying cartons of beer and soda.

James went back to counting tips while Roger banged cans into the bar fridge.

"How'd we do?" Roger finally asked.

"Cash—thirty. Credit—one-eighty-six."

"Then my labors were not in vain."

"You can go home. I'll get Max to stock the bar tomorrow."

"Now you tell me. I'm almost done."

James concentrated on his paperwork but could feel the probes of Roger's eyes.

"You want to get a drink?" He came around from behind the bar, wiping his hands on a towel. "After the night we had, I feel we deserve it."

Roger had never before asked him out. In all the months they've been working together, he usually shot out of the restaurant as soon as his shift ended, hurrying off to some new club or cast party.

"I still have paperwork," James said.

Roger started breaking down the cartons. "I don't want to get all maudlin and everything, but I wanted to say I'm sorry. About your grandmother."

"Thanks."

"I never really knew my grandmother. She died when I was four. Cancer." Roger scratched his forehead with a folded beer carton. "Or no, maybe it was diabetes. Or ... what's that thing where your face goes slack on one side? Stroke. Yes, that's it. My mother brought me to the hospital and I asked if grandma was melting." He started stacking the cartons on the bar top. "How did your grandma die?"

"Um. It was a heart attack. On a city bus."

"Quick. Boom. Splat." Roger slapped the bar for emphasis. "Best way to go."

"Well, not splat, I hope."

"Heart attack victims seldom remain upright."

"I don't know."

"If she fell to the floor, there most definitely was a splat. Though she might've just slumped in her seat. Did she slump?"

James pressed his pen harder into his ledger.

"Well, slump or splat, you got off lucky. No hospital visits. No endless physical therapy. You might even get to sue the bus company."

James continued filling out the closing reports. He could feel Roger gearing up for one of his monologues. His voice always became more pronounced with a slight British accent. Sometimes he would quote directly from one of his plays, mentioning its title and the theatre company that produced it. Other times, he would rehearse dialogue from a new play. It could be entertaining, but James had no patience for it tonight.

Roger poured himself a glass of red and plopped down on a bar stool. "I suppose I missed out on something—not having a grandmother. I might have developed a taste for hard candy and the smell of Ben-Gay. Or learned how to play Parcheesi and unlock the subtle plot-points of *Murder, She Wrote*. Maybe that's why I have this horrible fear of aging. If I'd been confronted by the ravages of time as a tot, I might not need a hundred-dollar moisturizer today. At any rate, there's a void in my life—a grandmotherly void. But you. You've had so many years with your grandmother. Cheers to that." He raised his glass along with an eyebrow, inviting James to agree with him. James concentrated on his paperwork but kept Roger in his peripheral view.

"I didn't know my grandfather either." Roger stared out among the audience of empty tables. "Died before I was born. And my other set of grandparents.... Well, they were estranged. Lost in the holocaust of divorce, as so many are. Your parents are still married, right?"

James gave a slight nod of his head.

"So lucky." Roger gestured to the ceiling, as if calling on the gods to validate his statement. "But really. What good are grandparents? They're old and smelly. Forgetful. You can't actually be seen with them in public. Well, you can, but no one is going to cruise you with Nana on your arm. And what are you going to talk about—the Cold War? Depression staples? I don't know anything about making soup with old shoes." Roger took off his apron and folded it on the bar. "Yep, James. You are one lucky ducky. Sure you don't want to come for a drink?"

He had to admire how Roger turned every situation into his own personal tragedy. Just like his grandma, he had a flair for the dramatic. It wasn't lost on him that Roger was trying to make him laugh. At death. At family ties. At all the uncomfortable realities. It was very Zen. Daiyu used to say, *the disciple who contemplates death is free from craving.* He would encourage James to meditate on photos of corpses and decaying bodies: bloated flesh and blackened skin, teeth pressing through the gauzy skin of a cheek.

He shuffled his papers into a large pile and headed to his office. "Just let me put these away and I'll come with."

2: Liquid Desire

Roger stood on a dry patch underneath the awning and waited for James. Rain was falling in big, spastic droplets, giving the sidewalk an undulating sheen. All down Smith Street, the metal gates of the shops winked in the streetlights, while the newer shops, the ones without gates, glowed from inside like secret eggs waiting to hatch.

He already regretted inviting James for a drink. But what was he supposed to do after witnessing him openly weeping over the server reports—both hands covering his mouth like some mystic ape refusing to speak his sadness? In spite of a reputation for being self-absorbed, Roger did have some latent strings of empathy that could be plucked, even by a bald and befuddled Buddhist. In the words of Arthur Miller, "attention must finally be paid to such a person." Otherwise, they found themselves on the wrong end of a hosepipe. And though the restaurant didn't have a gas furnace, he couldn't abide the thought of coming into work one day and finding James's poly-wool blend pant legs sticking out from the oven door.

A damp tingle of water was beginning to seep into his shoes. He started thinking of excuses to leave, but guilt—that sticky gum of human interaction—fixed him in place. Through the steamy window, he watched James carrying soiled napkins and a single teaspoon into the kitchen. He was supposed to be setting the alarm and locking up, not purging the restaurant of all its filth. But James couldn't turn off his tidiness—his OCD was OOC. It might have been a coping mechanism for grief, which a more understanding person would have excused, but Roger didn't have patience for grief.

His years in the theatre had taught him that in the fifth act—everybody died. It was the whimpering way of the world: the vine withered, the stalk crumbled, the flower lost its petals and went to seed. To decry death was like lamenting that saggy pouch of skin below one's chin, or the proliferation of hairs in one's nose—at some point, the body always betrayed us. We all had to go, gently or not, into that good night, so one might as well do it on the down-low and not make a fuss.

When it came to dying, Roger preferred the Irish Goodbye, or, the more refined French Exit, which was the same as the Irish Goodbye but, because it was French, had extra panache. Just leave the party without a postscript. Funerals, wakes, graveside elegies, bedside ablutions, casseroles and covered dishes—all of it was a tedious epilogue and ultimately, a selfish endeavor. Mourners were merely trying to comfort themselves about their own deaths, which all the sympathy in the world could not rescind. Roger believed death was a furtive, essentially private affair. It should take you unawares in the night, like a randy boy scout sharing your tent on a camping trip.

He had observed James and Sherry consoling each other in corners, looking wet-eyed and wistful talking about their belated grandmothers. Of course, it was hard to tell if James's histrionics were due to immoderate grief or immodest lust. Roger surmised more of the latter. And for that, he truly felt sorry. For James had as much chance of getting with Sherry as a dog had of riding a bicycle. Not that Sherry was a super beauty, but she was safely out of James's league. She had one of those Scandinavian faces—big eyes and heavy cheekbones—resembling an astonished Little Match Girl who had just been told she had a venereal disease.

Roger held to a severe caste system about physical appearance. Dating outside of your caste was not only an affront to the eyes but an abomination of evolutionary norms. Yet, he did allow for some autonomy: a six could date a seven, and a seven, if rich or famous enough, might capture a nine, but a five mating with a ten was an unholy hybrid, a kind of bestiality only to be attempted by the truly desperate or the profoundly drunk.

James continued to bend his lanky frame over tablecloths, straightening their edges and brushing away crumbs, while Roger fumed and thought about: the email invitations for his play opening; the Jelly sandals he had to purchase for the beach scene; the joke in act one that needed punching up; the new shoes he would have to buy if James kept him waiting any longer in the rain.

Across the street, a man held a magazine over his girlfriend's head. The corners of the magazine bent, channeling water onto the girlfriend's shoulders and down her shirt. Still, the man's intentions were good. Roger wondered if he would ever find someone to make such a well-intentioned futile gesture for him. Where was the person to stand behind him and protect him from the elements? To try his best while making it worse?

It had been over three years since his relationship with Nathan came to its fizzling, dribbling end, and there hadn't been anyone since. Not to say he hadn't been with men, but not anyone he wanted to live with again. Not anyone that could make him spark and gush. He had thought it was going to be easy to find another lover. When he met Nathan, things had just fallen into place, from sex, to love, to the mutual commingling of their lives. But dating in the new millennium had proven exceedingly difficult. One could find the sex, and sometimes inklings of love slipped in between morning orgasms and Sunday brunches, but truly needing someone, having your happiness and theirs mutually intertwined was a chasm that couldn't be bridged. Everyone had their list of needs that had to be fulfilled before they could span the gap between self and other. Of course, Roger had his list too, though as the years went by, he kept crossing things off. What had been dealbreakers in his twenties became, in his thirties, endearing little quirks. Must-have attributes turned into unrealistic fancies. Lines that couldn't be crossed were sprinted over with ease. If things kept this pace, by the time he reached forty, he'd be ready to date a paraplegic dwarf who lived in his mother's basement.

To avoid striving beyond his caste, he usually never dated anyone better-looking. Roger considered himself a solid seven—an eight in rural and Midwestern states, and perhaps a six-and-a-half in certain sections of Chelsea and at Swedish Gymnastic Tournaments. The one time he might have gotten a bit uppity and stretched beyond his means was with Diego, an actor in his current play. Roger had made the mistake of becoming involved with Diego and was now in the process of de-involving himself, which was easier than anticipated, yet not without its moments of doubt.

It wasn't as if they were so far apart in appearance. They both had long hair and goatees, though Diego's hair was thicker and some ten years younger. A fact not lost on Roger every time he watched the twenty-eight-year-old run his hands through his mane, or tuck a heavy lock behind one ear. Sometimes, he didn't know if he was watching a play or a Pantene commercial. Garrick, the director, constantly advised Diego to bring it down a notch, both his performance and his hair, which Diego often tied in a high ponytail, sticking up from his head like a gleaming black horn. Still, for Roger, it was like looking back in time. He too had graduated from the same acting school. He too was an only child from a single-parent home. He too was always being told to bring it down a notch.

Diego, when he had a good night's sleep and wasn't hungover, could be considered a nine. Perhaps even a ten, if it wasn't for his one crooked tooth and a slight malformation of his nose, the result of rollerblading into the glass door at a General Nutrition Store. Sometimes Roger would keep a mental list of Diego's physical flaws just to assure himself that he wasn't dating an alien species from the planet Perfection. He lived in mortal fear of people saying, "Look at that hideous troll with that beautiful boy." Sometimes, an errant pimple would pop up in the deep crevasse between Diego's pectoral muscles. Roger would feel very tender toward that pimple, kissing and licking it in the hopes that it would fester and multiply, knocking off a few points of perfection. He often teased him about it, accusing him of having a devil's tit. Which would send Diego running to the bathroom for a jar of Dead Sea Mud and a scrubby pad.

It wasn't so much the physical differences that troubled Roger, but the temporal—Diego, for all his overacting, still had potential, which was a commodity given to the young free of charge. It became much scarcer the closer one got to middle age. Watching Diego show up to rehearsals after a full night and day of partying, made Roger want a do-over for his twenties. If he had given up acting sooner, a profession for which he was ill-suited and untalented; if he'd taken playwriting more seriously, and not spent his youth chasing after beautiful men and wild parties; if he'd gone to graduate school, he could at least be teaching right now and getting big-budgeted university productions, instead of little black box showcases that couldn't even afford gels for their lights or Jellys for their actors.

In spite of these regrets, he did have several productions under his belt at small theatres around the city. Roger had acquired a reputation for sex comedies and portrayals of urban gay life. He had a small following, if not among the glitterati, then among the latexed and leatherati. Diego had seen his play *Phaedra or Phallus*, which ran for six weeks in the East Village, and decided to audition for his current play: *Three Nights of Sand*. From the very first read-through, he latched onto Roger with industrial-strength suction: asking endless questions about his character, giving gushing praise about the dialogue, and taking a biographical interest in Roger's life. In the spirit of professionalism, Roger tried to maintain a distance, but Diego's perfect pectorals and muscular ass appealed to quite a different spirit.

He soon discovered one significant difference between his younger self and Diego—Diego was more sexually experimental. Which was a nice way of saying that he was a pig. If sex was an ice cream store, Diego had sampled all thirty-one flavors. Butt plugs and tit clamps, blindfolds and paddles, were as common to him as shoes and socks. And quite disconcertingly, these items started appearing on his bedside table as not-so-subtle suggestions for their post-rehearsal frolics. It was all rather unerotic to Roger, who thought sex the one event that didn't require accessories. He'd never heard of a butt plug until well into his thirties, and still had no occasion to use one. If Diego was a version of his younger self, he was his younger self sent to summer camp with the Marquis de Sade.

Part of the allure of dallying with youth consisted in introducing them to pleasure, and being present at the self-discovery of their bodies. But introducing Diego to pleasure was like teaching a whore the virtues of the missionary position. For Diego, sucking and fucking were adolescent activities long ago discarded; they held a place in his sexual repertoire slightly above dry humping and heavy petting. It got so that every time Diego reached over and opened his bedside table, Roger lost his erection. This didn't dissuade Diego, who had a drawer full of satisfaction at his fingertips. Though Roger was old-fashioned enough to be both offended and humiliated by the presence of a dildo in the bedroom. If one was going to compete with silicone fibers that pulsed, vibrated, and afterward could blend up a smoothie, it seemed as if the game was rigged.

Presently, they were just friends without benefits. Cordial in rehearsals. Nodding to each other when they passed. Picking up each other's dropped pencils, and occasionally smiling over the coffee cart. Roger found it was surprisingly easy to be polite to someone once your fist had been up their ass. After rehearsals, he would sit in the back row and wave goodnight as Diego went home with one of the other members of the cast. And before the auditorium door slammed shut, he'd breathe a sigh of relief.

Diego wasn't his only good-looking boyfriend. Most of Roger's lovers had been straight-of-nose, flat-of-abs, and well below the required thirteen percent body fat for the athletically inclined. This didn't mean he was necessarily a shallow person. Or that shallowness itself was something to avoid. Everyone knew the most interesting coral and vibrant sea creatures were found in the shallowest of waters. Life itself originated in a few inches of solar heated tide pools. Only in the murky depths did one find those solitary monsters, piebald and blind from living in their cold dark pits. As far as Roger was concerned, depth was vastly overrated.

Finally, the lights went out inside the restaurant. He watched as James carefully placed his fingers over the alarm keypad as if entering the launch codes for a missile attack.

"Okay. Where are we going?" James asked, turning the key in the lock. The streetlight shone directly in his face and Roger studied the smudge marks on his glasses. James suggested they go to Vegas, the new bar that had just opened across the street. But Roger didn't want to make his first appearance there accompanied by bald and befuddled James.

"Vegas is too much of a scene," he said.

James looked across the street at the silhouettes in the foggy window, pursed his lips at the neon 'V' over the door. "Is that a scene?" he asked.

"Yeah. For Brooklyn. It's a scene."

"I guess I wouldn't know a scene if I saw one."

They ended up down the street at their usual place—The Roxy. A former pawnshop, The Roxy's sign depicted a set of gold wedding bands superimposed over a fan of dollar bills. Inside, it was your basic black box with barstools. Halfway into their generous Manhattans, James started talking about his trip back home and his ex-girlfriend.

"Tracy told me I'm not her type. What does that mean—*type*?" He tucked his elbows into his sides and made a big 'Y' with his hands, resembling a very confused seal begging for fish.

"Well, everybody has a type," Roger sipped the sides of his drink. "Certain people you're attracted to and certain ones you're not: facial features, body parts, personality traits. It's not always about the soul, James."

This was where James gave his usual speech about inner qualities, and our superficial culture not allowing us to have deeper relationships. Roger thought if James spent a little more time contemplating his outer qualities, he might find someone to appreciate his inner ones. Not that he was repulsive. He just had the distinction of looking like a young Henry Kissinger… without hair. Now, Henry got a lot of play in his day, but unless James was instantly catapulted to Secretary of State, Roger didn't foresee much sex in his future.

Of course, there was only so much one could do if one was balding and Kissingeresque. James experimented with funky little caps that might be called "jaunty." He'd lost quite a bit of weight through swimming and yoga, but at twenty-six, he looked strangely inappropriate: awkward and uncomfortable in his newly elongated body. At forty-six, if he took care of himself, he might pass for distinguished. That was one of the advantages of being a heterosexual male. Straight guys got to metamorphose into distinguished gentlemen, whereas gay guys had two options: hang on to youth by stomach crunch and hair plug or become a mustachioed leather daddy. There really wasn't a way to grow old gracefully in gay culture. No cardigan sweaters for the gay set. Roger swirled his cherry at the bottom of his glass. At least James had his forties to look forward to. Whereas Roger, who was far closer to forty, regarded the coming of that age like an approaching meteor, falling on him in slow motion.

"Okay. It's not *just* about the soul," James said. "Physical attraction does play a part. But you have to go beyond the body. Otherwise it's empty."

"We are conditioned from infancy." Roger signaled for another round. "All of our emotional and sexual patterns are set by the age of three. Have you ever noticed how many men end up with wives who look like their mothers? There's a reason for that." He surveyed the bar, hoping to discover a man accompanied by both his wife and mother to solidify his argument. Unfortunately, the room was practically empty. Five morose college girls lounged on top of the three Lay-Z-Boy chairs like lionesses of the Serengeti.

"We can't break out of it," Roger said. "Or if we do, we choose the exact opposite of our parents, which is still reacting to them. Scratch anybody's lover, and underneath you'll find Mama with a rolling pin or Daddy with a belt."

"Whatever." James pushed up his glasses and pulled down his white button-down shirt. "If we're hardwired from childhood, then Tracy would have known I wasn't her type from the beginning, and she never would've gotten together with me."

Roger surmised Tracy's story: thirty-something divorcee, gets a hostess job and seeks to recapture her self-esteem by dating a younger man. Every Mrs. Stone has her spring. It was as common as Vagisil.

"Anyway." James shrugged. "I don't want to talk about it."

They both gazed into their drinks as if their next lovers were trapped inside the amber liquid.

It was raining harder when they left the bar, so they ran down the block to James's car, both a little tipsy. Only after nearly side-swiping a Miata did Roger realize that James was somewhat beyond tipsy. And that riding in a car in the middle of a deluge with a drunken, grieving Buddhist might not be the safest way to travel.

Rain pounded the windshield; Roger braced his hands on the dash. At a flooded area of Flatbush Avenue next to the park, James floored it, water pelting the sides of the car like machine-gun fire.

"It's white-water rafting," James yelled, lifting his hands off the wheel. Roger locked his grip on the dash and told him to slow down.

When they pulled up at his building, Roger unclenched his fingers from the dashboard. James continued smiling at the windshield, tapping out some imagined song on the steering column. Currents of water rolled over the curb and encircled the gray plane trees on his street. He offered to make coffee and told James to come inside until the storm died down.

"I don't drink coffee *now*," James replied indignantly, as if Roger had just asked him to fart in a cup.

"Okay, tea then. I'll make decaf tea."

Roger dunked teabags into two mugs of water and stuck them in the microwave. They sat at his chipped Formica table, and James talked about some exotic tea his father had given him: Darjeeling with Ylang Ylang or Oolong with Chai. Then he brought up Tracy's selfishness for not attending his grandmother's funeral. Roger told him if only he spent as much time contemplating the female psyche as he did dissecting various infusions of tea, he might find a woman willing to accompany him to social events.

James wrapped his hands around his mug and laughed. He often broke out in laughter, like something was out of control inside. The staff at Bartholomew called him Mr. Giggles behind his back.

"This is a nice place," James said, scanning Roger's small, unnice kitchen.

"It used to be a single-family townhouse. Then they turned each floor into separate units. I think this was a child's bedroom."

"You want to hear my idea for a short film?" James had been hinting around for weeks that he was working on some new idea, but he never wanted to talk about it. He made vague noises about going to NYU Film School, but whenever Roger tried to engage him in specifics, James demurred, as if such questions were too pedestrian to discuss.

"Do tell," Roger said.

"Okay. It takes place during World War I. This guy's a piano player for silent films. One day, he sees a woman sitting in the audience and falls deeply in love with her."

Roger felt his eyes rolling and his eyebrows reaching for the ceiling.

"What? It could happen." James brandished his big 'Y' hands. "She's his type, to use your expression. She's got his mother's eyes and his father's nose."

James went on to describe how the girl was married to a soldier, and how the piano player came to be devastated when she arrived at the movie house with her war hero husband in tow. Throughout the telling of this tale, all Roger could think about was his sink full of dirty dishes. He wondered if it would be rude to start washing them now.

"Well, it's a very romantic story," Roger said. "Traditionally romantic."

James slammed his mug on the table and braced the air with his hands. "Traditional, yes! But I'm doing the whole thing with puppets."

Roger coaxed his eyebrows lower. He could feel this was a big reveal. Doors were opening, shades were rising, and the lights were turning on in the house of James. "Why puppets?" he asked.

"Actors are bullshit. I can't deal with them."

"So you want to make this into a comedy—froggy romance, piggy heartbreak?"

"No no. Totally serious. I design puppets. I make them out of *papier mâché.*"

"I've worked with you all this time and you've never told me any of this."

"People make fun of puppets. But that's the thing. I want them to take puppets seriously. What do you think?" James clapped his cheeks with both hands and stared across the table at Roger, a grin spreading across his face as if he'd just disclosed a dirty secret.

Truth or kindness, Roger thought, as he examined the flecks of gold in his tabletop. Truth or kindness. "It'll never work, James. No one takes pup-pets seriously any more than they take mimes seriously."

"What's wrong with mimes?"

"You need real actors, with real emotions and intricate facial expressions to pull off a scenario like that." Roger got up to rinse his mug at the sink.

"I don't work well with people."

"You work every day with people. You deal with customers. You manage employees."

"I'm not good at it. Everybody hates me. You hated me the first month. Remember, you told me to stop micromanaging you."

"Well, we get along fine now."

"Because I don't manage you at all. I let you do whatever you want."

"See. You've learned a lot already." Roger dried his hands on a towel.

"Tracy told me she was screwing other guys." James dunked his teabag up and down in his mug. "All through our relationship. Guys I knew. Some I worked with. Some from other restaurants."

"Sounds like quite a list."

"It was." James giggled to himself. "She said she'd changed. And she had. She was wearing black pants and a gold blazer."

"Not the most flattering color combination."

"I hardly recognized her. She used to be all flowy dresses and sandals, and now she looked like ... a real estate person. She got her license and said she was engaged to the manager at the office. When I asked, 'What about us?' she told me we were never really a couple. And named all the guys to prove it."

"What did you say?"

"I congratulated her on her engagement."

"What about the guys?"

"I didn't say anything. I left."

"You didn't curse her out? Call her a liar and a slut?"

"I wasn't trying to hurt her."

"She hurt you. Deliberately it sounds like."

James got up to rinse his cup. "Responding to anger with anger only creates more anger."

"At least it makes you feel better."

"Let me wash these dishes. They're starting to smell."

"James." Roger slapped the counter. "You're too good for your own good."

James got the soap from under the sink, squirted a few lines on the dishes, and turned on the water.

"Stop." Roger shut off the faucet. "You don't have to do my dishes. You don't have to play victim all the time."

"Just because someone wants something different than me doesn't mean I'm a victim."

James made a move to pick up a dish, but Roger grabbed his hands. "James, you have to stop being so insecure. I see it when Bart yells at you. That old man tonight. Max. Me. You can't let people walk all over you."

James slid his hands around Roger's. They were caught in the slipperiness of the soap. "My security doesn't depend on whether or not someone yells at me."

The over-the-sink light slanted off James's forehead, giving him a noble but forlorn aspect—a naive prince lost in a wicked forest. Unconsciously, Roger stroked his hand.

"Wow. You really have no malice."

And then something happened that in all probabilities, in all possible worlds, in all realms of the imagination, Roger could never have conceived: he leaned in and kissed James on the lips. And then something even more extraordinary happened: James kissed him back. And soon they were not standing by the dirty dishes but sitting in a chair, Roger straddling James's lap, all the while kissing and touching and groping, Roger thinking: *I'm kissing Henry Kissinger. I'm kissing Henry Kissinger in my kitchen.*

James was a pretty good kisser. He would stop every once in a while and look Roger in the face, just to make sure it was a guy, with a goatee and two-day beard stubble that he was kissing. And Roger would look back at him, just to make sure that it was a geek, with big glasses and a bald head that he was kissing. And then they'd start back up again.

He could feel the heat pouring off James. He ran his hands up and down his back; it was like touching a loaf of bread still warm from the oven. From James's recent weight loss, the skin of his back was loose. Roger could grab great handfuls of it and pull it out from his body.

They kissed for a long while, then rested their foreheads against each other. James was breathing heavily, making little sounds like steam going through cold pipes. Roger had to hug him hard at one point just to get him to calm down. It was as if his body was starving and Roger was feeding it with kisses and caresses that James kept trying too fast to eat. He took off James's glasses and stroked the smooth, oily top of his head. More than awakening feelings in James, Roger believed he was creating new ones, planting himself on virgin soil, giving gifts to the natives.

He unbuttoned James's shirt and ran his hand over his chest. It had just the beginning of definition, like two soft parentheses. His long body was pliable. It moved under his fingers, retreating and advancing in bumps of pleasure. His eyes were closed. Roger wondered if he was imagining Tracy doing these things to him. Or Sherry. When Roger put his tongue on his nipple, James let out a gasp, like a tea kettle boiling for a single second. And that was the value of virgins. By awakening in them a never-before-experienced passion, you could recreate passion anew for yourself.

There was a point in every sexual encounter when a decision needed to be made: go further or not? That point was soon coming, and Roger knew he had to be the instigator. He took action and unbuttoned James's pants. He slid them to the floor and knelt between his legs. The first thing he noticed was that James's boxers had pictures of World War I airplanes, giving their encounter a kind of historical significance. He briefly imagined pleasuring the Red Baron in the cockpit of The Albatros D. The second thing he noticed was that James had great legs.

How did a geek like James end up with linebacker legs? As a kid, he'd told Roger the he played the tuba in his school band. Maybe marching down Main Street built up those calves. Or he came from a long line of mountaintop goat herders. It didn't matter to Roger's tongue, which found much to appreciate in James's inner thigh.

James began breathing faster, sporadically, like an engine trying to click into third gear; needing to go faster but not finding the place. When Roger took his penis in his mouth, James came with a faint, high-pitched cry that was surprisingly calm, compared to all the sounds he made earlier.

"Oh my god. What happened?"

Roger looked up and swallowed. "You came in my mouth."

"I'm sorry. I didn't mean to do that."

"No worries."

"That was … Thank you." James stood up and pulled up his pants. "Wow. I don't know what to say. I'm kinda light-headed."

Roger picked himself off the floor and stood next to James, waiting for something, some kind of gesture toward him. He had never seen someone open up so fully and yet remain so distant. He felt powerful, like a god bestowing radiance. But also alone—a stone god that could only move others and not be moved himself.

James gave him a strong, brotherly hug, his neck still wet with perspiration, his chest scooping big gulps of air. He put his hands on Roger's shoulders and brought their foreheads together, like two survivors of an unexplainable calamity.

"Is it all right if I go?" he said.

Even though he asked it as a question, it was not a question.

At the door, the awkwardness of protocol asserted itself. How to say goodbye? If they were acquaintances, they would shake hands; if they were friends, they would hug; and if they were lovers, they would kiss. As they were none of the above or some hybrid combination, James just held up his arms in a big "Y" gesture and said, "Wow."

Roger went to the window and watched him running through the rain to his car. He imagined walking next to him, holding a coat over his head.

He got into his car. Roger could see his face in the car light, all shiny with water. He looked scared, his features scrunched up like a puppy emerging from his birth sack. He lifted the bottom of his T-shirt and dried his head, then held the shirt in his mouth and gazed at the steering wheel. He wiped his glasses and started the car. Soon, the light went out inside the car, and Roger saw only the outline of a body through the windshield.

He sat in front of the window for a long time watching James. All the lights in the living room were off; no one could see in. His chin rested on the sill, and he inhaled the sharp smell of ozone. He didn't want to leave the window until James had left the road. Then he would go back to the kitchen, wash the rest of his dishes, and hope for sleep. But James remained parked, headlights glaring off the car in front of him. Droplets of water streaked the apartment window, and Roger followed their journey down to the end of the glass.

He couldn't help feeling that regardless of their differences, some private communication had been shared. These bodies, so mutually undesirable and ill-fitting, had managed to speak to each other despite incomprehensible languages and foreign terrain. It was as if for a few moments they'd left their physical selves and connected as pure voices. But now, they were back to skin and bone and bald heads and big glasses—unreachable in their own private compartments.

He wondered what James was doing in the car. Was he crying? Was he in shock? A truck turned down the street and briefly caught James in its lights. Roger saw he was singing: mouth open, head bobbing, hands tapping the steering wheel. The bastard was singing to the radio.

Eventually, he pulled away. Roger watched the cherry taillights disappear into the night. And then he started singing too: quiet, unfocused sounds without words, like scatting for an audience of ants. It was a liquid melody of tones and notes coming from some hidden place. A place with a very small opening that could only let out the smallest of sounds—a happy place. He brought his hand to his face. It smelled exactly like wet dog and Dial soap. It smelled like James.

3: The Greatest Show on Earth

Goatees were flying through the air, flapping their mustachioed wings, bearing down their bearded menace upon him. James was running in a field of breasts, perfectly rounded, achingly soft. Every time he stepped on one, it squirted out a stream of frothy hot milk. The goatees dived and nipped at his ears, their bristly whiskers grazing his cheeks. Just as the largest was about to suck him into its gaping maw, he woke with a start.

Streaks of sunlight fell across the ceiling and he was hard as a rock.

Images of the nightmare broke apart and gradually reconstructed themselves into the hazy surroundings of his studio apartment. His 408 square foot claim on New York City. He took deep breaths, breathing from one nostril and then the other as Daiyu had taught him. The objects in the room slowly came into focus: the white stucco walls thumbtacked with character sketches; his work table piled with shredded newspapers and puppet parts; his meditation corner with braided rug and incense; and his wall of shoe boxes, each dated and numbered, containing one of his many puppets—a hundred and forty-four to be exact. The decision to bring them was a tough one. Stupid, perhaps, but he didn't want to leave them with his parents. What if they sold the house? Or his mother turned his room into the candle making business she was always threatening to start? In truth, he didn't want to be separated from them. They were his three dimensional photo album. Since the fifth grade, he had been making puppets of family, friends and even enemies. Playing with them gave him the opportunity to recreate events from his past, or imagine possible future ones. Some people journaled or kept a diary—James made puppets. Before the move, he carefully packed each puppet box into sixteen larger boxes and loaded them onto a U-Haul and drove to New York.

It gave him some comfort to acknowledge his things, though not enough to erase the details of the previous evening, which were emerging from the soil of his brain like ugly shoots of poisonous flowers. He rolled off the damp spot on his futon and into a fetal ball. He could still feel the scratch of beard stubble on his thighs, the warm elastic touch of a tongue, the wet suction of a mouth. What had seemed like innocent abandon last night— his sadness sliding down Roger's throat as easily as flushing a toilet—now, in the rational light of day, triggered some troublesome questions: Did he violate Roger? Use him? Provoke unrealistic expectations? And the most persistent question of all, the one that lingered in the clammy consciousness of every man, whispering what to wear, how to speak, and the kind of dressing to put on one's salad: Does this make me gay?

He knew the old sayings: a mouth was just a mouth, any hole will do. It should have felt good. Who didn't like blowjobs? But it didn't feel good. It didn't feel exactly bad; it just felt weird. Roger's eyes looking up at him: *See what I'm doing? You like it? You like it.*

He liked it, but he didn't want it. How do you say that to someone who has your dick in their mouth? When someone has your dick in their mouth, you have to choose your words carefully.

It was a kind of violence. He remembered clutching Roger's head and pushing himself down the back of his throat—that tight burning explosion. Yet, he couldn't ascertain who was committing the violence. Was it him, pounding Roger's skull? Or was it Roger, sucking out his last drop of manhood? One moment he was being comforted and praised, the next suctioned and drained. And the two moments felt oddly alike. It seemed like Roger was trying to take something from him: his virility, his dignity, his manly essence—and it became crucial that he keep it. A woman loses her virginity by the taking of her maidenhood, but does a man lose his manhood by the taking of his essence? Of course, there were a hundred ways to compromise one's manhood, from making a sibilant S to wearing the wrong color tie. Being a man left one constantly in the precarious position of not being a man. One was simultaneously being and not being, depending on the observer of one's being—a thoroughly Heideggerian concept that required a PhD in masculinity to contemplate. The term dick-raped, as in his dick had been raped, kept coming to mind. His manhood violated by the plush of Roger's mouth. Though it was more like Roger was a sneaky timeshare salesman, luring him in with the promise of sympathy and booze and gradually selling him on the benefits of blowjobs.

Outside, the garbage men shook bottles and cans into their truck. The gears of their great machine bellowed and churned its many loads. James wished he could wrap his thoughts in a plastic bag and hand them over for recycling. What a difference a blowjob makes. What responsibility. What pressure. He knew there would be repercussions. Roger would be expecting things. What kinds of things, he couldn't imagine. What does one expect after giving a blowjob: candy, flowers, a diamond-encrusted spittoon?

He went to his meditation corner, folded his legs, put his hands on his knees, and breathed out an elongated om. Usually, this was how he started his mornings, clearing his mind of troublesome thoughts and expelling the flinty voices of recrimination. The voices that said: you are attached to desire; you are holding onto feelings of hostility and resentment; you are thinking too much about blowjobs. James was particularly good at merging Buddhist practice with Jewish guilt.

He straightened his spine and did his self-reporting: heart pounding; cheek itching; a sharp pain in his knee; a single drop of sweat ran down the small of his back. He focused on sound: the roar of a car engine; the chirp of a bird. It was Sunday. The restaurant was closed. He had the whole day to build puppets and work on his film. *Breathe in—inspiration. Breathe out—recrimination, accusation, stimulation, ejaculation ....* And—he was back to blowjobs.

In college, his first girlfriend gave him tons of BJs with no expectations. In fact, that was the extent of their sex life as she was plagued by recurring yeast infections. Joanne claimed she loved giving head, but in practice made it seem like community service. Methodical about everything, she insisted on the same position—James kneeling on the bed, her sitting cross-legged in front of him, so her neck wouldn't get stiff. She didn't like to kneel as she thought it made her "too subservient." This arrangement worked fine at the beginning. James was forty-five pounds heavier then and didn't like the pressure of his squishy belly against her flat stomach. She was the fragile beauty that he needed to protect, and he was the person she needed protection from.

Though grateful to have found a girl so accommodating, he gradually grew tired of this position. His friends in Film History thought he was nuts: "Who gets tired of blowjobs?" They were fat, oily kids who spent too much time ranking the greatest movies and eating fake-buttered popcorn. Getting a blowjob from a girl was as foreign to them as the mating dance of bumblebees. At least he had a girlfriend. A dean's listed English student with a taste for Virginia Woolf and Djuna Barnes, Joanne had wild, frizzy hair and a thin, tightly wound body. For a fat guy in Film History, she was practically a goddess.

Throughout their relationship, he'd tried to convince himself that penetrative sex didn't matter. He concentrated on raising his chakras. In his meditations, he focused on the sacral chakra. He channeled his sexual energy up and onto his breath, expelling it through the air. He planned his future with Joanne. She would be an English professor with several books of deep textual analysis on Woolf's diaries, and he would be an indie director who taught classes in animation technique. *Breathe in—academia. Breathe out—vagina.*

On their second anniversary, his senior year at Michigan, Joanne asked what he wanted as a present. James said he'd like to have sex, real sex, as in intercourse. She claimed that oral sex was real sex: "What's not real about my mouth on your dick?" He replied that if they were ever going to have kids, perhaps she should familiarize herself with the act of penetration. Joanne wound the elastic even tighter on her ponytail and explained that "children are to women as cotton fields were to Negroes." After that, their relationship slowly deteriorated.

When he started dating Tracy, a woman for whom penetration held no political agenda, he thought he had hit the jackpot. Tracy would go down on him in any configuration, though she would never let him cum in her mouth. Usually, after he got hard, she wanted him inside the designated orifice and getting to work pronto. Sex with Tracy was like a horse race where the goal was to come in last. She required as much thrusting and manipulation as it took to launch a rocket into space. At first, he viewed her contractions and gyrations as signs of passion, but it soon became onerous. And, as with most tedious jobs, he sought to get off early.

In retrospect, it seemed Joanne and Tracy might not have loved him as much as he'd believed, or even found him desirable. And now, he had to add Roger to his slim cast of conquests. That Roger could find him desirable was even more farfetched. He remembered him saying in his kitchen, "Your legs are the best thing I've seen all day." An apparent compliment, unless he had spent the day cleaning leaf mold from his gutters. It was odd that Roger considered him attractive. He usually dated underwear models and personal trainers. Why he had chosen James over the buff actors in his plays, over all the club kids, whom he talked about like so much muscular poultry: pecs and lats, abs and delts, was a mystery. There would have to be repercussions. You didn't just stick your cock down someone's throat without consequences. He would be punished for his misuse of Roger's mouth. Maybe his act of lust had damaged Roger's larynx and he would have to pay exorbitant medical bills. But most likely, the guilt from shattering Roger's romantic feelings would be crushing enough. That was if Roger held romantic feelings. He thought about Roger holding his hands in the soapy water; telling him he was too good; tenderly licking his thigh. Just the thought that Roger could possibly entertain romantic feelings gave him an illicit thrill. He was the center of someone's desire. He was breaking hearts. Moreover, he was breaking the heart of one of the beautiful people. He curled the braided rug between his fingers and picked at its rubbery undersides.

It was odd to think that in all the months they had worked together, Roger had barely shared a cup of coffee with him, and yet, last night he was drinking his most intimate fluids. All the months he had been in New York waiting for something to happen—for someone to find him—for those marvelous acts of serendipity supposedly occurring every day in the city: *I was just standing in line at the bank when I met my future wife; my girlfriend was a client at our gallery; the guy behind me at a Broadway show kicked my seat and three weeks later we moved in together.* All that romance seemed to have been happening to other people. But now, it had happened to James, albeit in the most confounding way possible. It was as if the universe was trying to trick him. He had asked for flowers and was given stems. He had wanted a home and was given a hut. He had desired succor and instead got sucked.

It embarrassed him to think about it. He was ashamed of his own need. Sitting in Roger's kitchen, all unbuttoned, his penis peeking out of his shirttails like some beggar's hand. What was he supposed to do as Roger hugged his legs, kissed his thighs, cupped his balls? How could he say stop when his body was pointing at the ceiling and shouting go? Any refusal would've made him look like some disingenuous coquette.

It was all about mechanics—anyone, anything, could have been down there: Abe Vigoda with no teeth, an Ewok with super suction, a Gremlin without a gag reflex—it didn't matter. It wasn't attraction so much as manipulation. If Roger would have stopped, he gladly would have gone home happy. If Roger would have laughed and said, "I've seen better cocks in infant nurseries," he would have breathed a sigh of relief. But Roger seemed just as needy. Seeing his own needs mirrored in someone else, seeing loneliness and desperation in someone so adept made the connection stronger. Even with friends and lovers, irony and artistic success, Roger was still missing something. It was into this void that they had consolidated, two holes swallowing each other.

After a breakfast of jasmine tea and muesli, he went to his work table and continued building his latest puppet for the WWI film he had told Roger about. He wetted a few newspaper strips and smoothed them around her hips; he wanted a little more fullness there. The process of building the body of a puppet was sacred. James always started from scratch, and in the construction found the soul of the character. He never replaced the bodies with different heads, even though the puppets were clothed and their bodies often indistinguishable to the untrained eye. James could always see the difference: the rounded shoulders he gave to his father; the elongated neck of his mother; the paunch he put on Bankman, the protagonist from his award-winning college film. All of these puppets were born from a few lumps of paper, their bodies gradually layered and molded into fully formed individuals. At each joint in the arms, legs, and waist, he attached wires so the puppets could move in multiple directions. Only in motion do things really come alive. It was this discovery that precipitated his interest in animation.

He examined the new torso, which belonged to the girl the piano player fell in love with. The breasts looked a little too pointy, but it was hard to tell until the body was painted. James painted all of his puppets from head to toe, whether or not the parts were visible. Puppets weren't real to him unless every part was real.

He wondered how to paint the nipples. It would depend on her coloring. At first, he was thinking mauve, but now he leaned toward a lighter completion: pink pincushion nipples with spirals of red rims. He often received distinct ideas about a puppet based on specific body parts: belly buttons, earlobes, or pubic hair. All of his puppets had fully formed genitalia. It was part of the process of knowing their stories, their movements, the emotions rooted in their bodies. And though it gave him some pause when building puppets of his family, he approached it with the mind of a creator—he owned everything and therefore had no reason to be ashamed.

His work was interrupted several hours later by the phone. Surprisingly, the call was from Roger. Even more surprisingly, Roger wanted him to come to his play rehearsal. He agreed only because it gave him an opportunity to clarify that what had happened in his kitchen could never happen again, and to reinforce the idea of friends with absolutely no benefits. Before he hung up, Roger mysteriously told him to dress all in black.

James found him at the agreed-upon coffee shop a few blocks from the theatre. Roger was hammering the straw of his iced cappuccino into its plastic cup, wearing the aforementioned black pants and a black t-shirt. Together, they looked like they were going to cater a hipster bar mitzvah.

"Let's go," Roger said. "We have to hurry."

If there were any hint that Roger was troubled by their previous encounter, James couldn't detect it. He decided not to broach the subject and suppressed any anxiety he had about confronting him. If anything, Roger acted completely engrossed in the drama he was creating in his head about the drama he had created on stage. As they walked, he explained that his cast had requested a rehearsal without him. They found his presence intimidating, and the director asked to work alone with them tonight. Roger was planning on sneaking in and spying on the proceedings.

He brought him to a grey stone building with Greek columns and large palladium windows. Etched in the upper facade was the name Prospect Lyceum. Roger explained that it used to be a turn-of-the-century public bathhouse now converted into performance spaces. They went to a door at the back and Roger whisked him up a tiny stairwell and into an empty lighting booth. As they crept into the darkened booth, he pointed to a milk crate for James to sit on and gave the hand signal to zip his lips.

James hunkered down and tried to make himself small, his head just visible above the levers and dials of the lighting board. Roger positioned himself against the wall on the far side of the streaky window. He sat on a stool with a notepad and pen, looking grim and determined. James could understand his anxiety. He had talked about the play enough at work, describing his initial excitement at finding a production company, and his disappointment when he didn't get to choose the director but had to accept the husband of one of the trustees. Roger worried that a straight director couldn't appreciate his gay sensibility but had since come to revise his opinion of Garrick. Whether because he proved to be exceedingly perceptive or secretly closeted, James didn't know. But he was aware of Roger's many complaints about casting, blocking, and the general laziness of the actors.

The play was about an older gay man suffering from dementia, who falls in love with his nurse. He wants one last adventure, and during a weekend on Fire Island, both decide to tell their long-term partners they're dumping them and moving to Bolivia. James didn't have much trouble discerning the action even though they'd arrived in the middle of a scene.

An older actor with huge rose-colored sunglasses was walking through the audience brandishing a floppy foot-long dildo. "Blow, winds and crack your cheeks. Rage. Blow. You are a cataract. And you a hurricano." After each line, he reached into a plastic shopping bag and handed a brightly colored dildo to a person in the audience. "You will be the steeple. And you the sulph'rous, thought-extinguished fires."

"Warren, that's great," said Garrick. He spoke with a British accent and carried a Styrofoam coffee cup, from which he took careful sips. "Can you bop someone on the head with your dildo-thingy?" He tapped his cup.

"I can, if you don't think we'll get sued."

"Oh, and Warren?" said a woman sitting in the front row holding a large binder. "The line is 'thought-executed fires,' not extinguished."

"My God. I'm even forgetting my Shakespeare."

They rehearsed the scene again, Roger making occasional grumbles about Garrick breaking the fourth wall and moving the action into the audience: "What is this? Cirque du Soleil?" When Warren made it onto the stage, the lights came up on a bright blue backdrop of sky and a canvas tarp stretched across the floor. It perfectly captured the colors of the beach.

An actor with long hair and a goatee, who looked like a more muscular version of Roger, hurried onto the stage.

"Papi. Papi. What are you doing? I been looking for you."

"Ah, Bolivar. My sweet Bolivian rebel." He rubbed the dildo on the actor's neck and gave him a lascivious look. "Come to bed, we must."

"Heriberto." He grabbed the dildo from him. "Where you get this?"

"You like? I have dozens." He tossed several more at his feet. "This one is for remembrance. And this one is for thoughts. There's fennel and columbine. And rue for you ..."

"Look, Papi. Look at me." He held Warren's face in his hands. "You steal all this? Where you find?" He gestured to the stage littered with disembodied cocks.

"Why at the dildo store, of course."

He started picking up the dildos and putting them in the bag. "How much you spend? I hide your wallet. Where you get the money?"

"They still accept checks at the dildo store."

"Excuse me, Garrick." Warren broke character. "Am I wearing Speedos or board shorts? Because if I'm in Speedos, I don't know where I'm keeping the checkbook."

Garrick walked to the front of the stage. "We haven't confirmed that yet. I need to talk to Roger."

"The script says Speedos," said the woman with the binder.

"I'm sorry. My family jewels won't fit into a Speedo."

A heated discussion ensued about the virtues and drawbacks of Speedos: exposure vs. coverage, packages vs. pockets. It reminded James of his own difficulties directing actors for his short films in college. For his studio class, he wrote and directed a short about five friends who run over a dog. The dog was still alive, and they had to decide what to do. The cast's schedules were impossible to organize. Everyone had opinions about dialogue, camera angles, and light exposure. In the end, the film was so far from what he'd envisioned that he didn't want to put his name in the credits.

"Fucking prima donnas," Roger said to himself.

Garrick told everyone to take a ten-minute break, and the actors migrated to their stashes of trail mix and water bottles. In the audience, Warren, Goatee and two other actors, gathered in the aisle and talked about Roger.

"Everything is about sex with him," said Warren. "Sometimes I don't know if this is a play or a porno."

A bald actor held up his hands as if receiving revelations from God, and did a spot-on impersonation of Roger. "Warren, when you drink the coffee, make love to the cup."

"You're terrible," said the other one with a gray beard.

"Philip. When you dry your hands on the kitchen towel, find the desire in the terrycloth."

Everyone cracked up, including Garrick, who was going over notes with the binder woman. They both smiled and shook their heads.

Philip took a long swallow of water and wiped his grey beard with the back of his hand. "Has anyone counted the blowjobs in this play?"

"For Roger, the blowjob is a literary device," said Warren. "It's both epiphany and metaphor."

"Or a substitute for epiphanies and metaphors," said the bald actor.

Roger slapped James on the leg. "Come on. Let's go."

They circumspectly made their way down the back stairs, almost running into two of the younger actors smoking what smelled like a joint by the back door. They waited in the stairwell until rehearsal started again, Roger fuming and slapping his leg with his yellow pad.

Outside, he started walking toward the subway. James followed, not wanting to leave him alone, yet, not knowing what to do. He didn't want to risk saying the wrong thing, so he matched footsteps and chose silence. He felt responsible for Roger's safety, and somehow just walking next to him was reassuring—he could stop him if he ran headlong into a bus.

When they got a block from the train station, James asked if he wanted to come over to his place. He explained about a new tea he had purchased, which was somehow both relaxing to your muscles and stimulating to your brain. Roger shrugged his shoulders, as if it didn't matter if he accompanied James to the sixth circle of hell.

At his apartment, James made matcha and chrysanthemum tea, served on his Japanese tea set. The set was a gift from Daiyu upon completing his meditations on Right Livelihood. He whisked the tea in a bowl until it was green and foamy, and then poured it into tiny wooden cups, elucidating the basic points of the ceremony just to have something to fill the silence. He demonstrated how one held the cup to warm one's palms; how one studied the tea's color and consistency; how one let the aroma flow into one's nostrils; and finally how to take a small sip and feel the hot liquid glide down one's throat. Roger's response was to chug the tea, bang his cup on the table and say, "Hit me again, Barkeep."

After a protracted explanation of the benefits of Matcha, James was running out of topics of conversation. It was then that it occurred to him to show Roger his puppets.

Daiyu might have said that seeing Roger's play had ignited sparks of competition. That the professional setting and crowd of people recreating Roger's work had activated James's ego. But James told himself that he wanted to share his creativity. Roger knew only his dull manager side, and friendship required revealing layers.

It wasn't as if James didn't have some small successes to be proud of. Once he switched to working with puppets, his shorts began to get noticed. *Bankman* won second place at the Ann Arbor Film Festival. Animating puppets was a tedious, time-consuming process. Most animators use line drawings or clay figurines. James was one of the few to undertake the animation of puppets. It was a natural transition since he's been making puppets all of his life. Not just family members, but his marching band instructor, the bully in fifth grade who routinely punched him in the nuts, the girl who picked her scabs in civics class. All resided in his wall of boxes, and he chose carefully which ones to show Roger.

They sat on the floor while he unwrapped Bankman from the tissue paper. He was bald and thin, and truth be told, resembled James without glasses. In his generosity, James had bestowed upon him 20/20 vision. Bankman's story was about an uneventful day counting money as a clerk. Nothing much happened during his routine of addition and subtraction, stamping and stapling, and by the end of the day, he felt bereft—as if something was missing. He wanted Roger to ask about the film so he could bring out the DVD and they could watch it with their chrysanthemum tea, like real *auteurs*. But Roger didn't ask.

He did seem interested in the puppets, though. He studied Bankman's clothing and moved his arms and legs. "You made this yourself?"

"I did." James smiled like a parent at his child's first ballet recital.

"How do you get the arms and legs to move?"

"Wires. I put wires in the papier-mâché. Even the torso and head can turn and move." He pulled out another box and showed Roger Bossman. "This is the manager of the bank from the same film."

"Wow. You made his suit and tie. Even cufflinks."

"They're just some bits from my mom's old jewelry."

"Where did you find the shoes?"

"Those were old G.I. Joe boots that I painted and retrofitted."

"The clothing is remarkable. Maybe you should be a fashion designer."

James could feel heat spreading on his cheeks. "I have this one dress ... Let me show you." He went to box number sixty-four and brought out a puppet of his mother in her 1970s prom dress. He usually didn't show his family puppets to people, but he wanted Roger to see the dress. It had white peasant sleeves, a long crepe skirt, and tiny embroidered daisies on the bodice. He spent two days sewing those daisies.

"Va-va-voom," said Roger. "Who is she? The sexpot receptionist at the bank?"

"She's someone else."

"You've got the right idea, James." He shook the puppet and let her dress catch the wind. "Fuck actors. I wish I could put life-size puppets on the stage."

"Maybe soon, with holograms."

"The attention to detail is amazing." He ran a finger over the embroidery. "Did you ...? What's this? It feels like ..." He poked a finger inside the top. "This puppet has nipples."

"It just looks better that way." He took the puppet from Roger, smoothed out her dress, and put her back in the box. "For verisimilitude."

"That's taking attention to detail to the extreme." Roger picked up Bossman and started walking him across the floor. "Actors. They wouldn't know a literary device if it bit them in the ass. In my next play, I'm going to put a blowjob in every scene. You know why?"

James moved his head imperceptibly.

"Because it's subtext. Nothing has greater subtext than a blowjob." And you know what that subtext is?"

Given their recent experience, James was getting a bit nervous about all the blowjob talk. He stared at the floor, trying to think of a way to change the subject.

"Tenderness. Compassion. Love. Violence. Anxiety. Depression. It's anything you want to make it. It's not just about the blowjob. Goddam-nit." Roger raised Bossman's arms in triumph and then brought them down and straightened out his suit. "What's this? Have you? No?" He passed his finger over Bossman's crotch. "Why you little devil."

James kept staring at the floor but could feel his face burning.

Roger unfastened Bossman's pants. "Holy fucking shit—look at the schlong on this guy. Right down to the pubes. You're a fucking puppet pervert."

James covered his face with his hands.

"Did you do everyone?" Roger picked up James's mother and lifted her dress. "A true seventies bush—you weren't kidding about verisimilitude."

"Okay. That's enough." James tried to grab the puppet, but Roger scurried away.

He pulled down Bankman's pants. "This one has a big schlong, too."

"Hey." James lifted a hand to stop Roger, but it was as if gravity had suddenly doubled and every movement required an effort beyond him. The energy of the room was turning violent, and he froze—a poor bald duck with his feathers shot off.

"My next play is going to be ALL blowjobs and fucking," said Roger. "Every scene, a Bacchanalian orgy. Take these characters." He held up James's mother and Bankman. The puppet's pants were still around his ankles. His mother's dress was exposing one of her breasts. "She's Ophelia. And this one is Hamlet. You could write an entire play based on their copulation. And it would be a fascinating exploration of character. More revealing than most other actions." He tapped Bankman's crotch. "Does this thing get erect?"

James shook his head.

He maneuvered Bankman's crotch into James's mother's face. "So get this. Look. It's brilliant. Hamlet wants Ophelia to suck his dick, but will she do it? The tension is dramatically interesting. Once that decision is made, there are a dozen more choices. Does she take it tenderly? Just the tip? Is she worried he'll think she's a slut? Or, is she so concerned with pleasing him that she swallows it whole hog? Licks his balls and fingers his taint?"

"And Hamlet." Roger lifted Bankman's hand to the puppet's eyes. "Is he emotionally distant so as not to be defiled by her? Or, is he so consumed by passion that he becomes ashamed? Does he stroke her hair? Enfold her with his legs? Maybe he pulls her onto him because he likes the gagging sounds."

James realized that playing with the puppets was Roger's way of rebuking the actor's comments, but it pained him to see his creations used in such a way.

"And when it comes to fucking." He took James's mother's legs, threw them in the air and put Bankman on top of her. James kept watching, his eyelids pinned open, unable to look away from the corruption of bodies—an autopsy of exposed organs and open chest cavities.

"Does he go in slow, out of concern for her? Or, because he's close to coming himself?" Roger manipulated the puppets with agonizing clarity. "Does he tease her on the surface? Or plow right in and take his pleasure? Does he pull her dress over her head?" Roger does this. "Is it to hide her face so he can't see who he's defiling? Or, because her cries of passion remind him of the rutting sounds he heard from Gertrude and Claudius's bedroom?"

James followed the stages of Roger's narration: his mother's rape or her carnal pleasure? Neither was a story he wanted to hear. Yet it began to dawn on him that Roger was merely putting into action what he himself had originally started. The body was *not* a neutral canvas. There was no such thing as a wholesome and uncorrupted natural state. Fingers were for grasping and genitals for fucking. You didn't make either without the intention of using them. Roger had plucked the story out of James's subconscious and wrote it bold.

Now, he was smashing the puppets together in rhythmic thrusts, his mother bent doggy style, her dress mercifully covering her head. "Does this seal their love? Or does it end it? Who's in control? Who's giving the most? Who's holding back? Who has no feelings to hold back? Don't tell me sex has no meaning. The universe spins and expands. Planets come together, stars explode, and people just keep on fucking. It's the greatest show on Earth." He held up his hands to hold back imaginary applause. Then threw the puppets in their respective containers. "When it's all over. We end up in a box."

James couldn't raise his head. He stared at the floor, exploring the nicks and chips in the wooden planks. He couldn't bring himself to look at his puppets, so casually tossed and tossed off. The images reverberated in his mind: his responsibility, his perversions, the sick miasma of his egocentric soul. "I want you to go," he whispered.

"What?" Roger said.

His insides sputtered and fizzed. He was afraid to speak for fear of what might become uncorked. "Just go. Please."

Roger brushed a lock of hair from his forehead. "What are you talking about?"

James stood up and yelled, "GO. GO. GO."

There was a small pause while his words bounced off the walls. And then Roger stepped around the boxes of puppets and fluttering tissue paper.

"You're a nutcase," he said. "A fruit and nut case."

The door slammed.

Roger's feet thundered down the stairs.

The outside door made a faint bump. And then there was just the sound of cars coming down the street and his own breath, exploding in his head.

He sat on the floor, the wreckage all around him: tissue paper and teacups. How could he ever look at these puppets again? Finally, he attempted a cleanup. He pulled up Bankman's pants. With masking tape, he removed the lint from his pants. He straightened his mother's dress, which, somehow throughout her ordeals, remained miraculously unscathed. If only he could say the same for his brain. He wrapped the puppets back in their tissue paper, closed the lids on their boxes, and put them away. It was several hours before he realized he might have overreacted.

4: The Gay Straight Men

Roger opened the frosted glass door of Bartholomew with some trepidation. Its cursive B mirroring the rolling, curlicued circuits of his mind. It would be his first time seeing James since the ill-fated night of puppet pornography. He might have taken things a bit too far, but he was making a point: sex was a profound experience with complex, multifaceted meanings and shouldn't be diminished. He had suspected that James was making a similar point with his puppets, saying that nipples and genitals were just as important as arms and legs, and the entirety of the human form should be taken into consideration. Perhaps he exaggerated his point, but who would have guessed James would turn out to be so prudish about puppets? Especially after Roger had given him a blowjob. Was this any way to say thank you?

With all the conflict going on with his cast, Roger had relegated the blowjob to a distant file in his brain labeled "things to consider later." He didn't have time to recategorize their relationship: employee/boss, friend/friend with benefits. But he did register the unusualness of the act. It wasn't as if he went around doling out blowjobs like air-kisses and Kleenex. Ordinarily, he would only bend the knee for guys he felt a deep attraction to. What provoked him to genuflect for James he decided was a certain sense of pity. Something needy and childlike in James touched his heart. Like those commercials for the Humane Society with the puppies in cages. He would give every one of those dogs blowjobs if it would ease their suffering. In James's case, he concluded, it was a palliative blowjob and needed no further categorization.

He was relieved not to find James at the podium. It gave him a moment to breathe, make himself a Diet Coke, and gather his courage before facing this man/child, boss/friend, friend/lover, lover/whatever.

Sherry was sitting at table twelve, rolling silverware in napkins, a small pyramid of white linen tubes rising by her side. The chairs had already been taken down and the tables freshly clothed. He greeted her and settled down to help with the roll-ups.

"Thanks for setting up. You must have gotten here early."

She plucked a knife and fork from the tray and robotically folded the napkin around them. "I needed to get out of the house."

"Is it Sean?"

"He's in his manic phase. Last night he threatened to jump off the fire escape."

"Ah, the artistic temperament."

"I had to coax him in by telling him he's one of the greatest artists of his generation."

Roger raised an eyebrow. "Is he?"

"How should I know? I'm from Iowa. But it got him off the fire escape."

"The things we do for love."

She blew out a long stream of air, as if all the things she had done for love were exhausting her. Little red dots formed on her milk-white skin. "I hardly slept at all this week. He's up till all hours hammering and welding."

Roger considered the empty triangle of his napkin and carefully dropped two pieces of silverware inside. "Art used to be a peaceful process: oils on canvas, figures in clay. Postmodernism ruined all that. Now every artist needs a combustion engine, ten coaxial cables, and a hundred pounds of shark intestines."

"He keeps changing his mind, destroying one project and starting another." She waved a roll-up in the air. "I was showing him how to make soap because he wanted to ..."

"Wait. You make soap?"

"Sure. My grandmother taught me."

"You're not going to tell me you can't buy soap in Idaho?"

"Iowa." She threw a napkin at him. "I make most of my own beauty products. Saves money and no animals have to suffer to make me beautiful."

"Someone always suffers for beauty. If not a poor animal, then the sap who falls in love with it."

"Someday, I want to start a natural cosmetics company. I have a whole line of products in mind: soap, makeup, moisturizers. I'll make you some soap. What do you want to smell like?"

Roger threw up his hands against an imaginary marquee. "Overwhelming Success."

"A lot of sweat and guts goes into making a success. Might not smell too great."

"Don't tell me how the sausage is made, Blanche. Just buy me a hotdog."

"You're such a weirdo." She squinched up her face and bugged out her eyes like some deranged milkmaid who'd just discovered the cream had curdled. "Anyway. Sean wanted to make a life-size female figure from soap that would stand in a shower stall and people could turn on a hose and lather her up. But he got frustrated and threw my boiling pot of oil and lye out the window. It landed on the neighbor's patio, and ungelled soap bits got all over their lawn chairs. I had to go over and apologize."

"*You* had to apologize?"

"Well, someone had to. I told them I was letting it cool on the sill, and it fell on accident. And then I spent the morning scraping off chunks of soap from their patio."

"Oh, Babygirl. You've got to get out of there."

"That's what my friend Trish says."

"He's dangerous."

"Isn't that part of the artistic temperament?"

When Sherry first started working at the restaurant, Roger thought she was a bit pretentious. Friendly enough in her Midwestern way, but most times quiet and aloof. Always texting on her cell when she had a free moment. She had come from a three-star restaurant in Manhattan and claimed she wanted some place quieter and more relaxed. After work, she would rush out with barely a good-bye, as if not to sully her hands with the riff-raff. It was only several months later that she told him Sean wanted her home at a certain time. He texted her constantly with love poems, threats, and queries about where she put the household bleach. In previous discussions, Roger had hinted at the controlling nature of their relationship, but now he realized he would have to be more blunt. "Picasso and Miles Davis beat up their women. William Burroughs shot his wife in the head. If he's throwing pots out windows, you could be next."

"Trish says she and I should get a place together."

"Has he threatened you?"

"Not in so many words."

"In any words?"

"He gets agitated and says things but he doesn't mean it."

"Listen to me. Leave. Even if it's only for a few weeks. Until his show goes up."

"But he gets crazy when I'm not there."

Roger leaned into the table. "And how's his sanity when you're there?"

Sherry fingered a fork and blew air through her lips.

"Tell him it's for his own good. It'll give him more time to work on his projects. And it will give you a good night's sleep."

She stared at the brick wall and widened her saucer-shaped eyes in contemplation. She was too young to have a forty-something, manic-depressive boyfriend, but from what he knew of her past, this one wasn't the worst. This one wasn't addicted to meth. This one didn't crash her car into an Indian burial mound.

"Oh. I forgot to ask." She hit the air with her hand. "How's your show going?"

"Never mind about that. Promise me you're not going to stay with that man."

Her hands tapped the table in some rhythmic combination that brought the topic to a close. She pulled from her purse what looked like a scrunched-up bar rag, but it turned out to be her work shirt. She refused to dry-clean because of the chemicals and spent a good fifteen minutes ironing her shirts during pre-shift. Roger always complained that this allowed her to avoid sidework but didn't say anything this time.

"I'm going to get dressed before Melissa comes. I'll stock the bar when I get back." She threw her shirt over her shoulder and ambled downstairs.

He never could tell if she was flirting or if it was just her natural exuberance, but there was always a sexual ripple running through the cornfield of her Midwest congeniality. He went to the supply closet for the precut squares of white paper and laid them over the tablecloths. Then he set the tables with bread plates, roll-ups and water glasses.

On some level, he could sympathize with Sean and the frustrations of a struggling artist. He never threw a pot out the window, but he had been guilty of visiting his frustrations on his partner. His five-year experiment in romantic cohabitation with Nathan was over before it dawned on him what he had lost. And, as he trekked from boy-toy to boy-toy, he sometimes wished he still felt the weight of one steady man to hold him. Though, in day-to-day practice, it became oppressive. He often counted his years with Nathan as one long prison sentence, if prison served a pasta course and then made you watch two hours of Will and Grace. Though now, three years a free man and outside of Nathan's connubial orbit, he couldn't watch an episode of Will and Grace without a wistful feeling creeping up the back of his neck.

Nathan used to call him an angry bear. He would imitate him and paw at the ceiling and growl whenever Roger went off on one of his rants against the theatre establishment or some short-sighted director. In retrospect, he could see his rants as, if not abusive, debilitating. He recognized his flight to anger as a form of self-protection. Though what he was protecting himself from he didn't know. Like most children, he spent his childhood being angry at his mother for one reason or another. They were both such different people, it was hard to believe they were related. In fact, he used to fantasize about having a different mother: more glamorous, more educated and fun-loving, more like Rhoda Morgenstern or Cher. Maybe it was because he never knew his father, who left before he was born. A father was the perfect foil for a gay boy, but he was left to take all his frustrations out on his mother, who never graduated high school and worked all of her life as a payables clerk at Pearl Trim and Textile. She had always regarded his theatrical ambitions as somewhat suspicious and somehow pathetic. Though, she did her duty and drove him to dance classes, voice lessons, and numerous children's theatre rehearsals across suburban Philadelphia. She wasn't a devotee of theatre herself but thought it would cure him of his heroic shyness and maybe garner him some friends. Little did she realize that among the bullies and jocks on the playground, acting the Mouse King in *The Nutcracker* didn't give one much status. In fact, it actually caused one to be made to eat dirt, if one was foolish enough to wear one's mouse costume to school.

She managed to attend all of his shows in gymnasiums and defunct movie houses, where he played various supporting characters: Prince Valiant, a studious caterpillar, one of the Lost Boys. She applauded and smiled in all the appropriate places, but never considered it a vocation. When he decided to study acting in college, she refused any support and told him he was ruining his life. Since moving to Florida, she had never seen any of the plays he'd written, and had little to say about the clippings he would send of his reviews. But he still remembered the one time she had made the effort to see him act in a play. It wasn't something he thought about often. It was another lost connection, like those friends and colleagues extinguished by AIDS. Nothing he wanted to dwell on for long. He kept waiting for the right moment to tell his mother that he was not infected but, in her timidity, she never asked. His gayness, like his theatre career, was something to be avoided—the chip in the china cup that one made an effort to ignore.

The last time she saw him was when she came up from Philly with his great-aunt Jinx. Roger had told her about his good fortune landing a plum role in an off-off-Broadway play after graduating from college. The playwright/director was an avant-garde impresario who even managed to pay his actors. He never expected her to come. Since he'd moved to New York, she hadn't paid him a single visit. Even when he'd won starring roles at college in traditional plays like *The Glass Menagerie* and *Our Town*. She was in the process of selling her tiny bungalow on Fritzwater Street and moving to a retirement community in central Florida. He assumed the next time he'd see her would be when he went home to clean out his boxes in the basement.

He was more than mildly shocked one night when he peered into the audience and spotted his mother with his Aunt Jinx. They were sitting on the bleacher seats looking distraught and greatly in need of lower back support: their pocketbooks stationed on their laps, their wool coats still buttoned to the neck. It occurred to him that he might have overstated certain aspects of the production. His mother didn't know anything about New York theatre and probably heard "famous director" and "paying job" and thought he was performing on Broadway at the Biltmore. He'd left out the fact that his role required him to be naked on stage except for a giant prosthetic phallus protruding some two feet in front of him on an upward curve. Also absent from his description was the white Kabuki makeup the actors wore, the set which consisted of hundreds of colored strings stretched across the stage at odd angles, and that all the dialogue was pre-recorded voices in foreign languages. He remembered telling her it was a journey play based on Odysseus. He omitted the part of the journey that required him to fit his phallus into milk cans, rings of fire, black holes, and even a life-size inflatable cow.

That night, Roger gave the most understated and elegant performance he could give with a two-foot dildo strapped to his loins. After the play ended, he hung up his phallus, washed off his Kabuki makeup, and went to find his mother. She was still in the same spot in the audience: purse on lap, coat fully buttoned, likewise his aunt. A small crowd of hipsters was milling about, talking on cell phones to other small crowds of hipsters at craft beer tastings and dubstep music venues around the city.

"There he is," she said, and lumbered down the three steps to meet him. Though it had been over two years since he'd last seen her, she looked much the same. Her hair still dyed with Nice n' Easy honeysuckle blonde and combed in bangs, her eyes with slightly larger bags.

"Hi, Jinx." He fanned his hand in the air.

"Hi, yourself," said Jinx. "That's some play there."

"If I knew you were coming I'd have comped your tickets." Roger crossed his arms and smiled, in a way that invited more compliments but also ready to be offended by them.

"I never knew you spoke so many languages," said Jinx.

"Oh. That wasn't me."

"See." His mother elbowed Jinx. "I knew he couldn't speak all those languages. He barely passed freshman Spanish."

"It was five pre-recorded voices. Two were women."

"Well, your hair looked good on stage," his mother said. "Like you just washed it this morning."

"We can go to a restaurant down the street if you're hungry," he offered.

His mother clutched her purse. "Oh. I can't eat past seven these days."

"There's a bar nearby if you just want a drink?"

She made a face. "I just wanted to see one of your shows before I go to Florida."

He saw the familiar fear in her eyes: afraid to say the wrong thing, uncomfortable with the strange people around her, perceiving them as alien life forms with superior intelligence. She was so afraid of provoking his disapproval that she couldn't see her own.

As a child, his disapproval of his mother was monumental: her elastic-waist stretch pants, her Jell-O with shredded carrots, her spray-painted plastic flowers, and those damn Hummel figurines. As he grew, his disapproval accelerated, like dark energy in an expanding universe. Disapproval became a kind of protection against becoming an unhappy person with no knowledge of the better things in life. On Sunday night, the family would gather around the TV set. He would look at his grandma nodding off, his aunt with a bowl of popcorn on her lap, his mom working on one of her puzzles of kittens in a basket, and he'd think: Do not be that. He struggled to create an alternative life. A life that included books and art and ideas and beauty. And when he finally achieved it, he and his mother no longer had anything in common.

He sent her off that evening, shaking her head into the bustling New York night. A couple of weeks later, he went back home to help her organize the house. They held a garage sale, sold most of her furniture, and donated the rest to Goodwill. That weekend, over fourteen years ago, was the last time he saw her. And though he thought about her often, he didn't really miss her. If he had to sacrifice the security of family and filial feelings for his life today, he would do it again in a heartbeat. The lucky people were the ones who didn't have to make this sacrifice. And maybe this was the cause of his anger—all the lucky people with parents as best friends and confidants, cheerleaders and support systems.

He placed the last roll-up on table twelve and went to check the reservation sheet. James's color-coded times were superimposed over a graphic of each table. He couldn't help but admire his attention to detail. Puppets with genitals, reservations with graphics—nothing escaped his notice. The restaurant didn't look too busy, and he would ask to go home early so he could work on his script. If he felt more comfortable with Sherry, he would have told her about his play—how the entire cast had turned on him—but talking about it only made it more real. And just like with the terrorists, admitting that someone hurt you was allowing them to win.

The door opened and Melissa breezed in, pushing three-year-old Barclay in a stroller, while six-year-old Brandon trudged behind. Melissa gave Brandon a pack of crayons and set him at a table to color. He always seemed unusually lethargic for a six-year-old; Roger could never tell if it was affected boredom or acute depression. Having a father as unpredictable as Bart could be exhausting for any child. Roger imagined Brandon spent most of his time trying to go unnoticed, which was a similar disposition the restaurant staff cultivated.

Melissa wheeled Barclay, who was fast asleep, to a corner by the bar.

"Where is everyone? Did he do the tasting already?"

"What tasting?"

"The new appetizer. For the Shawmut launch. Didn't you read my email?"

"I didn't get an email," Roger said, a note of suspicion rising in his voice. Melissa frequently operated on the premise that thinking of doing something was the same thing as actually doing it. "Is Shawmut having their launch here?"

Every year, the city's premier restaurant guide had a launch party for their new issue. The party was always held at an up-and-coming restaurant that received high ratings. Though it had never been held in Brooklyn, Melissa explained that this year, they had it on good authority it would be, and Bart naturally thought his restaurant would be the obvious choice.

"There's my little mama." Bart came bounding out of the kitchen carrying two plates of food. He was wearing his usual board shorts and flying disc t-shirt. His temper tantrum of the previous evening had been completely wiped from his memory, and he was back to being the irascible puppy, jumping on everyone's legs.

"Here it comes. Get your mouths watering and your tongues wagging." He set the plates down just as James was coming up from the basement.

"What's going on?" James made his big Y-arm gesture.

"My duck confit is going on. Wowing the Shawmut judges is going on. Get with the program, Mr. Magoo." He pointed to the cutlery tray. "Roger. Could you get us some forks?"

Roger retrieved forks while Melissa reiterated the intel about the Shawmut launch.

"That's exciting," James said. "When are we going to find out?"

"Any day now. I explained it all in the email."

"Oh. I didn't get it."

Bart and Melissa exchanged looks. "Honey. Pumpkin. Buttercup," Bart said. "Did you forget to press send? Again?" He pointed a fork in Melissa's direction and she fussed with Barclay's blanket.

James called downstairs for Sherry, and explained to Bart that Max wasn't scheduled for today.

"His loss. All of you will have to describe this orgasmic goodness to him. This duck … this duck … I can't say enough about this duck. I want to get a t-shirt that says: It's all about my duck. If a gram of cocaine and your mother's best hug got together and had a baby, it would be this duck. It's confit. Do you all know what that means?"

"It's pretentious?" Roger said, taking a bite.

Sherry came to the table and grabbed a fork. "Slow-roasted in its own fat."

"Yes. Slow-roasted for three hours, and then pan-seared to crisp the skin."

"We used to serve this at Jean-Georges, but yours is better."

"Better than Jo-Jo? Why, thank you, kind maiden. Finally, someone with a discerning palate." He flicked his fingers at Melissa.

"Delicious," said James.

"Is that rosemary I taste?" asked Sherry.

"I rubbed it with garlic, onion, and rosemary in all its cracks and crevices. And then I slapped its little bottom and let it soak overnight."

"Okay. Keep it G-rated. Your children are in earshot," said Melissa.

"You mean I can't say it tastes just like a woman after she's done an hour of strenuous Pilates?"

Melissa sighed and made air quotes. "Professional. Isn't that what we talked about?"

"I am being professional. Roger wants to know what a woman tastes like. Don't you, Champ?"

"Um… What makes you think I don't?"

"You with your manly chest and shoulders. I see you and think: sweaty ball sacks; hairy armpits. All those mens you've been with. You should be oiled in duck fat."

"So," Melissa interrupted. "This is the new appetizer. It's fourteen dollars. Expensive, but it's almost a meal in itself. Push it tonight as a special and ask for feedback."

"I want to get it perfect before Shawmut comes," Bart said. "Let me know what the hoi polloi think."

Roger did a mental eye-roll. The last thing he would ever do was bring criticism about Bart's food to his kitchen.

Sherry sucked on her fork, quizzically. "I wonder what it would taste like with some fruit flavor. A hint of berry or orange."

"That's a good idea, Milady."

"Yes. Great idea," James chimed in.

"I hate these crayons," Brandon whined. "Why can't we go now?" He threw a crayon at his sleeping brother, who woke up and started crying.

Melissa picked up the crayon and started wheeling Barclay out. "We're taking off. See you guys." As she was going to the door, she whispered to Bart, "I thought you were going to start wearing a chef's coat and pants, like we talked about?"

"Be good boys." He put a hand on Brandon's back, moving him along. "You don't want to make Mommy and Daddy get a divorce."

"Bart!"

"Bye, Dumpling." He stood at the door, waving a towel. "Remember to press send. Like we talked about."

After hearing their farewell, Roger gave Sherry a raised eyebrow, and they both smiled, knowing there would be much more to discuss later. He made a concerted effort to exclude James from their circle smirk, and took another bite of confit. "It's so tender. Don't you think?"

"Like a child's feelings," Sherry said.

"You little urchins made fast work of that." Bart scooped up the plates and regarded Sherry. "I'm going to add arugula salad with an orange vinaigrette and Madeiran slices to the dish."

Sherry tilted her head in surprise. "Great."

"What did Jo-Jo serve it with?"

"Oh. I think a frisée and cranberry compote."

"I'll write an insert to put in the menu," James said. "Duck Confit, arugula salad, orange vinaigrette, Madeiran slices."

"Team work makes the dream work." Bart swaggered into the kitchen, holding the plates above his head.

Roger strode past James, purposely avoiding his eyes and got a Diet Coke from the bar fridge. He angled his back in James's direction and readied himself to receive a heartfelt apology. But James merely dropped his fork in a bus tub and hurried downstairs. Roger reconstituted himself on the banquet and continued rolling silverware. Soon, Sherry joined him.

"What was going on with you and Bart?" he asked.

She demurely pursed her lips and rolled a napkin. "Just his usual silliness, I guess."

"Come on. He was aggressively flirting with you. Right in front of Melissa."

"He was aggressively flirting with *you*, more like it. Talking about dipping you in duck fat."

"Yes, but it didn't mean anything."

"And why should it with me?"

"Because there's the possibility he could act with you."

"And why not with you?"

He tapped a roll-up on the table. "Reason number one: I don't think he's gay."

"Why not? You think everyone else is?"

He stopped rolling and considered this. Had he been fooled by the wife and kids, the board shorts and Frisbee tournaments? New York City was a swirling cocktail of confusing masculinity. There were straight gay men—bearded, flannel-wearing guys who did wood carvings and religiously made their own homebrew. And then there were the gay straight men, effortlessly rocking pastel nail polish while double-fisting mimosas at a disco brunch. In fact, in this city, the more a guy looked like he could bench-press a small car, the more likely he was to also know every word to a Cher deep cut. And then there was James. Into which category did he fall? The tea set and puppets were definitely gay, but the khaki pants and lack of upper body strength suggested a man who considered ranch dressing a personality trait. He was an enigma, like a lumberjack who exclusively chopped tofu. Still, the more he thought about Bart, the more improbable it seemed that he was gay.

"Would you ever?" he asked.

"You mean if he didn't have a wife and kids and wasn't my boss?"

"Or even if."

"Hum. He's very tall."

"And you know what they say about tall men?"

Sherry rolled her eyes. "Big shoes."

"No. They're always looking down on you."

"I have enough men looking down on me." She ripped open another pack of napkins. "I've been thinking about what you said. Maybe I will stay with Trish. For a while. Until Sean's show is over. Give him some time to miss me."

"Good idea."

They rolled for a while in silence. Sherry clutched a napkin and giggled mischievously. "Would you ever? With Bart?"

Roger pictured Bart with his long legs in the air, his brows concentrated in that mean expression he gets just before he blows up. "It could be my mission. Converting one gay straight man at a time."

5: The Buddhist Guide to Blowjobs

James sat in his basement office, typing up the menu special. Every now and then, he looked up to see Roger and Sherry on the monitor. They were rolling silverware and laughing. It seemed to be their primary form of communication—always laughing in corners, at the hot line, by the coffee station, smiles passing between them like secret codes. He went back to typing. For companionship, he had the hum of the walk-in fridge and his desk of precisely organized documents. Sometimes he would open a drawer and examine the papers all sitting in their color-coded folders; it gave him a renewed sense of accomplishment. The world may be random and unpredictable, but these drawers were immutable.

This was Roger's first appearance at work since James had kicked him out of his apartment, and obviously an apology was in order. Over the past couple of days, he'd brooded about his lack of generosity and the feelings of jealousy Roger had unearthed. Generosity was one of the three pillars of Dharma, first on the list of spiritual perfections, and he had committed a serious breach. Daiyu used to say: *Were it not for guests, all houses would be graves.* James had broken the rules of hospitality. The first person to visit his New York apartment had been cast out in anger. He had failed to meet Roger with a generous spirit. And Roger had been quite generous with him. He invited James into his house, gave him a hot cup of tea and a blowjob—it didn't get more hospitable than that.

He was still reconciling his stance on oral sex—the Buddhist texts held strict prohibitions against it. He couldn't comprehend why anyone would want to suck a dick, but he was certainly grateful for the women in his life who had done so. And even though he usually returned the favor, he still worried about his performance: his tongue not finding the right rhythm, his jaw going numb. Being too focused on self and ego, he couldn't always lose himself in the present moment. Though when he managed to forget himself, he could take almost as much pleasure as he was giving. He imagined the giver of fellatio might have felt the same. Sex, whether oral or otherwise, was the one act where one could actually get as much pleasure in giving as receiving, which might make it the best example of generosity.

On his desk blotter, Melissa had scribbled some reservations that needed to be confirmed. He picked up the phone. Most of the calls were to regulars, so it was kind of like talking to old friends. He often thought of the confirmations as inviting friends to his house for dinner. "Hi Kathy. This is James at Bartholomew. So glad you could join us tonight. We'll see you at seven."

Roger and Sherry were now earnestly discussing something. The monitor showed them with solemn head shakes and stoic expressions. Sherry stared blankly at the wall, crushing a napkin in her hand. If Roger told her about their interlude, it would wreck his chances with her. He didn't want Sherry thinking he was a closet case. Or some sexually confused rube, prey to every gay guy's machinations. He tried to read their lips, but the picture wasn't clear enough. He wanted to believe that Roger wouldn't sabotage him. After all, they were both men searching for love. Granted, they might be searching for different manifestations: Roger in pursuit of hairy nipples, chiseled jawlines, and someone who knew all the lyrics to *Hello Dolly*, but hopefully he wouldn't stand in the way of a brother finding love of a more feminine variety. There was a code—of brothers—of bros—of brahs.

But Roger had his own code, and it usually involved describing his sexual liaisons right down to the spit-take. James had heard too often about the guy whose "cum tasted like Cool Ranch dressing." The man with "the hooked shaped penis." The tit-torturist whose nipples "pointed at the floor." He had little confidence that Roger would be discreet about their own encounter. Especially now that he felt wronged.

James called more numbers and spoke to people's voicemails. At one point his mind wandered and he almost said, so glad you could blow us tonight, but he recovered and stuck to the script.

Intellectually, he knew that coming in one man's mouth did not make you gay. Even coming in a hundred men's mouths did not make you gay. Though it probably meant you had a large and attractive penis. Being gay was about desiring the same sex, and, he was still very much attracted to women. In fact, if he wasn't so attracted to one particular woman, he wouldn't be so worried about receiving a blowjob from Roger. In that context, it was really his heterosexual attraction that was making him obsess about gay sex.

He opened a drawer and arranged the paper clips in symmetrical rows inside their box. On the monitor, Roger was setting tables. He heard Sherry's feet coming down the stairs and the ironing board groaning with her pressings. Sometimes she would iron in just her bra and pants. On these occasions, he usually found an excuse to walk by and check the shelves, but today he didn't trust himself to say the right thing.

With the calls finished, he started reconciling the inventory sheets. He was so involved counting orders of morel mushrooms and broccoli florets that he didn't hear Sherry knock. He looked up and she was standing in front of his desk—shirt finely pressed, eyes brimming with understanding.

"How you holding up?" she said, tying a fresh apron around her middle.

It took him a beat to realize she was referring to his dead grandmother and not the accumulating workload on his desk. "Oh. You know." He sighed. "Surviving."

She returned a sympathetic nod. "Yeah. I know."

He hated milking the dead grandma theme, but every time he saw Sherry, he was reminded of their mutual grief, and then in turn of his particular loss. Which brought on a wave of sorrow accompanied by a rush of desire, fantasies about how their mutual mourning might lead to a mutual commingling. He imagined brushing her hand as they looked at old photographs of their grandmothers. Maybe a day at the cemetery, where she cried on his shoulder and he valiantly adjusted his erection away from her leg.

"I had a dream about her last night." Which was true, if by dream he meant fleeting thought.

"That's how they speak to us." She slapped the desk, making vibrations that carried through the wood into his stomach. "When my grandma passed, I dreamed she baked molasses cookies. She was stirring everything into a big bowl, and then she handed the spatula to me." Sherry looked to the ceiling as if her grandma might be reaching down right now, spatula in hand. "Then there was this image of her wrapping a shawl around me." She crossed her arms around her chest. "What was yours?"

"I was in this dark room. And my grandma was rocking in a chair, saying, over and over, 'Don't be a putz. Don't be a putz.'"

Sherry pursed her lips.

"I wish I would've spent more time with her." He glanced at the columns of numbers on his screen. His grandma would have hated this job. She had an automatic dislike for anything conventional, which was probably why she tolerated his father turning Buddhist. And why, after Tracy dumped him, she encouraged James to "leave this hick town and go to New York." She would call him every weekend, hoping for stories of celebrity sightings or raucous parties. When he had nothing to talk about but grease traps and health inspections, she accused him of wasting his life. Eventually, he stopped answering her calls.

"You know what you need? I've got just the thing." Sherry ran out of the office, and he heard her rummaging in her locker. She came back with a purse that could double as a medic bag. She unfastened the nylon straps and brought out a small bottle. On each of his wrists, she put a small drop of oil and massaged it in.

"What's this?"

"It's basil oil. My own recipe. It's calming."

He lifted his hand to his nose. "I smell like a Caprese salad."

She put a drop on his forehead, her thumb caressing the spot between his brows, her breath feathering his cheek.

"You made this?"

"It's one of my potions."

"So you're a witch?"

"A good witch. With lots of white magic." She put her fingertips over his heart and held them there—listening. "You can still talk to your grandmother," she said. "Open your heart and she'll come to you in dreams. In reflections. Even through certain animals. Once, when I was having a really bad day, I saw the spirit of my grandmother in a squirrel with a white patch on its head."

"How did you know it was your grandmother?"

"She always wore a small white hat she called a fascinator."

"That's crazy."

"The universe is a crazy place. Sniffing herbs can clear your mind. Squirrels can become your grandmother. And why not? If it makes you feel better?"

Why not indeed? Though, he wasn't looking forward to seeing his grandma gathering nuts in the park.

Sherry leaned in and studied the conformation sheet. "If we're not busy tonight, can you send me home early?" she asked. "I need to do something before Sean gets back."

"Sure. I wouldn't want to steal his muse." Unless, he thought, it was for a night of illicit sex leading to marriage with children and years of eternal devotion.

"These days I'm more of a nursemaid than a muse."

"Don't you pose for him?" James flashed on images of Sherry draped over various pieces of furniture.

"He claims me as inspiration but he's obsessed with Slinkies right now, so ...." She rolled her eyes and put some oil on her wrists, rubbing them together like sticks. "Actually, I'm going to stay at a friend's place for a while to give him more room to work. Do you think I could leave early tonight? I need to move some stuff."

This was the opportunity he had been waiting for—a crack in Sherry's romantic edifice, through which he might pull her out and build a house around her. No, that was wrong. He would let her build her own house. He would just ask for some small shelter within: a den, a nook, a linen closet with a little shelf on which to lay his head.

When eight o'clock rolled around, he told Sherry she could leave. He watched her pacing in front of the to-go containers, whispering into her phone. He knelt close by and pretended to count the stock on the bottom shelf. Her socks had cats' faces peeking out from around her ankles. He could only hear a few monosyllables, but she clearly was making plans to sneak away without Sean knowing. When the conversation ended, she grabbed her medic bag and hurried out the door.

By nine, the regulars were already on dessert, and they only had one more reservation on the book: Felix and Darlene, who ran a seafood grill in Park Slope. Many smaller Brooklyn restaurants closed on Mondays, and their owners would often pay their respects to Bartholomew. As the only restaurant in Brooklyn with a twenty-six-point Shawmut rating, Bart was blazing a trail they needed to follow.

He walked by one of Roger's tables and heard him telling a guest that they didn't have any steak sauce in house. It was one of Bart's pet peeves, not to allow guests to ruin his dry-aged, grass-fed beef with cheap condiments. But, a few moments later, when the old man with the bushy eyebrows stopped James and asked again, he told him "just a moment" and went to the bodega across the street and bought some A-1 sauce. He didn't know why he did it. Maybe it was a passive-aggressive way to assert himself with Bart. He understood how an overbearing sauce could spoil the taste of a fine cut of meat, but he also didn't like to be inhospitable. After his altercation with Roger, he needed to practice generosity. And the old man looked so pleased when he set the bottle on the table. If he couldn't be a good host in his own home, at least he could be one here.

Felix gave him a firm handshake, and Darlene an even firmer one. He escorted them to the best table by the window and held out the chair for her. She yanked the chair from his grip and commandeered it under the table herself. With her short grey hair and big glasses, everyone assumed Darlene was a lesbian-in-waiting. Felix himself joked that he met his wife at a softball game: "Changed her from a pitcher to a catcher with my seductive charm" was how he put it. Darlene, for her part, always responded in kind: "It wasn't your charm, Fel. Your penis just reminded me of my ex-girlfriend's fingers."

At any rate, they had three kids, so James assumed the speculation was all in good fun. Of course, Roger had insisted: "I guarantee you, as soon as their youngest is in college, Darlene is buying a Jeep Wrangler and going fishing every weekend. And not necessarily on a lake."

Darlene and Felix, like Melissa and Bart, were typical of many husband-and-wife teams in Brooklyn restaurants: the husband as chef and the wife as general manager. It was a kind of mother-and-son dynamic, where the husband got to play the creative genius and the wife the stern supervisor, handling the practical matters and enabling the genius to be creative. Sixty percent of new restaurants failed in the first year, and eighty percent after three years—a statistic Melissa was fond of mentioning at staff meetings. Still, it didn't stop every disgruntled sous-chef in Manhattan from crossing the East River and trying to beat the odds.

He set the menus on the table and went to inform Bart. When industry people arrived, he usually sent out appetizers and sometimes even prepared tasting menus.

In the kitchen, Bart was playing catch with Eric and Jorge. They stood at three corners of the prep table, tossing a bag of chicken livers. Bart holstered the livers in an apron pocket and hurried out to greet them.

"Felix, you mad dog. Tell me all the news."

"You heard about Green, no doubt."

Green was Bart's biggest competition on the street. It was run by the husband-and-wife team of Aaron and Carrie: the two most hated people in the Brooklyn culinary scene. They were notoriously competitive with other restaurants and downright mercenary with their staff. When their bistro first opened and they were interviewed by the Times, they claimed to be the only restaurant in Brooklyn with "true farm-to-table fare." And the first restaurant in the borough to combine "organic eating with elevated cuisine." This naturally pissed off the dozen other restaurants in the borough that were doing the exact same thing.

"What about those charlatans?" Bart took a step back from the table and folded his hands behind his back.

"They're hosting the Shawmut launch."

"Really?"

"Yeah. They scored a twenty-eight in the ratings this year. Can you believe it?"

James noticed Bart's fists flexing behind his back, and he took a moment to come to the table and refill the water glasses, giving him a chance to escape.

"I have to get back to the kitchen. I want you to try my new appetizer."

As Bart was walking back, the bushy eyebrowed man stopped him. "Are you the chef?"

"I am indeed."

"I just want to tell you that was the best steak I've ever had. My compliments to you."

"Thank you, sir. We aim to please." Bart reached across the table and extracted the bottle of A-1 sauce. "Enjoy your evening."

James watched him hold up the bottle to Roger and point to the kitchen.

There was no music to this moment, but nonetheless he heard the soundtrack to *Jaws*. He followed them, determined to make a full confession about the steak sauce.

As he approached the kitchen, he heard Bart yelling. He took a few cleansing breaths. Again, that Daffy-Duck-with-his-feathers-shot-off feeling assailed him. Daiyu said: *Let the world pass over you like the reflection of birds flying over water*. But when the birds were pecking and hurling abuse, it was hard to be reflective.

He heard a shattering, presumably the A-1 bottle smashing in the sink. He leaned against the wall outside the kitchen and gripped his thighs.

"This is my restaurant," Bart said. "I decide what goes on the plates."

"I'm sorry," Roger said. "I forgot about the steak sauce rule."

James couldn't believe Roger was protecting him. It made no sense. He started to wonder if he had dreamed buying the steak sauce. He pressed his back against the wall and listened. Bart was calling Roger a moron, a blockhead, and threatening to fire him. This was the moment when he needed to rush in—face his fears—and confess. It didn't matter that when Bart got angry his eyes turned into primordial black holes that sucked you into their madness and made you feel your molecules were splitting apart. One time, he came into the kitchen and Bart was yelling at Eric. A bowl of chopped cauliflower stood between them; Bart was saying, "I wanted florets not wedges." He picked up handfuls of the stuff and threw them in the air. Pieces of cauliflower rained down on Eric's shoulders and dangled in his hair like protracted bits of brain. Another time, Bart was so distraught when a customer sent back his rib-eye that he ripped it in two with his bare hands and chucked the bloody pieces at the wall.

Of course, none of this mattered now because Roger was in trouble. Roger, who opened his rehearsal to him, who shared his art and exposed himself to ridicule, who gave him tea and blowjobs and advice about women—Roger needed his help. But first, he had to calm down. He took deep cleansing breaths and tried to think soothing thoughts.

Bart was now listing all the ingredients in the steak sauce and telling Roger exactly how it ruined the meat. When he got into professor mode, all bets were off. His mother had always told him to take responsibility for his actions. She used to be perpetually late picking him up from after-school daycare, always making excuses about traffic or faculty meetings, but that didn't stop James from noticing her new manicure or the packages from Maryann's Fashions in the back seat of the car. It was slowly dawning on him that women had been deceiving him in one way or another for his entire life.

Roger came out of the kitchen and breezed past him; James realized he'd missed his moment. A couple was at the door and Roger was heading in their direction. James grabbed two menus and sat the guests himself. There were only so many favors his conscience could allow.

For the rest of the night, he maintained a protective circle around Roger, bringing bread to his tables, filling water glasses, running Felix and Darlene's food from the kitchen so he didn't have to interact with Bart. Still, every time he tried to talk to him, Roger averted his eyes and walked away.

After Felix and Darlene left, and the restaurant emptied out, he cornered Roger by the cappuccino machine. "I'm just going to tell Bart that I got the steak sauce. Okay?"

"Do what you want." Roger waved a hand and headed downstairs to the wine room.

In the kitchen, Eric was sharing a joint with Jorge, both defiantly ashing into the sink. Bart was nowhere to be seen. When he asked, Eric told him that Bart had gone out the back door as soon as the last entrée had been plated.

He went to the computer to print out the sales report and watched the long spool of paper fold over itself. *Karma is like a shadow. The smallest act can grow into something large and serious.* James felt he had a shadow of bad behavior looming over him. Not only had he been inhospitable to Roger, but he had caused him to be dishonored at work. He imagined his bad behavior growing and impacting Roger's life: he would become a recluse, never venturing into another friend's house; he would nurture resentment of future coworkers; he would develop an unnatural fear of steak sauce. He checked the sales figures for the night and waited at the bar.

Eric and Jorge charged out of the kitchen, jostling each other with goofy smiles and friendly jabs. He called to them, but they were too involved in their private joke to respond.

He knew he had to do something to compensate Roger. Buy him a drink? Bake him a cake? He wanted to make things right and went down to the wine room.

"I think we need to talk." James stood in the doorway, careful not to touch the wobbly metal shelves, whose smallest movement caused the wine bottles to clink against each other. Roger ignored him and continued loading his bucket with wine. Empty boxes were stacked waist high between them. He thought about telling Roger to break them down, but decided that issuing commands might not be a good prelude to an apology. "You're angry with me. I get that. I just wanted to apologize. I should have never let you take the blame for the steak sauce."

Roger picked up a bottle of Chianti and studied its label.

James toed the cardboard on the floor and braced a hand on the door frame. "I also wanted to apologize for what happened the other night. I overreacted. I shouldn't have kicked you out of my place. I'm a bit sensitive when it comes to my puppets."

"You think?"

"I haven't shown them to many people. I'm not used to them being ... handled. But that's no excuse. I got defensive. Maybe even a little jealous. So, yeah. I'm sorry."

He turned towards James. "You're sorry for what now?"

"For the steak sauce. For telling you to leave. For overreacting. For not defending you to Bart. I was wrong on all counts. Is there something else?"

Roger stowed away the Chianti. "Nope. That about covers it."

"But you can't be talking to Sherry. There's a code..." He leaned on one of the empty boxes and it buckled under his weight.

"Now you're telling me who I can talk to?"

He broke down the box and folded it into a flat square. "Just about certain things."

"Oh yeah? What things?"

"You know what things."

"You mean about your thousand creepy puppets?"

"You didn't think they were so creepy when you were engaging them in copulation."

Roger exhaled, dismissing his words as if they were no more than a burp at a cocktail party. "Then what then?"

He threw the cardboard down. "You know perfectly well what I'm talking about. There are certain things ... between men. Honor. Loyalty. Solidarity."

"What? Are we in the French Foreign Legion now?"

James rested a hand on one of the shelves, which set in motion a round of clinking bottles, causing his thoughts to scatter and disseminate.

"You mean about me sucking your cock?" Roger said. "And licking your balls? And rubbing your nipples? And making you moan in that little high-pitched..."

"All right all ready." He steadied the shelves to stop the clinking. "Just don't tell her. Okay?"

Roger put a few more bottles in his bucket. "Why not?"

"I just ... it's not her business."

"You're ashamed."

"No, I ..."

"What if I already told her?"

"You had no right." He stepped around the boxes. "That was between you and me. This puts me in a very bad position at work."

"What does it have to do with work?"

"It ... everything. It has everything to do with work and my position as manager."

"You're ashamed of what happened between us."

"Not ashamed. I just don't want you telling people."

"Isn't that the definition of ashamed?"

"As a manager. It's not supposed to happen."

"As a heterosexual man, it's not supposed to happen."

He blew air between his lips and pressed his fingers against his palms. "I was drunk."

"And you want me to forget about it and not tell anyone?"

"Yes."

"Because it was so disgusting and embarrassing for you."

"No. It was ... fine—weird and awkward, but a perfectly fine expression of generosity and ... kindness. You were very kind to me. But I'm not gay. And I don't want people thinking I'm hiding or confused or in the closet."

Roger gave a defensive smile. "You don't want Sherry thinking that."

"Look. I was raised by the most liberal-minded parents in academia. If I were gay, it wouldn't be an issue. My mom would knit me a rainbow flag. My dad would buy me a leather-bound edition of Angels in America. I just want you to understand that. And I hope we can still be friends and put everything behind us because I really like you .... Just not in that way."

They studied the pieces of cardboard on the floor.

"I didn't tell her about the sex," Roger finally said. "I might have mentioned something about the puppets. But that was all."

James breathed a sigh of relief. "So she thinks I'm some maniacal puppet master."

"Well, you are." Roger reached around him, grabbed a bottle of Cabernet and set it in the bucket.

"I should never have shown them to you."

"I'm glad you did. They're very special. Your films must be ... they must be extraordinary."

Blood rushed to his cheeks. This was quite a compliment coming from Roger, who had been known to criticize a cloudless sunny day for being too prosaic.

"You have a gift. I'm sorry I was so careless. I should have respected your art."

James had never thought of his puppets as art. A craft perhaps. A profession maybe. But art had never occurred to him. The movies he someday made with the puppets would be art, but the puppets themselves were just a hobby.

"You should think about mounting them in some kind of display or installation and seeing if a gallery would be interested. They have a Henry Darger quality."

He had never heard of Henry Darger, and couldn't imagine his puppets in an art gallery, so he stuck to the question at hand. "Why did you take the blame for me? With Bart?"

"I don't know. He's harder on you than he is on me." Roger kicked the bucket out of the way. "I didn't want you getting into trouble." He stood there with a goofy smile on his face, his toe poking the bucket, his fingers tapping his leg.

"How can I make it up to you?" James said.

Roger looked into his bucket and seemed to be taking a kind of inventory. "Do me one favor."

"Sure. Anything."

"Let me kiss you."

He realized that a rejection at this point could send their relationship on a downhill trajectory from which it might never recover. He imagined further insubordination, complaints to Bart, incriminations to Sherry. The situation was delicate. Everything was at risk. He felt like Roger had just rescued him from one burning building and set him down in another.

"Why?"

"Just to see what it's like sober. If it's not an issue for you, then it's no big deal."

James stood there silently calculating how to escape the flames.

Roger reached out and touched his neck. Pulled his face down. He felt the bristly mustache tickle his nose and almost started laughing. He half expected Roger to pull back and yell, Psyche! But Roger's mouth kept pressing its whiskered barbs around his lips, searching for an opening.

Their feet pushed around the cardboard on the floor. He was glad that Roger wasn't angry anymore. Grateful that he had recognized his puppets as art. But there was only so much gratitude he could muster. He started to recoil when Roger's tongue touched his teeth, when his arms cradled the small of his back and pulled him in.

He told himself it was just body parts congregating with other body parts, nerve axons firing into connective tissue, electrochemical impulses canoodling. In the grand scheme of things, it was no more significant than two paramecium conjugating in a Petri dish. Though in the immediate here and now, there was something thrilling in being desired this much. In being pursued beyond the bounds of social propriety, workplace decorum, and sexual orientation. He felt Roger's taproot of loneliness reaching through the soil. This willingness to give oneself over—to connect—to merge. To crawl out of these separate bodies—these shells. It was as if he was privy to Roger's secret house; he could open all of his drawers and cupboards and plunge his hands inside.

Roger put a hand on his shoulder and pushed him down. And quite unexpectedly he went. Knees releasing, obeying the pressure of Roger's hands. This was what was expected. This was compensation. Roger opened his pants and he felt the cold sting of the zipper on his cheek. He was face to face with Roger's penis. Or more problematically, face to penis.

He had never been this close to another penis, and watched as the whole apparatus unfurled before him, all wiry hairs and blue veins, like some wrinkly old man slowly pulling himself out of the bedclothes.

Through the act of giving, we learn to remove our attachments. James thought about what he was attached to: his identity as a straight man. He self-reported his feelings: aversion, fear, jealousy. *Fear and disgust are all parts of life. Become aware of these reactions so you can be free of them.* Could he do it? Could he lose these adverse reactions and free himself of attachment? It was just skin, over tissue, engorged with blood.

Generosity was the act of giving without the expectation of receiving. Whenever he would come to Daiyu with a problem, Daiyu would ask: *What have you given today? To whom have you sent Loving-Kindness?* Though Daiyu most certainly would not have considered a blowjob an act of loving-kindness. They had discussed oral sex quite extensively when he was with Joanne, and Daiyu had counseled that as long as oral sex didn't go against the main precept of not harming any being, it could reasonably be sanctioned. James continued the practice with a mostly guilt-free conscience, concluding that misplacing his penis in Joanne's mouth rather than her textually sanctioned vagina was allowing her an expression of generosity. And now the karmic wheel was turning on him to reciprocate.

He took just the tip. There was no taste. Just a slight musty smell like old blankets in an attic. His tongue pushed against it and it grew. His lips pulsed around it and his saliva began to increase. It could be anything in his mouth: a popsicle, a Tootsie Pop, a chicken leg. When in doubt, everything tasted like chicken. He lost his balance and held onto Roger's thighs, which felt taught, hairy, and somewhat moist.

Giving quietly supports the endeavor to free the mind from defilements. It was the first of the Three Meritorious Deeds, and the first of the Ten Perfections. *The perfection of giving is to be practiced by relinquishing one's happiness to others.* James could feel his happiness slipping away every time Roger hit the back of his throat. Sometimes a little hum escaped Roger's lips. Unexpectedly, James began to appreciate that hum. He endeavored to move his mouth in such a way as to make the sound repeat. Similar to playing an instrument, Roger was the tuba he could make music with. One could receive pleasure by giving pleasure. In giving one's self, a kind of loving-kindness was exchanged.

Tenderly, Roger stroked the top of his head. He reached around to the back of his neck and pressed James closer. He slid down James's throat; James gagged and pulled back. His eyes watered and he coughed, regarding the instrument in front of him with a look of defiance. Roger tapped him on the check, as if to remind him of his duty. If it was a finger or a cane it might have been almost charming. "Pardon me. Do you have any Grey Poupon?"

And so he kept going. After all, one did all kinds of unpleasant things for friends: walked their dog, moved their furniture, picked them up at the airport. This was just another obligation. Roger had done the same for him. He thought about Sherry. Roger's little moans and spasms becoming her little moans and spasms. The tremors in his bony knees turning into her smooth ones. Their two bodies conflating and rearranging themselves in his psyche, their parts forming and reforming themselves. A blowjob couldn't be gay if you were thinking about pussy while doing it. Could it? It was the kind of rationalization that put the dick back into contradiction.

If penises had no taste, he couldn't say the same for semen, which landed on his tongue like some briny pudding doused in bleach, Roger grabbing the sides of his head and releasing one staccato grunt. He had the urge to spit it out but after Roger kissed the top of his head, it seemed a mean-spirited gesture. He sat back on the floor while Roger redressed himself. James could feel his eyes scanning him but he kept his gaze downward; meeting Roger's eyes would make the moment too raw. When he finally looked up, Roger was gone.

Eventually, he swallowed the astringent and bitter sample, which conformed somewhat to Roger's personality. He wondered if every man's semen was indicative of his character. If being nice gave you better-tasting spunk. In which case, Tom Hanks must taste like vanilla ice cream. Though he had no desire for further exploration, he couldn't help but feel slightly poisoned, as if Roger's spunk was working its way through his internal organs, turning everything gay: tap dancing on his stomach, coating his large intestine with glitter, bedazzling his colon. After he heard Roger slam the door upstairs, he went to the walk-in fridge and downed a bottle of tomato juice.

6: The Heterosexual Storybook

Sherry was stocking his cabinets with food, laying in what looked like enough supplies for a nuclear winter, if said winter were to be spent in a diabetic coma. Sugared cereals, fruit roll-ups, pop tarts—it seemed you could take the girl out of the Midwest but you couldn't take the High Fructose Corn Syrup out of the girl. Roger was still in his flannel robe staring into the murky waters of his first cup of coffee, not yet cognizant enough to comment on the situation.

She had called him two days ago, desperately looking for a place to stay when her friend Trish had unexpectedly let her down. After taking his advice and leaving Sean's, she was supposed to have hidden out on Trish's couch, but Trish's roommate had an impromptu visit from her sister and her kids, so the couch, floor, and all other horizontal surfaces were subsequently occupied. Hence, because he felt partially responsible for her leaving Sean, and since, the futon in his windowless office was just going spare, Roger offered her its use until she could find safe lodgings elsewhere.

With his art show approaching, Sean was becoming more and more unstable. From what she described, it seemed like the last scene of *Long Day's Journey* with Mary Tyrone as a frustrated installation artist. His new concept revolved around The Eternal Spring, and what had finally convinced her to leave was Sean slicing open their mattress and extracting the springs to use for his ideal woman. Roger agreed that this could be a disturbing omen, and didn't want to expose Sherry to whatever Sean might decide to slice open next.

"Thanks again, for letting me stay here," she said. "It'll only be until Trish and I can find a place together."

"So you're not planning on going back? Even after his show opens?" He was examining one of her packages, a box of chocolate chip cookies with "birthday frosting."

"The whole troubled artist thing is weighing me down."

"Stay as long as you like. I'm not using the office as much now that my show's in rehearsals."

She broke open the cookie package and offered him one. "How's that going? Must be exciting."

He took a bite of cookie, which tasted like something a Teletubby might throw up after a night eating gummy bears and rainbow sprinkles. "The director's rewriting my script, my entire cast hates me, and I haven't been able to come up with an ending that works. So I guess it's going as well as expected." He dropped the cookie half on the table where it sent out a sprinkle of crumbs.

"At least you're not threatening to jump off the fire escape."

"If I didn't live on the first floor, I'd have been out the window years ago."

She poured herself a cup of coffee and dunked a cookie. "I still feel bad about leaving him."

The last couple of days had been spent catching him up on her relationship with Sean. Things she hadn't told him when they were just work buddies could now be disclosed over morning coffee and late-night TV viewing. He had become so familiar with the intimacies of her relationship with Sean and his drug-addled behavior that he'd come to view himself as her personal domestic abuse counselor.

She pointed a cookie in Roger's direction. "I've always had a soft spot for creative types."

"If you were smart, you'd have a soft spot for investment bankers."

"And how many investment bankers have you fallen in love with?"

"Not nearly enough." He stood and cinched his robe. He didn't particularly welcome another confessional moment. "Learn from my mistakes."

"And who are your current mistakes?" She closed the cookie package and put them in the cupboard.

"You wouldn't believe me if I told you."

He started to walk out, but she blocked the doorway. "So tell me."

Somehow, in the short time she'd been living with him, they'd settled into a domesticated version of Thelma and Louise, without the requisite robbery and murder. She was Geena Davis, all pouty lips and perky aphorisms, and he was Susan Sarandon, sour grapes and saggy tits. They had long conversations about fashion, love, and life's regrets. He appreciated that for every disappointment, she could procure an oil, cream, or stick of incense that would solve the problem. His medicine cabinet was now overflowing with her "potions." Every time he opened the door, some lotion, poultice, or little baggy of dried herbs would fall out and remind him that he needed to scrub, oil, or exfoliate some negativity from his being. He remembered his promise to James not to reveal anything about their liaison. And as much as he wanted to give her the blow-by-blow of James's blowjob, he held back. However, their new level of intimacy obliged him to at least partially answer her question.

"James," he confessed.

"James who?"

"Our intrepid leader? Our Captain, O Captain?" When these denominations received no reaction, he blurted out, "Our manager?"

Her eyes widened as if he'd just confessed to being an Al-Qaeda operative. "You're kidding."

"Wish that I were."

"What on Earth? Why?"

"If I knew the answer to that, I could write a dozen country songs." Not to involve himself in a conversation that might betray James's confidence, he pushed past her and closed the bathroom door.

The floor was damp from Sherry's recent shower. She had forgotten to put the curtain inside the tub. Beads of water lingered on the tile. He turned the faucet to hot. His dick was still sore from James's teeth. That's what happened when one fooled around with untutored virgins. He let the spray pummel his back. Was it just James's virginity that made him attractive? To be the first cock to plant itself in his geeky soil? Was it the power to turn a straight man gay—or bring a gay man to self-discovery? The bathroom steamed up with a fog of possibilities.

What he remembered most about their encounter was James looking up at him, his doe eyes trapped behind those wire-rimmed glasses, an expression that said: *Am I doing this right? Are you feeling good?* James wanted to please. Nothing critical in his countenance, no ulterior motives, no imagining someone else, just the desire to make another human feel good. The purity of the gesture stunned him.

He lathered with Sherry's olive oil soap and handled his body with a newfound care. The softness of the soap diminishing all his imagined flaws and imperfections. The water flowed down his back, smoothing out the wrinkles of worry and making him glow and shine. He thought about James. And how beautiful he looked with his cock in his mouth.

On his way to the restaurant, he decided to strike a more casual note. He knew that if he approached James with too much feeling it would be awkward. Complex emotions needed to be distilled into something graspable and fun. When two people shared a profound moment, it was better to break the ice with humor. He opened the door, and seeing James stationed per usual at the podium, came up behind and swatted his ass.

"Hello, Ducky." Roger always maintained that the best way to break the ice was with a sledgehammer.

"Hey!" James turned an angry shade of crimson and held up a finger. "Not appropriate."

Roger planted his elbows on the podium. "After all that's happened, are we really going to talk about what's appropriate?"

James bowed his head and exhaled into the reservation book. "Get to work."

"How about we go to the Roxy after?"

James studied the reservations and lifted the phone. "I don't think so."

"Look." Roger ran a finger across the podium. "I know this is confusing. I don't want to pressure you or make a big deal, but we should have a conversation. We'll drink. We'll discuss. And while at work, I'll remain the soul of appropriate behavior." He attempted a winning smile, which James didn't see because he still had his face buried in the book.

"Right now, I need you to clean the bar. Take out the bottles. Wipe down the shelves, and wash the Speedrack."

"Max just did that last week."

"And now it's your turn. Get busy." He tapped his colored pencil for emphasis and entered numbers into the phone.

"So we're still on for after work?" Roger placed a tentative finger on the reservation book.

"No. I want to keep things professional from now on." He began talking to someone on the phone in his "professional" voice.

Roger strode silently to the bar and started pulling liquor bottles from the shelves. The liquids sloshed. The glasses clanked. He took out the plastic tub of cleaning supplies. A burning spread across his chest and constricted his throat. Dismissed! Like the hired help. That was what he got for trying to liberate the mind and body of that repressed paramecium. James was trying to erase the intimacy that had transpired between them with Windex and Lemon Pledge. He smacked the bar rag on the shelves and made streaks in the dust.

It was infuriating that he could be so affected by this butter-headed Buddhist. That he'd given himself over to an ape of insecurity, too timid to take responsibility for his own desire. That he wasted ten minutes of thought and two ounces of semen on this bald, bumbling, sexually confused bumpkin, defied belief. And for what? The taste of his ovo-lacto nutty-flavored spunk? The privilege of being flayed alive in his meat-grinder of a mouth? The sex was so bad it should have come with a warning label and protective gloves. He'd had better sex in teenage circle jerks: in bathroom stalls with hallucinating meth-heads, in compact cars with obese octogenarians, underneath Formica tables with halitosic Hassidim, with bath-a-phobic street performers still wearing their rainbow wigs, with gaseous cab drivers whose windows wouldn't roll, with flaccid grandfathers whose dentures slipped, with advertising executives in Gucci loafers, with middle-aged cost accountants in backwards baseball caps. With Republicans. With women. And even with himself.

He sprayed Windex across the mirror in big dripping swaths. Each swipe of his hand shook the wall behind the bar. This was his reward. After taking the fall for the steak sauce. After letting his cock be used as a chew toy. After listening to trite stories enacted by oedipal puppets, and getting down on his knees and bringing this hairy-hooved ogre to orgasm—this was his reward.

He wrapped a cloth around the bottles and wrung the necks of the decanters. Sherry kept glancing in his direction as she set the tables, but he avoided her gaze. Fool around with straight boys and something always goes crooked. Though applying the term straight to James was laughable. In the undifferentiated world of Buddhism, it might be a possibility, but in the realm of Rogerism, James was about as straight as the pubic hair ensconced in the sequined G-string of an African American drag queen performing "It's Raining Men" in ninety percent humidity. Being bad at blowjobs did not make you straight—it just made you incompetent.

And if *not* straight, then James was definitely closeted, which was just as problematic. He didn't have the energy to be the gay Yoda to his Luke Biwalker. To teach him about disco naps and douching, bicep curls and Crisco. How to trim both his pubes and chest hair, and the multiple uses of irony. Who wanted to endure the coming-out baby steps of a late-blooming latent twenty-six year-old, exhibiting all the recriminations, insecurities, self-doubt, projections of alienation, poor body image, and grandiose visions of public humiliation common to gay newbies, along with the exaggerated ego defenses, anti-defamation urges, inflated moral superiority and linguistic prohibitions, that finally culminated in a cologne-spritzing, ball shaving, ass bleaching, nipple piercing, penis pumping, rainbow banner waving, radical fairy? There were enough red flags to hold a communist parade.

He slammed the liquor bottles back on the shelves and let the sound ring through the room. He hoped the people on the phone with James would think the restaurant was under construction and cancel their reservations.

As the evening progressed, and some of his regulars came in—the ones he could joke with and tease, those who were interested in the progress of his play—his rage subsided. James had the good sense to keep his distance. He didn't say anything when Roger started mixing vodka/cranberries and drinking them at the computer terminal. Midway through the night, the pink elixirs had worked their magic; he forgot his anger and even offered to make one for James.

"Just don't let Bart catch you," James said, and walked off, shaking his head.

An hour later James discovered him in the walk-in fridge, eating one of the flans. He smiled sheepishly and offered James a trembling spoonful of custard.

He turned to leave.

"Are you okay?" Roger asked. "You've been weird all night."

"I've been weird? You're drinking on the job and stealing food."

"That's normal for me."

"You better get upstairs. Table three put down their card."

Earlier in the evening, Sherry had tried to convince him that James was experiencing massive hetero-doubts and that Roger should "give him time." In between seatings, they huddled by the to-go containers and analyzed the situation. He hadn't told her everything, namely the sexual stuff, but he mentioned enough that she understood this was more than just mere conjecture on his part.

"Strong feelings are scary." She was arranging sugar packets by color in their respective ramekins. "Especially if you have them about someone you're not supposed to."

"You think James has strong feelings?" Roger folded a sugar packet between his fingers.

"Why else would he be so reactive?"

Of course, he had experienced men falling in love with him before. He was a produced playwright with good hair and a big dick—he knew his street value. Even if his forceful personality frightened away more timorous suitors, there were always those stalwart devotees who found his disposition bracing—like a cold gust of wind sweeping over a vast churning ocean. Granted, these were mostly young men who harbored secret fantasies about their lacrosse coach telling them to "keep your head on a swivel." Or effete actors who wanted to be purified in the fires of the dramatic arts. But he couldn't deny the possibility of other kinds of men falling for him. Even pseudo-straight boys with smudges on their glasses. He kept thinking about James looking up from the floor, lips slightly parted. Not exactly desire *for* him but a desire to please him.

At the end of the night, he and Sherry sat on the banquette counting tips while James buried himself in server reports at the bar. Roger separated the house money and faced the bills, occasionally looking over at James for signs of reconciliation. But James was entering numbers in columns with fixed concentration, almost as if he were afraid to look in Roger's direction. Almost as if he were holding back *strong feelings*. Just exactly what these strong feelings entailed, Roger couldn't decide. He would have to proceed with caution. James had broken through a psychological barrier that many straight men were loath to cross—the penis penetration barrier. It was a truth universally acknowledged, at least by the male ego, that any hole infiltrated by a penis was subsequently exalted and simultaneously defiled.

Roger held a much different view. He believed that every man, as part of his personal development, should be required to fellate at least ten dicks, not only as an act of altruism but as a necessary community service. Think what it could do for the homeless alone. It was the perfect demonstration of empathy: knowing when to move from tongue to tip and cup the balls. Was there not a greater example of self-sacrifice and charity? If only George Bush could get down on his knees and fellate Osama bin Laden. If only Yasser Arafat could have felt the dull throbbing of Yitzhak Shamir's cock in the back of his throat—we would have had peace in the Middle East decades ago. Presidents and pundits, ambassadors and activists, needed to know that the solution to war and armed conflict was easily achieved. And that solution was: suck a dick.

He started to count his money, but after two, possibly three, vodka/cranberries, he was a little fuzzy; every time he counted, he came up with a different figure. It didn't help that Eric, upon Bart's departure from the kitchen, had turned up the radio and was blasting "Money Maker" by Ludacris.

James was tapping a ballpoint on the bar, waiting for the tip report. It came as a relief when he finally got fed up waiting and went downstairs to his office. At the sound of his feet safely clearing the stairs, Sherry brought her vodka/cranberry out of hiding and set it on the table. "You think he's mad at us?"

"He's scared. Of me. And my penis."

"Is your penis scary?" She gathered her money and started to face her bills. "I always thought gay penises were more tasteful and discreet."

"That's the problem. The gay penis is so subtle you don't even know it's inside you, until you develop an inexplicable urge to go to the gym and pluck your eyebrows."

"No wonder you're not getting laid."

"More to the point, I'm not getting loved."

"Oh, stop it." She threw a dollar at him. "These men fall in love and make you responsible for everything. God forbid you get tired or angry and can't give them the attention they need, then their whole world falls apart."

"Are you actually complaining about being loved too much?"

"Fucking right I am." She took a long pull on the straw in her drink. "I wish they would just fuck me and forget me."

"How do you bear such a burden?"

"Sean wasn't the only one. There was this graphic designer who kept putting my tits in his logos. Everything he designed had humongous breasts."

"How do you know they were your tits?"

She fanned herself with a stack of bills. "I was the only girl under twenty-five in Ottumwa with a D cup."

Roger smiled and folded the tip report around his money.

"And then there was the comic book artist who wanted to make me into a superhero."

"And what was your superpower?"

"I forget. Something shot out of my vagina. Lasers or feminist angst or something." She lifted up her glass. "Fuck love and the flipping bastards who stick you with it."

The drunker Sherry got, the more she cursed. With her big eyes and chubby cheeks, it was kind of like watching a baby smoke. "How many vodka/cranberries have you had?"

Before Sherry could formulate a response, the door opened and a man walked in carrying a board with a bunch of Slinkies attached.

"Sher. What d'you think? I've been working on this all week." It was Sean. He wore a paint-splattered denim shirt and sported sideburns a millimeter away from muttonchops. His hair was fastened on the top of his head with a binder clip.

She hurried behind the bar. "Jesus Fuck, Sean. Get out of here. I don't want to see you." She turned her back and started polishing glasses.

"Just look. I need your opinion. Gregory says it's my best work." He stood the board on table seven and leaned it against the wall. It was a woman's torso and legs. The arms and legs were depicted by flattened Slinkies. The breasts and vagina were pink Slinkies with knobs that pulled down. "Goddamnit, Sher. I'm on the verge of something here. I know it's a bit much with the boobs and vag and all..." He shifted his weight from one foot to the other. Roger didn't know many installation artists but he did know a few cokeheads, and Sean was doing a pretty good imitation of one.

Sherry continued to ignore him, while Roger slipped the tip envelopes into his pocket just in case.

Hearing the commotion, Eric and Jorge came out of the kitchen with towels slung over their shoulders.

"How about you gentlemen? What d'you think?" Sean gestured to his art. "She's the mystery of life. Woman as coils, uncoiling, coming undone and being put back together. A snake. A transformer. An eternal spring."

Eric and Jorge took a few steps closer to examine the art but didn't know how to respond. They kept smiling, unsure if it was a joke.

Sean walked over to Sherry at the bar. "This could be a whole series. Slinky Odalisque. Slinky Olympia. Les Demoiselles du Slinky."

She turned around. "That's what you think of me? Three-dimensional genitalia and no head?"

"It's a feminist statement."

She stuffed a bar rag into a glass and turned her back.

"I'm on the verge of something here. This is bigger than my paperclip women. Or my Post-It note women. It's an unexplored medium." He was hunched over the bar, bouncing on his heels. Roger took this opportunity to go to the podium and put one hand on the phone.

"Go home, Sean."

"You heard the lady," Eric said.

"What's going on?" James came up from the basement, working a ball-point pen through his fingers.

"I'm sorry, James." Sherry walked to the door. "He was just leaving."

"Stop saying that." Sean spun around and pointed to the Slinky woman. "Tell me what you think."

"I already told you. I hate it. Now get out."

James approached Sean. "Sir, I'm afraid I'm going to have to ask you to leave."

"And who are you?"

"I'm the manager."

"The manager." He turned to Sherry. "Really, babe? Don't you ever change your act?"

"Just go, Sean." Sherry held the door open.

"Again, Sir. We're closed. If you have personal business, I ask that you take it outside."

"Who's gonna make me?" Sean started to bob and weave. He was trapped between two tables and kept looking at his artwork and then back at Sherry. He bounced on either foot, the small space between the tables and wall unable to contain his energy. James turned sideways to allow him to pass but dropped his pen and fumbled forward to pick it up. Sean seemingly saw this as an attack and socked him in the face. James fell back against the tables, knocking over a few chairs.

"That's it. I'm calling the police." Roger picked up the phone.

"No. Don't," Sherry called out. "He's leaving now. Aren't you, Sean?"

Sean held his fist and stared at Sherry.

She stood with her back against the open door, arms folded. "It's not gonna work this time, Sean."

"Dude, there's cameras all over here." Eric pointed to the plastic disks on the ceiling. "You better go."

Sean held up his hands and backed away. He picked up his Slinky woman and shuffled out.

The Roxy was dead on a Wednesday night. There were a couple of old men at either end of the bar. A group of construction workers sat silent and exhausted at a table, their hard hats stacked in front of them.

Sherry and Roger were tucked inside a sticky booth by the window. Eric and Jorge had just left, leaving behind a half dozen empty beer pints. They'd spent the last hour rehashing the scene with Sean in drunken exclamations about what they should've done, should've said, and what they'd do if he ever came back. Sherry interrupted the proceedings just long enough to cuss out Sean or tell some embarrassing story about him. She had changed into a sleeveless t-shirt and Roger would playfully snap her bra strap whenever she got too excited. Everyone was worried about James, but too keyed up to mention him and bring down the party.

After Sean had stormed out, Eric gave James a frozen chicken breast to put on his face. Underneath his eye, a half circle darkened. Roger made him a cup of chamomile tea. When he tried to drink it, his hand shook so badly he spilled on his shirt. They all hovered around him: Sherry apologizing; Eric and Jorge telling him what a badass he was and giving him consoling punches in the arm. Finally, James pleaded with them to go. He said he would lock up and erase the surveillance tape, so Bart didn't see it in the morning. He promised to meet them at The Roxy but later texted that he was tired and on his way home.

Roger wasn't surprised. James seemed like he needed to be alone. His eyes kept welling up, which he blamed on the punch, but Roger knew better. It was the violence that had overwhelmed him. The shock of it. He imagined James going home and taking his puppets out of their boxes and having a tea party. The world was too harsh a place for people like James. Roger wanted to put an arm around his shoulder and pat his stomach. Kiss him on his sweaty head. None of which he could do as it would've made James even more uncomfortable.

"Hey. I have an idea." He hit the table, causing the glasses to jump, and pointed a finger at Sherry. "You need to suss out James for me."

"Me? I don't know anything about sussing."

"Just meet with him. Talk about all your gay friends. You know ..." Roger fingered the scarred wooden table. "See how he feels about me."

Sherry concentrated on his face, like she was looking at a child who still wanted to believe in Santa Claus. Then she said, "Let's blow this fucking place. I'm wiped."

She crawled over Roger and out of the booth. He grabbed her hand and hauled himself to standing. As they ambled out, the construction workers gazed at Sherry with hungry eyes. He put an arm around her waist and felt the heat of their stares burning into his back.

They walked down Smith Street, still holding hands, mainly for balance, but also in some spirit of camaraderie. They had survived the night as co-workers, friends, and even unwitting foils for James's attention—now they were verging on drunken bachelorettes. Most of the shops had their grates drawn. They passed another couple coming out of a bodega, who nodded and smiled in some alcoholic version of friendliness. A lady walking her dog beamed in their direction. This was the life of straight people: one big world of self-congratulation—everywhere they looked, they saw themselves. Two guys walking down the street holding hands would never have received such welcoming responses. In parts of the city, you could advertise your gayness without harassment, but it never garnered smiles of recognition or speechless aches of lust. Hand-holding gay couples remained somewhat of a social shock, like a child drooling in a wheelchair or an old man muttering to himself. This didn't happen with Sherry by his side. The street embraced their coupledom, and Roger soaked up the everyday affability that heterosexuals take for granted. Even their most embarrassing moments were part of the great human narrative: screaming in restaurants, crying in bars, public displays of every kind—all part of the heterosexual storybook. We read it and sympathize, as familiar to us as the lint in our navels.

The subway car was almost empty. Sherry rested her head on his shoulder and dozed off. He put his arm around her and felt the trace of wetness on her bicep. Across the aisle, in the dark train window, their reflection peered back at him. They resembled a model couple from the pages of a magazine. Not exactly *Vanity Fair* or *Vogue*, but something like *Vanlife* or *DIY Quarterly*; he could imagine them as the featured couple in an article on "How To Erect Your Own Yurt."

It occurred to him that he was probably a bit too old for getting drunk and sloppy on the subway. Straight men his age had families, steady jobs, and lace-up shoes with arch supports. Being gay allowed him to continue a protracted adolescence. And being a writer meant he could skip all the milestones and live in the terrarium of his own invention.

The air-conditioning chilled the sweat on his skin. He sat in the stainless steel arms of the train and waited for the next thing to happen. The doors slid open. The doors closed. A young man in a knit cap got on, bouncing to the music in his headphones. Further down, a middle-aged man with a toolbox nodded off. Roger let himself be carried by the movement. A plastic bottle pinballed its way down the aisle and rattled to a stop at his foot.

When the train arrived at their station, he pulled Sherry awake. They laughed and careened the few blocks to his apartment. She crawled up the stoop on all fours. Once inside, he led her to his bedroom, where they both collapsed on his unmade bed. Sherry mumbled something about going to her room and then put a pillow over her head. Roger kicked off his shoes and passed out.

A few hours later, as dawn poked through the Venetian blinds and hungry birds peeped at the windows, he awoke with one leg cast over Sherry's hip and his breath billowing in her hair. Her braid had come undone and the loose hair tickled his nostrils. He was semi-hard and she was softly grinding against him. He rolled to the far side of the bed and went back to sleep.

Later still, he awoke to a tickling on his stomach and felt fingers brushing his hairs back and forth—tracing little lines down to the top of his underwear and back. He scooped her up and went back to spooning. Her breasts were soft. He had forgotten what breasts felt like. It had been a long time since his teenage gropings and backseat bouncings. Not like the hard bumper-guards of gym-chiseled men, these fluttering, malleable things with the hard little tips were a nice surprise.

Roger let his hands do the feeling and luxuriated in his feelings. His body took over and his mind hit pause. Like two sleeping puppies, they nuzzled and pawed each other with their eyes closed. Roger couldn't help running his fingers over her soft skin—as if returning to the silk lining of a pocket. Somewhere between sleep and wake, their clothes came off, and their lips met.

They rolled around on his plaid sheets, braiding their bodies together like so many strands of hair. Sherry felt weightless. He couldn't account for the difference in their strength. When two bodies come together, it's easy to determine the stronger of the two. Roger, who was used to rolling around with guys twice his size, seemed big and bulky by comparison. He felt the delicate bones underneath her skin. There was no layer of muscle. He could easily break her arm or throw her across the room.

Sherry's energy, though active and sexually engaged, played out more submissively than a man's. Her body was pliable; she knew how to adjust herself to his weight and balance the heft of his body. Every gesture was accommodating, every shift, a little act of submission, causing Roger to be more vigorous and assertive. It was as if their bodies knew unconsciously who was the more powerful and acted accordingly.

Roger usually enjoyed being the weaker party in a sexual encounter. He relished the challenge of taking the stronger guy and turning him into a whimpering dishrag. The goal was to conquer through pleasure. Women, he imagined, might derive a similar satisfaction; only with Sherry, there was nothing to conquer; he was already the more powerful.

She rose up and straddled him with her smooth, muscular thighs. "You got a condom?" she asked.

Were they really going to do this? Up until now he had thought of it as a kind of make-out session sans clothes. But he didn't flinch. Such was his determination to trek into this uncharted territory, without compass, flashlight, or even a Lonely Planet Travel Guide. He pointed to the nightstand drawer; Sherry ripped open a condom with her teeth. As she put it on, he began to wilt. Now that his mind had had a chance to catch up with his body, he wanted a refund on this extreme vacation.

She started stroking him with her tiny fingers. Her baby hands and their ministrations reminded him of those little fish that flutter around whales, eating microbes off their backs. Yes, he was getting turned on by his own dick. He wondered if straight guys ever had this problem.

"Are you sure about this?" he asked.

"Not really." She sighed and eased herself onto him.

He let Sherry do all the work. For as friendly as the breasts looked with all their bouncy fullness, the vagina with its red folds and creases appeared rather angry. He remembered reading somewhere that you have to be more polite at the front door than the back. The whole apparatus seemed unnecessarily complicated—too many foyers and vestibules before the main entrance. Was this biology's way of increasing anticipation—an endless list of opening acts before the main concert?

After the initial shock of hotness, he forgot his trepidations. Sherry had her eyes closed and was slowly rotating her hips. Little things gripped him, as if going through a car wash and being wiped down with sponges. He could understand how people enjoyed this. How effortlessly everything was accomplished. Sherry leaned down on top of him for a long kiss; her stomach and chest pressed against him. With a guy, kissing would be awkward, if not altogether impossible.

Roger shifted positions. Sherry was so light, he could just lift her up and carry her around the room. With one fell swoop, she was underneath, first, with her legs on his shoulders, then around his waist. Their bodies were like a pair of figure skaters, moving in some rhythmic dance that struck Roger as more acrobatic than sexual. The whole thing would have made more sense if they were wearing leopard print leotards and peasant blouses.

Still, the dance continued, and to his amazement, he seemed to know all the moves. Thousands of years of biology had gone into his training. Sherry made quick, high-pitched gasps and crinkled up her face. Then those little sponges on the side of his cock. Her legs locked around Roger's waist—twirl, dip, salchow, somersault, triple lutz—he was barely trying, yet he seemed to be executing perfectly. No wonder clumsy fifteen-year-olds had a sex life.

If only the penetration of men could be so uncomplicated: the lubricant, whether tube or tongue, needed liberal application; the digital probe, not a strict necessity but a prudent recommendation, required the gradual introduction of one, two, even three fingers. And then there was the easing-in, inch by inch, the period of adjustment, the deep breaths, the are-you-okays, the faltering smile that could also be a grimace; the staccato thrusts, the wait-just-give-me-a-minute, the eventual eye-roll and flutter. And finally, once enveloped, the search for that particular spot that had to be palpated to life, eventually with some force. With Sherry, everything was accomplished with ease. It was an effortless dive into the deep end of the pool. In some ways, Roger felt more connected to her pleasure than he had with any man.

He eased her off the bed; she wrapped herself around him and up against the wall they went, her body, light, accommodating, and ready to receive. There was something aggravating about the male body—it always pushed you away: the legs didn't bend enough or stretch wide enough, bulging calves on your shoulders gave you a backache, you could never press the length of your bodies together. Men had all this musculature, and though beautiful, it did interfere with the hydraulics of fucking.

Standing, pressed up against the wall, his feet were sweating so much that he slipped, and they went tumbling to the floor. He was now beyond tired. He had to end this before he passed out.

"Maybe it's a sign we should stop," he said.

"I want you to come." She started in on the old hip rotation.

"What about you?"

"I already have. Twice."

Talk about stoking a guy's ego. Maybe she was lying. Who knew? Clearly she wasn't lying about wanting to make him come. She had him pinned down with her hands on his chest and was doing some combination of Watusi dance and round-the-world gyration. He wondered if he was up to the task. Suddenly he felt very much in need of a bulky, inflexible man. He started to call up images of pro athletes and dream boyfriends, but it was hard to think of wrestlers and linebackers with a pair of boobs softly bouncing in his face.

He finally alighted on Brian Boitano: Olympic gold medalist and Emmy winner for *Carmen On Ice*. Brian free-skated to him across the spot-lit arena, his peasant shirt billowing behind. He slowly pulled down his leotard and balanced his perfectly muscled bum on top of Roger's cock, the sharp metal of his skates dangerously near Roger's armpits. Then James's face appeared, pale and blotchy next to his cock. He remembered that *teakettle* whimper.

It was almost enough to bring him to climax. He grabbed Sherry's hips and thrust her up and down but with no results. Finally, he decided to just fake it. Why not? Women have been doing it for centuries. He rolled her onto her back, made some histrionic grunts and thrusts, and whipped the condom into the garbage. The fresh air burned his dick, and he collapsed on the floor.

They lay on their backs while the cloud of their actions slowly settled over them. He could feel the pivots and grooves of the hardwood floor, and some bumpy things sticking to his skin. Underneath his bed, constellations of dust gathered in swirls and drifts. He wanted to reach out and stir them up. Dust was mostly dead skin cells, the parts of him that had fallen off. He was going back to his atavistic self, the monster under the bed that turned out to be him. It didn't take much to become a different person.

Without a word, Sherry got up—all rubbery legs—and stumbled to the next room. He heard the groan of the futon receiving her weight, the fluff of the covers. And her mumbled curse as she drifted off.

Roger brushed off his shoulders and crawled into bed. He made a mental note to vacuum tomorrow, or at least to sweep. In seconds, he was asleep. In sleep, he dreamed of trains rattling, tea kettles whistling, and constellations of dust.

7: The Great Disappearing Act

The first thing she heard was the squeak of Roger's door and then running water in the kitchen. Shortly after, the gurgle of the coffee maker. She'd been awake for nearly an hour, staring at the ceiling, unable to decide on a course of action. Did she pretend that nothing happened? Act like she was too drunk to remember? Make some lame joke about walking funny? Or, should she run out, capture him in a braless bear hug and declare her undying affection? The possibilities swirled and comingled, while Sherry held an amethyst crystal to her chest, trying to feel the vibrations of a decision.

A familiar elation agitated her insides, igniting pulses of heat in her chest and stomach. She felt powerful last night: bringing Roger to climax. His first woman. At least the first one chosen in maturity. Roger had protected her from Sean. He had given her a place to stay. He made love to her all night. Or, a good part of it. It would be easy to vanish into that familiar euphoria and give in to the promise of Roger. She had to be careful though. She couldn't let herself get carried away like the other times. With Magda—her first and only girlfriend. With Freddy—her meth-addicted ex. And Jerome—the first boy to take her virginity. Really more of a man, thirty-one years to her fifteen. He came to her defense outside the 7/Eleven when the manager caught her stealing a forty of Miller Lite. He paid the man and told him she was his sister. They drank it together back behind the dumpster, where he slipped a hand down her pants. When he began moving his fingers, something shifted inside her. He kissed her, his tongue deep in her mouth and she was lost—she never knew that lost was just where she wanted to be. Since he was married, they couldn't go back to his place, so he drove to the old rock quarry and unrolled a sleeping bag in the bed of his pick-up truck. They fucked under the stars. It only hurt a little at first, and then not at all. It seemed as if they were making stars. She didn't know if the light was coming from the sky or behind her eyes. When the moon appeared over his shoulders, she understood that the universe had sanctioned their union.

She couldn't go a day without seeing him. That whole summer was spent watching him, waiting for him, and lying in the back of his pick-up making stars. On days when she couldn't see him, she used to walk by the auto parts store where he worked just to glimpse his truck in the parking lot. Her emotions seemed too big to carry by herself. She needed Jerome to help bear the burden. All the movies had told her that this was love, but it felt like something more arduous. When they were together, her chest overflowed, and when they were apart, something was cleaving it in two. It made it worse that she couldn't tell anyone. Certainly not her grandmother, who had raised her since she was eight, proclaiming all men "no good bastards." The prime examples being her grandfather, who passed out drunk on the railroad tracks, and her father, who left when she was five. And even though dating an older man would have given her some cachet with her girlfriends, she couldn't tell them about it because Jerome had two kids, and in Ottumwa, being a homewrecker was worse than being a slut and this admission would make her both.

If she went two days without talking to him, she began to lose her sense of self. She only seemed real when his hands were touching her. When his eyes probed her with wonder and he said things like: "You're the most beautiful thing I ever did see." "You're my angel." She couldn't concentrate on the simplest tasks. Her grandma would tell her to wash the porch and she'd just stand there with the hose in hand, thinking about Jerome.

Of course, it didn't end well. When Jerome called it off, she took her grandmother's car, her learner's permit barely dry, and drove it straight to the quarry, hoping to drown herself in its cerulean waters. Thankfully, she caught the axle on some rock outcropping and never made it over the edge. Had she been really committed, she would have just shoved some rocks in her pockets and jumped in, but a family in a minivan saw the whole thing and came to her rescue.

She caressed the crystal and studied the walls. Roger's office was covered with theatrical posters. From the wall above the futon, Marlon Brando in *A Streetcar Named Desire* looked down on her, all sultry eyes and bulging biceps. There were other men in various stages of undress; the office seemed more designed for wanking than writing, but who was she to judge the creative process? She didn't recognize most of the shows: *The Food Chain, Bug, The Cripple of Inishmaan*. A bare-chested Richard Gere in something called *Bent*. And, old Samuel Beckett, a wise raisin among these youthful grapes.

From the kitchen came the tinkling of a spoon in a cup—Roger stirring his coffee with artificial sweetener. She could walk out now. Come prancing down the hall, bare-legged, with a skinny tee barely covering her V. But her mascara felt chunky in the corners of her eyes, her teeth were unbrushed, and her hair smelled like beer. Her braid had come loose and she could feel the staticy split ends crackling around her face. A straight man wouldn't care, but gay guys had higher standards. They wanted their women dressed, coiffed, and ready to walk the runway. Every woman was a substitute for the dolls they weren't allowed to play with as children. She looked up at Brando, who didn't care about hair or makeup. She'd heard he had given up showering for months at a time. After sleeping several nights underneath his watchful eyes, they'd already formed a bond. His energy was speaking to her in dreams. She connected with him on the astral plane, where he was waiting to be reincarnated, desperate to experience sex again. Brando, she surmised, was a real pig, but she knew how to handle pigs. Roger, however, required considerably more finesse.

The one person she hadn't connected with on the astral plane was her grandmother. She hadn't appeared to her in a dream since she'd moved in with Sean. In that dream, she warned her about him: "He's a kook." And now she was mad because Sherry didn't listen. Her grandmother always could hold a grudge. Try as she might, she never found her mother on the astral plane. She was probably still mad at her. Though maybe Sherry couldn't recognize her; the only image that remained from those last days was her entwined with tubes. Her dad was still probably in the material world somewhere. Where? She had no idea. He left after her mom's first round of chemo. Her last memory was of him changing the tire on their Chevy Impala and giving her a stick of Juicy Fruit. When she told Roger about her childhood, he quoted some famous writer, who said: to lose one parent may be a misfortune, but to lose both looks like carelessness. They laughed and clinked their Cosmo glasses. She would much rather be careless than misfortunate.

A siren wailed down the street and she tried to connect psychically with the sick person inside. Those last days of hospital smells and beeping machines came rushing back. The good part was the nurses. They called her doll baby and honey-pie. Told her she was the prettiest girl in all of Iowa. She had long, blonde hair, frizzy and out of control. One of the nurses, Nurse Ingrid, gave her a barrette with a pink unicorn. One time, when her mother was out of the room for a procedure, Nurse Ingrid stayed and braided her hair. One long braid that cascaded down her back. She felt so grown up. When they wheeled her mom in on the gurney, she tried to show it to her. She kept whipping her braid around and dancing: "Mommy. Mommy. Look at my braid." But her mom was just a lump in the sheets.

After that, she spent most of her time with the nurses. She did dance moves for them that she copied from the Solid Gold Dancers on TV. They fed her candy and told her she looked like a young Mariel Hemingway. Nurse Ingrid usually found time to re-braid her hair. She helped out by walking the corridors with the physical therapy patients, telling them about her school projects. Even helping the older ones wheel their IV bags. She would follow the nurses on rounds and talk to patients. While Nurse Ingrid worked a ventilation tube down a man's throat, Sherry recounted how she beat her arch-rival Megan in a jump-rope contest. When a woman with stage four lymphoma was getting an enema, Sherry told her all the names of her doll-babies and their favorite outfits. And before one man's epidural, Sherry kept him rapt with her account of how she said to Megan, "Get off my case, toilet-face," to the cheers from students in fourth period lunch.

Her grandmother would eventually call her back to her mother's room, mainly just to sit and watch. Her mother couldn't speak much. Didn't really see her. She lay in the bed and tossed and moaned. Her grandmother would sometimes make her take her mother's hand, which was bony and hot. The sound of her labored breathing filled the room. Sometimes her eyes would lock with Sherry's and she'd say something incomprehensible.

The last time she saw her mother, she was unexpectantly coherent. Sherry asked her to braid her hair. Her mother was on a lot of painkillers, but she lifted herself up and fumbled with Sherry's tangled tresses, her hands doing more pulling than braiding. Finally, Sherry got frustrated and said, "You're doing it wrong. I hate you." She stormed out and went to find Nurse Ingrid. When she came back, her grandmother was sitting by the bedside, a handkerchief pressed to her face, crying.

Roger's desk was a jumble of papers: sketches of set designs and brochures of Fire Island. Sections of his script lay cross-hatched scene by scene in a small tower on top. She had tried to read some but quickly lost interest. Writing never held much appeal for her. Given the choice, she preferred images. An image you could point to and say that's a couch, a river, a naked breast, and have confidence that everyone else would see the same thing. But no one saw the same thing described in words. Everyone had a different couch, a different river, a pair of tits specific to them. When they'd first moved in together, Sean would sketch her constantly. She'd wake in the morning and he'd be scratching away at his pad. The first thing she heard was the rubbing of the charcoal and the rustling of paper. She felt real on paper, as if they were creating her together. She knew when it started like that it would be one of his good days. No catatonic silences. No angry rants about neighbors or the news. "Don't move, baby," he'd say. "I just want to capture the bones in your hip." He'd tell her how his next piece was going to be about "the transformative power of beauty." It went without saying that she was the beauty.

When he created his Post-It Note women, his paperclip women, his women of a thousand tiny While You Were Out Memos, she tried not to show her disappointment. He always claimed her as his sole inspiration: "That piece has the curve of your ass." "This piece has the jut of your chin." If she squinted and pressed her imagination, she could almost see it. But who wants to work that hard? For the most part, she saw yellow rectangles arranged in a vague female form. The rectangles had different kinds of writing on them: grocery lists, other people's names, business addresses— all things *not her*. He was abandoning her. Not only did she feel betrayed, but also a part of her was disintegrating.

It was his drawings that originally had brought them together. On their first date, he sketched her profile on a napkin. "Way better than Nefertiti." When they moved in together, he did her ass in oils, as the featured flower in a jungle of ass-flowers. That painting sold in the low four figures to a Boomer couple from Pennsylvania who collected erotic art. She often thought of them doing their sadomasochistic/Karma Sutra rituals while contemplating her ass.

He did other oils of her that first year. And he must have made at least fifty drawings. But they were all gone now. And though it was probably her fault, the loss made her stomach sour. At the time, she thought he'd just do more, but then the Post-It Note women took over his life. "It's a new phase, Babe. Woman as bureaucracy. Woman as routine." She couldn't help but interpret this as a comment on their relationship. Soon he was making weekly trips to Office Depot and obsessing over cardstock and color combinations.

Of course, she had to compliment these clerical objets d'art. Sean had grown dependent on her opinion. He said she had a good eye. He would ask her if the Post-Its should have bolder writing. Or if he should thicken certain areas on the silhouette. When they first met, he was so insecure about his process that she had to encourage him at every juncture. She would come home from the restaurant, and he'd show her his work for the day. In that period, he was layering paint on top of photographic images. He'd take multiple photos of the same image and arrange them across a canvas, applying different tints over them. It had the effect of movement. She would inspect the images closely. They were her in different poses: sleeping, sitting with her legs tucked under her chin, putting on makeup, buffing the skin off of her feet. It was fascinating to see how the camera caught her expressions: defiance and vulnerability—sadness. She never thought of herself as an angry person or a sad person, but studying these photos gave her insight. She would tell him to soften certain lines. To paint over certain parts of the face. She'd imagine she was creating different versions of herself with each painting. He took her suggestions, and the paintings were better for it—she had a talent for constructing character, adding details and depth where it was absent. Slowly, his confidence grew. And the paintings sold. Not for much, but every sale was an ego boost. She would help him by casting prosperity spells. They did these together, him lighting the green candles in one circle, her lighting the yellow candles in a wider circle and chanting the incantation. Then they would make love on the floor while the candles burned and their passion activated the spell.

Though sad to see the paintings go, there were always others in process. Another version of herself for them to construct together. But when he started on the Post-It women, everything changed. She couldn't get interested in these paper shadows. And he didn't seem to need her critique as much. She'd offer some simple advice while secretly thinking his other work was superior. Then he moved on to the paperclip women.

That was when she started cheating.

She was working at Jean-Georges, where one of the floor managers was a Vespa-driving playboy from Albania. All that was missing was a gold chain. Not her type, but persistent. She'd take persistent over Post-It anytime. She started coming home late, or going into work early to meet Gezim at his condo in Chinatown. He pronounced his name Gá-zeeme, but she liked to call him Jism—a moniker he wholeheartedly embraced, usually all over her tits. He had a copper coffee set, and after sex would make really strong coffee in cups with no handles. She would then ride on the back of his Vespa to work. When she told Roger about this, he said it was just like *Roman Holiday* and they watched the movie together, commenting on Audrey Hepburn's clothes and drooling over Gregory Peck. Unlike Audrey Hepburn's Vespa ride, hers didn't end happily. Sean started getting suspicious. Picking her up after work. Calling her every time she left the house. And then one afternoon, he was just there—waiting outside the restaurant, leaning on the flower boxes as she and Gezim pulled up. It looked bad. She was holding Gezim's waist. Before she could warn him about Sean, he gave her a peck on the lips as they dismounted the bike.

"What are you doing here?" She marched over to him, trying to marshal a believable stream of indignation.

He pushed her aside and went over to Gezim. "Did I just see you kiss my girlfriend?"

"Woah. Woah." Gezim held up his hands and was slowly backing away. "I don't want no trouble."

"You kissed my girlfriend."

"Knock it off, Sean," she called.

"I was just giving her ride."

"I bet you were. You oily prick."

Sean backed him up against his bike. He wasn't a large man, but he had a wild energy. His ropey arms tensed underneath his ripped t-shirt. His shoulders kept twitching, which was one of his ticks when becoming enraged. Gezim, though taller and more muscular, looked scared.

"We just went out for supplies," he said.

"Supplies? Where are they?" He slapped Gezim's bike and then tapped the sides of his torso. "Where? Where? I don't see any supplies."

Gezim pushed him away, which was all Sean needed to ignite. He reared back and socked him in the jaw. Gezim fell on his bike, holding his face.

"You crazy motherfucker. I call police." He looked at the window of the restaurant, where the cooks and food runners had gathered, and then at Sherry. "Call police."

She fluttered her hands helplessly at her sides. There was no way she was calling the police. She wanted to see this through to the end. Though custom dictated that she try and stop it, she needed to see who cared the most. She put her hand to her mouth and affected terror. How was love measured? In kindness and compassion, they say. Though it could also be measured in punches and fists. Sean was daring it all for her; she owed him his moment of glory.

Gezim was making a poor show, leaning on his Vespa, coddling his chin, but then he manned up and took a swing, which Sean sidestepped while delivering a punch to his gut. Gezim grabbed his shoulders and they knocked over the bike and grappled on the sidewalk.

She looked back and someone from the restaurant was phoning the police. "Sean. Stop. Come on. Let's go. The police are coming." She stood over him and clapped her hands. He had Gezim pinned and was punching his head. Little rabbit punches, nothing damaging, but a gesture nonetheless. The contest was over. The measure was made. She clapped again and he looked up at her, like a dog with a chewed-up shoe.

"Come on, Baby. He's nothing to me. Let's get out of here." She reached out her hand, and he slapped it away. He got up and started walking. She followed him, while the restaurant staff and a few bystanders burned holes into her back. If she had to quit her job, this was a spectacular way to go out. They would be talking about it for years to come. Though she probably couldn't count on Gezim for a reference.

Sean stalked through the crowds of Spring Street, dodging and swerving; she followed behind, giving him time to cool off. He was pulling on the leash, but she could still feel him attached. She followed him all the way to the river, where he plopped down on a bench and started those kind of dry-heaving tears that men get who want to cry but can't. That was her cue to comfort. She stroked his cheek. Looked longingly into his eyes, and told him how much she loved him until the dam broke and he started crying for real. She got the basil oil out of her purse and put some on his red knuckles. Daubed the scratches on his neck. He reluctantly gave himself over to her—a wounded baby. She was both healer and harmer, comforting mother and punishing father. She rocked him gently, while joggers cut a wide berth around their little island of misery.

When they returned home, Sean gathered all of his drawings of her and the remaining oils and burned them in a garbage can in front of their apartment. She watched him stare into the fire. The oil canvases created clouds of black smoke that blew across his face. He was burning his vision of her and it remained to be seen whether they could create another one.

After that, she took the job at Bartholomew to be within walking distance of home and to spend more time with Sean. In order to make up for her transgression, she had been spending every free hour with him, encouraging all his new projects, finding helpful things to say, and supplying ego-boosting blowjobs. The Post-It Note women had been replaced by Lego women, and then a coat-hanger woman with a Rubik's cube vagina. She had to admit the Rubik's cube was clever—some men could never figure out the puzzle. But with his move into metals, the opportunity of finding herself in his work had disappeared. Now, instead of waking to soft scribbles on paper, she awoke to the buzz of the power drill and the smell of burning solder.

A more accommodating person might have waited until after his show opened to leave, but Roger had convinced her. She didn't actually believe Sean would hurt her, but if she were going to end it, his erratic behavior provided a better excuse. To abandon him in the calm aftermath of his show would require more explanation, as well as provoke more resistance. Now, at least, he was distracted. Roger had been the voice of reason in all this turmoil. And didn't his attention and generosity reveal a deep concern, perhaps even some unacknowledged feelings? Right now, he could be waiting in the kitchen to talk to her about these feelings.

She fell back onto the bed and buried her face in the pillow. Roger had given her some old flannel sheets that smelled mildewy. The buttons on the futon dug into her back. She remembered she had to call Trish and set an appointment to look for apartments. This was her life now: sleeping on couches, at the mercy of disinterested friends. Alone and empty, she curled on her side and stuffed the pillow between her legs.

From the kitchen, Roger poured another cup of coffee; she heard the scrape of his chair and the clank of the pot against his mug. He was obviously waiting for her.

"Hi," she said, when she finally came out of the bathroom, after brushing her teeth, washing her face, and applying a new layer of mascara. She left her hair tousled around her shoulders.

Roger barely looked up from his yellow pad. He was staring fixedly at his pen. "I'm looking for a word for reticent."

"How about reticent?"

"It can't be an R word."

"If you're writing, I won't bother you. I only came for coffee." She pulled her t-shirt down.

"It's just a letter. Well, maybe a poem. Sit down."

She poured herself a mug and sat across from Roger. Leaning on the table, she felt the reassuring weight of her breasts pressing between her arms. "I haven't received a letter since the nineties. I miss them."

"This is something I was composing for James. I probably won't send it."

"For James?" She tried to keep a neutral face.

Roger turned over the pad. "I was wondering if you could take him aside and see how he feels about me?"

"You mean ask him if he wants to take you to the prom?"

"Not in so many words. Just ... just, you know, maybe see if he has ... feelings. Tell him it's okay to express those feelings. I think coming from you, he might believe it."

She blew on her coffee and tried to assess the situation: a few hours after having sex with her, Roger was composing poetry to James and asking her to be his matchmaker. She searched his face for any hint of an explanation about last night—how it affected their relationship, where they would go from here, but he seemed content to forget. Or maybe he actually didn't remember. Or maybe he didn't think it important enough to talk about. She started to feel the slippage again. She was disappearing in real time, in the daylight hours.

She gathered herself together and came back to Roger's pleading face. A scene was not going to get her what she wanted. She brushed her hair off her shoulders and said, "Sure. Sounds like fun. I'll put him through his paces and give you a complete report."

8: Back to the Garden

James was already starting to sweat. The sun bore down on his bare head, creating tiny sprouts of wetness, which bubbled on his scalp and threatened to tendril down the side of his face. He wished he had worn his jockey cap but didn't think it would be proper to eat with it on. And taking it off was too much like a big reveal: surprise—baldness. He would have chosen someplace inside with air-conditioning instead of this Brooklyn bucolic at high noon, except that Bart, after relieving his initial anger in a pot-throwing tirade, had convinced him to spy on the competition. He wanted to know why The *Shawmat Guide* would be holding its launch party at Green and not any of a dozen more established restaurants, particularly his. He gave him the company credit card with instructions to "have a long leisurely lunch and bring a friend." So James made the intrepid decision to invite Sherry, telling her it was a business lunch and giving her every opportunity to back out. He was unexpectedly surprised when she said yes without hesitation.

Now the sweat was rolling into his eyes, one of which was still discolored from his altercation with Sean. He thought about trying to cover it with makeup but decided it gave him a note of machismo. Considering that he had just fellated one man and been beaten up by another, he needed all the machismo he could get. The other good thing about his black eye was that it would remind Sherry how he had rushed to her defense. Of course, it might also remind her that he got his ass kicked rushing to her defense, and hence, was not the ideal defender, but he might score points with guilt.

Arriving ten minutes early, he'd already been waiting fifteen, trying to make himself comfortable on the tiny patio furniture in Green's outdoor garden. He hoped Aaron and Carrie wouldn't recognize him. He had never met them, but had talked to Carrie several times on the phone. She would often call Bartholomew on Saturday nights, asking if James had room for a couple of deuces she could send him, as Green was "entirely booked for the entire evening." Most often, the people never showed, and he surmised she was just trying to find out the status of their reservations.

It was easy for Green to be "entirely booked" as the restaurant only held six tables. In summer, they opened the back patio that held another five or six. The patio was the envy of Smith Street, featured in several magazine articles with photos of farm-to-table hipsters grinning over goat cheese salads. James couldn't understand the fuss.

He shifted his seat and nearly toppled over; the restaurant's chairs were the miniature folding kind that left you constantly off balance. He felt like some hairy hoofed goat trying to sit on a Victorian settee. In an effort to market his best features, he had talked himself into wearing shorts. A decision based solely on Roger's endorsement of his legs and some rather specious reasoning: if Roger found his hairy legs attractive, then Sherry would as well. In the past, listening to Roger had not always proved the best course of action, but if you can't trust a gay man's opinion on fashion, whose can you trust? Mostly it was his tone. Roger usually coated every utterance with a chrome-plated irony that bordered on ridicule. Yet when he said, "Your legs are the best thing I've seen all day," his voice grew quiet and direct, as if stating a simple fact. When it came to his appearance, James didn't have many positive facts on which to draw, so he gratefully accepted this one.

He was still terrorized by the memories of his high school locker room and the chafing of his red thighs—bat wings, the boys called it. They would point at his fat legs and say, "Hey Tubby, you better Gold Bond that shit." Those skinny boys with zits on their backs and hip bones like razor blades. The mouth of their rib cage poking through their skin. Sometimes they'd punch him in the gut just for fun. Or tweak his nipple. When he bent down to put on his underwear, he could feel his man-boobs swinging. And even though he had since firmed up, some vestige of repulsion still lingered around his body, and all male bodies. His flesh had always failed him; he took no comfort in it.

With his gray shorts, he wore a blue short-sleeved shirt. But now in the unremitting glare, he felt exposed—he was perhaps too gray—too gay. The shirt was an effeminate powder blue. His socks had little Polo players on them—who was he trying to fool?

There were still areas of his body that recalled Roger's touch. He cringed to remember: the pinpricks on his neck from Roger's beard stubble; his pointy chin digging in; fingers circling his balls; the wet smoothness of a tongue on his thigh. He was twenty-six years old and had never felt a tongue on his thigh. He had also never felt a cock down his throat, but that was a subject he was trying not to think about. Not when he had to muster enough courage to impress a beautiful woman. When the girl of his dreams would soon be walking through Green's twee garden gate, stepping over the dying pots of salvia and rosemary. And if Sherry wasn't exactly the girl of his dreams, he'd had enough dreams about her to put her a close second to Natalie Portman. He could question his masculinity, his sexuality, and everything else relating to his manhood, but he could not question his desire for Sherry. Even Roger's penis could not interfere with that.

A trial was how he thought about it, whenever he thought about it, which was not very often, and not obsessively as to indicate it meant any more than it did—which was nothing. Roger's penis was nothing. Just something he endured out of politeness, like kissing a mole-ridden auntie, or listening to the war stories of his old uncle. Daiyu used to say: *Accept what the universe offers. It's not about getting what you want, but liking what you have.* So the universe had offered Roger's penis, and just like Job, he endeavored to make the best of it.

If anything, the trial helped him appreciate what he'd been putting women through all these years. A blowjob looked simple from the receiving end. But on the other side, it was quite a complicated operation. Once you got over the initial gagging, you had to deal with keeping your mouth open until you thought your jaw would drop off. You had to coordinate your breathing to your partner's rhythm: breathing in when he was pulling out. If he paused too long in his forward thrust, you choked; if he held back too long, you didn't know when to take another breath. The instinctual reaction was to bite down, but obviously, that would be a bad blow job. And he wanted to be good. When the universe gave you dicks to suck, you cleared your throat and opened wide. They don't call it a job for nothing.

A few more tables were sat by a woman with frizzy hair, wearing a chef's coat. He assumed this was Carrie. Bart and Felix called "bullshit" on Carrie's chef coat. She had no culinary training and never worked in a kitchen, including in her own; Aaron did all the cooking, while Carrie paraded around front-of-house like an executive chef. As she walked by James's table, she stopped and offered him a drink, her smile cracking the composure of her placid face. He told her he was going to wait for his guest but asked to see the dinner menu. He hoped she didn't remember his voice from the phone. When she brought the menu, he slipped out the cardstock and folded it into his pocket. The first of Bart's missions accomplished—ascertaining Green's summer dishes.

As the minutes ticked by after twelve o'clock, James became antsy. A young waitress bounced from table to table, always stopping a few feet from him as if hitting an imaginary force field—*Hairy Goatman, don't approach.*

It was hard to believe oral sex ever became an accepted practice. Perhaps during ancient Greece and Rome, but he couldn't conceive of its popularity in the Middle Ages or Renaissance. Oral sex required aqueducts of fresh water and a highly developed sanitation system. Otherwise no one would entertain the thought: "Yes! That sweat-soaked, rash-chafed area where everyone pees and bleeds is the exact spot I want to put my mouth." He took a swig of water and paid a silent tribute to indoor plumbing.

The sun continued to bear down. The breeze gleefully fanned his leg hairs. At the only table near him, two older women were deeply occupied with their spaghetti primavera. He saw Carrie handing the waitress a water pitcher and pushing her in their direction. She somehow managed to overcome her fear and approach his table. While she filled his glass, he picked up the lunch menu and feigned an interest: teenage greens, young beets, baby carrots, and new potatoes—the enforced pedophilia of the culinary world. He decided when Sherry arrived he would order one of everything. That way he could take notes and report back to Bart on the quality of the dishes.

He closed the menu and looked into the branches of a looming tree. A spider had cast its web between two leaves. He couldn't see it but assumed it was hovering close, waiting for whatever meal blew its way. And when it came, it would eat without hesitation whatever it trapped. No questions. No judgment. Acceptance. He unstuck his sweaty legs from the plastic slats of the chair. Was Roger the spider ensnaring him in a net of guilt and shame? Or was James the spider that accepted whatever landed into his web? Some things, like a penis, could not be so easily accepted. To accept a penis required more than a minimal commitment. It wasn't like a party invitation. You couldn't just accept a penis one day and then cancel it the next. There were implications. Society demanded a choice. He needed to be branded with one of the LGBT letters. But why did it have to be like that? Why couldn't sexuality be like someone's income, impolite to mention and unethical to judge?

And what exactly was the big friggin' deal? So he had tried it—cock, dick, dong, dingus. Schlong, snausage, skin flute, schwantz. He had eaten the forbidden fruit. Drunk the Devil's nectar. Tasted treif. Partook of the delicacy that dare not speak its name—prick, probe, prong, pud. The Short Arm, The Baby Arm, The Third Arm of Justice. The Meat Puppet, Meat Musket, Man Meat, Master of Ceremonies. The Sperm Worm, Clam Hammer, Taco Warmer, Whore Thermometer. The Tallywacker, Wacky Weiner, Wonder Knocker-Upper. Vomit Rocket, Cranny Axe, Cum Gun, Custard Launcher. The Bone Phone, Quiver Bone, Boney Cannoli, Baloney Baton. The Chick Sickle, Disco Stick, Cheese Staff, Clit Tickler. Johnny Cockrane, Magic Johnson, Elmer the Glue Shooter. Weenie the Pooh. Rumpleforeskin. Urethra Franklin. Mr. Bendy, Mr. Wiggly Flops, Stretchy and the Twins. The Single Serving Soup Dispenser. The Heat-Seeking Moisture Missile. The Throbbing Purple Womb Ferret. The One-Eyed-Purple-Wonder-Weasel. The Purple-Headed Yogurt Dispenser. The Weapon of Ass Destruction. Mr. Sniffles.

So what? What was the big deal? Nobody ever said, "Ah, you ate broccoli that one time, now it has to be broccoli for every meal." No one insisted after one Jimmy Buffett concert, "You must forsake conventional footwear and wear flip-flops for life." People were given leeway to experiment and test. How did you know the fire was hot unless you touched it at least once? Yet, that same spirit of experimentation was not allowed when it came to gay sex. Suck one dick and you were already on your way to the Homo-Improvement Center being measured for assless chaps.

Finally, he spotted Sherry coming out of the dark dining room, squinting into the rays of the sun. She was wearing a filmy dress with an open back that revealed the shadows of her thick legs. Her braid angelically circled her head. When she saw him, she flashed her gap-toothed, dairy-maiden smile and sauntered to his table. She was wearing Roman sandals and black nail polish, and, as she sat down, he noticed a tiny freckle, not a blemish, on her left breast.

He spread his napkin over his naked knees and folded his hands in his lap. She picked out a bottle of white, and they ordered far too many dishes from the nervous waitress. They immediately started in on their habitual topics: restaurants and food. Sherry liked to try all kinds of new restaurants, and it gave him a chance to tell her about his personal ratings of the best chefs in the city.

Just as he'd worked his way up to number eight, Mario Batali, Carrie interrupted and set down an *amuse-bouche* of diced beets. She took a full minute to describe every ingredient, right down to the sprig of parsley. Then she glared, with sponge-like eyes, expecting to absorb whatever admiration and wonder spilled out of them.

When Carrie left, he asked, "So have you and the boyfriend worked things out?"

"I haven't spoken to him. I'm still at Roger's." His face must have registered surprise because she added, "Only until I can find a place with my friend Trish."

Roger had been off work for the last couple of days. He knew Sherry was crashing there but figured after a few nights, she would return to Sean. This new development was both promising and scary. Promising because it meant Sherry might finally be unencumbered. Yet scary because it gave Roger more opportunities to blather about blowjobs. James imagined him unburdening himself during a commercial break of Gilmore Girls.

"Good thing you left," he said. "That guy's dangerous."

"I think he's having a breakdown."

"I'm sure he had some good qualities. Otherwise, you wouldn't have been with him." He thought it best to keep her talking about the crazy boyfriend, as he was bound to look good in comparison.

The waitress poured their wine with a shaky hand and Sherry took a large sip.

"I feel bad leaving him right now but... I guess my taste in men is questionable."

This was music to his ears. Maybe she had a whole string of old boyfriends on the verge of nervous breakdowns. "My ex, Tracy, dumped me because she said I wasn't her type."

"That's harsh."

"I wasn't aware I was a type." James threw up his hands, almost knocking over his wine glass. "Let alone not her type. Do you think I'm a type? I mean, what kind of type do you think I am?" He imagined her taking his hand and saying, you're my type, James.

"You're such a wonderful guy, James. Standing up to Sean like you did. I can't thank you enough. You need to find someone who appreciates you."

"Where are these women?" He looked around the patio, then directly back at Sherry.

"Well, you can't limit yourself to only one type. Back in Iowa, I mostly dated guys in bands. I thought that was my type. The only other choices were farmboys and methheads. But then I came to New York and found all kinds of creative types. Actors and artists, playwrights and poets. You have to open yourself up to possibilities. Get out of your comfort zone."

He figured he pretty much deserved an Academy Award for acting outside of his comfort zone. And his tonsils had the scars to prove it. But that was a conversation for another time.

The waitress brought their dishes, setting each one down as if it were a Fabergé egg, and they took share plates and divvied up the food. James tried to figure out the dressing on the heirloom tomato salad. He inquired if Sherry tasted orange zest and she speculated it might be lemon rind. Bart would want a full report later and it needed to be thorough. They began dissecting all the dishes, and had a bit of a quibble about turmeric vs. cumin in the grilled chicken, but in most cases their palates were in agreement. To be with someone knowledgeable about food was a real treat. After scrutinizing the asparagus risotto, Sherry returned to the subject of types and asked if he had a specific physical type.

"Buddhism teaches that decisions based on physical attraction are deceptive," he said. "We should look for spiritual attraction in a mate."

"I thought I had that connection with Sean, because I helped him with his art, but I was just a kind of a ... sounding board."

"I felt that way. With my ex from college. We would have these long conversations about Foucault, Irigaray, Butler—all the feminist scholars— and I would think we really connected. But she didn't care what I thought. She was just using me to solidify her own ideas."

"That's exactly it." She speared a quinoa-filled dumpling and pointed it in his direction. "He was using me. He never saw me as a person. I was just a means to make a Slinky."

They chewed contemplatively for a while, occasionally commenting on a dish. They both liked the spaetzle. James told her about the history of the building. How it used to be an Italian restaurant, where wiseguys hung out, eating gabagool and proshoot. He even pointed out possible bullet holes in the painted brick facade.

"So how did you come to be a Buddhist?" she asked.

He explained about his dad converting and the rift it had caused in his family. His Jewish grandmother and his Lutheran mother.

"So you didn't like celebrate Christmas or anything?"

"We had a tree. My dad allowed Santa and the reindeer, but not the baby Jesus."

"What about your Mom?"

"Oh, she's an atheist. Mostly."

"What does it matter anyway?" Sherry poured them each more wine. "Buddhist/atheist, black/white, man or woman. They're just labels." She raised her glass in a toast. "To making our own definitions. To freedom."

He clinked her glass. "To freedom."

"Now that I'm away from Sean, I want to do all the things I never got to do when I first came to New York. Snort coke in bathrooms. Vomit in cabs. Have sex in the window of a fancy hotel. Pee in the street. Is that how you felt when you first came here?"

"Well, I haven't done any of those things ... I can't even pee if someone is in the next urinal."

"I don't want to be tied down to some man. Maybe I want to be with a woman?"

James paused over his teenage greens. "You do?"

"I want to keep my options open. Don't you?"

This had to be Roger's influence, his gaseous planet Gaytron pulling everything into its orbit. "Well, there are limits."

"Does there have to be? Didn't you just say that Buddhism teaches that the spiritual connection is the most important? And that all the physical stuff is just ... window-dressing?"

Sure, he believed the physical stuff was less important than the spiritual.

But he also believed you were born gay or straight and didn't have much say in the matter. Yes, Kinsey talked about a sliding scale and most people were somewhere in the middle, and certainly humans diverged now and then, as his own recent detour confirmed, but overall, the attraction for one sex over another was hardwired from birth. "Nature forms us in certain ways," he said. "It creates boundaries."

"Does it?" She chewed an asparagus tip thoughtfully. "Don't most feminists say that gender roles are formed by society?"

He wiped his mouth with his napkin and dried off his head. He couldn't believe he was having this conversation. A couple of days living with Roger, and Sherry was turning into a post-modern dyke. Roger was Kryptonite to heterosexuality. As much as he wanted his sexuality to be free-floating and undefined, he wanted Sherry's to be firmly planted in heterosexual soil.

"Let me ask you this: Do you find yourself just as attracted to women as men?"

She scooped up an artichoke leaf with her fingers. "I've been with women. When I first came to the city, there was this one woman who took me under her wing—Magda. She was the one who taught me how to make potions and things. She wore wife beaters and had this cut body with tattoos all up and down her arms." Sherry licked the butter off her fingers, and James pictured her and the tattooed woman doing indecent things with basil oil and potpourri.

"It's different with every person," she said. "This one's funny. That one's sweet. That one is really smart. Once you ignore the shell, your attraction isn't based on who has the biggest boobs or the best muscles."

"But it might be necessary to have boobs. Or other parts," James added, putting in an endorsement for genitals.

"Please tell me you're not one of those people who thinks that having a penis makes you a man?"

"Well." James raised his hands in a big 'Y' gesture. "Call me old fashioned, but ..."

"So when you're attracted to a woman, it's just about the vagina?"

"No. But I like it to be part of the package. When you look at real estate, the heating and plumbing might not be the first things that attract you, but you wouldn't buy a house without them."

She poured out the rest of the bottle and clutched the glass to her breasts.

"The heating and plumbing, eh?"

"You know ... infrastructure."

"I get it." She took a sip of wine and rocked back and forth. "Fucking metaphors." She said fucking the old-fashioned way, like it was an invocation. "You're saying you need heating and plumbing. It may not be the main thing but it's necessary to close the deal. And I'm saying, why be restricted to only one kind of heating and plumbing? *You* want radiant heat. *I* say, try forced air. *You* want a Jacuzzi. But a jet-stream shower might work just as well."

James was starting to lose himself in these metaphors. He couldn't understand why she was so committed to making him gay, but he enjoyed sparring with her. "What if I just *prefer* a Jacuzzi to a shower? Aren't I allowed to have a simple preference?"

She leaned into the table, arranging her arms around the various plates spread before them. "So. You can honestly say you've never felt an attraction for another man?"

James searched the crevices of his yuca chips for an answer. He wanted to confess the incidents with Roger—prove that he was indeed an open-minded metrosexual, willing to accommodate a diversity of plumbing fixtures. But something told him to hold back.

"Okay." He tapped the side of the table. "I wouldn't say attraction. More like beyond the physical—emotional. I've been emotionally attracted, I guess."

"Well that's the deepest part, isn't it?" Her smile widened. "You just haven't allowed yourself permission to express it ... physically."

"Maybe. Maybe you're right," he said, his own secret grin pulling his face upwards. "Maybe you'll have to show me how." He could easily be gay with this beautiful woman instructing him. He could be anything with her: transgender, concubine, slave. He was beginning to understand the justification for the Trojan War.

Sherry looked a bit confounded. He, too, was somewhat shocked at his bold statement. They each took a sip of wine, while a breeze lifted their napkins.

"So how are your potions?" he asked. "Have you made any new ones?"

"That's all on hold now that I've moved out of Sean's."

"I loved that basil oil. It was very calming. I would buy it in a store."

"Starting a business is so overwhelming. I've sold some items at farmer's markets but ... the whole process is just..." She moved the air with her hand.

"You should start a web page."

"That's what Trish says. I guess I'm just waiting to be inspired. All these people with startups and web pages. What chance do I have?"

"You have to define that for yourself. Success can mean different things to different people. Didn't you say we have to go beyond society's definitions?"

"Wow. My own words used against me."

The waitress came and cleared their plates. They remained silent while she stacked each of the plates into the crook of her skinny arm, ending up with a wobbly tower that looked like it could tip at any minute.

"Of course, there's nothing wrong with being a waiter," she said. "In Europe, it's a noble profession."

"I've been thinking the same thing." James put his palms on the table. "I *like* managing. I *like* the restaurant industry."

"But aren't you doing things with puppets?"

He noticed a tone change on the word puppet. "Well, I'm trying. To make an animated short film but you know ... life."

"Yeah, I know life."

"I came to New York... to go to film school. Now, it seems far-fetched."

"One thing I learned from Sean: to be an artist, you have to be selfish and single-minded."

"I don't even know where to begin. I need lights and camera equipment. At least in Ann Arbor I could use the university's."

"Roger could help you. He knows tons of people. He has connections all over the city."

He didn't want to tell her that Roger hated his film idea. And that asking him for a favor would be opening up a new set of entanglements and reciprocations that he didn't want to get into. He just called for the check and put down Bart's AmEx.

"Oh no," Sherry said. "I have to pay for this. For all your help with Sean."

"Don't worry. It's on Bart."

"You'll have to let me take you out to dinner then." She arranged her purse on her shoulder. "To make up for your eye. We'll go to Daniel or Boulay. One of your top ten chefs."

"Absolutely. If you really want to."

As they left Green, James glanced at the reservation book. The week looked busy but not completely full. Mostly deuces and four-tops. In red ink, he recognized a name affiliated with the Shawmut Guide. The Guide was supposed to be based on anonymous restaurant reviews by ordinary customers, but word on the street had it that certain reviews carried more weight. His reconnaissance was complete. He could give Bart a full report.

They strolled down Smith Street. The lunch had gone better than expected: they argued and confided, joked and flirted, and even made plans for a future date. He had to stop himself from taking her hand and swinging it in the air.

After a few blocks, they passed the shell of a new restaurant under renovation. The door was open, and James wanted to explore. Another bit of info he could give to Bart. Inside, it smelled like sawdust and dampness. There seemed to be no workmen around.

"More competition on the street," he said. "Bart won't be happy."

The restaurant was trying to be a Cape Cod fish shack. Lobsters with smiley faces were painted on the tongue-and-groove paneling. A nest of fishnets lay on the floor. Probably some future decorating scheme. They held plastic starfish and pink seahorses.

"Maybe you can get a job here as a Mermaid," James said.

"Maybe you can work here as Captain Nemo." She toed a starfish.

Brown paper covered the big windows and laser-like shafts of sun burst through tiny holes in the paper. A hundred pin pricks of light focused on their bodies, like they were starring in their own private rock concert. Schools of dust motes swirled in the light and James thought—do it. No questions. No judgment. Take what blows into your web. He scooped Sherry into his arms and kissed her. A full-on kiss, lasting so long, time seemed to have stopped.

She eventually pulled away but stood for several moments in his arms. Her head so close he could feel through his shirt her breath on his nipple. He didn't know what to do next and was relieved when she thanked him for lunch and bolted out the door.

He watched her go, a little surprised, a little confused, but mostly happy. He'd taken the plunge and kissed a beautiful girl. And surprise of all surprises, she'd kissed him back. He was sure of that: she had kissed him back.

He knelt down in the tangle of fishnets and tore out a pink seahorse. He tried to remember what had been here before. Was it a nail salon? A Pentecostal church? One of those vintage clothing stores that opened and closed every month? He thought about all the different businesses that might have resided in this building over the years: barber shops and Victrola repairs, candy stores and shoe-shine stands, video arcades and photocopy centers. It probably had changed its name and appearance hundreds of times; and yet through all of these transformations, all of the labels applied, it remained essentially itself, a basic building with walls, support beams, and electrical wires. He put the seahorse in his pocket, to keep as a reminder when the building changed into something else.

9: Survival of the Unfittest

The front door opened, and he heard Sherry stomp into the living room. When she didn't come to the kitchen right away, he went to find her.

"Roger. Do you see a man out there?" She was standing by the window lifting the slats in the blinds; the light from the streetlamp made lines on her white work shirt.

"It's too dark. I don't see anyone."

"I think some guy followed me home from the subway."

"What guy?"

"This guy. I walked by him getting off the train and he grunted at me and grabbed his crotch. Then a block from the station, I noticed him behind me. I think he followed me all the way home."

"Come on. I made us a pitcher of cosmos. I want to hear all about your lunch with James." He started walking toward the kitchen. "Why didn't you call?"

"My phone died." Roger handed her a drink, and she collapsed on one of the kitchen chairs. "But now he knows where I live."

He pushed a packet of Chips Ahoy towards her. "Have a cookie. Sugar makes everything better."

She obviously needed some time to compose herself. He waited while she broke a cookie in two and casually nibbled the ends. She had brought this chocolate-chipped contagion into his house and he'd spent the last hour wolfing down half the bag, thinking about the possible outcomes of her lunch. When she didn't call or respond to his texts, he considered going to Bartholomew and confronting her during her shift, but he needed to revise the final scene of his play, so he waited for Sherry and spent the evening fretting and speculating about James instead. He thought about their last sexual encounter, and after the sanguinary rush of James taking him by mouth subsided, he kept coming back to his wine room apology, and how James took ownership of his mistakes, without deflecting or defending; how easily he admitted he was wrong. This required a certain amount of emotional maturity and compassion. But did mature compassion lead to a newfound passion?

He hadn't realized how long he'd been waiting for a man to apologize to him. Perhaps ever since his father had left, and certainly since Nathan had moved out. On that fateful night, he came home and found him packing the brush heads of his electric toothbrush. Nathan informed him that he'd met someone else. Someone "who wasn't angry all the time." Someone "who wasn't so judgmental." Someone who actually wanted to spend time with him and "not keep holed up in a room staring at a computer screen." That night, he watched him leave, and over the next few weeks, stood by while the contents of the apartment went with him, presumably also to the new boyfriend's. Nathan felt entitled to take the things he'd paid for, and since Roger sunk most of his money into his plays, that turned out to be almost everything. One night, Roger came home and found all the pots and pans gone. The next day, the Tiffany lamps they picked out at a flea market in Chelsea. And then the leather couch, the velvet egg chairs, the white lacquer tulip table, the TV and speakers. Instead of renting a U-Haul, Nathan took things piecemeal in the new boyfriend's Grand Cherokee: coffee maker, vacuum cleaner, French country dishes, the shower curtain, a giant box of votive candles from IKEA, a stapler Nathan had won at a carnival in Rockland County. It got so that every time Roger came home, he was greeted by some new loss. The emptiness of his heart mirroring the emptiness of his apartment.

Sherry's blue eyes remained fixed on her Cosmo. "What if he comes back?"

He crunched the cookie bag closed. "Who? James?"

"No. The grunty guy from the subway."

"You think he's going to be lurking in the bushes?"

"You don't know what it's like for a woman. Guys think they can grope us or kiss us or follow us to our doorsteps." After James had planted that kiss on her and Sean had stalked her at work, she was starting to feel like a target. It brought back memories of Ottumwa and her ex, Freddy. He would follow her down the street in his car, yelling at her to get in. She stared at the elves on the cookie package as if they were possible predators.

"Are you ever going to tell me about James?" Roger asked.

"I'm not kidding. This whole thing with Sean is creeping me out. He called me like a hundred times today."

"You should block him."

"I know. I should." She took out another cookie, and dunked it into her Cosmo. "Can you show me how to do it?"

"You've never blocked anyone before?"

"I usually just light some sage and say a banishment spell."

"So why didn't you do that with Sean?"

"I left my banishment sage at his place. Which reminds me." She scrunched up her face. "You have to go with me to get my stuff."

"Sure."

"We have to do it tomorrow. That's when he goes to brunch with his mother."

"Tomorrow. Sure. Fine. Now, what happened with James?"

She regarded the elf on the cookie package, with his red cap and placid smile, and wondered what it would be like to live with him in a hollow tree and bake cookies all day. Definitely more peaceful. It took some time before Roger's question registered, and then she regretted having to answer it. "We had lunch at Green. The spaetzle was good."

"And? What about James?"

"Oh. He had the asparagus risotto."

Roger slapped his hands on the table and let out a growl. "Spill your guts, Blanche."

Men were all the same. Ordering you around like their servant. Her grandmother was right. More to the point, she didn't want to give Roger the satisfaction. Who was he to tell her what to say? She brushed away some crumbs from her shirt and watched him squirm. "I'm trying to give you the whole story. I'm painting a picture."

"Don't paint—sketch. Broad strokes."

"I can't eat any more of these." She got up and put the cookies in the cupboard. "There are no broad strokes in these situations. It's all squishy lines and squiggly dots and what you see in them."

"And what, pray tell, do you see?"

"Hard to say at the moment. I'll tell you one thing though, he was staring at my tits for practically the whole meal. You shouldn't have put me in that dress."

He remembered picking out her outfit that morning. She was going to wear some ruffled print skirt with a quilted vest that made her look like the serving wench at Medieval Times. He put her in a tight yellow dress emblazoned with red peppers. She said it was a bit cheap. But he told her about subliminal messaging and how it was good to associate yourself with food. "If women were really set on attracting men, they'd wear nothing but cherry pie and pork chops." He took an ankh on a thin gold chain, lifted it to just above her cleavage, and tied a knot in back. "You always want to draw the eye to the best merchandise." She said the outfit was sending mixed messages. "Aren't I supposed to be convincing James to be attracted to you?" Roger rubbed his fingers on the corners of his mouth and told her that in the theatre, the more attractive the messenger, the better received the message. Though now he realized that Sherry was probably right. He had costumed his actor for a scene about seduction instead of a scene about a friend offering advice.

"Did you talk about sexuality? About his feelings? For me?"

She opened the cupboard and peered at Roger's meager staples, as if the answers to his question could be found in old pasta boxes and dented sardine tins. She didn't know what to say. If she told him about the kiss, he might end up hating her. Accuse her of seducing James. If she told him James was assuredly gay, she would confirm his desires and render herself obsolete. There was a delicate balance that had to be struck. They still had yet to discuss their night of passion and its implications. She persuaded herself that when it came to fighting for Roger's affection, she had an advantage over James: she lived with Roger, had a rapport with him, a confessional friendship. They were both fatherless and bereft of family. And now, it appeared, they were both bisexual as well. When she thought about all the things they had in common, it seemed impossible that he could ignore the rightness of their union. She waggled the cupboard door back and forth and considered her next move. "He eventually admitted that he has an emotional attachment to you."

"Oh." Roger raised a hopeful eyebrow.

"If you want my personal opinion, I think he's overwhelmed and con-fused, and trying to repress his feelings." She jumped up and sat on the counter. "When you think of yourself as one kind of thing all your life, it's hard to imagine yourself as something else. Don't you agree?"

"Did you tell him what a great person I was? How talented and compas-sionate people find me?"

She started loosening the strands of her braids. "I told him about my experience with a female lover."

Roger cocked his head. "You had a female lover?"

"When I first came to the city, I lived with this cool lesbian. She's the one that got me into Wicca."

"I didn't know that."

"One of the best experiences of my life. So liberating. So freeing." She stretched through her shoulders. Magda was anything but liberating and freeing. She was a controlling bitch who dominated Sherry's existence her first years in the city. But Roger didn't need to know that. She shook out her hair and let it fall around her shoulders. "It taught me to open myself. I never thought of myself as gay, but when I allowed it to happen, it seemed like the most natural thing in the world."

"Always felt natural to me," Roger said.

"Of course, the first time was difficult."

"Couldn't part the beef curtains, eh?"

"Don't be gross." She combed her hair with her fingers. "I just had to get over my preconceptions of who I was. I had to stop thinking of myself as heterosexual Sherry and redefine myself as fluidly sexual Sherry. Once I did that, everything was easy."

"What did James say about your lesbian interlude?"

"Oh, he was salivating over it. But not in a gay pride way."

"Typical." Roger tapped the salt shaker on the table. "Maybe you weren't the best person to convince him. It was kind of like sending a cute little lamb to talk to the lion about vegetarianism."

She fingered the ankh that Roger had put on her that morning. "So I'm a cute little lamb, am I?"

"Thank you for offering yourself up for the sacrifice. I appreciate it."

"I think everyone is basically bi anyway. Whether they want to admit it or not. Don't you?" This was the hundred-thousand-dollar question. The one she'd been waiting to pose since their night of passion.

"Well..." Roger clutched the salt shaker as if it were a liferaft.

"I mean, if the other night was proof of anything ..." There she said it. She made it real. Now it was up to him to deal with it.

"I guess that's true in theory," he said. "All things being equal. But things are never equal." He slid the salt shaker across the table.

Sherry waited for him to say more, bouncing her legs against the cupboards, but Roger remained silent.

Finally, he stood up and did a fake stretch of his arms. "I'm turning in. I'm exhausted." He hurried to his room and shut the door.

She sat under the cold fluorescent lights and counted the fingers of grease on the walls. The feeling was so big inside her. Was it love—lust—or some yearning for something beyond her knowledge? Whatever it was, she just wanted to give it to Roger, but she couldn't take the chance that he would reject it—her—that would be too devastating. She went back to her room, unfolded the futon, and fell on the bed. The beefy men on Roger's posters looked down like sentinels sent to taunt her. His bulletin board filled with snapshots of old boyfriends ridiculed her desires. She needed a place of her own. Six years in the city and she had never lived by herself. It was always someone else's space, someone else's furniture, someone else's toiletries in the medicine cabinet, someone else's expectations she had to conform to.

She came to get away from Freddy. In a dream, her grandmother had sung, "New York New York, it's a helluva town." She could have gone to Chicago or Minneapolis, where most of the youth of Ottumwa migrated, but Freddy had friends in those cities; his band played gigs there. She wanted to put as much distance between them as possible. She wasn't exactly afraid of him, but afraid of what she became when with him: needy, servile, conforming to his desires. And since his only desires were playing music and doing drugs, that was all she did too. Listened to his band do covers of Soundgarden and Stone Temple Pilots while pinching a joint with her feathered roach clip. She made herself scarce when they did meth that the drummer cooked up at his cabin.

Freddy never hit her; he just ranted and kicked the furniture. Sometimes he'd throw beer bottles at the walls. Never in her direction, but she got the idea. One time he totaled her car driving into an Indian burial mound. She had left him twice before, but he always managed to pull her back in. "You're my everything." "I love you so much." "I'm nothing without you." Maybe the latter was true, but he wasn't really anything special with her, so after a while, his declarations lost their attraction. Still, she knew the only way to be clear of him for good was to get out of town.

She arrived in New York just after the millennium but before the dot-com crash and got a job at a fancy candle shop. Magda also worked there. And though they were polar opposites in almost every way: she: Rubenesque and shy, brimming with Midwestern good cheer; Magda: emaciated and tattooed, teaming with New Jersey attitude; they had a big sister/little sister vibe. She convinced Sherry to move out of her Hell's Kitchen SRO and into her drafty loft in Greenpoint. In retrospect, this proved advantageous, as a month later, the economy went into recession and the candle shop closed. Magda helped her apply for food stamps and navigate the bureaucracy of unemployment. They pooled their resources and holed up in her loft, living La Vie Bohème and growing dependent on each other.

How they became lovers happened gradually, over a period of months. Magda took her shopping at resale shops and food pantries. She invited her to meetings with her coven and taught her how to cast spells for money, jobs, and general good fortune. Magda had recently broken up with her girlfriend, and they stayed up late trashing their respective exes, commiserating over bottles of cheap wine and Ritz crackers. Sherry slept in what Magda called "the guest room," which was a mattress on the floor on the far side of the loft. Magda's bed was on the other side, and a living space with furniture around a TV sat in the middle. Sometimes they would fall asleep together on the couch, after Magda had given her a long lesson on reading Tarot cards or deciphering astrological charts. They would be at opposite ends, but their feet would sometimes rub against each other.

It was on one of these evenings that Sherry felt a warm hand massaging her foot and then traveling up her leg. She was too tired to stop it and just went with the flow. The next morning, Magda made her breakfast and tied on her wrist a 'hearthmate' bracelet. It was made with rope and twined with their hair and other charms, like pieces of wax from the candle shop where they first met and grass from the park where they took their walks.

She told her she had foreseen their romance in the cards, and the cards predicted they would be a powerful and lasting couple.

To disagree with this assessment would have put quite a strain on their living situation. Magda didn't handle rejection well. One of the witches in her coven didn't show up for her Equinox celebration, and Magda burned her in effigy and spelled her with perpetual menstrual cramps. Being unemployed didn't leave Sherry many options. And Magda had furniture and a TV; it was comfortable enough for the time being.

The time being turned out to be two years. Two years of treading lightly and constantly checking in. Two years of a million little compliments and just as many apologies. Of running every sentence through the filter of: would Magda take offense? Of doing everything together, including trimming each other's toenails and waxing each other's pubic hair. Of learning the rules of Wicca, Tarot, Santeria, and various practices of astrology. Dozens of spells, hundreds of incantations, thousands of chants, all used to address grievances and achieve desires. Magda animated the world with auguries and secrets. A black bird landing at your feet, or a cool wind blowing from the north had meanings beyond the mundane. Trees contained troubled spirits and people could be controlled with magic. And even though she sometimes felt like a caged rat or a brainwashed cult member, Magda often made her feel like the most important person in her life, which was probably the thing she craved the most: to be someone's number one. By the time Sean came along, Magda's attention had already drifted elsewhere, to a new witch in the coven going through a traumatic divorce. In spite of everything, Sherry still looked back fondly on the experience, and she did learn a lot. Not just about the pagan arts, but about how desire could be cultivated. How unknown desires can be coaxed and stroked and brought into bloom, whether through necessity or by sheer force of will. All of this she was going to put to use with Roger.

The next morning found them quietly hurrying up the stairs of Sean's building to avoid being spotted by the neighbors. Roger was worried that some unexpected occurrence might have kept Sean at home. The last thing he wanted was to face some manic, coked-up artist, looking for an outlet to express his rage and frustration. Thankfully, when they entered the apartment and Sherry anxiously called out his name, there was no answer.

The living room had been turned into a studio. A plywood work table with cans of brushes and tubes of paint stood in the center. Sean's latest creations leaned against the walls: the paperclip women with wiry red and yellow hair; the Post-It Note women marked up with scribbles; a woman made out of coat hangers with a Rubik's Cube vagina; and of course the Slinky woman, thrown awkwardly into a corner, her breasts dangling downward on the floor.

"He wasn't always so into his art." She waved a hand at the paintings as if flicking away dust. "Well, he was, but he was also into me." She went to a wooden desk and pulled out some books, shoving them into the canvas sack she brought with her.

Roger didn't relish another discussion about Sean. They'd already had so many late-night confabs that her emotional wounds and disappointments were more vivid to him than his own.

"This changed everything," she said, pointing at the Post-It Note women and their iterations: the Rolodex card women, the women of a thousand pink While You Were Out Memos. Roger tried to see them as her rivals. He studied the yellow and pink rectangles, looking for some vague resemblance to Sherry, but he couldn't see any.

He followed her to the bedroom and watched her rummage in a dresser for socks. "If he hadn't started in on those ... junked-up doohickeys, I probably would have never cheated."

"You never told me that part."

"Yeah. Well. It happened." She sat on the bed, helplessly holding a sock in each hand. He felt compelled to join her. "Haven't you ever cheated on a boyfriend?"

"Actually, you'd think I would have, but when I love someone, I get imprinted like a baby duck."

"Baby ducks eventually grow up and fly away. She opened a garbage bag and began filling it with clothes from the dresser.

"So who was the guy?"

She gazed at the floor, which was littered with crumpled yellow papers. "He was one of the managers at Jean-Georges."

Roger thumped the mattress. "That's why Sean was so triggered when he found out James was the manager?"

"Yeah. Bad memories." She went to the closet and started flipping through the garments. "If he had a brain in his head, he'd have known I'd never fall for someone like James."

"Oh. And why is that?"

"Well. No offense, but he's not winning any beauty contests."

Roger was aware of James's limitations but didn't especially relish anyone else pointing them out. "I admit, he's not *conventionally* handsome."

"I don't know what convention you'd have to attend to find him handsome." She selected a blouse and then put it back. "Maybe a science-fiction convention."

"Granted, he's no skinny, coked-up artist with binder clips in his hair."

"What do you think of this blouse?" she held up a geometric print. "Sean got it for me when we went to the Mondrian show."

"Save it for when you're sixty and playing Canasta at the Senior Center."

She went back to perusing the closet. "One thing I'll say about Sean. At least, we had a deep physical attraction."

"I'm attracted to James. Deeply." He pushed himself forward on the bed.

"But are you? Really?"

"I think I know when I'm attracted to someone."

"It's just that comparing him to those pics of your exes, he doesn't exactly seem like your type."

Roger considered the photos in his office: the pool parties with Nathan; dance parties with other boys du jour. After Nathan, there was an infantry of men, who stormed his bed sheets and discharged themselves in various states of adoration and ambivalence. Afterward, they invariably withdrew, most before sunrise. He told himself that he didn't want another relationship, but that was only because one was never on offer. A relationship was an inconvenience in New York, like owning a car. You could get to every place faster without it, and you didn't have to worry about finding a place to park it once you'd arrived. In reaching the top rung of the corporate ladder or the pinnacle of artistic success, a romantic partner held you down. Though it wasn't like he had ascended to new heights without one.

"I used to believe in types," he said. "That we were imprinted by our parents or our first loves. But now I think we can override these ... proclivities."

"And that's what you're doing with James? Overriding your proclivities?"

"Maybe."

"So, you're opening yourself to new experiences." She gave him an over-the-shoulder smile.

He thought about James unwrapping those puppets from the tissue paper. Interceding for Max when Bart wanted to fire him. Risking his job to get steak sauce for an old man. How he abided Roger's lateness and drinking, and all his other infractions with grace and understanding. "There's something beyond the physical with him. His kindness. His carefulness. I don't know. It hits me at a deeper level."

She held up a beaded peasant skirt. "What about this?"

"Perfect. If you plan on telling fortunes in Times Square."

She stuffed the skirt back into the closet. "People can't just be attracted to personalities, you know. We're animals after all. We're designed to go after the strongest and fittest."

"And you think we can't change that?"

"Everyone always claims they value honesty, or kindness. Or a great sense of humor. But they expect it to come with flawless skin and a perfect set of teeth. The fat guy with a thousand jokes is out of luck. The hunchback with a heart of gold doesn't get to go to prom."

"That's what's wrong with people."

"We all come from nature." She took out a blouse, examined it, and put it back. "We have these ... desires. For the biggest and strongest, the youngest and most fertile. Maybe we can suppress them for a while, but, in the end, they're part of us."

"And what about the unfittest? What are the fat guy and the hunchback supposed to do?"

She paused with her hand on a velvet dress. "They don't mate. Or they don't mate consistently." She put the dress under her chin and studied herself in the mirror. "Otherwise, the world would be overrun with fat guys and hunchbacks."

A few weeks ago, he would have heartily agreed, but now he was seeing the world in a more expansive state. He had to rethink this philosophy.

"You like this?" She held up the velvet dress that laced up the front with string.

He shook his head.

"I give up." She dropped the dress on the floor. "You look and tell me if there's anything worth taking."

He went to the closet and searched through her wardrobe of ruffles and fringes, Indian prints and Peruvian vests. "This is cute." He held up a white t-shirt dress.

"You don't think it's too small?"

"It will hug you in all the right places."

"Let me try it on."

She shucked off her shorts and shirt and stood in her bra and panties, examining herself in the mirror. Roger could feel her looking at him but kept moving through the hangers. When she finally put on the dress, he gave her a nod of approval.

"What shoes go with this?"

He threw a pair of red wedgies at her feet.

When she had them on, she did a little spin. "What do you think?"

"It works."

She stared at him through the mirror. "You don't think it needs some jewelry? You have such a good eye for these things."

"No. Keep the focus on the body."

"So you want to focus on my body? Well, I'm all for that." She did a little bump and grind in the mirror.

He didn't know how to interpret these comments. Sherry had always been flirtatious, and Roger, safely ensconced in his gay armor, would usually flirt right back. Now, after their night together, her flirtation held something palpable.

"What about my hair? I'm thinking of getting bangs." She combed her fingers through her shoulder-length strands and held a clump over her eyes. "You think I should do bangs?"

"A short blunt cut just under the chin would highlight your cheekbones."

"Really? Sean would kill me. He always hated it when I cut my hair."

Roger kept perusing the garments in the closet. "And you want to please Sean because?"

"You're right. I don't have to please him anymore." She slipped the dress over her head and began folding it, carefully doubling it in half then quarters, as if the realization that she no longer had to please Sean diminished her somehow. Roger could smell her powdery deodorant filling up the room.

She cupped a hand underneath each breast and studied them in the mirror. "Do you think my boobs are lopsided?" She palmed each breast, turning from side to side.

"I'm no expert."

Every time I get my period, one of my tits gets lopsided." She walked over to him. "Here. Feel 'em."

"I'm not feeling your tits."

"That's not the attitude you took the other night."

Roger rolled his eyes and handed her a purple silk cocktail dress with a sequined bodice. "This might be an option."

"I bought this for a wedding years ago." She held it across her body. "You'll have to take me to some place fancy with this one."

"Try it on."

She shimmied the dress over her head and smoothed it out. "Oh, I like it. It's all sparkly." She looked at him through the mirror. "So? What do you think?"

"Well ..." He tried to keep a neutral face but felt his lips pursing and eyebrows rising.

"You hate everything." Sherry wiggled out of the dress and threw it on the floor. "Nothing is ever good enough for you. You want this. You want that. And the truth is that you don't really know what you want. And everyone else is supposed to kowtow to your whims."

"Okay. Keep the dress."

"You want me to be your doll. Your dress-up girl. Use me as bait to attract some guy you're obsessed with. Be your fuckbuddy when you're horny. And the whole time you don't care about my feelings." She stood in her bra and panties, her hips checked, her shoulders back, her entire body mobilized to strike.

Even though he had felt something like this churning under the surface, he didn't realize the extent of the maelstrom. He leaned on the closet and twisted the doorknob. He couldn't believe her impertinence. He had given her a place to stay, listened for hours to her complaints about Sean, and tried to be a good friend. He was about to release his own maelstrom when he remembered James's apology and thought to take a different approach.

"Okay. My actions might have been confusing. I see that. I'm sorry about the other night. I do care about your feelings, and I just want us to be friends."

"That's all I am—a friend."

"A good friend. I don't see ..."

"You don't see." She flopped down on the bed and screamed into the pillow.

"How can there be anything more?"

She jumped off the bed and paced around the room, kicking up discarded Post-It notes. "Stop with your rigid definitions. Your - your boundaries and fences and everything in its place. You have these limits on friendship and gayness and heterosexuality, but when you're drunk and horny—these limits disappear."

"I didn't mean to ... I didn't think ..."

"You didn't mean. You didn't think. But when your body wasn't thinking or meaning, it was busy getting busy with my body." She stopped in the middle of the room and starfished her arms. "Was it so terrible? Did I take advantage of you?"

"No. You didn't. But I just ..." This was precisely the conversation he'd been trying to avoid and it infuriated him that she had forced him to have it. "Motherfucker of God, we were drunk. That's just the occasion when boundaries disappear."

"We were free of inhibitions. We were beyond society's rules. Just two glorious, hungry bodies feeling and exploring each other."

"It wasn't the same for me."

"What was it then?"

"What was it?"

"What was it?"

Truth or kindness. Everything always came down to this. Desire consisted of the things you couldn't have. Sherry simply wanted him because she couldn't have him. And nothing he said would make a difference. "It wasn't unpleasant. It was just ... not me. It has nothing to do with you. I'm just not wired that way."

"You mean you can't override your natural proclivities?" Her eyes held a glint of triumph, and she sauntered around the room. "If you can't unwire your wires with me, how do you expect James to do the same thing with you?"

"Leave James out of this."

"Oh. That's different, is it?"

"Maybe. I don't know." He stared into the black hole of the closet. "I feel there's something between us."

"You know that for a fact, do you? Because he spent an entire lunch staring at my chest and then he grabbed me in his arms and kissed me."

"What?"

"I wasn't going to tell you. I didn't want to be the bearer of bad energy and all that. But yeah. After our lunch, we went into this empty restaurant under construction and he kissed me."

He walked to the window and looked down at the courtyard where a group of pigeons was pecking at a discarded burrito. She picked up her clothes from the floor and slowly dressed herself. Roger listened to the crawl of the fabric sliding over her skin, thinking about bodies and their sacks and layers. How to separate the container from the contained.

"What kind of a kiss?"

"On the lips. It lasted for about twenty seconds, which was how long it took me to get over the shock and pull myself away." She started throwing more clothes into the garbage bag.

He watched the birds with bits of tortilla in their beaks, flapping their wings and craning their necks. He wondered how much Sherry was exaggerating. It might have been an awkward goodbye kiss held for too long, like when a nervous salesman can't stop shaking your hand. Or it could have even been a lie, but he didn't think Sherry would go that far.

"He kissed me too," he said. "In the wine room at Bartholomew. And then he knelt down and took my dick in his mouth."

She twisted the end of the garbage bag and tied it in a knot. "I guess you win then."

As they walked to the subway, he kept imagining that kiss and Sherry's motivation for telling him. He didn't hold it against her, but he could see her intentions were by no means pure. They walked in silence, scraping the ground with their shoes.

10: Feeling Around the Edges

Roger examined the various food groups sitting on his kitchen counter: the leafy greens fluttered; the sauces shook; the sliced veggies winked. He contemplated cooking something spectacular, but his cracked kitchen tiles rebuked him, flooding his memory with the burnt offerings of previous culinary fiascos. Sherry was out canvassing apartments, leaving him free to sacrifice whatever animal, vegetable, or mineral that came to mind. It had been a week since her blow-up at Sean's, and things had been cool but cordial between them. They swept their fight under the rug and glided over it on tiptoes. She put most of her efforts into finding an apartment, and he put most of his efforts into not running away every time she came into a room. To live with someone not so secretly lusting after you made casual passings in the hallway and meetings at the breakfast table seemingly not so casual. He felt he had to put on pants every time he left his room.

Being Memorial Day, the restaurant was closed, and he had been shut up all weekend. He could have been on Fire Island with the rest of the gays—cast-mates Syd and Philip had invited him to respective parties—but he couldn't in good conscience frolic and imbibe in front of his actors while his play still remained unfinished, so he declined all offers and chained himself to the computer screen. It was a good thing he did because that morning James had called with the propitious message that he "needed to talk," provoking in Roger the desire to create an inspirational meal to accompany such an event. A meal where every bite of food, every sip of wine, would bring James and him closer to their inevitable union through the congress of mutual mastication.

He invited James to his place later that evening and hoofed it to a gourmet food store for supplies, which now sat on his kitchen counter in all their plastic-wrapped glory. Previously, ill-fated attempts with toasters and broilers, woks and blenders, had caused him to forsake cooking altogether. The only appliance in his kitchen still in working order was one exhausted smoke detector. Thankfully, grocery stores now had prepared foods, which enabled every culinary shlub to be a three-star chef. Gone were the days when a man had to galantine a chicken to show how much he cared.

Though, when he thought about all the hours he'd spent at the gym, the dentist, the hair salon, and tanning studio, another hour spent cooking foodstuffs seemed a step too far. The whole point of having good abs and straight teeth was that you didn't have to do anything else. You didn't have to help potential mates move, drive them to the airport, or visit with their relatives. And you certainly didn't have to cook elaborate dinners with unpronounceable ingredients. Yet, here he was—looking at half a pound of radicchio and wondering if it was salad or side.

The sun slanted through the blinds and cast stripes across the floor, illuminating the various polyp-shaped stains he wouldn't have time to mop up. James was due to arrive in fifteen minutes. And aided by his arsenal of precut, precooked, and prepackaged foods, Roger was ready to advance once again into the culinary arena. He would de-lid the receptacles, rip open the baggies, plate, reheat, and even stir things with a spoon. In spite of his previous failures, he remained confident in his ability to puncture a cellophane bag and drop it into the microwave.

Sherry had argued that microwaving wasn't really cooking but merely reheating. And Roger refuted this claim with the bravado of a master chef on Bravo TV. He declared himself *Maestro of the Micro*, an expertise demanding great skill and perseverance. Calculations had to be precise. Ten seconds too long, and you were eating your breakfast burrito off the oven door. An extra minute on a chocolate croissant, and you had chocolate pudding with croutons. And then there were the endless worries about containers. You had to know which ones melted into Dippy-Doo, and which ones appeared solid but secretly leaked microscopic particles. Roger was attracted to the danger as much as the convenience. One never knew if dinner would implode, melt, or give you cancer.

Acknowledging James's epicurean tastes, he had loaded up on everything gourmet and pre-made. He bought Vichyssoise because it sounded pretentious and required no reheating. With similar reasoning, he acquired a fennel/apple salad and olives for hors d'oeuvres. He contemplated getting a couple boxes of sushi and eliminating the microwave altogether, but decided one can't entertain a serious relationship without a hot entrée.

The olives almost undid him, though. At the store, he had hoped to just grab a random container, but the olives were displayed on colorful ceramic trays behind glass, like a jewelry case at Tiffany's. One had to negotiate with the counter person for their release. This required calling out olives by name and giving some indication of pounds and ounces, size, color, and stuffing. Such in-depth conversations seemed invasive. He imagined the counter girl thinking, *Oh, he's getting the olives with blue cheese; you know what that means.* It took away the surprise, like some over-enthusiastic guy explaining beforehand what he wanted to do in bed. Roger liked his food as he liked his men—uncomplicated and coming without explanation.

After the altercation with Sean, he felt unexpectedly protective of James. He brought him concealer for his black eye, which, after a couple of days, was still slightly dark. He maintained a constant watch and vowed that he would punch Sean in the face if he dared to set foot in the restaurant again. Or at least he'd aggressively dial 911. He even interceded when a customer got snippy with James and escorted the businessman and his frat-pack to the bar next door. The interlude in the wine room remained unspoken about, and Roger, in a feat of considerable self-control, made neither joke nor innuendo. He preferred to let it percolate between them—a memory that might resurface whenever he brushed James in the aisle or casually touched his shoulder: *Yes, my penis was in your mouth.* Mostly, they talked about his animations, and how to get into film school. After closing, over a cluttered table of cash and guest checks, they had long conversations about the kind of submission the schools wanted and how to film it. Roger mentioned that he could connect him with people who had secondhand equipment for sale or rent. And James, for his part, seemed to forego his previous decree of professionalism and eagerly participated in their talks, giving Roger all the more reason to suspect that something deeper was developing between them.

When he thought about Sherry's accusations—that he was mating with the unfittest of the species, falling for a guy so far beneath him on the scales of beauty as to be in an entirely different class, a featherweight compared to Roger's solid middleweight status—it all sounded rather inconsequential. Scales weren't always accurate. Sometimes they covered your eyes and kept you from seeing the important stuff. James was refreshingly uncritical. He didn't expect Roger to make witty comments or have discerning opinions on art or politics. He didn't care how Roger dressed or what his body mass index was. There were no appraising eyes focused on him, calculating his worth in comparison to the next guy. And Roger could love him or lust after him without being devastated when James didn't return his feelings. When their flirtation ended, heterosexuality would be to blame, and cushion whatever blow his ego would receive if he were rejected. He realized a relationship was probably impossible. These feelings were an excess of wealth burning holes in his pockets. He was gambling on James and betting to lose. After years of dating fascist university professors and fashionista artists, it was a comfortable bet.

As he set the kitchen table with his mismatched earthenware plates, he pondered Sherry's description of her lunch with James, and his promising confession of an "emotional attachment." In spite of that ill-timed kiss and James staring at her tits, he remained optimistic. The fact of the matter was that James had called *him*. And why else would he have called needing to talk so soon after admitting an "emotional attachment?" Granted, "emotional attachment" wasn't a blazing declaration. It sounded more like something you kept next to the vacuum cleaner: *You want to talk about love? Hold on, let me get my emotional attachment.* But he supposed it was the only way James's nascent gay psyche could formulate his feelings right now. Roger knew emotional attachments could eventually become permanent, just as anyone knew who had ever tried to remove the bristle end from a vacuum nozzle. He polished his wine glasses and texted Sherry not to come back too early.

Outside Roger's apartment, James lingered in the swampy vestibule, adding his warm breath to the already hot numbered buttons on the wall plate. He couldn't believe he was standing where Sherry stood on a daily basis, placing his hands on the same sticky door handle, rubbing his feet on the same gritty tiles. Over the last week, he'd been replaying the details of their lunch like it was the next installment of the Star Wars saga: the way she cut her food into tiny bites and then mixed it all together; how whenever she took a sip of wine her collarbone would turn red and he knew that her next sentence would contain a swear word. And of course—the kiss: her mouth slowly opening, tasting of garlic and avocados; her hands pressing on his chest, pushing into him or pushing him away, he couldn't tell. He had been living kissless in New York for over nine months; that one gesture had managed to crack his shell of solitude. And now, he was slowly picking his way out.

He thought about *Beauty and the Beast, The Phantom of the Opera, The Elephant Man*. Movies about sensitive men trapped in grotesque bodies, and the compassionate women who learned to love them in spite of horns, scars, and foreheads that look like fancy French pastries. He was hoping that Sherry would turn out to be one of these women.

He put a sweaty finger alongside the hot metal buttons marking the entrance to her bower, her lair, her sanctum sanctorum. Of course, it wasn't just *her* apartment; Roger occupied the space as well. And it was with Roger whom he needed to talk. After the kiss, he was the first person James had thought about. He needed his advice. Though apprehensive about how he'd react, he also wanted to share his happiness. In spite of everything, Roger remained his only friend. He continued to regard what had happened in the wine room as a kind of reciprocation. He was returning a favor, like after a friend buys you lunch. Though he could see that Roger might have a different interpretation—a blowjob was not a ham sandwich.

He just hoped he didn't feel slighted. The last thing he wanted was for Roger to tell Sherry about their relations. Which was why this talk was important. Not only did he need Roger's advice about how to proceed with Sherry, he also needed him to keep silent about their own relations. His plan was to confess his feelings for Sherry and then swear him to secrecy.

He pressed his finger on the buzzer and a trickle of sweat ran down his ribs. It was too hot for long pants and long sleeves, but this meeting required full coverage. This meeting required riot gear and a Kevlar bodysuit. The lock clicked with an ominous yowl, and James wished he had doubled up on his underwear.

At Roger's doorway, he didn't know how to greet him. Should they hug, air-kiss, or shake hands? Roger opted for a pat on the shoulder and led him down the hall to the kitchen. The hallway seemed to go on for miles. Painted dark red and padded with a plush crimson runner, it was like going for a long walk down somebody's throat.

When they finally made it to the kitchen, James noticed the table set with plates and wine glasses; fluffy lettuce had been carefully placed in bowls. "Oh, is this dinner?" He wasn't expecting dinner. He assumed they'd head out for a drink, where he could announce his news in a public space with lots of witnesses.

"I wanted to surprise you. Here, have an olive." Roger shoved a saucer of olives at him. "They're stuffed with all kinds of complicated things."

"So am I," James said, and took a seat at the table. The same table where a few weeks ago he had sat, drunk and depressed, and allowed Roger to unbuckle his pants and have his way with him. He lifted his collar, remembering how scratchy his neck had felt from Roger's beard stubble. And then he flashed on what had happened in the wine room, and the smell of musty blankets filled his memory. He tapped it all down. After finally having a chance with a beautiful woman, he wasn't about to turn gay now.

Throughout dinner, Roger brought out course after course. It was touching to see the trouble he took, even if he didn't make it himself. They talked about work-related things: was the restaurant slowing down? Was anything nefarious going on with Green and the Shawmut Restaurant Guide? How jealous was Bart? James looked for an opportunity to bring up Sherry and his feelings, but Roger was being so solicitous that he didn't want to put a damper on things. Now that Roger was opening up, he couldn't help but be drawn in.

"I was dating this bodybuilder once," Roger said. "Gorgeous but so much work. Had to eat every three hours—only lean proteins. After a play, before a concert, I always had to make sure he was fed or by intermission he'd turn cranky and hostile. It was kind of like taking care of an infant."

James stirred his soup carefully. "Didn't you feel insecure dating someone like that? Didn't you worry he'd find someone ... like ... another bodybuilder?"

"At first I did. I thought I needed to have sixteen-inch biceps and eight percent body fat. But then I realized he wasn't working at improving himself for my benefit. He wasn't studying the history of drama. Or having informed opinions on world events. There comes a time when you have to focus on how they're meeting your needs rather than you meeting theirs."

James wondered how Sherry met his needs, but he couldn't come up with anything specific. He was just happy to be around her.

After dinner, while the microwave hummed with two mugs of jasmine tea, and the plates collected in the sink, he told Roger that he'd have to make dinner for him sometime.

"I'm hoping you can do better than that." Roger smiled.

He leaned back in his chair and hung on to the chrome edge of the table. The last shards of sunlight made sketchy patterns on the walls. Now would be a good time to tell him about Sherry.

"You want to go to the living room?" Roger asked, taking the two mugs from the microwave. "I've got *Spike and Mike's Festival of Animation* on DVD."

"Where did you find that?"

"I have a friend who does PR for them. I thought you should study your competition."

For years, James had contemplated submitting his short films to Spike and Mike's. Animators from all over the world showed their shorts at these festivals. They featured 2D animation, computer animation, and the kind of stop-motion animation that James did. This was a grand gesture on Roger's part, a knowing gesture—a gesture with consequences.

They settled themselves in the living room. James made sure to grab the chair, leaving Roger the couch. Roger opened a tin of biscotti.

"I thought you hated animation," James said.

"A story is a story." Roger waved a chocolate-tipped cookie. "Whether it be told with actors, puppets, or line drawings."

The first two shorts were technically accomplished and structured entirely for laughs. James couldn't concentrate. He had been over this in his head a thousand times and couldn't think of any way to keep Roger's friendship while courting Sherry's girlfriendship.

Roger had his arm slung over the back of the couch, a puzzled expression on his face as he studied the angst-ridden gopher on screen. He'd probably have an hour critique for every ten minutes of film. James scrutinized Roger's wiry body, like a scrub brush, all bristly and hard. His face sprouted a dark shadow of hair above his goatee.

"Can we stop this for a while?" James blurted out.

Roger aimed the remote and paused the DVD.

James put his hands on his knees and stared at the happy little cookies in the biscotti tin. "I have to tell you something, and I don't know how you'll take it."

"Try me." Roger smiled.

"Okay. First off, I want you to know that I really value our friendship, and I don't want anything to mess that up."

"Why would anything mess that up?"

"I need your advice."

"I am a compendium of information from Dear Abby to Penthouse Forum."

"I'm interested in someone."

"Yes?"

"And I don't want any weirdness about it."

"There won't be if we're honest with each other. With our feelings..."

"Yes. Exactly."

"I know all of this must seem a little strange to you. Believe me, it's strange for ..."

"It's Sherry."

Roger rose a bit in his seat as if he might levitate. James saw imaginary clouds of steam bursting from his ears. "Sherry?"

James pushed into his chair and gripped the armrests, as if preparing for heavy turbulence. "She kissed me and that means something, right?" He described their romantic lunch at Green and the kiss in the fish shack. It gave him a secret thrill to recount these events to someone else.

Roger gestated on the couch. His face inscrutable as stone. "I see," he said to the black TV screen. He reached for the remote and started the DVD.

On screen, a dog-faced husband was being henpecked by a fish-faced wife. The husband kept digging a hole with a shovel until he was buried underground and couldn't hear his wife nagging him.

Roger hit pause on the remote. "So what was all that stuff you were doing with me? Experimentation? Idle curiosity? Are you on the bi now, gay later plan?"

"I never meant to lead you on. I just... didn't know how to stop it."

"Saying 'stop' might have worked."

"I didn't want to hurt your feelings."

"I didn't know I was so repugnant to you." He grabbed the remote and hit play. On screen, the wife was now crying about how much she missed her husband. Big tears spilled from her fishy eyes, and she swam longingly through all the rooms.

James observed the wheels turning in Roger's head, the color rising on his cheeks. He had obviously upset him, which was unkind after Roger had gone to the trouble of making dinner. It occurred to him that no one outside of his mother had ever made him dinner. Once, when he was sick, Joanne made him split pea soup, but as soon as he got well, she withheld her culinary favors. Tracy had sometimes cooked breakfast, but dinners happened at a restaurant or in her kitchen with James slaving behind the stove. Roger was the only person who had ever cooked him dinner.

He lunged for the remote and hit pause. "You're not repugnant. I was being polite. I didn't want to offend you."

"I must have missed the chapter on cocksucking in Emily Post's Book of Etiquette."

James could see Roger bundling himself in layers of sarcasm, covering up whatever openness and vulnerability he'd previously exhibited. But he did have a point. How ineffectual—how phony James must seem. He was either the world's biggest tease or the world's biggest closet case. No explanation was going to satisfy Roger. Even the truth sounded ridiculous. He leaned in with his elbows on his knees.

"Roger, you're my only friend. I didn't know what to do." The words hung in the air like something solid between them. They sounded desperate and pathetic, but James conceded their validity. If he was going to be honest about Sherry, he would also have to be honest about Roger. "I liked the attention."

Roger's eyes probed for more explanation. James scanned the room for answers, for something that he could relate to in Roger's world. An Elvis lamp did a hip thrust on top of a decoupaged end table. Bookcases held titles on theatre and philosophy. The walls were covered with posters from Roger's plays: half-naked men with squinty eyes and prominent chins. Everything made him feel deficient.

"I didn't want you to dump me as a friend," he said.

"The idea was to just string me along until what?—I proposed marriage?"

"I thought you'd get tired. You have a new boyfriend every month. Muscle-bound party boys with glitter on their chests. What were you doing with me? I was some freaky flavor of the week. You were bound to move on."

"But I haven't." Roger pulled out a thread from the fabric of the couch. He held it taut between his fingers.

"Not yet, you haven't."

Silence.

James started the film again. On screen, the fishwife's tears poured from the windows and washed away the soil, uncovering the husband enjoying a fine cigar underground. She then started berating him for smoking.

Roger swiped the remote and hit pause. "You're afraid."

He could see Roger gearing up for another onslaught and wished he had a white flag to wave. "If that's what you think..."

"You're afraid of these new feelings, and you don't know how to deal."

"I just want to be friends, is all."

Roger rubbed his thumb over the side of the remote. "How can we now?"

James regarded Roger's play posters: *Dark Stranger*, *Total Eclipse*, *Mephisto, My Love*. He felt like a cockroach caught by a cat. A cat who was saying, "I don't want to eat you," all the while batting him around with his paws. "So it was just about sex? Nothing else meant anything to you but the sex?"

"Don't flatter yourself. The sex was nothing. The sex was minor."

"Then why are you pushing for it?"

Roger raised his feet and slammed them on the floor. "That's not what I'm pushing for."

James thought about his friends from college. Not one of them had contacted him since he left Michigan. He had slipped from their memories like a boring preview before the feature presentation. "If you really cared who I was on the inside," he said, "you'd want to spend time with me regardless of whether we had sex."

"And if *you* really cared who *I* was on the inside," Roger said, "sex would be an expression of that friendship regardless of what I looked like on the outside." Even as the words left his mouth, he realized their futility. He could no more make James desire him than he could make himself desire Sherry. Than Sherry could make herself desire James. Everyone was locked in their own prisons of yearning and expectation, waiting for the perfect combination of looks and personality to free them.

"Aren't you the one always saying appearances don't matter? It's the inside that counts? Well, what's wrong with my insides? Aren't I smart, creative, and kind?"

"Yes."

"If you're so concerned with everyone's goddamned inner qualities, why can't you appreciate mine?"

James sank lower in his chair. If he could pick it up and carry it out the door, he would have. Perhaps they both wanted the same thing. They just went about it in different ways. Roger sought to find it through sex, and James through friendship.

He shrugged. "I gave it a shot. Didn't I?"

"And? Was it so terrible?"

"And." James felt the air with his hands, searching to grab onto the right words. "I just want to be friends."

"What if Sherry told you she only wanted to be your platonic friend? Would you still want to be around her?"

"Yes. I would put my sexual feelings aside for the sake of a more meaningful friendship."

Roger stood up and brushed his hand on his pants. "I need a drink."

James watched him stalk to the kitchen. He fingered the fringe on the Elvis lamp next to his chair. Could anyone put their sexual feelings aside? That was the crux of the matter. If people could put their sexual feelings aside, most marriages would never break up; advertisers would actually have to discuss the merits of their products; and there would be no need for porn. It was wishful thinking to believe Roger could ignore his sexual feelings. And, as validating as it first seemed, being the object of desire exhausted him. Even if the universe had decided to reverse roles in the movie of his life, and made him the Beauty and someone else the Beast, the responsibility was too much.

He had always thought of his body as a shell. This was what he told himself when women ignored him or suddenly developed surprisingly busy schedules whenever he asked them out. He always hoped that once they discovered the man underneath the shell, they would be pleasantly surprised. He knew that his shell wasn't all that attractive, but for some reason, Roger wanted to touch it. He understood this kind of blind hope. Even after being told that he was interested in someone else, Roger was still holding on. This was his chance to do for Roger what all along he had been asking women to do for him. If the body was only a shell, what difference did it make which shell he groped around the edges of?

But of course it did make a difference. These shells determined our destiny. Biology maintained a strict caste system: man/woman, gay/straight, beautiful/ugly. No matter how much we wished it wasn't true—and in this moment, he really wanted to love Roger as fully and deeply as he desired— we were all trapped inside our shells.

Roger came back with two beers and handed one to James. "So, you want to know how she feels about you?"

"What?"

He snapped open his beer and took a long swallow. "You think you have a chance with her?"

"I think she likes me." James gripped the can and let the coldness seep into his palms. "You think she doesn't?"

"Only one way to find out."

"How?"

"I ask her."

This was more involvement than he wanted Roger to have, but at least he didn't seem angry anymore. "It's so high school. You ask, 'Do you like him?' and then come reporting back to me."

"You could listen in. Hear what she says yourself."

"What do you mean?"

Roger folded a pillow on his lap and rested his elbows on it. "I could put you in the bedroom, leave the door open. Talk to Sherry in the kitchen. You'll hear everything."

"I don't think she'd like me spying on her."

"It's up to you." He took another long swallow. "You can find out tonight how she feels. Or you can live in limbo."

James scratched the nubby fabric of the chair. He was actually quite comfortable in limbo. Just to have a few days, or weeks, to contemplate possibilities. To study Sherry's language and gestures—the thrill of that gap-toothed smile. To plan their future date, or dates. He'd already thought of three places to take her: Daniel, a picnic in Prospect Park, and a Broadway show. He still hadn't been to a Broadway show. When he thought about all the things he'd never done in New York, it seemed like he'd been waiting for a girl like Sherry to make them worthwhile.

"You think about it. Sherry won't be home for a while." Roger picked up the remote and pressed play.

They'd finished last year's Spike and Mike festival and were watching the previous one when Roger heard the creaking of the gate. "Come on." He grabbed James by the hand and pulled him to the bedroom. "Just stand out of sight." He left the door ajar and went to the kitchen. At some point in their viewing, between evil cats and dirty birdies, James had tacitly agreed to Roger's plan.

From the fridge, he got a can of Guinness and weighed it in his hands. Truth or kindness seemed to be his perpetual dilemma, yet, he always chose truth. There were other ways to break the news to James. He could let Sherry manage it, or allow nature to run its course. There was no need to stage a scene of betrayal and have James pummeled by the truth. On the other hand, this would free him from weeks, maybe months of false hope, and spare him a greater heartache. In the long run, Roger surmised, truth was always kinder. He opened the beer and let the foam spill into the sink.

Sherry slammed the front door, threw some packages in her room, and clomped to the kitchen.

"You won't believe the dumps I've seen."

"I'm just pouring a beer. You want half? I can't afford the carbs." He got her a glass, and they sat at the table. "I told you it wasn't going to be easy."

She brushed back her hair and exhaled. "Warehouses turned into lofts with bathrooms in the hall. One-bedrooms divided into studios and broom closets turned into bedrooms. People are living like animals in cages. We did see one place that was livable. I put you down as a reference. Said I lived here two years. Hope you don't mind."

"I'll tell them you were a model tenant."

"I'm not sure we'll get it." She took a big swallow of beer and wiped the foam from her lips. "Trish's credit isn't good."

"Don't worry, you can stay here until you find a place."

She reached across the table and grabbed his arm. "Thank you. I'm not sure I could've done this—left Sean and all—without your help."

"No biggie."

"And about the other day. I'm sorry if I ..."

"We don't have to talk about it." Roger pushed back his chair, hoping the noise might distract James from what was just said. The situation could backfire if Sherry started blabbing about their ill-timed peccadillo. He dragged the table an inch closer, making more noise. "The past is a country best left unvisited."

She brushed something off her blouse and regarded the stack of dishes in the sink. "So, did you impress James with your master microwaving skills?"

"No explosions anyway."

"And? Did you make any inroads? Did I pave the way for you?"

"He was very preoccupied by that kiss you gave him."

"I didn't *give* him anything."

"He thinks it meant something."

"Oh my God." She put her hands over her face.

"He's looking forward to your second date."

"There wasn't even a first date."

Roger lifted his beer can in a toast. "You can admit it. Maybe there was a little spark between you two."

"Ple-ase. He sweats non-stop. You should have seen him—his head was a sprinkler system. And the hair on his legs—it was like a shag carpet. I know that's your thing—bears and otters and chipmunks but ..."

"Just to be clear, there are no chipmunks in gay iconography."

"Really? Why not?"

"Chipmunks have buck teeth."

Sherry crinkled her brow.

"Not good for ..." Roger mimed sucking a cock.

"Oh. Well. Whatever. And..." she palmed the air. "...when he kissed me, he smelled like ... I don't know ... it was like ..."

He wanted to say wet dog but held his tongue.

"Uh-uh. Not for me." She made a sticking-out-tongue-face. "Blech."

"Okay. Okay. I believe you. Let's change the subject." He wasn't expecting such a vehement rejection. The Guinness was starting to rise in his throat.

They talked more about apartments and neighborhoods. Sherry chattered on, occasionally knocking his leg under the table. She wanted his advice on brokers and credit checks, how much information to give land-lords, what rules she should make, if any, for her new roommate, should they sign up for Internet cable or DSL. At certain points, she clutched his arm dramatically. He felt like he might be substituting for Sean in the boy-friend department. Or maybe it was a residual from their sexcapade, trying to keep the intimacy going any way possible. He listened and advised as much as he could, but after a while, he threw his can in the garbage and said he was going to bed.

"Let me give you a goodnight hug." She wrapped her arms around him, her head just under his chin. He felt the soft crush of her breasts. It was strange holding something smaller and lighter. Also a bit unnerving. With it came the added responsibility that you must take care of this thing. There was the unspoken expectation that you could be relied on: for chores, ad-vice, emotional support. All the heavy lifting. Along with plunging the toilet, fixing the flat tire, programming the remote, killing the bugs, and shoveling the snow. These small vulnerable things needed so much. He was beginning to understand why so many men ran away.

She let go, giving his chest a quick cat-bump with her head, and walked to her room.

In the bedroom, he closed the door. It took him a minute to locate James, who was sitting on the floor by the laundry hamper, knees against his chest, the empty beer can rolling at his feet.

"I have to go home," he whispered.

Roger put his finger to his lips and mouthed: *Wait till Sherry goes to sleep.* He wanted to put an arm around him or offer a solid hand on his shoulder, but James seemed to be holding up the wall with his back, and any slight movement would topple him. His statue-like composure was on the verge of cracking. Roger could visualize little fissures running through his body. He crouched down and spoke low. "I'm sorry. I didn't think it would go that way."

"You knew it would go that way."

"I suspected ... but I ..."

"You told her to go to lunch with me."

There was no short explanation. And with Sherry down the hall, they couldn't really talk. James leaned his head against the wall and shifted his vision just left of Roger's face, as if erasing him.

When he heard the shower turn on in the bathroom, Roger retrieved the DVD and started it on the TV in the bedroom. He tried to get James to sit on the bed and watch, but he remained on the floor, defiant and numb. Roger hoped the sound from one of the animations would pique his interest, especially classics by John Dilworth, whom James had once praised as groundbreaking for his use of horror. But trees with human lips and misshapen fetuses didn't draw his attention. He just kept pressing his back against the wall. At one point, Roger was going to turn off the cartoons; there was only so much existential angst he could take from fluffy bunnies and spunky lizards. Just as he was patting down the mattress for the remote, James got up to leave. He was going to walk out without so much as a goodbye when an animated short came on that had been recently nominated for an Academy Award.

"Look," Roger said. "This is that guy you hate." How he'd managed to remember so much about cartoon directors surprised him. But James seldom said anything negative, so when he did, Roger took note.

The film was composed of simple line drawings, often the same drawing in each frame, giving a wavy quality to the images. There was a lot of absurdist humor that required a deep reading of Heidegger and Sartre to appreciate. James gave a little huff and glared at the TV, his nostrils becoming pinched. Roger could read the reel of rebukes playing on his face.

"Here. Have a biscotti and calm down."

"If you can't draw, you shouldn't be doing line animation." He grabbed the tin and sat on the bed.

When the short ended, another one came on that James admired. A lushly drawn story from Japan about a man who had a cherry tree growing out of his head. James crossed his legs Indian style and munched on a cookie. After each film ended, Roger expected him to leave, but instead, he grudgingly took over more of the bed: leaning back on his arms, lying on his side, and finally resting his head on the cookie tin and falling asleep.

He looked serene in sleep. All the tension washed out of his face. All the effort of his enforced maturity relaxed. Roger could picture the little boy making puppets for his grandmother. The weird kid collecting leaf samples at recess. The lonely child lost in his imaginary world. The same imaginary world that drew Roger to theatre and movies. It might have been the veneer of alienation that attracted him to James as much as his creativity. And so he felt the need to protect him. He wondered what it was that made him want to comfort this body and not the more feminine body down the hall. And maybe that was the distinction of love—it felt necessary.

He removed James's glasses and put them on the nightstand. His head was sweating and he wiped the droplets with his finger. Felt the subtle indentations in his skull and the sharp bristles. He breathed in his wet dog scent and held it inside, committing every molecule to memory.

11: The Theatre Bug

The ride to the theatre was tense. They inched along in Brooklyn rush hour, dozens of cars deep at every traffic light. James gripped the wheel and stared fixedly at the chrome bumpers ahead, not so much as blinking in Roger's direction. Even after three weeks, the scene that Roger had staged with Sherry was still fresh in his mind. He kept replaying it as one would pick off a scab, the crescendo of pain ending with her exclamation of "blech." Not even a real word, but a discharge in the back of her throat. He had resolved to distance himself from both Sherry and Roger. But, over time, Roger had a way of breaking down barriers. He was like the ocean in that regard: inevitable and supremely salty.

James kept him at bay for a while: secluding himself in his office, giving only the most perfunctory responses on the floor. Roger would come up to his podium and ask, "Aren't you ever going to speak to me again?" To which James would reply, "Table eight needs water. Go." One day, on his podium, he found a cupcake, on top of which were figurines of Christopher Robin and Winnie the Pooh holding hands. He supposed it was some reference to friendship and in full view of Roger, took the cupcake and dumped it in the garbage. Another time, Roger asked, "What's a four-letter word that ends in 'k' and means intercourse?" James walked away while Roger called after him, "It's talk. Have you ever heard of it? Human communication. The basis of all civilization."

But there was only so much opposition he could muster. In truth, after so many years of chasing after women who wouldn't give him the time of day, he quite enjoyed someone pursuing him in such a vigorous fashion. Roger would sit on his desk and play Pac Man with his stapler, discussing ideas for his piano man film, while James pretended to fill out inventory sheets.

"You know, instead of love at first sight, maybe the woman asks the piano man about a song he was playing. And they strike up a conversation about music."

James knew long conversations didn't work in animations, but he kept quiet and continued inputting his spreadsheets.

"Or maybe." Roger held up the stapler, clapping it like a maraca. "The piano man sees her crying. And it stirs something in him. His own grief perhaps."

One day, Roger cornered him at the coffee station and asked what animations on the Spike and Mike CD he liked best, obliquely reminding him of that thoughtful gift. James replied just to shut him up, but eventually they got to talking about the various shorts, which led to longer critiques, and James was reeled into a dialogue he had emphatically tried to avoid. One can hold back the ocean only so long.

Sherry, he would never forgive. It was one thing to ask a friend to ingratiate you with someone, and quite another to lie about your feelings and lead a person on. James felt decidedly used and was glad she saw fit to keep her distance. Now, whenever he saw her, he felt a discharge in the back of his throat and his own feelings of "blech" erupting forward.

A white van cut him off and he laid on the horn. And then felt bad about laying on the horn.

"I'll introduce you to Erin, the stage manager," Roger said. "She works as a PA and knows tons of people in the industry."

"Uh huh."

"She may have some ideas where you can get film equipment."

"Uh huh."

"Please stop uh-huhing me. I can't stand it if you're going to spend the whole night uh-huhing me."

"Okay." James turned up the radio—Terry Gross was talking about gentrification.

They stopped at the traffic light by the park. A water seller walked between cars, absently looking into windows, waving a splayed hand of bottles. Roger recalled the rainy night when James offered him a ride; they drove down this same street and ended up in his kitchen drinking tea and kissing. That one improbable choice led to so many other improbable choices. And now here he was, infatuated with a confused straight boy who couldn't decide if he hated him or loved him.

Across from the park, the art deco facade of The Brooklyn Public Library was held captive by a wooden fence. Its gold hieroglyphics of Athena, Zeus, and the proletariat of America in the process of being restored.

"I hope you keep working on your film, whether you get into film school or not."

"What happened to 'It'll never work. No one takes puppets seriously?'"

"That was before I saw your puppets and took them seriously."

The theatre was a mess when they entered: T-shirts and hoodies thrown over seatbacks, Par Cans stacked in the aisles, Styrofoam cups and water bottles balanced on metal chairs, and waiting to fall off the edge of the stage. Technically, Roger shouldn't even be here; he should be home writing the final scene. With only a few weeks until opening, the cast was ready to mutiny, and Garrick was breathing down his neck. He was risking his career and reputation, but he wanted one more chance to show James his baby in utero. Through all their late-night conversations, he had come to value his weirdo, outsider perspective. He wanted his opinion on the second act, which would help him decide how to finish the final scene.

The cast was huddled in the first two rows running lines. The crew, a ragtag group of students from Brooklyn College willing to work for course credit, was on stage with Erin going over cues. Erin was one of those "indeterminate" people. She might be young or middle-aged, plump or heavyset, and no one would have been surprised to find out she was actually a man. It was difficult to pin a description on her. If Roger ever needed anyone to secretly plant a bomb at the United Nations, he would've chosen Erin. Her blonde hair was cropped short and she wore work boots with jean shorts; she often smelled of the kind of cold cream that came in gallon tubs. The cast had given up speculating on whether she was gay or straight. Most decided that she probably cared for a dozen cats and left it at that. Nevertheless, she was an exceptional stage manager and an anal-retentive expert at organization. Roger and Garrick often joked that she probably kept her feces in numbered bags cross-referenced by date, color, and consistency.

Roger went directly to her, and James shuffled behind. "Hey Erin. Did you see the Jellies I got for Hal?"

She looked up from her cue book. The other techies slouched even deeper into their black t-shirts. "Um, yeah. The Jellies are size nine and Hal is an eleven and a half. Not going to work."

"I never would've guessed. He's so insecure for someone with big feet." Even though Hal possessed all the gay culture requisites to give him high status: youth, abs, and a jawline so chiseled you could cut paper on it, he was deeply unsure of himself. It was a winning combination for playing the gullible volleyball player that Terry and Luca brought home from the beach.

"Don't worry. I have an uncle who has a pair. I can borrow from him." She turned back to her group. "Cue 145 is a seven-count, lights up downstage left."

"Good job." Roger patted the back of a greasy-haired kid who smelled of pot and B.O.—the L'Air du Temps of techies.

As he approached Garrick and the cast, Diego smiled at him. He didn't know in what capacity he was going to introduce James: friend, boyfriend, boss. Though he and Diego had ended their extracurricular entanglements, some residual notes of competition remained. While Roger was relieved to see Diego hooking up with size eleven Hal, he didn't want him judging James on the same superficial level. He secretly wished he had thought to redress James in something other than a Peerless Produce t-shirt and pleated khakis. The cast was doing speed-lines; everyone was spitting out dialogue with machine-gun enunciation so introductions had to be postponed. Garrick got up and took Roger aside.

"I was thinking about the drag show. What if one of the boys' drag names is Katrina? And they wear a wind-blown costume, carrying a net of black babies?"

"Interesting." Roger tried to nod in a thoughtful way as if he were actually contemplating the theatrical value of a net of black babies. Garrick was a "neo-Marxist, proto-feminist, former Act-Up activist," which was not a satiric description but an actual quote from his director's bio. To say he had no sense of humor was like saying Mother Teresa dabbled in works of charity. In the 1990's, he was notorious for a production of *Much Ado About Nothing* where all the characters were dying of an incurable disease.

The double marriage in the finale where both couples were covered with Kaposi-Sarcoma lesions created a minor uproar with both AIDS activists and Shakespearian purists. He was constantly pressuring Roger to make his text more political, like insisting that Luca refer to his penis as a Weapon of Mass Destruction, only to later reveal that he was packing nothing more destructive than a firecracker. "Let me mull it over." Roger flourished a hand in James's direction. "By the way, this is James. He's going to sit in on rehearsal."

Garrick gave a head nod and turned back to the cast. "Okay, everybody. Take ten. When we come back, we're starting Act Two, scene one." He put an arm around Roger and let his glasses-on-a-chain fall to his chest. "How's that final scene coming?"

"Any day now. I swear."

"We're down to the wire here. I caution to tell you the cast is getting agitated. And from a directorial point of view, it's hard to orchestrate a character's journey if I don't know his final destination."

"I hear you. A few more days and I'll give you the scene. I promise."

He guided James to a seat in the middle row, where hopefully no one would notice his pleated khakis or sullen attitude. He gathered his notepad and script from his satchel and professionally put one seat between them. He had a queasy feeling in his stomach, the confluence of an inexplicable need to impress James, and, at the same time, for his cast, especially Diego, to be impressed by James. He knew that James didn't have stunning beauty like Diego, who was in his own right a minor Greek god—or more accurately, a major Puerto Rican one—but he hoped that James's presence would at least stop Diego's constant flirting and hinting at a one-night reconciliation.

Syd, standing a few rows ahead, tipped his water bottle in Roger's direction, and he recalled the night he snuck into the lighting booth and the sting of his mean-spirited impersonation. He wanted to make some crude sexual remark, like "Make love to the bottle, Syd," to let him know he was in on the joke, but held his tongue. Syd was known in certain circles as The Virgin Mary. A former dancer, with a dancer's perfect body, he was notorious for resisting the advances of the most eligible doctors at New York Presbyterian, where he now worked as a nurse. He spent most of his free time at the gym, where his mortifications of the flesh through bench press and bicep curl left him so defined his body seemed written in bold font.

The general speculation was that he hadn't had a boyfriend or even a casual fuck in years. In gay culture, this elevated him to the Mt. Everest of sexual conquests. Though Diego would fight to the death to refute this claim. He was always making reference to Syd's bald head and flaunting his own long locks in his presence. Due to their opposing sensibilities, Syd's abstinence and Diego's indulgence, the two actors frequently clashed in rehearsals. Originally, Roger hadn't thought it a good combination, but Garrick was set on making Syd and Diego the uber couple that comes uncoupled. He also wasn't opposed to capitalizing on their good looks. "Think of the tickets we could sell with those two on our poster. Plus, the diversity points: Black Goliath meets Hispanic David." Unfortunately, he didn't surmise that they actually embodied two sides of a more feminine ideal—the Madonna and the whore, and hence, had little chemistry onstage.

He looked up from his notes just in time to see Diego coming toward him, Coke can in hand, smiling like some demented alt-leisure spokesmodel. His tank top exposed articulated arms that resembled finely tooled machinery.

"Hello, Ruggero. How come you no say hi to me?"

"Hello, Diego."

"I want to ask you something." He stood in the row in front of them and propped one foot on a chair. His crotch was uncomfortably at eye level. "You know how we talk about Luca's bicho. How is really a bichito. So, how does a man with a bichito walk? Because, for me, you know, I have no experience with this kind of *aflicción*." He leaned back, pulling the fabric of his shorts around his prominent bulge.

"Instead of all the blood rushing between your legs, it stays in your head so you can think clearly and not say stupid stuff."

"Ah, *intellectual*." He turned to James. "Hello. Ruggero will not introduce us because he has no manners. I am Diego."

"Hi. James."

"Nice to meet you, Jay-ames." He pronounced his name with two syllables. "Ruggero doesn't want to introduce us because we used to be a couple. And now he is embarrassed."

"I'm not embarrassed."

Diego leaned in with his elbow on his thigh. "But there is nothing to be embarrassed about. We are artists. The playwright and the actor. We let our creativity juices flow. I always let my juices flow." He stroked his goatee. "Is a good thing, no?"

"Certainly," James said. He seemed to be enjoying Diego a little too much. "So you and Roger were a couple?"

"Si. I was his muse."

"You were not my muse."

"But the passion between us, it burn out. Strong at first. A Fuego! But then like two suns close together, we eat each other. Don't worry, Jay-ames. We are professional now. We work together as friends. You no need be jealous."

"Oh," James said. "Roger and I are just friends. We work together too."

Roger felt this comment like a small pin in his side.

"Ruggero." Diego slapped his leg. "Why you not tell me you doing another play?"

"Relax, Sarah Bernhardt. We work at the restaurant. He's the manager."

"So." He raised an eyebrow. "You are his boss? Must be hard for you. Ruggero doesn't like anyone to be the boss of him."

"Tell me about it," James said.

"It put many limits on sex play."

"Diego," Roger interrupted. "They need you on stage." He pointed to Garrick and the cast, who were glaring at him expectantly.

Diego ran down, put his arm on the stage, and lifted himself up in one athletic swoop. Philip and Warren were already onstage in their trial costumes. Philip wore a short silk robe and trim shorts that showed off his surprisingly muscular legs.

"What do you think of this?" asked Philip, modeling his outfit.

"That's perfect," said Garrick, taking a seat in front of Roger.

Warren, in baggy shorts and a loose Tommy Bahama shirt, looked up from his script and said, "I'm not wearing a Speedo. These balls are too old."

"That's fine," said Garrick. He turned back to Roger. "Is this okay?" Roger shrugged. "Erin? Can you make a note of these costumes?"

"Got it." Erin called from the front row, scribbling in her binder.

The crew had moved the railing upstage right and set a bar cart and three metal folding chairs in front to designate the deck of Herbert and Findley's Fire Island home. Philip was playing Findley, Warren's long-term partner; Diego was his nurse, Luca, with whom he'd fallen in love; and Syd was playing Terry, Luca's partner of several years.

"Erin?" Garrick called out. "Is there some reason we don't have deck chairs yet?"

"I'm working on it. You said the Adirondack chairs were too slouchy."

Roger whispered to Garrick's shoulder. "Shouldn't the lights be brighter? It's high noon after all?"

"Erin?" Garrick called. "Can we bring up the lights a bit?"

She spoke into her headset and the lights came up on stage.

"Perfect," said Garrick. "Okay. When you're ready, actors."

Warren and Diego took seats and held hands, while Philip paced behind the bar cart with a drink in hand. It was the scene where Herbert and Luca told Findley that they were planning on moving to Bolivia, and Herbert wanted to permanently separate and sell the summer house. The actors were playing it rather too glibly. The jokes were landing but not the fear and sorrow underneath. Roger underlined in the script some of the punchlines that might have to be removed. Again, Diego was proving to be the real star of the show; his performance continued to show depths of feeling. Roger wondered where this depth of feeling was in real life. When they were dating, the only depth Diego was concerned about had to do with his vibrating butt plug.

When the scene ended, Garrick came down to the front of the stage to give notes. "How did that feel?"

Diego sat on the edge of the stage. "I don't know what to do when Heriberto walks out. Should I stand still in shock? Or move in his direction?"

"One or the other. Make a choice and commit to it."

Philip leaned forward in his chair. "I'm having a bit of trouble justifying Findley's actions. He's coming off as kind of a gold-digging bitch."

"You think he doesn't actually love Herbert?" Garrick peered over his glasses.

"I always thought he did, but the way the scene is playing now, Warren is so strong in his convictions to leave, Findley seems selfish and vindictive."

"Maybe I can help." Roger raised his yellow pad. "I used to have more lines for Findley, about how he took care of Herbert when he had his first heart attack, how he slept in the hospital during his bypass surgery. Findley worked through their whole relationship as an elementary school teacher. He just didn't make enough to afford all the things Herbert wanted. But it's not like he didn't contribute."

"I see. That gives me more to work with."

"I might add those back in."

Warren walked downstage holding his script. "For god's sakes don't go adding more lines. And, while we're on the subject, can we please get an arrival date on the final scene?"

"Yes," Syd chimed in from the audience. "I need to know what happens to my character."

Garrick held up his hands. "Let's not gang up on Roger. He assured me the scene will be finished in two days."

"No offense, but we've heard that before," said Warren.

"I'm sorry, guys," said Roger. "I know it's unprofessional, and I'm making your jobs ten times harder, but just bear with me a few more days."

"Is it two or a few?" said Philip.

Warren flapped his script. "I can barely remember the lines I've been working on for a month now."

"Tell me something," Roger said. "How would you all like the story to end? I'm curious. Any input you have would be helpful."

Syd came and sat in the front row. "I think Luca and Terry should stay together. Luca's motivation never made sense to me."

"He wants to go back to his home country—to his family," said Diego. "And this is the only way."

"He could go by himself. Save up his money. Why does he want to play nursemaid to this old man?"

"The money for one," said Vikram, who had joined their circle by the stage. Vikram or Vik, as everyone called him, was a Shakespearian actor who had just moved to New York from The Stratford Festival. He was slumming in Roger's play but had recently come out and was eager to immerse himself in gay culture. So much so that in his kissing scene with Hal, Garrick had to tell him to restrain himself. It was a bit incongruous to hear the pool boy talking like a Cambridge upperclassman, but Vik's Shakespearian training didn't include Long Island accents. Garrick liked him because he fit with his United Colors of Benetton method of casting: his darker Indian features making Hal's blondeness even more fragile and ethereal.

"He really love Heriberto." said Diego.

"If they go to Bolivia without the money then I'd believe it," said Syd.

"But we'd need to know the ending to determine that."

"I think he really loves Herbert," said Philip. "I don't care what these cynics say. I'd like to see them run away together."

Heads turned toward Warren. Usually the most opinionated of the group, and always ready to argue with conventional wisdom, he pulled up one of the metal chairs. "Personally, if I were Herbert and had a partner of twenty-six years who still loved me, and cared for me when I was sick, and let me have sex with anyone I wanted, I would count myself the luckiest man alive. He has so much—this man, yet still he's greedy for more. But at the same time," he clutched the script, "I understand that he's doing this for Luca as much as for himself. He wants to give him the gift of reuniting with his home and family, to the detriment of his own health. It's noble and loving, but pushes the boundaries of what's believable. I guess you have to choose between realism and fantasy."

"Or pessimism and optimism," said Philip.

"Or selfishness and altruism," said Vik.

"Thanks, guys." Roger tapped his pen on his yellow pad, even more confused than before. "You've given me a lot to think about."

"Just give us the scene," said Warren.

"Okay," said Garrick. "Let's take fifteen and set up for the drag show. Get whatever costumes you have ready. I want to see them."

The actors scattered to the four corners of the auditorium. Roger sat by himself and wrote down some notes. All of his life he'd been realistic about love. His experience told him that even when it worked, it never lasted. And if it lasted, it turned into something else—something other than love: friendship, estrangement, hatred. When critics disparaged his plays for being "too dark," "without hope," or having "no moments of grace," his reaction was to say, "It's not my job to give you grace or hope. It's my job to give you truth." Everyone always wanted kindness at the expense of truth.

James got up to go to the bathroom, and on his return, Erin conscripted him to help with the lights. One of the scoops was hanging loose, and some ParCans needed to be refocused. He was a head taller than the other crew members, so he obliged. Roger watched him climb the ladder, his footing unsure on every step. He reached up to adjust the light, while Erin gave directions. A sliver of his stomach was exposed, revealing delicate wisps of hair, soft and vulnerable, the kind you could easily wet with your tongue.

Who would have thought that this long torso would spill into that bowl of a belly? Or those skinny arms would be paired with such thick legs? His body was a constant surprise. He had absolutely no ass, which didn't coincide with current standards of beauty, but Roger could surmise its advantages. The prime one being deeper penetration.

James refocused the light and tweaked the shutters to Erin's specifications, his wide bony shoulders poking out of his t-shirt like the plates on a Stegosaurus. He came down and they moved the ladder underneath the scoop. The lighting guy held the base and Erin passed up the wrench. James was confident with tools, his hands cinching the bolt in steady rotations. He lost himself in the task, fastening the clip, securing the gel. His expression took on a quality of deliberate concentration.

Downstage right, Diego was practicing dance steps with big-footed Hal, doing a kind of Macarena with hip thrusts and hand gestures. With his buzz cut and pale skin, Hal was innocent and beautiful enough to make anyone fall in love with him. These were the bodies he should be attracted to. In Diego's case, this was the body he used to be attracted to: the V of his waist, the O's of his chest, and ovals on his arms. It all measured up and was totally predictable. You knew exactly where a line would stop and the next one would begin.

Diego dipped Hal and then pulled him close to his chest. Back and forth they spun out and came together, their wavy edges fitting like the cardboard pieces of a puzzle. And even though Diego was dark and Hal light—perfect little fish from vastly different gene pools—they had a similarity about them—the blandness of perfection. These muscle-bound bodies assaulted you with their perfection. It finally occurred to him how boring it was—the flesh, stiff and unyielding. Touching it always felt removed from the person inside, like an extra layer of armor that had to be penetrated. With Diego, often Roger didn't know if he was fucking a man or a leather couch. But James's body was a marvel of incongruities. It moved under his fingers. It relented. It squished. Its undulations connected him to the deep circuitry inside.

James came back to his seat. There seemed to be a softening of his demeanor, perhaps even a tiny smile on his face.

"Did you talk to Erin about film equipment?"

"The subject never came up so I ..."

"Come on." Roger pulled him up and started walking.

Erin was backstage sorting through the props for the drag show. Roger was glad to see there wasn't a net of black babies. He asked her where James could find equipment on the cheap and she wrote two names and numbers on a three-by-five card.

"Be sure to tell Carmine that you're not a collection agency and that I sent you. Otherwise, he'll hang up the phone."

"Thank you." James held the card as if it were a treasure map.

"Oh, Roger," Erin said. "Can you close up tonight? I have to leave early. I'd ask Garrick but you know..." She fluttered her hands in the universal gesture for flakiness.

Roger agreed, and she gave him a set of keys, color-coded and labeled for each door.

The drag scene was disorganized. Nobody had proper costumes, and Garrick was constantly pushing a political agenda. Roger agreed to have Warren and Philip be Barbara Bush and Osama bin Laden's wife. The niqab was practical and worked to cover Philip's beard. There was still no consensus on the others. He was thinking of cutting it. By the end of the night, everyone was exhausted. When Garrick called time, most of the cast couldn't wait to leave. Roger didn't have the heart, or the balls, to tell them to pick up their cups and bottles, so he got a garbage bag and went around the theatre himself. Penance for being a bad playwright.

The lighting guy came up to James and slapped his shoulder. "Thanks, man, for all your help tonight."

"No worries." James raised his fist in techie solidarity.

After he left, Roger said, "I'm going to have to tell Garrick to set a height requirement for future interns."

"Noah was schooling me about the difference between Lekos and Gobos. He knows his stuff."

"It's just unfortunate that he can't reach his stuff."

Diego made his way over. He stretched a leg on the back of a chair and grabbed his foot. "Did you see a difference tonight? I think I found a whole new level to Luca."

"You're definitely moving in the right direction." It was sometimes charming how much Diego needed his approval.

He grabbed his leg from behind to stretch his quads and bumped into

Hal walking up the aisle. Hal slapped his calf and kept moving. "It's like everything he does, he does to compensate. He needs to be the best-looking, the most famous, the richest man in the room. All to make up for his bichito."

"Keep exploring. You're onto something."

He rolled his neck and shook out his body. "I feel sorry for these men. Is tragic." He put a hand on Roger's knee and gave him a concerned look. "You coming across the street to drink, Paptito? You too, Jay-ames. You the boss. Tell him what to do."

"Maybe," Roger said. "After I lock up."

Diego wrapped an arm around Philip, who, always hungry for affection, rubbed his bicep and walked him out.

James turned to Roger. "Was he trying to imply that you have a small penis?"

"He thinks you haven't seen it."

The shock of knowledge sent them both into peals of laughter. All of a sudden, they were an old couple with an intimate secret, laughing at the folly of the world.

"What's so funny?" Garrick came up behind Roger and dropped his own coffee cup in the garbage bag.

"Apparently, it's my penis."

"It's very small," James added.

Garrick took off his glasses and let them drop on their chain. "The world of art was created by small penises, my friend."

"Didn't Picasso have a big dick?"

"Au contraire, Cubism was his way of making it look bigger."

"And Jackson Pollock was trying to obliterate the penis altogether."

"Nothing says 'size doesn't matter' more than a bunch of wiggly lines going in all directions."

They broke into easy laughter, and James smiled along with them.

Garrick shouldered his backpack, squared his shoulders and gave Roger a stern look. "The final scene by next rehearsal, mister?"

"I promise. Or you can cut my dick off."

"Great." He headed for the door. "I'll bring a pair of rusty scissors just in case."

Roger started straightening up the chairs in the audience.

James picked up a Styrofoam cup from the floor and tossed it in the garbage bag. "Do you know how you're going to end the play?"

"I've written out a couple of different scenes. I'm not sure which is right. How do you think I should end it?"

"The audience is going to be rooting for Luca and Herbert to stay together. They'll be disappointed if that doesn't happen."

"But isn't that too expected?"

"It's their story, right? They're the—what-do-you-call it?"

"The protagonists."

"Right. Everything is building to be about their story. But if Luca and Herbert don't get together, then Findley and Herbert are the protagonists."

"Findley isn't a protagonist."

James plopped down with his arms on the back of a chair and rested his chin on his wrist. "So, what makes a protagonist?"

"Usually, a choice. The character with the biggest conflict about that choice and how it changes him."

"So if they don't get together, Herbert would have to choose to stay with Findley."

"I suppose."

"Then nothing in his life really changes."

Roger gazed up at the grid of hanging lights and electric cords. "Fair point." He settled into a chair a few rows away. "What do you think about the second act?"

"The drag show is funny. I didn't get that Phillip was Osama bin Laden's wife."

"It probably needs some dialogue. I was thinking about making them all female world leaders: Margaret Thatcher, Golda Meir. Vic would make a great Indira Gandhi."

"Syd could be Oprah."

"That's perfect." Roger folded his arms and regarded James. "It seems you've been bitten by the theatre bug."

"Maybe."

"Well, watch out. It bites back." Roger gathered his script and yellow pad and put them in his satchel, and headed backstage to turn off the lights. James meandered behind. He switched off the circuit breakers, and block by block the theatre grew darker. James was standing next to him deep in thought.

"All these people working on their art while doing day jobs."

"That's what we do."

"Makes me think ... I'm a coward."

"You could do the same. You *are* doing the same."

"Not really."

"It's a long process. We all go through ups and downs. Get your equipment. That's a start."

He closed the final circuit and he and James stood in the dark, the red glow of the exit lights playing on their faces. It always spooked him a little to be in a dark theatre. The infinity of it. The scary thing about darkness is that one loses oneself. One melds with the furniture. You can be anything in the dark.

He turned to go and felt James reaching around his waist. It wasn't a tentative gesture but a sweep. They were kissing before he knew they were kissing. His yellow pad somehow bunched between them, until it slowly slid down to the floor, where it landed on their feet.

Some bodies vibrate with energy and that energy engulfs you. It commands. James pushed Roger against the wall, pressing his body against him, pushing with his lips.

His hands were under James's shirt, feeling his body come alive with sensations. The hairs, the pimples on his back. The hard ridges of his shoulder blades. Finally, they broke apart. He rested his head on James's chest and breathed in his scent of damp cotton and wet dog. The metronome of his heart kept the time between them.

"So who's the protagonist?" James whispered.

"Huh?"

"With us? Who's the protagonist?"

The word "us" reverberated in his ears. A susurration of flapping wings and rolling marbles. "Whoever has the greatest conflict," Roger said.

James kissed him again. "Do I seem conflicted?"

Roger looked into his wide brown eyes for some hint of indecision but found none.

"Let's go back to my place," James said.

The keys shook in his hand as he locked the theatre's steel door. His lips tingled and swelled. He licked them, and the night air vibrated around his mouth. Another kiss.

James was parked just down the street. He followed silently. Traffic roared past, a language of lights and noise and revving engines that said go go go.

12: Reprogrammed

Sunlight poured through the windows, blurring the cracks in the walls and the spaces between the floorboards. It was the best time of day for James to work on his puppets, and it lasted only until the sun fell behind the building across the street. The subway thundered past, vibrating the windows every twelve minutes. Five more trains and the light would be gone.

At his work table, he drew a goatee on the piano man's face with a fine-point marker. Then he would razor off the plastic hair and replace it with real brown curls from an old Belle doll. Why the puppet had to look like Roger, he wasn't sure. He had a vision of him playing the piano with wild hair flying.

The Sherry puppet lay on the table next to his acrylics, her nipples freshly painted, her skin a liquid puddle of perfection. Though now she seemed impossible, like winning the lottery or being able to afford an apartment in Manhattan. It was perhaps time to get sensible. Time to stop dreaming of what he couldn't have and settle for what he could get.

Roger had left that morning, after they had breakfast at the deli. They sat at a plastic table eating fried egg sandwiches wrapped in wax paper and drinking coffee from Styrofoam cups. Boxes of laundry detergent and bottles of dishwashing liquid surrounded them: All, Cheer, Dawn, Joy, Gain. The universe seemed to be sending a message, and the message was: be happy. Roger talked about possible fixes for his final scene, but James could only concentrate on their knees pressing underneath the table. Some egg dripped into Roger's beard. He almost reached over to wipe it off but hand-

178

ed him a napkin instead.

Before Roger left, he wrapped an arm around James's waist and gave him a squeeze. Told him he'd see him later at work. James thought it strange that they would soon be back at the restaurant, filling water pitchers and carrying plates, but with this extra layer of knowledge: how they looked naked; the taste of their breath in the morning; the smell of their sweat. Roger's had sharp vinegary notes that penetrated the back of his brain. He could still smell it on his hands—tomcat and earth. Roger had fallen asleep on his chest, with his leg flung over James's groin, his breath tickling his chest hairs. James couldn't sleep while he held him—he seemed too valuable. And he couldn't push him off for fear of waking him. He wanted to remain in the moment of this perfect man trusting him with sleep.

It was difficult at first, when they had come back to his place. They fell onto the bed, but James didn't want to take off his shirt. Even though they had been with each other before in various stages of undress, this new situation—in a bed, face to face—called for greater scrutiny. Roger whipped off his shirt and pressed his tight body against him, making James feel soft and flabby—embarrassed in ways he never was with a woman. Confronted with a better example of manhood, he didn't quite feel manly. He felt gleefully submissive. A relief, in fact, to let someone else take control.

Roger slowly peeled James's t-shirt over his head. Unbuckled his pants and pulled them off. He traced his fingers over James's torso, a craniometer measuring every bump and cranny. "What don't you like about your body?" he said.

"Everything."

"Like what?"

"I have stretch marks on my stomach."

"You do?"

"From when I was fat."

"Oh, yes." Roger ran his fingers over the wavy lines on the sides of his belly. He kissed them, moving his tongue from James's navel to his sides and back again. It tickled at first, and then it felt like rushing through water.

"These remind me of quarter-sawn cuts in the grain of a fine oak panel." Roger kept tracing the lines, sending shivers and goosebumps up his sides. "What else don't you like?"

"I have the same marks on my shoulders."

Roger turned him over, fingering his shoulders and then massaging, pressing with his thumbs. "You have really big shoulders. You must have grown right out of your skin."

"I was a confused teenager."

"These are massive. No reason to be ashamed of them." Roger massaged deep into his tissue, and then lightly kissed all across his back and up his neck. "Okay. What else?"

"You don't have ..."

"Shut up. Just tell me what you hate about your body."

James had never thought about it so bluntly, but he did hate his body. He always had. He hated his childhood of Husky pants and extra-large shirts. Of prickly heat and ripping zippers. Roger's luxuriating in his body seemed a trick. Or worse—a fetish.

"Come on. Tell me." Roger started to pat him down. "Where is it? The part you hate the most?" Roger started grabbing him in various places: stomach, hips, thighs. This turned into tickling with James scrunching up into a ball, laughing, and finally crying out. "My head. Okay. My head."

Roger ran two fingers over his scalp. "Your head is very symmetrical." He kept smoothing his fingers. James felt electricity raising bumps on his skin. He rammed his head into Roger's hand like a dog to its master. More kisses, each a tingly fire. And then Roger straddled his torso. "Anything else?"

"You really don't have to..."

"I want to. I enjoy it. Your body." Roger was smiling, tracing a line down his center and following the patterns of sparse hair on his chest.

James laughed. A deep, rich laugh that reverberated with all the fat jokes. All the names: tubby, lard-ass, doughboy. He laughed at all the years he sat alone at the lunch table. All the times he kept his shirt on at the beach. The guys who used to poke him in the belly and say, "Poppin' Fresh." The scornful looks from every girl in high school. Those dateless Saturday nights with a bag of Doritos and a quart of Ben and Jerry's. The laughs started to come out in barks. Roger was pleasantly occupied stroking his chest, and James stopped his hand. "You can't change everything in one night."

"But I can have fun trying." Roger put his lips on his nipple. James grabbed the back of his head. Ran his fingers through Roger's thick hair. Pulled it. Massaged it and claimed it for himself. Then he yanked him up and they kissed.

Somewhere in the kissing, their undershorts came off. It was strange to feel a man's hard penis on his stomach—the weight of it, the heat. The way it bobbed, like it had a mind of its own. They kept kissing and touching; the penis kept insisting. Attention must be paid. Roger had paid attention to his member, and he returned the favor, but without enthusiasm. A fact that made him feel guilty. And also a little relieved that there was something of Roger's he could resist.

"How about your legs?" Roger asked. "What do you think about those?"

"They've always been too big. I had problems buying jeans."

"They're quite muscular. I wish I had legs like these." He pulled James's legs onto his shoulders and kissed his calves.

It was an unwieldy position. He felt overwhelmed and vulnerable. He worried that he would fart. His legs would cramp. There were many ways to be out of control, but out of control with your legs in the air was the worst.

They kissed some more, and Roger's finger found its way inside him. He didn't even realize until he felt a tapping from within. Each tap created a spasm that felt weird. He wanted to tell Roger to stop, but the finger kept rubbing, and then the tap would send a spark to his brain, and language would be lost. He cried out once. He thought, I will not let this happen. This is too far. Roger had a kind of smirk on his face. The same smirk he had when he made fun of his puppets. Another tap. He choked back a cry. He would not give in.

Roger said, "Are you all right?" He nodded because the words wouldn't come. Then another couple of taps made him feel even weirder. Both full and loose at the same time. He couldn't decide if it was good or bad. It was a new feeling.

At some point, Roger went to his satchel, got a condom and lube. In retrospect, James wondered if he always carried such provisions or if he had planned this whole adventure. But in the moment, he was beyond thought. He was just a body to be practiced on.

Roger was inside him before he knew it. Like one of those doctors who distracts you when they want to give you a shot.

"Are you okay?" he asked again.

James nodded. He felt a burning sensation, and then as Roger started moving, more spasms trickled through his body. Did he like this? Didn't he like this? Was he supposed to like this? Occasionally, Roger would hit a spot, and it would vibrate in his genitals. Then he'd hit it again, and James would dissolve into pure sensation. He opened his eyes to Roger's labored breathing, his jaw extended, and all the tendons in his neck articulated. It was the atavistic instinct of catching prey on the savanna, of being devoured—the ugliness of desire baring down. He closed his eyes and waited for Roger to make those sparks, a machete chipping away at flint. Sweat from Roger's chest dripped onto his stomach. The smell of tomcat made him dizzy. He grabbed onto his arms, all bumps and ridges. Not the soft, straight arms he was used to holding. Not the smooth thighs he liked to caress. In the past, whenever he was close, he had always reached for breasts: buried his head in them, reveled in their softness—they were what carried him over the edge. But this time there was only the bristling animal—taut muscles and grinding teeth. All the visuals he associated with pleasure were gone. His circuits were being reprogrammed by the thrusting machinery of Roger's body.

He didn't want to come. To give Roger that power. He wanted to keep something back. But Roger grabbed hold of him, and he couldn't stop himself. Then he felt Roger grow big inside him. Subtle shudders rocked their bodies. Roger's eyebrows closed to a single line. To be the receiver of this felt both special and debased. He finally understood the concept of virginity—he was polluted. Despoiled by Roger's fecundity and also somehow elevated by it.

He worried that the condom had come off, but it hadn't. Roger whipped it off and collapsed on top of him.

His legs were still spasming when he brought them down. He wrapped his arm around Roger's wet back and held on. Somewhere on the floor that used condom was drying with their mutual secretions. He resisted the urge to throw it away.

The sun had moved far below the adjacent building when he realized it was time for work. He couldn't decide if the puppet's new goatee looked sinister or sexy. Or if sinister-sexy was a look he was going for. With a Filbert brush, he'd added more hair to the chest and stomach. He would augment the genitals later—Roger was uncircumcised. He laid the newly hirsute piano man next to the perfectly breasted Sherry—two ends of a spectrum in his recently expanding universe—and went to get dressed.

Outside, it was a balmy seventy-five degrees, and he chose to walk to the restaurant. He needed to be aware of the changes on the street; it was a constant topic of interest with customers. "Do you know what's going into the old dry cleaners?" "Did you see what they're building on the corner of Wyckoff?" Strolling from his 'hood down Smith Street was like walking into the future. On his end, the street was mostly rundown apartment buildings, whose first floors might contain a sporadic deli or laundromat. Subsequent blocks became lined with mom-and-pop stores, resale shops, and tax offices, the occasional pizza-by-the-slice, and seedy bar. Then into the gentrified blocks, alive with yoga studios and children's boutiques, tea shops, and a United Nations of restaurants. Finally, came the chain stores: Rite Aid and Dunkin' Donuts, TD Banks and Kinko's Copies. It was the mercurial nature of the city. Every thirty years, New York reinvented itself. He remembered people telling him that Park Avenue used to border a park. And Penn Station was a Beaux-Arts jewel before they tore it down and put in the rat tunnels under Madison Square Garden. Change was nothing new; it was the raison d'être of the city—the only constant in the universe. This very island was once attached to Africa. Prior to that, the Earth was a churning ball of molten lava. And even earlier, a few dust particles clumping together around a newly ignited sun.

He walked past a sign in a shoe repair shop that said, "Realtors Not Welcome." Many buildings were under renovation. He wrote down the addresses to check later who was moving in. Several neighborhood blogs kept track of the permits issued and sales recorded. Some storefronts had courtesy signs: Future Site of Boomtown Bar, Get Ready for Powerhouse Pilates.

He passed Green and noticed that they had added an artichoke salad to the menu. A few doors down, an old-fashioned diner had just opened advertising fifteen-dollar omelets and twenty-dollar hamburgers. The seafood shack where he'd kissed Sherry was nearing completion. Their sign was up: Davy Jones' Locker, with a picture of a treasure chest filled with smiling shrimp and lobsters. That kiss seemed a millennium ago, a moment in a history book depicted as vainglorious and foolish: *unused to the harsh winter, the colonists had perished.* Like so many explorers, he'd reached beyond his means. Fought the prevailing elements and lost. Sherry was the Promised Land he could never reach. And now, forces were pulling him in a new direction. He could either fight the current or allow himself to be carried away.

At work, he started right away confirming reservations. He brought the master sheet to the podium and made the calls from upstairs in order to keep an eye on the door. He listened for new signs of irony in his voice. When he said, "We look forward to seeing you tonight," he wondered if there was an extra exuberance. Not that gays were necessarily exuberant, but he expected something to have changed. He disliked heavily affected voices and wanted a world-weary quality, like Gore Vidal after three martinis.

He hoped to have gained something through this new gay experience: distinguishing the difference between silk and rayon; being able to hear a Madonna song from a thousand feet away. He wanted to "read someone for filth" or develop a really devastating side-eye. Of course, it might not be all good news. He might become more sensitive to clashing colors. Spotting a bad haircut at the farmer's market could ruin his day. Not reaching his ideal body fat ratio might depress him for weeks. Cher canceling her farewell tour, missing Barney's warehouse sale, a zit on his nose—Roger was teaching him that the gay world was fraught with perils.

Bart came out of the kitchen, wiping his hands on a towel. "How many resees for tonight?" He put an arm around James and gaped at the book.

"Twenty. Everyone is coming between seven and eight."

"Don't worry, Champ. I've had two Red Bulls and I'm wearing my elastic jockstrap." He shook James's shoulders. Bart was normally pretty handsy—in everyone's personal space—but today it felt uncomfortable. "And," he gave James another squeeze, "I've got a super-duper idea for the Shawmut launch. To show those philistines what real food is made of."

James shrugged off Bart's hands. "What is it?"

"Tell you later. It's still percolating. But make sure Roger and Sherry can come to the event. I'll need them by 1 p.m."

James made a notation on a post-it and stuck it to the reservation book. "Oh. I wanted to ask you to have off on the fifteenth? My parents are coming into town for their anniversary and I got tickets for *Mamma Mia*." He kept his eyes focused on the book so as not to startle Bart out of his good mood.

"No worries. Just clear it with the queen first." Bart only called Melissa 'the queen' when he was mad at her. He gave James a playful punch and sauntered out.

James wondered if all the touching and grabbing straight men affected was some acceptable expression of homoeroticism. Or was it just a kind of dominance? He flashed on Roger's long strokes pumping into him. Sex itself might be a form of dominance; only he hadn't recognized it before because he was the dominant one.

As he hung up with the last reservation, Roger walked in—right on time. After their night together, James worried he might be harder to manage. Or he would be overly demonstrative on the floor. There were a hundred ways the situation could backfire, not the least of which was Bart finding out he was sexually fraternizing with an employee.

"This is for you." Roger leaned on the podium and presented him with a single rose, its stem wrapped in cellophane.

"What's … the occasion?" He knew the occasion and immediately regretted bringing it up.

"I just felt like giving you something."

He shuffled to the bar a bit stupefied and looked for a container. No one had given him flowers before, much less a long-stemmed rose. Joanne had bought him a small basil plant one time, but that was only to season her tofu scramble. This was another new mile marker on the twisting highway of homosexuality—his first celebratory flower. And, what was being celebrated was his deflowering. Odd how a man could lay claim to you with just a flower. And how accepting said flower was a kind of capitulation. He never realized all the bouquets he'd given women were really property flags—the longer the stem, the deeper one planted one's flag.

He filled a wine decanter with water and set the rose inside. It was still closed, pinkish-red in color—the end of its ruffled folds reminded him of Roger's uncircumcised cock.

"Are you okay about last night?"

James moved the rose next to the computer station out of people's direct line of vision. "I'm okay if you're okay."

"I thought after you had some time to think about it, you might be a bit freaked out."

"No. My freak is in." The incongruity of Roger's daytime face was starting to mix with Roger's orgasm face.

"I wanted to tell you I had a nice time. A really nice time."

Perhaps even more bizarre than being fucked by a man was being courted by one. Roger had a goofy expression on his face. Did all men look so pathetic? James kept waiting for a joke or some irony to camouflage the schmaltz. In fact, Roger's usual sarcasm would have made the exchange more bearable. Earnestness was not a look he wore with ease. A feeling of power overwhelmed him—he could crush Roger with just one comment.

There seemed to be more that Roger wanted to say, but thankfully, their conversation was interrupted by Sherry walking in the door.

She swung her backpack onto the banquette. "Sorry I'm late. No rest for the homeless."

"Just in time to help with the chairs," Roger said.

James, wanting to limit interactions with her, headed for the basement. "I'm going down. Don't take any reservations between seven and eight. We're fully booked."

They worked in silence for a while. Sherry picked each chair off the table and let it drop with a thud. Roger did the same, and the room was filled with the sound of chairs hitting the floor. She had been up until 3 a.m. waiting for him to come home, the latest episode of *Deadwood* paused in the DVR. They played a drinking game where every time a character said "cocksucker," they would take a sip. She finally fell asleep on the couch. A call or text might have been nice, but she wasn't going to turn into a nagging housewife.

"What happened to you last night?" She set the last chair down with deliberate control so it made no sound. "When I left this morning, you still weren't home."

He adjusted a table on the banquette and pretended he didn't hear. "Did you get that apartment?"

"No. Trish's credit. She and I spent the morning looking in Crown Heights."

"Find anything?"

"We put in applications." She brought over a stack of tablecloths and started sailing them over the tables. Roger followed suit. The flapping fabric made fluttering sounds in the air. "Are you ever going to tell me what you did last night?"

"Let's just say it was a good night for love."

"For love? Are we talking about ...?" She tilted her head at the floor to indicate James in the basement, and Roger's face erupted in a sickening grin. This was moving faster than expected. She floated a few more tablecloths on the tables and waited for the details. When Roger just stood there smoothing out fabric and smiling, she prodded him again. "Are we talking about first base, second base, or what?"

"I think it's safe to say it was a home run—all bases loaded. All loads taken." Roger kept grinning like the Grinch with a sack full of toys.

"Well, this is a surprise." She tried to picture exactly what had happened. She knew that Roger considered himself a top, but couldn't fathom how James would bottom his first time out. And if Roger bottomed, that would mean he was really making an exception and might not be in it for the long haul.

Roger made his way to the glass racks stacked on the bar and started polishing wine glasses. She followed and set out a latté pitcher of hot water. They hovered the glasses over the steaming pitcher and rubbed them with napkins. She was determined to be as supportive as possible until Roger discovered the flaws in his Frankenstein monster. "So. Was it everything you expected?"

"You know." He watched a wine goblet fill with steam. "It was different. I'm usually more focused on my own pleasure, but he was so insecure about his body, I felt I had to give him something—some confidence. And I could. I could give him a whole new sense of himself. I made him beautiful. It was very powerful."

"*You* made him beautiful?"

"He was beautiful. I was absolutely attracted. And I showed him that." He set a wine glass on the shelf. "I don't think anyone had ever done that for him. You know, showed appreciation for his body."

Sherry scrubbed the rim of her glass with fervent strokes. "Wow."

"I wasn't concerned about how he was making me feel because I was feeling so good making him feel good."

"Sounds like charity work."

"Tis better to giveth than to receive." He put another glass on the shelf.

"So you're the Mother Teresa of sex now?"

"I don't think Mother Teresa did much butt-fucking."

She held a glass up to the light. "Maybe you just need to bottom more."

"Oh. I didn't bottom. I told you—my g-spot is naught."

"So James…?"

Roger nodded. "He was quite the little trooper. First time and everything."

"So what does this mean? Are you a couple now?"

He threw down the napkin. "I don't know. He's a bit overwhelmed. Understandably. I'm giving him some time to digest."

"And recover. I know what a beast you can be." She gave him a playful nudge, which he ignored and started setting wine glasses on tables. She still hadn't been able to talk to Roger about their night together. Every time she brought it up, he froze her out. She just wanted some acknowledgment that it had happened; she was starting to think she'd dreamed the whole thing. But a second sense told her not to push the issue; she would have to wait until he finished his adventures with James. "Maybe that's why he's being so weird. Have you noticed? He won't even look at me."

Roger paused and contemplated the cluster of glass stems threaded through his fingers. "Yeah. He's nervous about fraternizing too much with the staff. We talked about him keeping a more professional distance."

"Was that before or after you stuck your penis in him?"

Roger continued setting the glasses. She continued polishing, each passing moment of silence pushing them farther apart. She was starting to get short of breath. That old feeling of erasure was coming on. No one in the restaurant gave a good goddamn about her. Like with Sean's oil paintings, she was being incinerated. A wine glass snapped off in her hand. "Shit."

"Are you okay?"

"Guess I don't know my own strength." She threw the two halves of the glass in the garbage. "In case you were wondering, I didn't watch Deadwood."

"You should've. Don't let me come between you and Al Swearengen."

"We can watch it some other time." Her finger was bleeding a bit, but she didn't want Roger to see. She wrapped it in a napkin and went to the kitchen to get a Band-Aid.

As she was rummaging in the first aid kit on the wall, Bart called her over. "Can I borrow your palate for a minute, milady?"

"Sure." She put on a Band-Aid and went over to Bart, who was standing with a spoon in hand.

"It's crab bisque. Tell me what you think." He raised the spoon to her lips.

She wasn't really in the mood for one of his tasting games, but she didn't want to upset him. "Mmm. I love the nutmeg."

"Yes." He clenched a fist in victory. "I thought that was a baller move."

"Is there sherry?"

"Holy smokes. I forgot. There must always be sherry." He turned to Eric, who was chopping scallions for the mise en place. "Go to the wine store down the street and get a bottle of Taylor's sherry. If they don't have it, go to the one on Atlantic." He handed him a twenty from his wallet and sent him on his way. "Thank you. You saved me a world of embarrassment. It takes a Sherry to think of sherry."

"I never heard of sherry wine until I came to New York. Good thing, or I might have been chugging it all through high school."

"You deserve a better varietal than that." Bart looked down at her from his considerable height, and she remembered what Roger had said about tall men.

"Do I?" She fingered the ankh around her neck. It had become a kind of talisman ever since Roger had fastened it around her. Even though there were no windows in the kitchen, she could feel light seeping into her pores. "I knew a girl back in Ottumwa called Merlot. It was what her parents were drinking on the night she was conceived."

"Good thing it wasn't Mad Dog."

"People used to call her Merle Lot the Har-lot."

He laughed with appreciation. "You come from a rich and colorful people."

"I come from pure, unfiltered white trash."

Bart tapped the spoon on the side of the pot and tossed it in the sink. "One man's trash is another man's treasure."

This was getting weird. Bart had always been flirty—boys/girls—it made no difference, but there was a new intensity here. And, as much as she enjoyed the ride, she didn't want to get back on that particular roller coaster.

"I have to get back to setting up. Roger will kill me if I don't help." She breezed out of the kitchen and went back to the dining room, thinking that Roger would make some snide comment about her avoiding work, but he was happily rolling silverware, lost in his own thoughts.

After they closed, James counted cash at the bar with Roger's penis-rose staring him in the face. Business had been brisk but died off early. Roger was a trooper all night: seating tables, opening wine for Sherry. He didn't question James's directions and carried them out with a cheerful attitude. If this was all it took to motivate a waiter, he might have to add anal sex to the employee training manual.

Still, Roger's attentiveness made James uneasy. One time, he dropped a pen and Roger handed it to him with a flourish. When he stepped away for a minute, Roger answered the phone and took a to-go order, and even entered it into the computer. He left the printout on his podium with a smiley face and a dozen x's and o's. He understood Roger's attentions; he had acted in a similar fashion with past girlfriends. But having these same gestures directed at him felt infantilizing and controlling. Roger was putting too much pressure on James to like him. He finally understood why Joanne would sometimes yell at him to back off.

Sherry, however, was off her game. When the rush came, she was sluggish taking orders and sent all of her tickets to the kitchen at once, creating a backup. Normally this would have sent Bart into a fury, but he ignored it. After the rush, she neglected her tables and kept finding excuses to go into the kitchen. Once, she cornered James at the to-go rack and told him about a dream she had concerning her dead grandmother. It was a long and convoluted story, fuzzy on details; when it was over, she gave him a hug and said she would always be here if he needed to talk. He couldn't square her demeanor with her "blech" comment at Roger's. His emotional pendulum had swung, and he felt nothing but a kind of revulsion. She must have registered this because at the end of the night, she left without picking up her tips or saying goodbye. He put her cash in an envelope, glad not to have another interaction with her.

Roger came over and dropped his cash on the bar. "So. You feel up for a drink?"

He looked so hopeful; James couldn't refuse. "The Roxy?"

"How about we go to a bar in the city? I want to introduce you to gay nightlife."

The bar didn't conform to James's expectations, which enabled him to breathe a sigh of relief. The dress code posted by the door didn't include mandatory leather chaps or jockstraps. In fact, it said, no oversized jeans, no sleeveless shirts, workout gear, bandanas, or baseball caps. Roger held the door and James proceeded in cautiously. The walls were not painted black and splashed with cum stains, but covered in a red brocade wallpaper. Each room contained antique-y couches and end tables, and looked just like your grandma's house, if your grandma lived in an Edwardian mansion. And finally, instead of a sex dungeon, the back room contained a baby grand piano where patrons gathered to sing show tunes.

"This is your regular hangout?" he asked.

"Not exactly, but there's a big theatre crowd here."

Everyone was wearing polo shirts and printed shorts, and looked like they just got back from a scramble on the back nine. James felt underdressed without a class ring or a yachting pin.

They found a quiet corner with a couple of wingback chairs. Roger went to the bar and brought back a couple of gin and tonics.

"Are you sure you're okay?" he said, putting a hand on James's knee.

"Do you mind if we take things slow?"

Roger pointed to the tasseled drapes and black-tied servers. "Any slower and we'd be on the Sewanee River."

"Everything is very ... new right now. I need some time to adjust."

"You're not pulling the-cat's-on-the-roof-and-we-can't-get-him-down-thing?"

"What?"

"Instead of telling me the cat's dead, you're saying it's on the roof."

"No. The cat isn't dead. I just need time."

"Take all the time you need." He reached out and held James's hand. "Has a guy ever held your hand in public?"

"Not since my father took me to kindergarten."

"Is it weird?"

"Not unless you make me call you Daddy."

Roger raised an eyebrow. "You may find you want to in certain situations."

He escorted James to the piano, with a gentle hand on his back, where a group had gathered singing "Marry Me A Little." It was Sondheim night. Roger joined in the singing. James didn't know the words but laughed in all the right places. The piano player was a jowly man with gin blossoms, who smiled equally at those who sang their hearts out and those making fools of themselves. These were often one and the same. They went through the entire score of *Company*, ending on "Being Alive," where everyone belted and gesticulated, trying to prove they were more alive than the next person. Or at least more dramatic. As a teenager, he had listened to Radiohead or Counting Crows, thinking his life was insignificant, thinking no one loved him. Now he was beginning to realize that it wasn't being loved that made you more alive but perhaps loving someone else. After *Company*, they moved through the Sondheim repertoire until James got hit in the face with somebody's jazz hands, and they decided to leave for their own safety.

Climbing down the narrow stoop, they entered into the night, unhurried, affectionate. James slapped his hands on his thighs, a little bit drunk. Roger had supplied him with enough gin and tonics to lubricate without being lubricious. The streets were black rivers fed by concrete tributaries; they walked their banks, exploring the flora and fauna in shop windows. Chrome-legged couches, gold leaf stationery, copper cook pots, electronic watches, pearl embroidered underwear—the teeming urban landscape. In the distance, garbage trucks moaned like great beasts from the past.

James sang: "'Everybody says don't. Everybody says don't. Everybody says don't step on the grass. Don't disturb the peace. Don't do something else.' What's that from?"

"*Anyone Can Whistle*. It was a big flop in its day. Hardly ever revived."

The filmy light of the streetlamps enclosed them in little bubbles.

"Too bad. That's a great song."

"The books to his musicals were always problematic."

"How do you know all those songs?"

"It's in the gay handbook. You have to know the lyrics to at least twenty Broadway shows before you're allowed to give a blowjob."

"I don't know any musicals." He let the ramifications of that statement settle between them.

They waded across Park Avenue and stopped on the median waiting for the light to change. Cars floated by, briefly holding them in their halogen gaze. Red begonias swirled at their feet. Roger reached up and kissed him, cradling his neck with both hands. Their lips both sticky with gin, their bodies sweaty. James steadied himself by grasping Roger's waist. He tried to make himself open. He felt the bristliness of Roger's beard, which gave him pause, and then he opened wider and pulled Roger close. The walk sign flashed. Cars stopped, pinning them in a spotlight of attention. This was the romantic New York moment he'd envisioned having when he first came to the city. And now it had finally happened.

Over the next few days, James vacillated between Roger's rapt attention and his own stoic ambivalence. He would often look up from his podium to catch Roger's smiling face, shining down like a great sun awaiting worship. Sometimes, in the middle of a sentence, Roger would pause with a lingering glance, as if James should guess his prevailing thought. Other times, in the kitchen, or next to the computer terminal, he would feel a hot hand on the small of his back and turn to see Roger standing next to him. Most times he didn't even turn because he couldn't bear to look at those appraising eyes. He'd just stand impassively and absorb his sexual radiation. He was the rabbit in the field and Roger the great hawk circling. At the end of each shift, Roger would stay until everyone else had left just so he could hug James goodbye and kiss him lightly on the cheek, as a reminder he was waiting for James to "adjust" so they could continue their animal relations.

His connection with Roger did spur him to focus more on his animations. And so today, he was going to look at film equipment. As he turned his car onto New Utrecht Avenue, he considered that maybe he should just give himself over to a relationship with Roger. If only it wouldn't have led to more lingering glances and pauses filled with emotion—these were actually more uncomfortable than being fucked in the ass. In fact, he might have even considered letting Roger fuck him again if he could avoid the emotional baggage that came with it.

He pulled up to the storefront in Bensonhurst where he was supposed to meet Erin's friend with the film equipment. Carmine was his name. He lived above a shop with a maroon awning that said: Boutique and Hosiery. A gate obscured the window, but through the holes, he could see mannequins in filmy negligees and a selection of amputated feet in gold-toed socks.

He shifted into park and let the last gusts of air-conditioning blow onto his face. He unfastened his seatbelt and felt a twinge inside—a memory of Roger's little sparks chipping away at him. So much depended on context. So much was up for interpretation. Roger had made him feel desired, attractive, maybe even loved, or at least liked with enthusiasm. That thing moving inside him—the rhythm, the heat and pressure of it—could he get used to it, even enjoy it? Maybe he had already enjoyed it; only he had no context in which to interpret it.

Things were never just black or white. There were shades and shadows, a whole spectrum of colors. Things were never one thing or another. There were in-betweens. A wave was also a particle and a particle was also a wave. Maybe he could slip between the cracks. Maybe he could be both. He could live on each coast. He could dare to eat a peach AND a pear.

It really wasn't so bad. At its core, it was an expression of love. Imperfect. Awkward. At times uncomfortable. Who was he to question love? Things shifted. People changed. His father used to be a Buddhist and now he was a Jew. Buildings repurposed themselves. A bail bonds office became a Michelin-star restaurant. Cities annexed their borders. Civilizations collapsed, making room for other civilizations. What had heterosexuality ever done for him? Throw off the chains. Crawl out of the box. It was all in the looking. *Suffering isn't the result of what happens, it's the result of our resistance to what happens.*

He turned off the engine and rang Carmine's bell. Climbing up the stairs, he could already smell the cannabis, skunky and sweet. When Carmine opened the door, notes of B.O. were added to the mix.

"You the guy that wants the Sony HDR." He was wearing a Nicks jersey dotted with red sauce. "It's on the shelf there." He pointed to a metal bookcase that was filled with camcorders, light panels, and viewfinders.

James picked it up and looked through the lens.

"Be careful. I just got that in. I can let you have it for half of retail." Carmine turned it on and showed him how everything worked. It was one of the best camcorders on the market. James couldn't believe his luck. He also bought a tripod, reflector, a mini spot, and some editing software, effectively cleaning out his bank account.

Loading the equipment into his car, it occurred to him that if it weren't for Roger he never would have found this stuff. He might not even have had the inspiration to keep working on his film. He wedged the tripod between the two bucket seats and thought about what this meant for the future: Roger monitoring his progress, critiquing his results, pushing him to change this or that detail. His puppets would no longer be his own private project but a shared concern. He laid the reflector in the window well of the backseat. It might be refreshing to have a collaborator. Joanne had always thought his puppets were a joke, and Tracy was too self-involved to take an interest, but now he would have to report to Roger. Not necessarily a bad thing. A new thing, in a long list of new things.

He tried to imagine waking up next to him every morning. Feeling the

Membrum Virile between them like some panting dog. Roger's tomcat scent filling the sheets. His razor stubble grazing his chest, the hard little bumps of his biceps. Picking up his sweaty t-shirts from the floor, maybe last night's condom. He could adjust to the sex, but the requisite romantic acts seemed more uncomfortable: spooning cake into Roger's goateed mouth at a friend's birthday party; introducing him as boyfriend or partner at events; sharing the same box of popcorn at the movies; watching TV on the couch, with Roger's feet on his lap, massaging his hairy toes.

It seemed like the universe was pushing him to succumb. And yet.... He did have a choice. He didn't have to accept whatever the universe offered. Whatever blew into his web. He wanted to believe bodies were just the clothing of the soul. That the soul was the true object of desire. But the soul didn't have hairy toes. You can't desire in the abstract. You desire in the body. And *his* body was loath to accept hairy toes.

All these years he'd wanted women to love him in spite of his looks. And yet, he'd only loved conventionally beautiful women. He'd never fallen for an elephant woman. Nature drove his desires, and he went along for the ride, all the while thinking he was making choices when he was merely obeying the commands of hormones and neurotransmitters—the culmination of thousands of years of chemical configurations.

And now.... And now.... What could he do?

He closed the passenger door and regarded the mannequins in the window. Through the gauzy material, he could see the space where their nipples should be. He imagined them covered with wild, dark hairs. He waved a silent goodbye to the ladies and started his engine.

13: Who You Gonna Call?

They were standing at the computer station watching table six fumble through a first date. It was just her and Max. Bart had packed up his knives and gone home; Eric and Jorge were scrubbing down the kitchen and had already taken the trash through the dining room, and still the couple didn't get the hint. It seemed like hours ago that Max had picked up their credit card receipt— fortunately, they had left a good tip—and cleared everything from the table, including the salt shaker. Sherry could see they both didn't want the date to end but were scared to take the next step. They looked like young techno geeks who had been staring at a computer screen all week and now found it hard to adjust to a 3D world. She wanted to tell them to go next door for a drink, and after a couple of margaritas, things would figure themselves out.

"Do you think I should turn off the music?" Max asked.

"Yes. Do it."

She didn't know why she was in such a hurry. Roger was away for the next two days, celebrating the Fourth of July on Fire Island with some of his castmates. There was nothing to do at his apartment aside from watching TV and snooping through his belongings. Most of which she'd already explored, looking for something that would make her feel closer to him, some bit of information that would bring him back to her for a moment. His closet didn't reveal much. The pockets of his coats held only old Kleenex and abandoned breath mints. In the boxes stashed under his bed, she found cards and letters from old friends and boyfriends: mostly holiday greetings and postcards. One letter from Nathan listed all the reasons why he wanted to end their relationship. She already knew Roger was angry and reclusive; she couldn't believe it took Nathan five years to figure it out.

She examined snapshots of Roger as a child, where he looked like an awkward little girl, and a few photos from his time in children's theatre playing Prince Valiant and an urchin in Olivier. Then there were the photos on beaches and circuit parties, with half-naked boys and disposable boyfriends. She studied closely the pics of him and Nathan: at restaurants, on hotel balconies, in parks. They seemed like any long-term couple desperately recording their happiness. She and Sean had the same pics. Manuscripts of his old plays were scattered about, but the characters were too much in their heads to hold her interest. Hardly any women. He needed some goddess energy. And while she wanted to be the one to give it to him, she doubted he was ready to receive it. Yet.

Max shut off the music and she could hear Jorge in the kitchen running the dishwasher. He came back and started wiping the bar.

"So what are you up to tonight, Max?"

"Big plans. Me and the boys are going to this new place in Chinatown."

"Oh. That sounds like fun." She always thought Max had a little crush on her, but never took the time to cultivate it.

"I'd invite you but it's kind of a guy's thing. We're on the prowl for strange. Bringing a girl might muddy the waters."

She couldn't believe his stupidity. A woman friend was an icebreaker. Women talked to other women. Then their guy friend conveniently interrupted the conversation and an introduction was made, assuring the guy was safe and made credible by having a female friend. But she didn't have the energy to explain it to him. She sauntered into the kitchen. Eric was wiping the counters and Jorge was scrubbing pots too big for the dishwasher.

"Hiya." She leaned on the counter and pressed her breasts together. A strong smell of bleach cut through the air.

"Hey. I just wiped that," Eric said.

She removed her hands. "You guys going to The Roxy tonight?"

"We're going to this new club in Chinatown where the women are muy caliente. Isn't that right, Jorgito?" He looked to Jorge, who gave him a playful squirt with the dish hose.

"There are women at The Roxy, you know. Maybe those college students will be back. I was talking to one the other night. I could break the ice for you."

"Those skanks?" Eric slapped his towel on the stove. "Wasn't feeling it."

She walked over to Jorge and rested her hip against the sink. "You don't think there are any pretty girls in Brooklyn? You have to go all the way to Chinatown?" She arched her back slightly.

Jorge grinned and glanced at Eric. "I try Chinatown."

"Brooklyn girls suck." Eric threw his towel in the bucket. "We're going to meet some fine Manhattan women with important jobs and big bank accounts."

"And what makes you think these fine Manhattan women want you?"

"Because they're lonely and I'm cute." He pointed a finger at his face.

She shook her head and walked out.

Finally, the couple was rising and making their way to the door, their oversized sneakers squeaking on the floorboards. She barely had the energy to wish them good night.

James came up and asked why the music was off.

"Max turned it off to get that couple out of the restaurant." She figured he deserved to have her snitch on him after not inviting her out.

"We had to do something." Max lifted his hands to his head. "They were never going to leave."

James fixed him with a disdainful look. "Please, don't do that again." He took their paperwork and started filling out the tip sheets.

Max turned to Sherry. "You mind if I take off? We got a big night planned."

Before she could answer, he was in the kitchen rounding up Eric and Jorge and pushing them out the door.

She poured herself a diet Coke and sat down on the banquette for the first time that night. James was at table twelve, absorbed in the paperwork. She took off a clog and rubbed her foot.

"You'll notice that I did nearly double the covers."

"I did notice that."

"He spends all of his time talking to the regulars."

"Yes, but that's what keeps them coming back."

"I know. But other customers might not like it when they can't get a table because his aren't turning."

"Uh huh."

She wasn't going to make a big deal. She and Roger had complained about it before. James seemingly didn't want to discuss it. She stretched a leg across the banquette. "You remember when I was telling you about the woman I used to live with? Magda? You asked if I had a preference, and I wasn't entirely honest. I enjoyed Magda all right, but I also felt a little trapped by her. Controlled. You know?"

"Uh huh."

"She was a big personality. Weird and charismatic. I got taken up with it."

James kept punching numbers into the calculator.

"I was new to New York. Lonely. Overwhelmed. A girl from a small town in the Midwest. We have that in common." She extended her arm in James's general direction. "What did I know about life in the big city? And here was this cultured, intelligent person who knew things. Survival skills that I didn't have an inkling about. Saying she wanted me. Was in love with me. Under different circumstances, I don't think I would have been so taken with her."

James was facing the bills, making piles on the table. He looked up and gave her a nod.

"Do you think you might be going through something similar?"

"We have enough cash; do you want your tips tonight or by check?"

"Tonight, please."

He handed her a stack of bills.

She rolled it and stuck it in her pocket. "Hey. You wanta get a drink next door? I could give you my perspective on bisexuality."

"Thanks, but I just got a bunch of new film equipment I want to try out."

"Oh, right. Your film. How's that going?"

"So far so good."

"You know. I never took you out for that dinner I promised. For defending me with Sean."

He wrapped some rubber bands around the envelopes, pushed the table away and stood up. "We'll have to do it sometime. Have a good night. I'm going to put this in the safe." And with that, he picked up his papers and hurried downstairs.

When she got back to Roger's place, she turned on the A/C and started *Deadwood*. She got the vodka bottle and shot glass ready, determined to play their drinking game without him. By the sixth or seventh "cocksucker," she was starting to feel woozy. Underneath the rattle and hum of the air-conditioning, she heard other sounds, like people screaming and calling for help. She turned off the machine and the voices thankfully stopped. But then she got hot, so she stripped down to her bra and panties. *Deadwood* was becoming a blur and she lost track of the storyline, not to mention the individual cocksuckers. The humidity started to itch her skin. She put the A/C back on, and lay down on the couch. She must've fallen asleep because when she woke, the TV was black and the voices were calling again: distant pleas for help and faraway screams, coming out of the A/C. Of course, this was New York; people were probably calling for help all across the city. Maybe she was connecting with them psychically, picking up on their vibrations.

She let the voices wash over her. She wondered if she should call someone. You were always supposed to call someone. But she didn't even know where these people were or if they even existed. They were probably coming from the psychic pain of New York. The pain of all the souls beleaguered by this cruel city. She listened closely to their distress, the whir and buzz of it. She wondered who she would call if *she* needed help. Everyone needs someone in case of emergency. That's what the forms say. She couldn't call her mother or her grandmother—both dead. She couldn't call Magda. She tried that a while back and found out she'd changed her number and address. One of the witches in her coven told her she'd moved upstate but wouldn't divulge the address. Freddy, she heard, had moved to Green Bay; she hadn't had contact with him or his band in years. Jerome? Lost. Her father was out there somewhere. Presumably. But he was also lost. So many people... James wanted nothing more to do with her. Roger was... where the hell was Roger? She'd lost all of them.

She grabbed a pillow and put it between her legs. Tried to remember one of Magda's spells of protection. She needed her crystal and a white candle. But she was too tired to get them. Words jumbled in her head: Hecate, owl, scorpion, snake. She couldn't remember the whole thing. She started to repeat to herself: protect me from harm, protect me from harm. And then she thought about Sean. She could call him. He was probably better now. His show had opened. He'd be happy to hear from her. She felt around for her phone, in the couch cushions and underneath on the floor, but gave up and drifted off to sleep.

The next morning, she awoke, still on the couch, sunlight channeling through the slats of the blinds. The first thing she saw was the vodka bottle shining on the coffee table like an Absolute rebuke, and then her clothes strewn over the floor. The Elvis lamp was knocked on its side and the air-conditioning blew full blast, sending chills down her bare legs. She turned it off and stumbled to her room. The futon looked sad; she didn't feel like pulling it down. She walked down the hallway to Roger's room, her legs stiff and jangly, and collapsed on his bed. His sheets smelled faintly of hair gel and his peculiar scent of ammonia and earth.

It was afternoon when she woke again. The sheets kicked to the floor. The restaurant was closed and the whole day stretched out before her like one long highway to nowhere. At some point, she had turned on the air-conditioner but the voices were gone. She remembered the question from last night and reached for her phone to text Trish, who responded that she was busy with her nieces and nephews. She fell back into bed and listened to the weed wackers rev outside the window. The question from last night kept returning to her consciousness: Who could she call if she needed help? She gathered the sheet and tucked it between her legs, curled her hands in the fabric and put a pillow over her face. With Roger gone, it seemed strange to be in his bed—a delicious violation. He probably hadn't given her one thought. Did you even exist if no one thought about you?

She didn't even care if he was in love with James. She just wanted to sit in the kitchen and discuss the details of their relationship. Dissect every utterance and gesture for meaning and purpose. But a shift had happened. They were now on separate tectonic plates, slowly grinding away from each other. This felt like another kind of death. It seemed unfair, after all the effort she had put into bringing him and James together. Yes, she'd done it with the knowledge that they wouldn't last, but he never would have gotten so close to James without her intervention. And still, he dropped her like a piece of hot garbage. He would probably do the same to James. Poor gullible James. It briefly crossed her mind to steal him away from Roger, if only to save him the heartbreak. But the effort it would take to win James back seemed overwhelming.

She curled onto her side. Roger was the one who had convinced her to leave Sean. If he hadn't stuck his nose in, she would have been at Sean's art opening: standing beside his work, fielding questions about which parts of the sculptures were hers, pouring glasses of white wine and nodding at the compliments. The show had opened and he didn't even send her an invitation. In fact, she hadn't had any contact with him in over six weeks. She was curious to see what the pieces looked like. After all, she was part of the process, his muse. Those pieces were part of her too. Originally, she was glad Sean didn't send her an invitation. She didn't want to answer a bunch of questions about why she left—face his anger and sadness. But after the opening, he probably wouldn't be at the gallery. She could just slip in and see the works on her own. It would be like visiting old friends, ones she'd lived with for so long and saw change and grow. Afterwards, she could call him and tell him what she thought of the pieces. They could discuss the individual trajectories of each work. It would be like old times. And if he was still angry, she would deal with it. Let him yell and call her a "sadistic bitch." Let him rant and throw things. It was preferable to the static emptiness stretching out before her. She would cry and apologize. He would tell her how much he missed her, how devastated he was. Then they would fuck like animals. Sean would be so grateful; he'd ask her to move back in. And Roger would feel guilty for abandoning her. It was a win/win.

When she arrived at the gallery, a crowd was already milling about outside: girls with Che Guevara T-shirts wearing bandanas, and boys with bushy beards and pukka shell necklaces. She didn't expect so many people on a holiday. Actually, she thought the gallery would be closed, but she'd called ahead and a baby-voiced girl told her they were holding a special event open to the public. Only when she saw the signs: Stop the Death, and Make Art Not War, did she realize it was a fundraiser to help Iraqi refugees. There was a lot of talk about Bush and capitalism and how Dick Cheney should be tried for war crimes. Across the street stood an abandoned warehouse with a sign advertising Retail Space Available. Some Bushwick guys in baseball hats gathered on the stoop of the aluminum-sided townhouse next door. They held beer bottles and solo cups and seemed more interested in the young girls coming into their neighborhood than in helping refugees. Every so often a "muy caliente" or a "mamacita" would hail from their direction.

The gallery was a former auto repair shop; its garage door was rolled up, making a large opening to the street. She wondered if Sean was inside. He wasn't political; she had never heard him say anything about the Iraq War, so the event was an odd choice. A placard hung over the entryway with the show's title: Feminista. Sean's bio was on a pony wall underneath. He'd always dabbled in feminism as a way to get permission to sexually objectify women, but now he seemed to be going full tilt.

She stood behind two girls contemplating his coat hanger woman with the Rubik's Cube vagina. One had a tiny pink backpack, the other a large lunchbox purse. She remembered Roger saying: "A purse was for a woman what a sports car was for a man—a substitute for genitalia." In which case, Lunchbox wasn't doing herself any favors. Unless she only wanted to be eaten out, then she was right on trend.

She eavesdropped on the girls' conversation. They couldn't have been more than twenty.

"I like how he depicts women of color," said Tiny Backpack.

"How can you tell?" said Lunchbox.

"Duh. The coat hangers are brown."

They moved off and she continued to study the sculpture. Something looked different. The wires coiled in a smaller circumference. It was highly unlike Sean to minimize tits. Maybe it was a concession to feminism.

White walls divided the space into separate rooms according to materials: paper, plastic, and metal. She noticed all the usual suspects: the Post-It Note women, the paper clip women, the pink eraser women, the While You Were Out women. They were indeed her old friends. She had witnessed their creation, and took joy in seeing them displayed and lit. It would always be something binding her and Sean together—their art babies.

A large group congregated in back where the star of the show—the Slinky Woman—hung on a wall under the gaze of several spotlights. A table with wine and sparkling water had been set up in the middle of the room, making it seem from certain angles that Slinky Woman was birthing into the world a bounty of Merlot and Pellegrino. Sean was standing next to the table talking in hushed tones with Gregory, his agent. Their backs were to her and a young woman with curly auburn hair stood nearby, probably Gregory's assistant. He always had some poor intern fresh out of Parsons doing his bidding. Sean handed them both glasses of wine and they made a toast. Her stomach started to churn and she turned around and pretended interest in one of the paperclip women—one with pink paperclip nipples and a wild mane of red wiry hair. Sean didn't look as forlorn as she'd expected. He could be covering up, but it was hard to get a read. Naturally, he would be putting on a brave face in public. She started to have doubts about coming. She wasn't ready to see Sean and dredge up all the emotions of leaving him and missing him. Something started to rise in the back of her throat; she hurried out of the room and onto the street.

She held onto a parking meter for support, and concentrated on the sun-heated metal burning her hand instead of the bile rising in her stomach. She still felt a bit hungover from last night and probably should have eaten something more than chocolate chip cookies before she left. She rummaged in her purse for basil oil and applied some to her wrists and forehead. She needed her healing crystals, her Yemayá beads, her evil eye amulet. She refused to upchuck in front of all these tattooed hipsters, even though it might give her caché as a heroin addict. She leaned against the parking meter and let its searing heat pour into her back, taking her mind off the nausea. If Sean found out she threw up at his art show, he'd probably want to use it as material for his next project: Vomit Woman.

Just as she was swallowing her own bile, Gregory walked out the door and caught her in the lenses of his black horn-rimmed glasses.

"Why Sherry, I'm surprised to see you here." He fingered the lapel of his tight summer suit.

Gregory had always despised her. She was the thing that came between Sean and his art production. Over the years, Sean had confided in him about their fights, or whenever he felt she wasn't giving him enough attention—sometimes just a hesitation in praise could send him into a tailspin that would make him stop working for weeks—so she always took Gregory's animus in stride. But he was the last person she wanted to see with vomit in her throat.

"Sean invited me," she lied.

He looked her up and down as if she were a sculpture by a six-year-old being passed off as outsider art. "He never could resist the drama, could he?"

She stood up straight and pressed her breasts against the fabric of her dress. It was a loose-fitting housecoat that she got at the Goodwill; it could almost pass as a sundress as the waist was cinched, but its primary function was comfort. She wasn't expecting to run into anyone she knew today.

"You're looking very ... fetching."

She reached up and felt the elastic in the back of her head and tried to fluff up her hair. "Thanks." She wasn't sure Gregory was gay or straight or if she was wasting the effort. Sean always took him for straight. But she imagined his sexuality had something to do with jacking off into rare sterling silver teaspoons.

"What do you think of all the changes he made?" Gregory tilted his head and the sun articulated fine silver hairs on his jawline. "I think they're a remarkable improvement."

"I haven't ... actually gone in yet." She lied again.

"He's reconceptualized every piece. His best work to date. A whole new inspiration."

Sherry managed her best defensive smile.

"Come on. Let me show you." He put a hand on her shoulder and directed her inside. "Almost half the pieces have been sold already."

He maneuvered her inside, trailing a strong scent of powdery cologne that almost made her retch again. She tried to think of an excuse to leave, but Gregory's hand pressed into her back. At each piece, he flourished a hand and pontificated. "You see, the legs have been elongated, the buttocks minimized. She's been reconceptualized in the traditional sense. This could be a woman out of Botticelli or Ingres had they worked with such materials."

She tried to imagine Venus with paperclip breasts and a Post-It note snatch, but all she could focus on was Gregory's chunky class ring with its red stone and prominent D for Dartmouth. He flashed a scythe of a smile and brought her to the Lego women. "I love the way the bricks form a more compact shape. It's like she's a toy as well as a child. He's captured the enforced subjugation of women by making them playthings. A kind of hard, geometric doll that can be taken apart and reassembled."

It was her body and it wasn't her body. She glanced at the shapes and tried to fit herself inside. She thought about all the sketches Sean had made of her and how he would tape them to the walls of his workspace. She remembered the first time he built a Lego woman silhouette. He held it against her and traced the lines of her body with his finger. He was so excited to have captured a woman's curves in block rendering that he danced her around the apartment. They drank Gatorade mixed with tequila. But Gregory was right—the figures had changed. They were smaller, the hips slimmer, the silhouettes more girlish.

"These, of course, are my favorites," Gregory brought her to the paper-clip women. "The addition of the hair gives the objects a Medusa quality. They are warding off the evil eye and at the same time invoking it."

True enough. The red, green, and yellow hair was striking. When Sean had first conceived the figures, he wanted them to be all straight lines and elongated silhouettes, but she could see the curly wires added a touch of chaos and foreboding. It was slowly dawning on her that he had erased her from every part of his work. How long had it been? Only one full moon had passed and he had excised her image from years of work.

Gregory continued to lecture. Other people stopped to listen. He was so full of bluster and self-assurance, she even found herself interested, as if he were describing something other than her total annihilation. She was too thick and round to be the ideal woman—too full of folds and flabby parts to be contained in ideal geometric shapes. Gregory's pontification made clear that she was the wrong subject for Sean's art. By the time they made it to the last room, she felt like a blob of primordial goo ready to ooze back into some prehistoric ocean.

His fingers were slowly tapping out some stealthy melody on her back. She shifted a few steps to another piece and breathed through the cramp in her stomach.

"I hope you don't mind my saying," he slithered behind her, "but I was sorry to hear about your breakup."

"I just wanted to give him some space to finish his work."

Gregory raised a dark eyebrow and adjusted his glasses.

She shrugged. "Sean and I have always had our ups and downs."

"Well, if there's anything I can do to help." He rubbed his exposed clavicle. "If you need a job or anything..."

"I have a job."

"You're still at the restaurant?"

"Yes."

"Well, my door is always open."

She didn't trust his kindness. At the same time, she wasn't blind to the possible sexual undertones. "I really have to go. I have an appointment in the..."

"Nonsense." He grabbed her arm. "Sean would never forgive me if I let you slip away. You have to at least say hello."

He escorted her to the wine table, where Sean was chatting with one of the pukka shell boys. Next to him was Gregory's assistant. Very closely next to him. Close enough for Sean to have his arm around her. In fact, Sean did have his arm around her. Around her slim hips.

As they approached, Sean disengaged and set his glass on the table. She registered the note of panic in his eyes, and everything became clear.

"Look who I found," Gregory said, and thrust her forward like a ticking bomb.

"Hello." Sean froze his facial expression.

"Hello," she said, while staring directly at Gregory's assistant, who was obviously not Gregory's assistant. In spite of the army pants and T-shirt, she wasn't as young as she had first suspected. Perhaps late twenties. The most striking thing about her was her mane of curly auburn hair, which spiraled out in all directions, just like the paperclip women. Not only was this the woman who had replaced her in Sean's bed but also in his art. She could see traces of her everywhere in the show—the ideal woman—the classic woman—the geometric woman who can be taken apart and reassembled in perfect mathematical form.

"This is Margaret," Sean said.

"Pleased to meet you." Margret smiled but didn't offer a hand.

"Margaret works for a non-profit that helps Iraqi refugees," Gregory interjected. "She organized this event."

And with that, Sherry could not contain herself any longer. It all came rising out of her: anger, rejection, shame, fear, embarrassment. She could have turned her head away, but she bent over the wine table and unleashed a fountain of vomit. It fell on the glasses and turned the white wine a cloudy red, and the red wine into sangria. It poured into the ice buckets and stained the tablecloth with a rash of red and brown dots. Some even managed to splash up and get caught in the spirals of the Slinky Woman.

When it was over, she wiped her mouth with the back of her hand, looked at Margaret and said, "Pleased to meet you too."

Then she turned and walked out.

The crowd, which had been watching the spectacle with concern and horror, backed away as if she were a giant chicken with the bird flu. In spite of this, she felt like a queen—a triumphant, vomitous queen.

14: The Playground

The bar was half full when they arrived. The lights low but colorful. The professional gays had all left for private parties or dance clubs. The remaining crowd slouched against the brick wall, dots of light from the disco balls playing on their faces. Roger wondered if it was a mistake to bring James here. It had taken some convincing. Over two weeks had passed since they had consummated their relationship; if more time followed, they would merge back into work buddies, and James would continue on his happy heterosexual way, their night of passion a distant blip on his sexual radar. The interval between friend and lover was a short one.

He hoped that exposing James to gay society might make him more comfortable with his tentative sexuality, and that familiarity would breed consent. Hal's birthday party seemed an innocuous enough occasion. The cast had gathered at a friendly neighborhood bar, free of go-go boys jiggling their thongs and shirtless men glistening with meth-sweat. He tried to imagine James dancing shirtless under the colored lights but couldn't picture it. He was beginning to see the virtue in not sexualizing the body— in making oneself the desirer instead of the desired. Historically this had been the providence of straight men, who knew that being desired was a loser's game. They didn't wait to be chosen, but did the picking and choosing themselves.

Whether it was prudery or privilege, he had always considered it unattractive for men to be flaunting their bodies. Modesty was masculine. He appreciated James's unassuming demeanor, even if it came dressed in a white button-down shirt and pleated khakis. Roger abhorred fashion queens. He'd always believed what was underneath a man's clothing mattered more. And nothing was more appealing than a muscular man who didn't know how to dress. It provided teachable moments for bonding. Though now, he was coming to the conclusion that what was underneath the muscles might be even more important.

They searched for Hal's party under a falling snow of disco lights. It was Philip's idea to celebrate his birthday and, surprisingly, everyone had made themselves available. Roger attributed this to their time on Fire Island at Garrick and his wife's house. Over the Fourth, the couple had invited the cast for a two-night getaway, which turned out to be a real bonding experience. There were only three extra bedrooms for seven people, so everyone was obliged to share. Diego angled to share with Roger, but Roger, not wanting to ignite any lingering embers, opted to sleep on the sofa bed in the great room, leaving the rest to battle for partners. Because of their past animosity, it was obvious to all that Syd and Diego couldn't share a room. And Hal, due to his past with Diego and the subsequent fallout, wouldn't couple (again) with him. So they rock/paper/scissored it, and Philip and Hal ended up together. Despite their more than forty-year age difference, they became very palsy-walsy on the trip, which led to much speculation among the cast, which was never confirmed or denied by the pair. That Philip had organized this birthday party was confirmation enough for Roger.

When they couldn't find them on the first floor, Roger directed James up the metal staircase to the second, watching his little ass clench and unclench underneath his khakis. It was odd how he could find a half-naked man thrusting his hips on a dance floor decidedly unsexy, and yet be attracted to a baggy-shirted man shuffling around in leisure slacks. Everyone claimed confidence was sexy, but it took far more confidence to acknowledge one's anxieties than it did to cover them with a false swagger. Perhaps he had stumbled upon the central allure of James.

He saw his people dominating a banquette with several round tables pushed together.

"There he is," Syd called out, waving a muscular arm protruding from a minuscule tank top. He seemed to have gotten over his feud with Diego and was back to his gregarious self. "Come. Sit next to me."

The collection of empty glasses soldiering across the tables might have been responsible for his transformation. Discarded shreds of wrapping paper bunched at people's feet. Hal had several bows stuck to his shirt, and one on his head, presumably from gifts already opened.

"You remember James?" Roger said.

"Welcome back." Philip flashed his lecherous blue eyes and stroked his gray beard.

James and Roger scooped up some chairs and squeezed between Syd and Warren.

"James is the boss of Roger," Diego announced to the table.

"Now there's a daunting job." Warren folded his hands over his stomach.

Syd grasped Roger's arm. "We're trying to figure out our *Sex and the City* characters."

"We all agree Diego is Samantha," Philip said, straightening his pin-striped shirt.

"The whore." Roger nodded, and Diego raised his glass.

"Hal is Charlotte," said Syd.

"Because I'm sweet and beautiful."

"No. Because you're a dimwit," said Warren.

"Hey. It's his birthday. Be nice." Philip turned to Hal and grabbed his chin. "He's just jealous because you're young and handsome and have the body of a god."

"I think my eight-pack is finally coming in." Hal, feeling his birthday drinks, lifted his polo shirt to show off the bumps on his stomach, which everyone scrutinized with zeal.

"Impressive," said Vik, "but I think that's more like a seven-and-a-half-pack."

"No. I can see a muscle forming," said Philip.

"That's not a stomach muscle," said Warren. "That's a tumor from all the cum he's swallowed."

"Too bad none of it was your cum, Warren." Diego grinned, reminding the table that he had gone home with Hal on at least one occasion.

"Ooh, the shade," added Vik, practicing his new gay slang.

Syd took a big sip of his Cosmo. "Anyway. Obviously Warren is Miranda..."

"The older, grayer version." Warren pressed his fingers to his chest.

"You left out fatter," said Hal.

"Hah." Philip rubbed Hal's stomach. "Score one for youth."

"Philip is Charlotte when he's not being a creepy letch. Vik is Miranda transitioning into Samantha.

"Give me time. I'm just getting started."

"And Roger is ..." He squinched up his face in thought. "Miranda?"

"I thought I was Carrie."

Syd raised a benevolent hand. "Well, you *are* a writer."

"What do you think, Jay-ames?" said Diego. "Is he Miranda or Carrie?"

"There are no wrong answers," said Vik.

"Just hurt feelings and bruised egos." Warren rubbed his fingers together.

James adjusted his glasses and wiped his palms on his pants. "I've never seen the show."

Gasps of disbelief circled the table; everyone regarded this as a personal affront. It *was* the most popular show on television, generating dozens of hot-takes, puff-pieces, and feminist critiques. Viewing parties were held all over the country, where women and gays discussed the four characters' exploits as if they were gospels for living. It signified a kind of gay blasphemy for James to admit he'd never watched the show.

"Not even like one episode?" Hal's face started to crumble.

"Incroyable." Warren threw back his head.

Syd tented his hands. "I can explain. It's basically..."

"Three whores and their mother," said Vik.

"Thank you, Borat." Syd threw a cocktail napkin in his direction. "No. It's four women: one promiscuous, one intellectual, one naive, and one ... romantic?"

"A whore, a prude, a dumbass, and a dork," said Warren.

"Now. Which one is Ruggero?"

James looked to Roger for help, but Roger was even more interested than the table in seeing how James would answer. "Go ahead, label me."

"I'd say Roger is ... romantic." James blushed at this admission.

"I guess that makes two Carries." Syd threaded an arm through Roger's.

"No chica. You don't get to make yourself Carrie." Diego eyeballed everyone for confirmation. "The show is called *Sex and the City*, not *Lonely People Jack Off in Locker Rooms*."

This started a heated debate around the tables, with Diego labeling Syd the minor character of Big's ex-wife, and Syd labeling Diego as Miranda's

Ukrainian maid who can't speak English.

Roger stood up. "I'm going to get some drinks. Hal you want anything?"

James also stood. "I'll go with you."

"Nice pants." Warren felt the material. "Are those fully pleated or is parachute coming back?"

Roger turned to Hal and made the universal sign of drink. "Last chance, birthday boy?"

"Strawberry mojito, s'il vous plaît." He handed Roger his empty glass.

At the bar, they vied for the bartender's attention. "I'm sorry about all that," Roger said. "Usually, they're not so keyed up."

"They're like a pack of rabid dogs snapping at each other."

"We'll just have one drink and then go."

A bartender in a leather harness and a Hello Kitty necklace took their order. He made Roger and Hal's drinks, and then was waylaid by a group of friends, who smothered him with air kisses and marveled at his neck gear.

Roger took the two drinks and said, "I'll meet you at the table."

When he came back, the group was deep in discussion about the Oscars. Warren was still fuming about *Brokeback Mountain* losing best picture.

"Listen, guys." Roger handed Hal his drink. "Go easy on James. He's not used to so much ... drama."

"He does know you're a playwright?" asked Warren.

"And that we are ..." Vik spread his arms. "...thespians."

Diego leaned back in his chair and crossed his arms. "Ruggero is so overprotective of this little lamb. Like we are the big bad wolf."

"He just wants to make a good impression on his boss," said Philip.

"I think his boss have already made impression on him." Diego grinned and stroked his chest.

"Come on," said Warren. "Just because you sleep with everyone you work with doesn't mean that Roger does."

"I do not sleep with everyone, Viejo. Some I would not touch with a ten-foot dick."

"And we can all breathe a sigh of relief about that," said Syd.

Vik rapped on the table. "So spill the T. Are you fucking this guy or not?"

Six sets of eyes focused on him. Six torsos leaned in. And twelve ears tilted to receive the T. In the gay world, one could sleep with pretty much anyone, but who one admitted to sleeping with was a whole different matter. The room got quiet enough to hear the lyrics of Pink's "Stupid Girls" on the sound system.

Roger took a sip of his drink. "We're having a moment."

"See. I knew it."

"Really?" Hal looked broken-hearted.

"Heaven help us," said Warren.

"Pleated khakis," Vik mumbled to himself.

Philip clapped his hands. "Come on now. Roger is a grown man. He can have his pick of any man he chooses ..."

"Present company excluded," said Warren.

"Present company rejected." Syd cast a side-eye at Diego.

"And if he chooses ... pleated khakis, then we have to accept pleated khakis."

"No." Hal banged the table, clinking the glassware. "No. I'm sorry. It just doesn't make sense." He clasped his hands behind his neck and growled in frustration.

"There, there." Philip rubbed his back. "I'm sure they have lots in common."

"They both breathe oxygen and exhale carbon dioxide," said Vik.

"Unless James has gills," said Warren.

Hal shook his head and whimpered. "What can they possibly have to talk about?"

"Certainly not their workout routines," said Syd.

"Or their hair products," said Diego.

"Or where to shop for pants," said Vik.

Roger looked past the men milling around and spotted James at the bar. He did look like a Bible salesman at a stripper convention. He understood his friends' reaction. A month ago, he would've felt the same. But it was James's reaction to his friends that took him by surprise—a bit of the old Buddhist judgment there. With the exception of Vikram, he had known these guys for years. Syd and Warren had acted in his previous plays. Philip had given him his first professional theatre job. Hal had taken one of his acting classes at the YMCA and then become his personal trainer. To greater and lesser degrees, they were angry and somewhat bitter—but such was life in the theatre. Such was what happened when you lived with constant rejection and the daily dwindling of your dreams. When you juggled three jobs and took acting and voice classes at night, Alexander technique on weekends, the gym every other day, and made it to every audition only to be told "no" a dozen times a week. He didn't know anyone involved in theatre who wasn't angry. Or for that matter, anyone gay who didn't have something seething in their gut. He never regarded it as a fault, just the substance in which everyone swam.

Their stories were the same as his. They had all been bullied as children, condemned to feel worthless, inadequate, odd—rejected by their families, shunned from every social group, their desires turned into a sickness, their relationships made deviant. They were diagnosed as mentally ill or perverted, or less than men. So they built a culture where beauty and art would raise them above their oppressors—where the set of criteria they invented could be used to undermine their bullies, and the world would be forced to acknowledge them. They carried the hierarchies they experienced as children into adulthood. Some sought to become more perfect versions of their bullies. Some internalized the bullying and continued berating themselves. Others confronted their abuse in sexual reenactments of their childhood persecution. What James saw as combative was a result of decades of living in combat. Even when they won the battle, gays were still reliving the war. Every rebuke, every criticism, had to be contested and defied—challenged by arcane knowledge, specialized talent, obscure hobbies, or obsessive concessions to beauty and fitness. They fought with each other because they'd spent their lives fighting with the world.

Roger understood this, and yet could see how superficial and mean-spirited it could seem to someone who had grown up sheltered within their family's love and acceptance, who had a place in society and saw themselves reflected in its most mundane depictions. He watched James with his skinny arms and pleated khakis, carrying his drink through the crowd of muscled men in micro tees, who were ten times more insecure than he would ever be.

"Okay, Mean Girls. He's coming back. Change the subject."

Diego held up his hands. "Let me tell you about this guy I was fucking the other night."

"You mean Garrick?" said Warren.

"That was last night," said Philip. "He's talking about the night before."

James set down his drink and took his place at the table.

"Listen, Abuelas, this is the closest you get to sex all year, so take an ear." Diego pushed back his chair and put himself upstage of the table to better act out his scene. "So I'm doing it with this cute Julliard student and he starts saying, 'I want to go away with you? Will you take me?' 'Take this cock,' I say, and keep pounding his culo. He kind of start whimpering, 'Can we see a movie? Let's go to *The Fast and Furious*.' I think maybe this his way of giving direction. So I speed up. Then he say, "Can we go to the Berkshires? Will you take me to *Tinkle-wood*?" I have no idea if he asking for me to pee on him or ..."

"Tanglewood," said Warren. "It's a classical music venue in the Berkshires."

"Ah, gracias. So he keeps talking about renting a cabin and having picnics on the grass, and I start to lose my erection."

"Erectile dysfunction. Oh my," said Syd.

"I say, 'Take that cock, pato' and do him harder." Diego demonstrates with several hips thrusts. "But he keeps talking about maple syrup and flannel blankets and violin concertos—worse dirty talk ever. I did not even cum."

"Remind me never to take you camping," said Vik.

"He's probably waiting right now for you to call him and take him to a movie," said Hal.

"That poor Julliard student," said Roger. "Just waiting by the phone to go to *Tinklewood*."

"Sad, really," said Warren. "The kid just wanted intimacy."

"Sometimes guys think they want sex, but really they just want to talk," said Philip. "It was often like that at The Adonis."

"What's The Adonis?" asked Hal.

"That's where your Auntie Philip cut her teeth. Or perfected her suck, as they say." Warren gave Philip his over-to-you gesture.

"Let's not go into it," said Philip. "Ancient history."

"I want to know," said Hal.

"Go on, Obe Wan Gaynobi," said Roger. "Instruct your disciple,"

Philip cradled his glass in both hands and rotated it back and forth. "They were porn houses. The Circus, The Cameo, The Playground, The Victory—I can't remember them all. This neighborhood used to be full of them. Men would come for a blowjob or a handy-jay, and ... that was that. But other times. Maybe it was the dark, or the sex sounds, or the flickering image of naked women on the screen that made them open up. I had some great conversations there."

"With the semen drying on their stomachs," Warren started to half-sing. "Ah yes, I remember it well."

"The Victory is now a children's theatre."

"Between Madame Tussauds and Disney, this whole neighborhood is a children's theatre."

"That's kind of gross," said Syd. "Sitting on seats where hundreds of men blew their jizz."

"And you never sat in the row underneath the balcony, lest you get rained on by the tiny droplets of manhood streaming down. Spunk showers, we called them."

"Weren't some of those guys homeless and mentally ill? I can't imagine it—the smells." Syd shuddered as if shaking off a bad memory.

Hal nodded his head. "And deodorant didn't work as well back then either." Everyone gave him varying looks of incredulity. "It's true. People smelled in the seventies."

"They smelled like Brute by Fabergé," said Philip.

"Or English Leather," said Warren. "God. What I'd give to bury my face in a crotch doused in English Leather." He rested his chin in his palm.

"I still get a chubby when I smell Drakkar Noir," said Roger.

"That was more eighties." Philip fondled his beard. "Jersey boys and their Drakkar Noir."

"And Polo," added Warren. "The eighties were all about lemons and limes."

"And boy, did some of us get lemons."

Warren put up a hand. "Let's not go down that road."

The whole table quieted down out of respect for his command.

"And what do boys smell like today?" asked Hal.

"Self-righteousness and wheatgrass," said Roger.

Warren raised his hands and looked at Hal. "You'll have to tell me. I haven't had a lover in fifteen years. Once you pass the age of fifty, you're rendered invisible."

"Oh, I wouldn't say that," said Philip. "I've always managed to find ... companionship."

Hal twirled his straw. "That's because you take care of yourself. You do push-ups and go to the gym."

"Ah, yes." Warren tipped an imaginary hat. "It's my fault for growing old ungracefully. I should be spending my time doing stomach crunches and bleaching my asshole like Philip here."

"No one's saying that." Philip gave Hal a harsh look. "You have to make an effort, though."

"It's difficult to find quality people," Syd said.

"Well, if *you* can't find anybody," Warren's eyes grew big in his head, "I don't know what chance I have."

"He can't find because he look for perfection." Diego jabbed a thumb in Syd's direction.

"Excuse me. Have you ever been with anyone over thirty?"

"Si. I been with many old mens. Ruggero is twelve years older."

Roger raised a finger. "Um, ten, actually. If anyone cares about numbers."

Warren's left eye was starting to droop, a sure sign he had too much to drink. "And have you fucked any fatties or real uggoes?"

"I date a guy with ... how you say ... manboobs."

Syd and Hal each let out a simultaneous "eeww."

"He was nice guy but ..." Diego shrugged. "I am not the Salvation Army."

"That's misogyny," Warren said. "You despise the feminine."

"I wouldn't call it misogyny," said Vik. "It's natural to be attracted to the strongest and healthiest of our tribe."

Warren pushed his empty glass away. "Don't tell me we can't change our nature. We all have impulses to violence, yet a civil society tries to repress them." He was starting to sweat, the thin strands of his gray hair sticking to his scalp. "No one should be denied love because of race or religion, or because they're old, fat, or ugly."

"Uh oh. Here we go." Hal grabbed his drink and hunkered down, straw to mouth.

"Sex isn't a right," said Syd. "You can't guilt someone into being attracted to you."

"Warren, I agree with you up to a point." Philip raised a finger and circled the room full of men. "But you have to take responsibility for finding love. There's someone for everyone. Your future lover may be walking toward you right now. You just have to open yourself up so you can see him."

"He's not going to find me if the culture is telling him to ignore anyone with manboobs."

"What are you saying?" said Roger. "We all need to fuck someone with Down Syndrome to prove we're good people?"

"I'd fuck a Down's Syndrome," said Hal. "At least I'd let him blow me."

"Ah, the soul of generosity." Philip patted his leg. "But Warren is right. We should try to be more accepting."

Syd fluttered both hands in Philip's direction. "Right. Humbert Humbert. When's the last time you dated anyone under forty?"

"We all have certain ... people we're attracted to."

"Si, Papi—the good-looking ones."

Hal rotated his straw around his glass. "I've been with some pretty ugly twenty-year-olds."

"Nobody is ugly at twenty," said Warren. "Every puppy is cute."

"We all have certain types," said Vik.

"And what's your type?" asked Philip.

"My type? Oh. Well. I only date white guys."

A collective wave passed around the table as each looked to the others in disbelief.

Syd put a hand on his chest. "So you've never been with a brown or black man?"

"I have. But it wasn't my thing."

"*It* wasn't your thing," said Syd, eyes widening.

"Raaaa-cism," Warren sang.

"I believe everyone is equal under the law," said Vik, "but not between the sheets."

"You're not attracted to other Indian men?" asked Hal.

"Well, maybe Abhishek Bachchan. But for the most part, I prefer white guys."

Warren focused a malicious eye on Vik. "You've internalized society's bigotry and are perpetuating it on others."

"Think that if you want, but practically speaking, there are just way more white guys in America. And every Indian gay I know is tied up in knots about his sexuality. 'I can't tell Baba. Dida will disown me.' Who wants to deal with that?"

"Ruggero say the same thing. That everyone have a type."

Roger put his arm around the back of James's chair. "We can sometimes stretch our boundaries."

"We have to face facts," said Syd. "We all *have* types and *are* types."

Warren gripped the table. "Please don't tell me you only date white guys too?"

"No. Though I know a lot of brothers who only date other brothers."

Vik stopped the air with his hands. "And yet, I'm the racist for only dating white guys?"

"I see that in personal ads," Hal said. "Brother for brother. It always sounds so incestuous." He took a deep pull on his straw.

"I don't think there's anything wrong with having a type, though reducing it to race is limiting." Syd plucked his t-shirt away from his pectorals. "There are certain things I want in a man and I'm not going to settle."

"Such as?" asked Warren.

"He has to be in shape."

"Meaning he has to be an amateur bodybuilder like yourself."

"He has to have the same commitment to fitness as I do, yes. He has to be educated. Intelligent. Sophisticated. Have a professional job. Decent money."

Warren tented his hands. "And how much money is decent?"

"Net worth? High six figures."

Warren slapped the table. "That isn't a type. It's a unicorn."

Syd folded his hands in his lap. "Now you know why I'm single."

"I noticed you didn't mention anything about kindness," Philip said. "Compassion? Empathy? Humor?"

"Oh. Those old things?"

"With all due respect, kindness doesn't make your dick hard." Vik rattled his ice. "If humor were so attractive, personal ads would be full of jokes instead of eight-inch penises."

"You go to brunch with the funny guy," said Hal. "You go to bed with the sexy guy."

Diego pushed his empty glass to the center of the table. "I no have a type. I date anybody: rich, poor, black, white, old, young. I no discriminate."

"As long as they're attractive," said Roger.

"Por cierto. I am not an animal. I do not just go into the field and fuck any beast with his ass in the air."

"It has to be an attractive ass," said Philip. "Well-muscled and in proportion."

"Exactamente."

Hal nods. "Goes without saying."

"Y. Also. He have to be masculine."

"Ah Hah." Warren pointed. "There it is. Straight-acting."

"I no say straight acting."

"These days," said Philip, "the straight men are more feminine than the gay ones."

"But you object to a man being feminine," said Warren. "More misogyny."

"Of course. I want a man to be masculine. If I want something feminine, I go for woman."

"Gender conformity," said Warren.

"Is that why you didn't return my calls?" asked Hal.

The table paused, and all heads turned in Diego's direction.

"What calls? What he talking about?"

"After we... never mind."

"He can't help it," Roger said. "Diego's brain is hardwired to delete your number right after he fucks you"

"You never returned my calls. My many many calls."

"Dios mio, este pato es molesto."

"It happens a lot," said Hal, cradling his glass. "Men come up to me in bars and after I say a few words, they just walk away."

Philip rubbed his back. "That's horrible."

"One guy said, 'Take the purse out of your mouth.'"

"I think we're making too much of this," said Vik. "People reject us for all kinds of reasons."

"Trabajamos juntos. Eres demasiado joven. Hay muchas razones."

"It's not immoral for someone not to be attracted to you," said Syd.

Warren rubbed his hands on his legs. "Well, I'd like to make it so. Everyone who's ever rejected me should be sent to jail."

"They're gonna have to build more jails."

"It's just as immoral for someone to refuse to serve me in a restaurant for being gay or disabled as it is for someone to refuse to service me in bed because I'm old, fat, or ugly."

Collective sighs and groans made their way around the table.

"Viejo, you have lost your mind."

"Much as I might want it to be," said Philip, "a blowjob is not a constitutional right."

"I don't see anything wrong with tearing down the beautiful people. They hold all the wealth. They need to spread it around."

Hal grabbed the bow from his head and threw it on the table. He scrutinized Warren. "We're all limited by something. I'm too feminine. Phillip is old. Vik is short. Syd is bald. Diego is dumb. Roger has bad teeth. And you're fat with man boobs. We can't demand people find us attractive in spite of our deformities." Heads turned in disbelief at the harshness of 'deformities.' "And we can't just wish them away. We must live with them. That," he picked up his strawberry mojito and twirled his straw, "is our cross to bear."

Roger noticed James growing increasingly uncomfortable and tried to defuse the situation. "Wouldn't it be great if by government decree, George Clooney had to blow three guys a year?"

"Make it Jake Gyllenhaal," said Warren. "Make it fuck three guys. And make one of them me and you got my vote."

"Seriously." Roger glanced at James. "I think we should all try to be more accepting and less judgmental."

"Ruggero? You? Less judgmental?"

"The Supreme Court is less judgmental," said Syd.

Diego leaned back in his chair and folded his hands. "Even when we were together you make me feel bad for not meeting your expectations."

"Do tell," said Vik.

"What are you talking about? I did nothing but praise you night and day."

"Ah, but ... 'Diego,' you say, 'If only you were a few inches taller. You'd be perfect.' 'Diego, what is the diet of Latino men that keeps them so short?'"

"It was a joke, for Christsakes."

"But you're at least six feet tall," said Philip.

"Um, five eleven, actually," said Roger. "If anyone cares about numbers."

"Ruggero like mens over six feet two. That his type."

The whole table turned and looked at James.

"Uh oh," said Hal.

"I see," said Philip.

"That explains it," said Syd.

Roger pretended to find something interesting in his glass.

"And what do you think, Jay-ames? Do you want to tear down the beautiful people?"

James let out the breath he'd been holding in. "I don't think we should tear down anyone. Too much time is spent on physical appearance."

Syd rolled his eyes. "Of course, he would say that."

"Typical," said Hal.

"Why of course?" asked James.

"Well, you and Warren have a vested interest in changing the game."

James pursed his lips and nodded. "What interest would that be?"

Syd held up his hand to testify. "Don't make me explain it to you, Hunty. That's not my job."

"He means you and Warren don't conform to the norms of ... aesthetics," said Vik.

"Khaki pants," Hal blurted out.

"I think it's time for me to go." James stood with his hands resting on the back of his chair. "Thank you, gentlemen for an enlightening evening."

"Don't go," said Philip. "They didn't mean to be insulting." He looked around the table for others to speak up.

"Stay," said Warren. "We have to fight these beauty Nazis."

James gave Warren a salute and walked off.

"Good going, guys." Roger stood and leveled an icy stare at the table. He sighed and turned to go.

Warren called out, "Hold on. When do we get the scene?"

"Yes," said Syd. "When are you going to give us the scene?"

"When you all stop being such cunts."

Roger sidled through the crowd and hurried downstairs, just in time to see James walking out the door. He caught up on the street and matched steps alongside him. They walked in silence for a while, the humid air sticking to their air-conditioned skin. A fishy scent blew in from the river as they stomped out their thoughts in tandem.

"It got a little intense in there," Roger said. "I think they're all mad at me for not delivering the final scene."

James stopped beside a reeking mound of garbage. "They're horrible people. How do you stand them?" He continued on as if he knew the answer. As if Roger was a horrible person too.

And maybe he was. Maybe gay men were characteristically sex-crazed and superficial, obsessed with body parts and beauty, afraid of intimacy and apple pie. Maybe all they could do was snipe and bolster their fragile egos, while scoping out the latest sexual conquest to eradicate their feelings of inadequacy. This was a critique as old as Larry Kramer, and one he had some sympathy with. He could understand how an outsider might regard their quips and banter as *Lord of the Flies* behavior—where only the wittiest and most beautiful survived. But he didn't know how to justify it to James. How to explain the hurt behind the humor. How to separate what was harmful from what was playful. There was an art to distinguish the performance from the pain—the deception versus the self-deception—it was often the distinction between having a sense of humor and not.

They turned down Eighth Avenue, the silence exploding between them. The street as familiar to Roger as a favorite novel, one he could start reading at any place and be totally immersed. He'd been walking these dirty blocks since high school and his first visits to the city. He would cut classes and take the bus from Philly, sometimes with friends, sometimes alone. Just for the day. Usually to wait in line for half-price tickets at the discount booth in Duffy Sq. He saw *The Iceman Cometh* with a gruffly eloquent Jason Robards. *Streetcar*, with a much too sensitive Aiden Quinn. *Sunday in the Park, A Chorus Line, Glen Garry Glen Ross, Hurley Burly, Torch Song Trilogy*. Before the shows, he'd walk the neighborhood and secretly ogle the men in leather jackets and tight jeans. Avert his eyes from the ones with canes, or the sunken faces swallowed in layers of clothes. He'd pass the marquees of the triple X theatres but was scared to go in. When he finally moved here for college, he braved some of them. Most were on the brink of being condemned: needles littered the bathrooms, vomit dried in the aisles. A balcony had collapsed in one. He was too afraid to do anything. Anyone who approached him, he turned away.

He stopped and pointed at the huge glass wall of the Rite Aid store. "This was where The Adonis was."

They peered through the windows at the fluorescent aisles of soaps and toothpaste. The store occupied half the block, along with a Blockbuster Video. The theatre and surrounding buildings had been leveled. Set back from the drug store, a twenty-story apartment building towered above.

Roger reached out his fingers, as if he could bring back the theatre by touch. "It was four stories tall and had a huge palladium window over the marquee framed by Greek columns."

"Did you 'cut your teeth' there?" said James.

"I went a few times, but Syd was right. They were mostly full of addicts and bums."

It seemed unreal now, as if these places had never existed. Philip and Warren had stirred up memories of a time he seldom thought about. He tried to recall: Did it say *Adonis* in blue neon or plain white letters? Was there a bodega next door or a camera shop? He gazed down the avenue. They used to call it The Minnesota Strip because of all the girls who came from the Midwest and ended up hooking on the street. The ladies of the evening were long gone, but some nights you could spot one by the bus terminal. People said they were all out in Queens now.

If he thought really hard, he could almost picture the theatre marquees: *Sex Ecstasy, Sextacular Acts, Gates of Flesh, Naked Souls Mating*, Go-Go Boys, Grope-Rooms, Active Cruising Lounge. Words that imprinted his adolescent brain with the mysteries of sex and the insignia of death. Interspersed between these were peep shows, strip clubs, X-rated video and magazine shops. All this desire and decadence lived just a few steps away from F. Murray Abraham in *Macbeth* and Rex Harrison in *Heartbreak House*. The passions of New York were brazenly displayed on its most populous streets, where tourists gawked and dignitaries rode. Where the proletariat celebrated New Year's Eve. It disturbed and titillated his young mind that at The Crossroads of the World, sex was center stage.

They kept walking. Roger contemplated the facades, trying to remember the seedy past of each of the buildings, as if they were shunned relatives no longer invited to the family picnic. After eighteen years, it seemed that he too had reinvented himself along with New York. What bothered him was not so much that the buildings had been repurposed but that they had been replaced. You had no idea of their history because the veneer of that history had been eradicated.

"You know Philip's lover died of AIDS. He took care of him for years."

"I'm sorry to hear that."

"And Warren was involved in ACT-UP, picketing City Hall, protesting at the mayor's office. He lost a lover too, and many friends."

"If you're trying to make excuses for their behavior, it's not working."

Roger stopped and pointed to a red and yellow striped building that held New York Sightseeing Tours. "This used to be the Hollywood Twin."

James glanced at the building and nodded.

"It was an art house for a while. On day trips from Philly, I used to watch old movies here. Then it turned into a porno theatre. One twin was gay. One was straight. Just like in real life."

The building used to be blue and white striped. He saw *All About Eve* here on the big screen, which convinced him to become an actor. Also, every one of Tennessee Williams' plays that had been turned into movies, and a hypnotic Kate Hepburn making her *Long Day's Journey into Night*.

He took a few steps and then some detail would pull him back: a fleck of blue paint from the old color, the memory of a warm hand sliding down his pants in the dark. He was living in two worlds as the palimpsest of the sullied past imposed itself on the sterile present.

When he first moved to the city, the theatre community was shrouded in death. Someone was always inviting him to a funeral or a memorial service, mostly for men he didn't know or knew only in passing, or through the very act of their passing. When you thought about it, a funeral was the best place to learn about someone: all their friends and family were there, everyone wanted to talk about the deceased, and no one shut you down if you asked prying questions. In fact, the more questions you asked, the more concerned you appeared. Death was the one time when a person's life was considered an open book.

Roger went mostly to find out about upcoming acting jobs. He'd stand behind some famous producer or director with a solemn expression on his face and listen to their conversation. He never uncovered any work, and the experience always left him anxious, juggling between stoic grief and suppressed fear. There was much drinking afterward, huddled twelve to a table at claustrophobic bars. And much pairing off with co-mourners for drunken, defiant, comfort sex. Nothing makes you hornier than seeing a youthful colleague laid out in a box. Less attractive men, who were good listeners with sympathetic expressions, found themselves very much in demand—the rising tide of AIDS lifting their boat. The rules of attraction had changed from big shoulders and slim hips to friendly ears and compassionate eyes. When you were looking for a shoulder to cry on—size didn't seem to matter. For some, memorials and protest marches replaced bathhouses and porn theatres. But most, including Roger, kept to themselves. It was the age of the VCR, where desire sprang fully formed from a black plastic box that you played in the privacy of your home.

He focused his sexual energy on his acting, taking provocative roles or finding provocation in the dull ones. He caused a minor stir in college by playing George from *Our Town* as a compulsive masturbator. This added an extra dimension to the funeral scene where his wife was laid out for viewing. Later, he channeled the bulk of his desire into writing. Still, he felt he had missed out. Like a hippy who never went to Woodstock, he never got to roll in the mud with all the cool people. He'd never experienced the freedom of "sex without fear" that Warren and Philip had talked about. Nor had he come of age in the AZT protease-inhibited millennium, like Diego, where sex wasn't synonymous with death. He was born in the only pocket of time in the twentieth century where sex killed. Of course, better to be born knowing that fact than to be ignorant, like so many others just a few years older.

He pointed to a cluster of buildings across the street. "That was the block with The Eros and The Venus." The Eros had been turned into a restaurant called The Playwright's Tavern, where no playwright ever ventured. And The Venus had become a trattoria. As with everything that reaches middle age, New York had substituted food for sex. And turned lust into enchantment. The brazen slut had transformed itself into a Disney princess.

"Between the two theatres, where that gift shop is, used to be this wild bar called Cats."

James gazed down the street in the direction of the subway.

"They had go-go boys on the bar, and after hours you could buy them for twenty bucks." It was now a shop called Gift Expressions, which, if he concentrated really hard, might still be something pornographic.

James kicked a plastic water bottle across the sidewalk.

"What's the matter? All this sex talk making you uncomfortable?"

"The whole night has been nothing but sex talk."

"I see. All *you people* talk about is sex."

"I didn't say you people."

"No. But it was implied."

"You're being ridiculous." He walked ahead.

"You're going to have to decide, James. Are you with Them or with Us?"

"Don't turn the tables. This is about your friends being horrible people."

"No. This is about me being horrible people. That's what you're thinking."

James scoffed and sped up.

"And you're right. I am horrible. And I'm not going to change for any Midwestern milquetoast so you'd better get used to it."

"I never asked you to change. Stop being so dramatic."

"Oh. Right. Because I'm gay. I'm dramatic." He leaped over to one of the metal grates on a shop window and started pounding. "Look at the queer. He's being dramatic. He's having a sissy fit." A couple across the street gawked at them and kept walking. Then he started frantically tap dancing. "It's what we do. We can't help it. Step-ball-change."

James crossed his arms and rested his chin in his hand. "Are you done?"

"No. I'm not done. Because after the dancing comes the fucking." He grabbed one of the garbage cans with a swing-top lid and started humping it. "That's all we think about. Sex sex sex. We want to fuck everything."

"You're a child."

"You hate my friends. You hate my writing. You hate everything about me." He kicked the can and it jumped a few paces on the sidewalk.

"I don't hate you or your writing." James walked a few steps like he was going to leave and then came back. "I'm afraid of you. That's what I am. And everything you're doing now is making me more afraid."

"Yeah. Well, I'm afraid of *you*." He turned his back and looked at the can. The admission surprised him, but as soon as he said it, he realized its truth. "I'm afraid you'll decide I'm too mean. I'm afraid you'll change me and make me nice. I'm afraid this is just a phase and in another two weeks, you'll go back to being straight."

"You're the first person I've met who's afraid of being nice."

"It gives me the shudders."

"Well, I'm nice. If you're saying you don't like nice, you must not like me."

"You can be nice." He turned to James and leaned on the can. "I like it that you're nice. I just don't want you to turn me nice. But if you're nice and I'm a horrible person, how can we ever be a couple?"

"So that's what you want? To be a couple?"

Roger shrugged.

James studied the oncoming traffic. Car lights reflected in his glasses. "I guess we'll have to work on that."

"Take my hand." Roger held out his hand. A hot wind rustled some take-out menus down the street. James's shirt billowed out.

"What?"

People on the sidewalk curved around them. "Take my hand. If we're a couple, then we'll walk down the street as a couple."

James took his hand. It felt hot. The hair on their arms brushed together. They continued walking. Roger had seldom walked down the street holding hands with a man. He had tried it with a few long-term boyfriends, at the start of giddy romance, but as their passion waned, so too did the need for public displays of it. He could feel the awkwardness in the swing of James's arm. But he wanted to test his resolve. If he was unsure about being gay, better to find out sooner than later.

They continued on, trying to match each other's steps, pulling away and then coming together, shoulders bumping, hands brushing thighs. Whenever a person walked toward them, he could feel James stiffen. He froze a bit too. Men holding hands was a gesture that called attention to itself. And it wasn't always safe. Just a few months ago, two men were brutally beaten for holding hands along the Westside Highway. He was relieved that James had complied, even if he kept focused straight ahead and never looked at Roger.

There was still a crowd at a dive bar called Smith's; a greasy smell of buffalo wings wafted through its doors. They crossed 44th Street and he couldn't believe his eyes. The marquee was still in place: the New York skyline, red neon against a black background surrounded by stars and moons. Somewhere in the back of his mind he remembered it used to be a neon naked woman, but the Times Square clean-up crew must have changed it. The Playground was the last surviving porn theatre on the street. He'd heard there was one still standing, but the details had slipped his mind.

Colored neon in the windows flashed Girls Girls Girls—Live Live Live. Fantasy Booths. Preview Booths. 128 Channels. The canned lights under the marquee felt hot on his face. They lit up blue veins on James's temple. He refused to look at the theatre and instead focused next door on something called The Funny Store. Its window crowded with rubber chickens and fake vomit.

"Let's go in," Roger said.

"What?"

"Come on. We have to."

"Are you insane?" James dropped his hand. "It's disgusting. Probably dangerous."

"All this time you've been in the city, isn't it about time you did something dangerous?"

James stared at the colors reflecting on the sidewalk, his face a mask of pinks and purples.

"We may never see another one. It's *The Last Picture Show.*"

Roger went into the glass vestibule, its walls made opaque by a floor-to-ceiling poster of a girl on a swing saying: Welcome to the Playground. James followed.

The lobby had been turned into a porn shop, every inch of space given over to the paraphernalia of the trade: lubes and dildos, vibrators and Fleshlights. Shelves of DVDs lined the walls. A man with a beer gut and strings of greasy hair sat behind a plywood counter working a Sudoku. "No girls tonight," he said. "We're showing a movie. Ten dollars." He pointed to a poster behind him: The New Devil in Miss Jones, which appeared to be a remake of the 1970s classic.

Roger paid for both of them, and the man ripped two blue tickets off a roll. On the other side of the room, in front of a wall of rubber bras and leather harnesses, two young guys concentrated on a soccer game on a small TV. One leaned on a mop in a bucket; the other sat on a stool behind a display case. Inside the case was a selection of dusty video cassettes and old porn mags in plastic covers. The theatre was behind a black curtain next to a sign that read: No Drugs. No Alcohol. No Soliciting.

James feigned an interest in the DVDs, while Roger waited for him to work up the courage to go inside. Nurses, teachers, secretaries, librarians— it was odd that merely having a job was considered sexy. Though with its cowboys, businessmen, doctors, and construction workers, gay porn was no different. There seemed to be no professions that hadn't been eroticized. It confirmed his suspicion that all men thought about every day at work was sex.

He tapped James on the back and led the way through the curtain.

After the constrictions of the lobby, he wasn't expecting such a big room. The theatre looked like it might have held five hundred people in its heyday. The walls were painted matte black, but underneath he could see plaster angels. Greek keys wound across the balcony, and the deep recesses of the coffered ceiling framed a couple of dark chandeliers. The back wall was given over to a set of booths, which he figured was where they kept the live girls when they had them. One door was ripped off and a man sat in the tiny room, dozing in his underwear, like a saint in a crèche.

Some of the seats had been torn out and the slope of the floor leveled to allow for video booths down both sides of the auditorium. Between the double row of booths was a narrow passage, two tunnels from which you could hear the squeaking of hinges and tentative padding of feet. Roger tried to coax James down one, but he refused. An orgy was happening on screen, and a dozen heads looked to be in the seats. Some were bowed in sleep, a couple bobbed in masturbatory fashion but most were still. In the front row, a woman or a man in a long dark wig, rose from the floor in front of one of the heads. She wobbled on unsure heels into the tunnel of the video booths. Roger found an empty row; his foot kicked an empty liquor bottle and sent it clanking across the floor. He took a seat centered in front of the screen. James hesitated in the aisle but eventually joined him.

The movie seemed to be about a shy, awkward, but inexplicably hot woman, who kept being overtaken by sexual fantasies. She worked for a publishing house that was absurdly located in a secluded mansion in the Californian mountains. The women who worked with her were all in their twenties and dressed like corporate dominatrixes. No cardigan sweaters with cat hair for these editors. The men were average-looking with big dicks. He understood why straight guys didn't want to look at beautiful men, but couldn't figure out why they wanted to see big dicks. Didn't watching better-endowed men make them insecure? After a few more scenes, Roger began to understand the crucial role of the penis. It was always attached to an off-camera body or a barely visible face, so every man could imagine that the penis was his: *that's what my dick looks like going inside of her.* Even the lesbian scenes required a penis in the form of dildos and strap-ons. And even the strap-ons required servicing, as if part of an ancient covenant—no dick shall go unlicked.

James was staring stone-faced at the screen. Roger rested his leg against him but he moved away. A man came down the aisle and stood at the end of the row, massaging himself through his board shorts. His smile showed at least two missing teeth. Roger waved him away. James closed his eyes as if he were in pain.

The scene switched to Miss Jones being confronted by Miss Devilin, a Mephistophelian figure in Double-D cups. Miss Devilin gave her one wish and she asked to be consumed by desire. Cut to sex scene with the lesbian devil.

In an effort to give James the full experience of New York history, Roger reached over and put a hand on his crotch and was confronted with the sharp rebuke of his fully erect penis. James slapped his hand away and crossed his legs. He seemed embarrassed, though not nearly as much as Roger.

This called for a complete reassessment of the situation. All his preconceived notions had to be reevaluated. The chickens had come home to roost and they all had raging hard-ons for big-titted blondes. Of course, what was he expecting fooling around with a straight guy? That the sheer power of his charisma could convert James? Make a transubstantiation? Turn a desire for pussy into penis with some artsy conversation and a few furtive blowjobs? He would have understood a little excitement, even made allowances for a semi-chubby, but the implications of a fully engorged, splitting-the-pants-seams penis was something he could not ignore. He finally saw the value in pleated khakis, at least in their ability to hide erections. All this time he thought he was bringing James to a deeper understanding of his true self, but maybe he had been forcing him into something untoward. Maybe James ultimately desired to be the penis between two lesbians.

Roger slouched in his seat and watched these women pleasure each other for the enjoyment of straight men everywhere. He could always spot fake acting and these actors needed extensive lessons in the Stanislavski Method. This scene was more about positions than pleasure. No real communication was happening; certainly, no one was consumed. They were hitting their marks like beautifully trained seals. Could he be manipulating James in a similar fashion? If James found these inflated bimbos sexy, how could he find Roger sexy? He recalled their night together and James's cries of pleasure and satisfaction. Could he have misinterpreted those for surprise and remorse? Granted, so much about sex was a matter of interpretation, but either James was the Olivier of sexual performance, or they had found a genuine connection.

He watched the women going through their routine: upside-down, face to crotch, doggie style. The mechanics, if not igniting passion in them, could well ignite passion in others. Just as certain dolts teared up watching the Lifetime Channel or laughed at Adam Sandler movies—fake emotions could inspire real ones. Illusions inspired reality—that was the magic of art. It created desire. Or, alternatively, desire already existed in the body as a collection of hormones and chemical reactions and art gave it a target and direction. The body created desire—the need for release—and society determined what kinds of releases were acceptable. The process of maturity and civilization transformed our roiling, churning chemicals into a set of acceptable desires. Though sometimes an urge rampant in the veins overrode societal programming and caused you to fuck a sheep or a watermelon. The body sought release by any means possible. Maybe instead of creating desire *in* James, he was a release of desire *for* James. Maybe he was no more than a watermelon.

The same man with missing teeth came down the other side of the aisle and stood in front of James, rubbing his crotch. He had a vacant, almost serene expression, as if performing some perfunctory obligation. He had a quite large protuberance in his pants, and he smiled as he brought it out. James bolted up and ran out of the theatre. Roger pushed aside the toothless guy, ran up the aisle, through the velvet curtains and followed James to the street.

Rumbling tires and beeping horns replaced the cum cries in the theatre. Roger adjusted his eyes to the glare of the lights.

"Slow down," he called out.

"I'm going home," James called over his shoulder.

"Wait. I'll come with."

"I need to be alone." James turned around and hurried down the street. His white shirt reflected off the car lights and ballooned in the wind. He swerved and pivoted, dodging pedestrians, never stopping or slowing, a fading dot on the streetscape.

Roger watched him fade away. He wasn't going to dramatically chase him through the streets. He turned and began walking toward the subway. How does one fight biology? Even when genuine feelings arise—love, compassion, companionship—they can't compete with hormones and brain chemistry. He looked up at the former porn houses and strip clubs and sex shops; they had all been supplanted, surpassed even. People had come along and said we do not want these anymore. And down they fell.

He passed the New Victory Theatre on 42nd Street. Its marquee read *The Mouse Queen: An Aesop's Fables Classic*. He examined the poster of the actors wearing top hats with giant mouse ears. And a puppet of the queen herself, who looked to be a cardboard figurine in a funnel-shaped skirt. Maybe he would buy tickets and take James. Even if he didn't agree with the transformation, it gave him a kind of hope. Things could change. Impulses could be altered, or at least diverted. Or at least subverted. Actors could be mice and mice could become queens.

15: Waiting for the Film to Develop

James waited in between a red Honda and a white van, while the sun reached just below the car's visor and stung his eyes. He should never have driven into Manhattan—only cabbies and chauffeurs chanced it here—but Sherry had asked him to dinner and he decided to take the opportunity to tell her exactly what he thought of her lies and manipulations. He'd had enough of both her and Roger and was determined to set boundaries and affirm his right to be treated with honesty and respect. And when he accomplished this goal, he wanted to jump in the car, rev his engine and screech into the night. Much more satisfying than the click of the subway turnstile, the anemic beep of a Metro Card.

There shouldn't have been this much traffic on a Sunday, except that everyone was coming back from their weekends in the Hamptons or beach houses on the Jersey Shore. The Lincoln and Midtown tunnels, the Queensboro and Brooklyn bridges, funneled all and sundry into the great sewer of Manhattan, where everyone circled the drain like so much detritus.

As he crawled down Forty-Fourth Street, he could see that Times Square was still in the process of reinventing itself. Many buildings were under construction and dumpsters lined the streets, taking up valuable parking spots. Whole sections of sidewalks were cordoned off by orange cones, causing pedestrians to walk the streets. A traveler trundled her Gucci suitcase roadside, followed by a man pushing a dolly with boxes piled to his forehead. Down the block, a giant hole opened up where a building once stood, its carcass being picked apart by mechanical cranes. He had the feeling he was walking into the center of something. Not exactly the heart of America, but more like its brain. The dendrites and ganglia of the control center. The software that kept the wheels of suffering rolling.

The Buddha said: *If you are filled with desire, your sorrows swell like the grass after the rain.* James could feel Times Square swelling and exploding with fantasies and aspirations. It was the Cineplex of American desire. The whole Bhavachakra of America's shadow-self had been animated here, from the tap shoes of Broadway babies to the moans of copulating whores, to the earnest shrieks of the Little Mermaid. Everything the psyche repressed was found here, built of neon lights, and wrapped in advertisements for Coca-Cola and Yahoo Mail. Giant billboards looked down from Olympian heights, with their stories of family fidelity and personal trauma: lion kings and musical weddings, wicked witches and disfigured composers. Desire in the American psyche had gravitated from illicit sex to emotional wounds.

He tried to imagine the Times Square Roger had talked about: the Deep Throats and Mrs. Joneses, and before that: the Ziegfeld girls and Yankee Doodle Dandies, but it was beyond comprehension—the brain had been reprogrammed. Unlike Roger, he didn't see Disneyfication as a suppression of sex but as a shift in focus. Families were falling apart, the American Dream was unattainable, people were feeling alienated and exploited, so America's shadow space celebrated familial dependency and overcoming trauma. Whatever we repressed, sputtered back up the drain and splashed out on the marquees of Broadway. The great wheel of becoming spun, the spunky gal turned into the deep-throated whore turned into the misunderstood witch.

The light changed and he moved three car spaces. The big white bride on the *Momma Mia* billboard flashed her connubial teeth, reminding him that his parents were coming into town next week to celebrate their thirtieth anniversary. Hopefully, orchestra seats and dinner would ease their criticism of his life choices.

Another light change, another three spaces. He should just pull into a garage, but he couldn't afford it. Especially since he wasn't sure Sherry would keep her promise of paying for dinner. She could only get an early reservation, and not at Daniel's flagship restaurant but at his more proletarian offshoot in the theatre district. After what he planned to say, he could easily imagine her walking out and sticking him with the check. And when she did, he wanted the comfort of his car, even if he had to walk ten blocks to get it. He would drive out of town—a solitary cowboy on his two hundred and fifty horses.

A police officer was directing traffic across Eighth Avenue and motioned him forward. He inched along with the other cars, compressed between the tall buildings like motorized cattle being led to the killing floor. Agreeing to dinner was probably a mistake, but he didn't want to have this conversation at work. It was too personal: the way she manipulated him at Roger's bidding; the way she came on to him with tiny touches and those stories about her grandmother.

He cut over to the side streets off Ninth Avenue in search of the elusive parking spot. On the passenger seat, his phone buzzed. He thought it might be Roger, but it was a notice about his cell phone minutes. Since the night at The Playground, Roger had been sending various disgruntled messages, implying that James was irrational and overreaching. James had texted back that he needed time. He couldn't be expected to process all that had happened in a few days. Give him a few decades and he'd get back to Roger. As an old man, he could recline in his rocker and think to himself: *Remember the time you got shtupped and kind of liked it? Those crazy oughts. People were out of their minds. Our country had been attacked, hurricanes had destroyed our cities, and Ben Stiller was the highest-grossing movie star.* He could look back on it all while his wife made hot chocolate for his grandkids and his children argued about the mileage on their flying cars.

He slow-cruised the streets, holding tight to the steering wheel, contemplating the implications of getting buggered, banged, screwed, drilled, shagged, shafted, stuffed, and shtupped. Not really pleasant connotations. If being penetrated was supposed to be enjoyable, why did all the ways of describing it sound so brutal? Who really wanted to be pounded, porked, cornholed, mounted, nailed, pumped, and reamed? They really should think up better ways to advertise the experience. No wonder people felt demoralized after sex when the vocabulary used to describe it was degrading and sadistic. He turned the corner and maneuvered down the tight side street, wondering how much better it would be to be transported. To get ecstatic. To be blissed. *I was transported last night, getting ecstatic with this guy. He was uplifting me, perceiving me, joying me, filling me with his honor and acclaim.* James would much rather be blissed than banged. Joyed than drilled. Perceived instead of pumped. He couldn't help thinking guys would stand a much better chance of getting laid if they stopped talking about sex like it was a search and destroy mission.

It was no surprise that after ditching Roger at the porn house, their work relationship had become strained. Roger acted aloof and perfunctory, and James couldn't tell if he was giving him space or giving him up. No doubt this was a result of his request for more time. But it might also be that Roger was losing patience. In which case, James couldn't blame him. To finally consummate a relationship only to be told that your partner wanted time apart would cause any zealot to lose their zeal. The only hint he had that Roger was still interested came when he found himself in the spotlight of his gaze. Roger would be standing behind a customer, waiting for them to order, and simultaneously following James around the room. Appraising and gazing, forever judging: a *whore, a prude, a dumbass, and a dork. Pleated khakis.* He was probably undressing and redressing him in more fashionable attire. Finding all the faults, mentally fixing the defects. And now, of course, he was sending his undercover agent Sherry to do some more reprogramming.

He tried to fit into a spot between a dumpster and a moving van. He turned his wheel back and forth to inch his way in, only to have to inch his way out again when he found he couldn't fit, much like he felt trying to have a conversation with Roger's friends. He should just get it over with and declare that he was a homophobe. It pained him to admit, but what else would you call someone who didn't like being around gay men? He believed in equal rights, marriage equality and all the rest, but he would rather spend a night in jail than have drinks again with Roger's friends. They were teenage girls on testosterone: all they thought about was gossip, clothes, and boys. And ripping each other apart for their own amusement. If this was what it was like to be gay, he'd rather take up gun ownership and NASCAR. He'd participate in Civil War reenactments before attending another queer cocktail party. He didn't so much mind a cock up his ass but spare him the company of catty queens.

Between Tenth and Eleventh Avenues, he finally found a spot. He squeezed in, kissing the bumper of a green Taurus in front. The restaurant was almost to Fifth, but he didn't hurry; it was too hot to run in dress pants. Roger's friends had made wearing khakis impossible, and Sherry's criticism put shorts out of the question. The only pants he had left were a black wool blend, which held in heat like a Dutch oven. Every step recalled Sherry's complaints about his hairy legs, his sweat like a sprinkler. More droplets trickled down his sides. It was as if his body was taunting Sherry— You don't like my sweat? I'll drown myself in it.

He arrived twenty minutes late. The restaurant was fifties modern, done in browns and oranges with paneled walls and lots of mirrors. A chic host, whose pants seemed made of some flow-y material they only gave to good-looking men with hairless legs, escorted him to the table. Sherry was already waiting and jumped up to give him a hug. He kept her at arm's length, defying her to say something about his saturated, sweaty self.

"We have to celebrate." She held up a green cocktail. "I'm moving out of Roger's."

The host asked if James would like a drink, and he ordered what Sherry was drinking.

"Trish and I finally found a place." She described the apartment, the drawbacks: small kitchen, no light; the good points: lax on credit checks.

When the waitress brought his drink, he clinked her glass. "I'm sure Roger will miss you."

"I doubt that." She gave a sideways smile. "But let's not talk about him. How are you? How are you coping? Did your grandma visit you in a dream yet?"

Again with the dead grandmother shtick. "Look, before we say anything. I just want to tell you that I know what went on between you and Roger."

She raised an angry eyebrow. "He told you? Why would he do that?"

The question he wanted to focus on was why she had pretended to like him. And if it was part of Roger's instructions or something she took upon herself.

She did her little doggy shake. "I don't even know what's going on between me and Roger. Except that he treats me like crap."

"I thought you were going to tell me how wonderful he is."

"As if." She took a big sip of her cocktail. "He's a user. It took me a while to figure that out. That's all I'll say on the subject. Now let's order." She opened her menu. "Everyone says we have to try the Peekytoe crab cakes."

He perused the menu while digesting this new information: Roger the user, who had been letting Sherry stay at his place rent-free for almost two months. Though if they had a fight and she was no longer doing his bidding, what was she doing here? He'd noticed at work that they hadn't been spending as much time together. No more little chats by the cappuccino machine, no more arguing about *America's Next Top Model,* or leaving the restaurant arm in arm on their way out the door.

They ordered a bottle of wine, and over appetizers, she described the apartment in greater detail. It was a sublet so she could move in the middle of the month. He waited for more clues about why she was mad at Roger, but they weren't forthcoming. He wanted to bring up the comments she had made about him, but he couldn't find a way to introduce the subject organically. *Yes, the crab cakes look delicious, but inside, they are filled with vile and disgusting things—just like you with your lies and deceit.*

By the time the entrées came, Sherry's conversational steam was still sputtering along. He'd ordered raviolis au chèvre. And she'd ordered capon ballotine, which he couldn't help thinking of as a guillotine of cock.

"I can't believe he told you about me and him," she said, cutting through her cock. "Though, I shouldn't be surprised since he told me about you and him."

James set down his fork and gripped the edge of the table. "Pardon?"

"You and him. He told me about your thing."

"He told you about ...? What did he tell you?"

"Just that he's in lust with you and that you and him had fooled around but you're not sure you want to take it further." She put a morsel of food into her mouth and chewed thoughtfully.

His plate of ravioli swirled before his eyes like a battlefield.

"I'm sorry," she said. "I didn't mean to embarrass you, but you should know that when it comes to sex, Roger doesn't keep secrets. I think he only has sex with people so he can talk about it later." She daubed her lips with her napkin. "We both learned the hard way on that." Her gap-tooth smile brightened, and a gleam peeked into her eyes.

"I don't know what I learned." James stared at his plate; a split-open ravioli was oozing goat cheese.

"I mean, God knows what he's saying about our sex. I can only imagine the things he's told you."

"Wait. Are you saying that ... you and Roger ...?"

"You said you knew."

"You and Roger ...?"

"Only once. I thought it might have led to more. He really made it seem like he cared. I guess he did the same to you. Roger gets these obsessions with people, but they burn out quickly."

"Excuse me." He got up in a daze and walked toward the door. Behind him, Sherry was saying something but it was all white noise in the distance. On the street, he joined the pedestrians and was enveloped by the ostensibly normal people, who didn't live in the bizarro world where *Roger fucked Sherry*. He couldn't wrap his head around it. Of all the fantastic manifestations of the universe—waves are particles and particles are waves—this was the most unthinkable. *Roger fucked Sherry*. He would have believed Roger had fucked a sheep, or even a jar of spaghetti sauce, before he fucked Sherry.

He felt a tugging on his arm and she was next to him, a bit out of breath from running. "What's the matter? You just walk out? You said you knew."

He stopped in front of a theatre, where a poster for *Awake and Sing* displayed a young man in Depression-era clothes looming over a tenement, his empty pockets turned inside out. "I didn't know *that*."

"Well, now you do. He screwed us both."

He joyed her. He blissed her. James didn't want to hear anymore but Sherry kept talking. The street became more and more crowded as people rushed to make their curtain times. He dodged around them with Sherry nipping at his heels.

"Look. There's no reason to overreact..."

He turned down Broadway, shoulder to shoulder with people, and tried to lose himself in the crowd.

"It's really none of your business," she said. "I don't know why you're getting so upset."

"Weren't you just coming on to me?" They stopped at Forty-Third Street, six people deep waiting for the light. "Haven't you been coming on to me for weeks? Didn't you kiss me in the fish shack?"

"So I got drunk and slept with Roger. So what? You don't have a claim on me."

"I wouldn't want to claim you."

A family of possible Mormons, all carrying bags from the M&M Store, slowly began inching away.

"Don't judge me." She poked him in the side. "You slept with him too."

The light changed, and a couple in matching Hard Rock Cafe caps gave them dirty looks. The crowd thinned a bit at the subway station, where he hoped she would leave him. But she kept following. Across the street, signs were up at the New Amsterdam: out with *The Lion King*, in with *Mary Poppins*.

"You have no right to act all morally superior when you did the same thing."

He stopped in his tracks and turned around. "I didn't lie about my feelings. I didn't lead you on and make you believe something that didn't exist."

"Who says I was lying?"

People swirled around their little blood clot in traffic. Sherry stood with a hand on her hip. "After our lunch, you never asked me out. You ignored me at work. There was no follow-up. I thought it was because you had changed your mind."

"No. It was because I heard what you told Roger about me." With that little bombshell, he dropped the mic and walked off. Across the street was a giant hole, surrounded by wooden barricades. Something used to be there, but now it was gone; he couldn't remember what it was.

"What are you talking about?" The click of her heels sounded behind him.

He turned around. "My hairy legs like a carpet. I sweat like a sprinkler. Blech. I heard it all." He turned to go but the light changed and traffic on Eighth Avenue started whizzing by.

"What were you doing? Spying on Roger and me?

"I was in the bedroom. Roger tried to tell me you weren't into me, but I didn't believe him. So he set it up so I could hear with my own ears."

"Such a great friend." She tossed a hand to the sky.

He crossed the street. The Port Authority loomed to his left. He wished he could hop on a bus and leave the city. Just like he left Ann Arbor. A new place. A fresh start. Maybe Santa Fe, where he could meditate in the desert and sell turquoise jewelry to witchy women with leathery skin.

"Could you just stop for a minute?"

He kept walking.

"Goddamnit. I have something to say, and I can't say it chasing you down the street."

He paused in front of a church. Leaned against its wrought iron fence, and studied the red bricks.

"Okay. Listen." She fingered the ankh between her breasts. "I said those things to make Roger think you were a dork. I know it was mean, but I was so infatuated with him I would've said anything. I didn't really believe it. I was just trying to make him lose interest in you."

"And what are you doing now?"

She expelled a long breath and gave another one of her dog-shakes, as if to roll off all the guilt and responsibility sticking to her. "Roger played us both. Don't you see that—he played us both."

James studied the stone archway of the church. A pigeon rested on its precipice.

"Anyway. I'm sorry," she said. "I didn't mean to hurt you. I just hope we can still work together without hostility."

"It doesn't matter."

She leaned with him on the fence and fanned her legs with the hem of her dress. "God, it's hot." She had a small bruise on her inner thigh.

James felt guilty for making her chase after him. And then he realized she had been running down the street for blocks, falling all over herself, trying to get his attention.

On the corner was a Papaya Dog. She shielded her eyes with a hand and looked in its direction. "I'm going to get a juice. You want one?"

"I'll get it. You paid for dinner."

He got the drinks and they headed toward the river, pursuing what little breeze there was. They sipped their juices in silence. Sherry followed by his side, forgoing confrontation for contemplation.

They passed parking garages and auto body shops, car washes and storage facilities. Several empty lots had been recently demolished and awaited redevelopment. Closer to the water, two new condo projects, twenty to thirty stories tall, sliced up the sky. Buyers on the river side had the view, and those on the other side looked down on a wasteland of warehouses and former crack dens. It was the New York version of a subdivision.

He didn't know whether to trust Sherry. It was flattering to believe she said those things out of interest in Roger rather than disgust for *him*, but it made her a rather dishonest and vengeful person. It seemed the more you got to know someone, the more awful they became. Everybody had ulterior motives. Everybody was playing a role. By the time you became familiar with a person, you had a hundred reasons to despise them.

They arrived at the river, where the sun chopped the water into diamond lights. Across the water, the towers on the Jersey shore looked like citadels guarding a prosaic, less treacherous world. They held the metal railing and watched people paddle in rented kayaks. Sherry's hair was loose and caught the breeze; it pin-wheeled around her face, catching in the corners of her mouth. On her shoulder rested one solitary freckle. It made the smooth skin surrounding it all the more creamy, reminding him of the relationship between beauty and imperfection. Or more precisely, the tradeoff. Maybe he needed to start dating the deformed and misshapen. He wondered if he was spiritually enlightened enough to appreciate the elegance of a severed limb. Or to be enraptured by the mottled skin of a burn victim.

The Buddha said: *When a man's passion is aroused nothing prevents him from ruining himself. Even jumping into the jaws of a tiger.* Was he ruining himself with Sherry or just acknowledging his body's reactions? Maybe passion was the only honest emotion. Pheromones talking to other pheromones. Optic nerves inducing hormones. Hormones increasing blood flow, accelerating heartbeats, engorging tissue—these things happened irrespective of moral conduct. Desire might be the one pure experience between people.

He leaned down and kissed her. Her lips were sticky from the papaya juice, but they opened for him. Her arms came around, and he felt the cold press of her paper cup against his spine. She was kissing him back. He moved closer, locking her tiny frame into his body as a chain locks into a gear.

"Let's go back to my place," he said, surprised at his boldness.

"Okay." She tossed her drink into a trash can.

The car was only a few blocks away; he hurried to it, walking slightly ahead of Sherry. Before he unlocked the door, he pushed her against the car and tried to kiss her again. She moved away, crying "hot," and tapped the burning fender. He thought she might leave, but she put her hands around his neck and kissed him again.

He drove in a blood-engorged trance—his dick practically steering the wheel by itself, the air-conditioning blowing full blast, cooling his hand on her bare thigh. They sped over the Brooklyn Bridge and into the brownstoned streets. He found parking in front of his apartment, as if the universe wanted to help him consummate the relationship. He walked around the car to open her door, but Sherry was already out and looking at the buildings. He had the urge to take her hand and walk her down Court Street so all his neighbors could see him with a beautiful woman, but decided he needed to close the deal first. Sherry might change her mind and slip into the subway.

Inside the apartment, he turned on the air conditioner, which came to life with a reluctant groan. He went to shut the windows and heard Sherry kicking off her shoes. When he turned around, she was standing on his meditation rug naked except for a pair of navy blue panties. She walked over to his mandala, which was made of a circle of Buddhas within a square within a circle within another square. He'd never had a naked woman in his apartment before, and he watched fascinated, as if studying a wild animal, riveted by what it might do next: *the naked woman is smelling a candle; the naked woman is picking up a book; the naked woman is lifting her leg and pointing her toe, her back slightly arched—this is the signal that she is ready to mate.*

"Would you like a glass of wine?" he said.

"No thanks."

The naked woman has now spied something interesting on the work table and heads in that direction.

He couldn't let her see his puppets. He rushed through the veldt of his studio apartment and scooped her into his arms. He kissed her, trying to find just the right amount of pressure between passion and plunder. His hand ran down the smoothness of her back, stopping at the rough edge of her panties.

They shuffled to the bed, where she scooted against the headboard and studied the sheets, tracing her finger as if some code was written in Braille. He shucked off his pants and shirt and joined her. The air conditioner blew cool air across their bodies. Her nipples were the color of bubblegum. He circled them with a finger, then his tongue. There was so much of her body to explore, whipped cream mounds of flesh, clefts and indentations of silky skin. A wet spot was forming on his boxer shorts and he hoped Sherry didn't notice. But she had her eyes closed, swaying her body with his touch.

He tasted her, from the powdery residue of her deodorant to her per-fumed navel. Just the friction of his cock through his underwear was bringing him close. He slipped off her panties and applied himself. She turned her face into the pillow and made breathy sounds. He felt like he was servicing some delicate machine that needed just the right cal-ibration. He worked his tongue in different motions, imagining he was an expert watchmaker presented with a valuable movement. He tinkered with the mainspring, adjusted the escapement, and finally worked his way to the tourbillon, that delicate mechanism that regulated the other gears and wheels.

Much was riding on his ability to set tongue into motion, not the least of which was to affirm his heterosexuality. He listened carefully to her breathing, her sounds, the whisking of her hands across the bed sheets. He tried to find the right oscillation, the perfect balance of friction and suction. At one point, her thighs closed around his head and he thought he'd achieved the desired results, but she was still distant. He might as well have been some oil change mechanic down in the pit servicing her parts. Perhaps this was how you experienced desire without attachment.

He scooted up to kiss her, and she turned away, giving him her artic-ulated neck. He asked about a condom and she pointed to the floor: "In my purse."

When he returned, ready for the moment that would unite or unravel them, she was on her stomach with her ass slightly raised. This was not what he'd anticipated, but he followed instructions. She bucked against him silently. It was over in less than a minute. He held onto her hips and felt everything drain out of him.

She curled onto her side. He snuggled up behind her, a big spoon to her difficult fork. He placed his chin above her head, his arm light-ly draped around her. The first time was always awkward. He felt each breath bringing him in contact with her warm back. His darker arm on her translucent white skin. His hairy legs next to her smooth suppleness. He felt joyfully debased—an animal ravaging an angel, their disparate substances merging and creating some kind of powerful amalgam. He was the beast, befouling the beautiful princess. His penis rose at the thrill, and he tucked it between her thighs. He was the lowly worm, crawling on the leafy bounty of her tree, the ogre, who had captured the maiden and hidden her in his lair.

His mind raced through a dozen scenarios trying to comprehend his feelings. One thing was clear: finally, after all this waiting, he had what he'd desired. And predictably, he still wanted more. His hands caressed her thighs; his breath fluttered through her hair. He realized this could be the start of a great romance, or the last gasp of a toxic fixation. The capitulation of a lonely woman, or the dawn of her burgeoning passion. He could believe it to be whatever he wanted. And, at least in this moment, believing would make it so.

They lay side by side, essentially two strangers, face to back—a horizontal line. Waiting for a new life to start or an old romance to end. Waiting for the film to develop on that fuzzy, unresolved image they carried inside of a perfect love. Mommies who didn't scorn and daddies who didn't leave. The long-sought-after beloved who would heal their psychic wounds, validate their insecurities and bring them steaming hot cups of happiness.

It was hard to give up on something you had wanted for so long. He pulled her into him and said: "Would you like to meet my parents?"

The next few days were frustrating. At work, Sherry was friendly, but not overtly so. He never knew where he stood or what was appropriate. And yet, he couldn't stop thinking about her. His hands still felt the heaviness of her breasts, his head, the clasp of her thighs. He recalled her taste, and the deep hollow between her breasts. When she leaned on the bar, he could barely stop himself from reaching out to touch her. As he printed the menus for the week, every dish reminded him of her, from the burnished figs to the prosciutto-wrapped melon. As he ran food from the kitchen, the strawberry dacquoise resembled her pink nipples, slightly rough and dimpled. The spun sugar on the chocolate torte called to mind strands of her blonde hair. The rack of lamb, her meaty thighs. All the objects of his world were infused with faint traces of Sherry's body. Even his speech couldn't escape her. Setting down plates at a table of senior ladies, he invited them to have a "bon appé-tit." When discussing the reservations with Bart, he told him, "We have seventeen breasts on the books." It was like being fifteen all over again.

Sherry, for her part, kept up a steady stream of smiles and banter, but every time he tried to steer the conversation to asking her out, she circumvented him and flitted away. He didn't want to force the issue or appear desperate, even though he daily clothed himself in rags of desperation. He wished he could ask Roger's advice, but that would only provoke his wrath and ruin their friendship. It might appear insensitive to have moved from Roger to Sherry in a matter of weeks. It might even *be* insensitive. He'd never had so much sex in such a short period of time; he didn't know the protocols. Was there a proper grieving period the body had to endure before making itself receptive to someone else? Maybe they made a cleansing bath bomb for such a circumstance—eau du slut.

The phone rang and he grabbed it with a sweaty palm. "Bartholomew. Bon Whore ... Bonjour. Excuse me."

For staff meal, Eric made white bean soup. When James sat down, he noticed that Roger and Sherry were stoically slurping their soup, looking past each other, continuing their feud. He was still a bit miffed that Roger hadn't told him about his relations with Sherry, and even a bit jealous about those relations, but he didn't want to bestir their calm waters with a boatload of questions.

Before he could lift a spoon to his lips, Sherry asked, "James, do you think we could fit Trish's couch into your hatchback?"

"How long is it?"

"I don't know. When I lie on it, I still have lots of room below my feet."

"I suppose. Where does she live?"

"She's in Prospect Heights, only about a mile from our new place. We're moving on Thursday." She shot a quick glance at Roger. "If you come in the morning, you can help me put together my bed." She rubbed something from the corner of her mouth. "I'm having it delivered."

James flashed on Sherry lying on a bed, and was too overcome to speak.

"How's the movie going?" Roger interjected.

Glad for the change in subject, James turned to Roger. "I'm getting used to the new equipment. The new camera is amazing."

"I knew Erin would fix you up."

He went on to explain his opening shot when he felt a foot creeping up his pant leg. He looked at the two people at the table and believed it could be any one of them. Roger was scraping his bowl with a spoon; Sherry was munching on a slice of baguette. He still found it incredible that they were interested in him. Even more so that he had slept with both. He briefly wished he could put Roger's brain in Sherry's body and thereby form some sort of synthesis of the ideal mate.

Roger started talking about how Hitchcock filmed *Rope* in what looked like one seamless shot, and the foot moved further up his calf. He wondered if he could know its owner just by its touch. Was there a difference between a man's and a woman's touch? He thought it was much more about the energy of the person. Roger had a more direct touch, while Sherry's was playful and evasive. The tentativeness of the foot gave Sherry away. That and the fact that the foot wasn't wearing socks and Roger had already put on dress shoes. He wondered if the touch was more erotic because it was attached to Sherry's body, a body he so desired. Couldn't Roger's foot massaging him be just as arousing?

Sherry took out a vial from her pocket and rubbed some oil on her wrists. "Here. Smell this." She put a hand under his nose. "Tell me what you think."

"Lavender and orange?"

"I'm thinking it would be a great yoni oil. Would you like my pussy to smell like this?"

At the mention of Sherry's pussy, he felt a burning in his cheeks.

"Would be an improvement over liver and onions," Roger threw down his napkin and left the table.

During a break in their shift. He noticed Sherry going downstairs and followed her into the walk-in fridge. She was getting cartons of milk, her cheeks already flushed from the cold.

"Do you need some help?"

"No. I have it." She held a quart of milk in each hand.

He grabbed her milk carton hands and bent down to kiss her, but she turned aside. "Not here. Someone could walk-in."

There was no better place for a walk-in than in a walk-in fridge, so he released her. "I'm going crazy not being able to touch you."

"Are you?" She tilted her head and studied his face. "You don't look crazy?"

"I followed you into a refrigerator."

"I'm no psychiatrist, but that's not a committable offensive."

"You're still coming on Sunday to meet my parents?"

She bounced the cartons and studied the floor. "Isn't it a bit early for me to be meeting your parents?"

"I know, but they never come to New York and I want them to see you." She was nodding her head but her body was saying no. "And you'll never guess. I managed to get a reservation at Fu Bar."

"Wow. How'd you swing that?"

"Bart knows the chef. He said if anyone's palate deserves to taste Fu Bar, it's yours."

The cartons were starting to slip from her arms; he moved to take them, but she backed away and held them against her chest.

"Are you losing interest?" He folded his hands behind his head, as if expecting a blow. "Just tell me now. Don't string me along."

She stepped around him and opened the door. "I'll come to your place tonight."

James glided through the rest of his shift, stealing glances at Sherry and trying to contain his excitement. As soon as he could close the restaurant, he left the paperwork unfinished and rushed home to make his apartment ready. He turned on the air conditioner, changed his sheets, took a quick shower, and hid the Roger and Sherry dolls in their boxes. When Sherry knocked on his door, his hand trembled on the knob.

"You're here." He hugged her and felt the soft crush of her breasts. She was wearing shorts and a tank top, and her back was damp with sweat from the walk from the subway. "Mmm. You feel good."

"If only you knew."

"What's going on?"

She positioned herself in front of the air-conditioner. "I'm freaked out about moving in with Trish. She just told me she wants to bring her sister's cat to the apartment."

"I thought you liked cats."

"I do but she never mentioned it before. What else is she going to spring on me?" Her hair was loose and she pulled it off her neck. "I never lived with a roommate. The whole thing is stressing me out."

"Can I get you something to drink?" He motioned to a bottle of wine he picked up on the way home.

"Just water." She walked around his work table, where he'd started to build the interior of the movie theatre. His new lights were focused on the set.

He handed her the water and sat on the bed. The only other place to sit was on his work stool, and he waited for her decision. "So you've never had a roommate? Not even in college?"

"I never went to college. In Ottumwa, you didn't need roommates."

"What about when you came to New York?"

"I met Magda a few weeks after being in the city." She fingered one of the movie audience puppets.

"And you lived with her until you met Sean?"

"Yep."

"Maybe you should just think of Trish as a new lover, and then it won't seem so strange."

"I miss Sean." She lowered her head, and he couldn't tell if she was about to cry.

He went over and put an arm around her. "I know. When your ex takes a new lover, it feels like breaking up all over again." During slow periods at work, they had discussed her humiliation at Sean's art show, for which he felt genuine compassion. It humanized her and made her even more attractive.

"But that's the thing, we didn't really break up. I moved out to give him space." She broke free of his embrace and paced the floor. "It was a warning, you know? To change his behavior."

"It's a process."

"He was supposed to miss me, and chase after me, and beg me to come back." She walked to the sink and filled her glass with water. "Not replace me with some woman he had waiting in the wings." She took a long swallow of water. James thought she might throw the glass, but she set it in the sink.

"I'm sorry he hurt you. I'll never hurt you like that."

She walked over to him. "You wouldn't, would you?" She wrapped her arms around him and put her head on his chest.

He stroked her hair.

"Fuck Sean," she said. "Kiss me."

They kissed. She jumped up and wrapped her legs around him; he struggled to hold her. They landed on the work table, but he thought better of it and brought her to the bed.

"Fuck him out of me." She slipped off her top and undid her bra.

He nuzzled her breasts and she grabbed his head. "This is …an exorcism. You understand?" He didn't, but nodded his head. She slid down her shorts. "Get inside me."

He shucked off his pants and did as told.

"Squeeze my tits." He caressed her. "Harder. Push them together." He applied more pressure. "Fuck you, Sean. Fuck you."

He kneaded her breasts, her beautiful breasts, until they felt like stones in his hands.

"I'm a whore. A slut. Garbage." She hit the mattress with her fist. "Say it!"

He tried to form the words, but they dried in his mouth. Whatever he thought about Sherry—beautiful, creamy-skinned, Sherry—it wasn't that.

"Say it!"

"Whore. Slut. You … garbage bag." He blew out a regretful stream of air.

"Pull my hair." He entwined his fingers in her hair. "Pull it. Sonofabitch."

He yanked her glossy strands, jerking her head sideways, all the while trying to keep the rhythm in his hips, which was a bit like walking and chewing gum at the same time.

"Faster. Machine gun fire." He grabbed her hips, but the gun analogy made him queasy. The thought of using his dick as a weapon caused it to recoil. He was doing something wrong. Violence against women. The slogans from marches he attended with Joanne flashed into mind: *Take Back the Night; Real Men Don't Hurt Women; No Excuse for Abuse.*

"Faster." She shook her head back and forth. "Fuck you, Sean. Fuck Post-Its. Fuck binder clips. Fuck goddamn Rubik's Cubes." She raised her head. "Slap me."

Holding her hips didn't exactly give him a free hand. Even if he wanted to, the coordination of such a movement was beyond him.

"Slap me."

He released her hips and fumbled forward on the bed, pushing his hand into her face.

"Come on, Moron."

He tapped her face.

"Harder."

He did it again, this time leaving a little red coloration. His dick stiffened, which made him even more uncomfortable. *Take a Stand. Violence is Never the Answer.*

"Fuck your mother." She thrashed and kicked, all the while he tried to keep his rhythm. "Hit me again."

He gave her a tap on her head because he couldn't stand to see a red mark on her face.

"Hit me, you bald sonofabitch."

Love shouldn't hurt. Break the Cycle. Don't Hit, Use Your Wit. He backhanded her face and her head swung into the mattress.

"That's it. You pig. You shit. You maggot."

He didn't know if she was talking to Sean or to him. She thrashed around some more, and he found himself grabbing her hands and pinning her to the bed. Naturally and spontaneously. It happened so fast. He only heard the sound of their bodies slapping together. His sweat dripped on her face.

"Choke me."

This request stopped his rhythm, and he looked in her wild eyes.

"Choke me. Please." She looked so innocent. So beseeching. Like he would be doing her the greatest favor. He wrapped a hand around her neck. *Stand up to Abuse. Women Deserve Better.*

She clutched his hands. "Tighter."

Her face started to turn red. He relaxed his grip, but she croaked out "tighter." He brought both hands to bear. Her beautiful face was turning shades of crimson and purple. Shades of Daffy Duck without his feathers. *Love Doesn't Look Like a Bruised Body. Violence is a Choice You Don't Have to Make.* He was losing his erection.

He removed his hands and she rose up. "Okay. Pound him outta me." She turned over on her knees. Somehow he managed to keep going.

She bucked against him and panted. "Fuck you, Sean." It seemed she was reaching an end. He hoped so, because his dick was starting to bend in the middle.

She was grunting in fits and bursts. "Sonofabitch. You shit. Douchebag motherfucker. Come on. Come on." Again, he didn't know if she was talking about Sean, him, or all men in general. But it seemed she was in another world, another place that he couldn't reach. He wasn't part of this interaction. It existed between her and all the men who had hurt her. He was just a vehicle to get her to a place. A place so abject and painful, he was relieved not to be part of it.

When it was over, she fell on her side and he held her from behind, wary of this violent animal he had perhaps subdued but not tamed.

They stayed this way for a long time, letting the cool air-conditioned air dry the sweat on their skin. As he was drifting off to sleep, he heard her say, softly to herself, "I'm so alone."

16: Green with Envy

The speaker stepped down from the makeshift platform and the crowd burst into tepid applause. Behind her was a dais artfully stacked with copies of Shawmut's new restaurant guide. This must've been the fifth speaker of the afternoon, and Roger's hands were getting chapped from clapping. He would need a tub of shea butter to recover. The book designer was now waxing orgasmic over deckle edges and French flaps, all of which sounded to Roger vaguely pornographic. He stuck his deckle edge into her French flaps and nine months later, a book was born. After the book designer, someone with the lavish title of Director of Integrity got up to speak. Roger was starting to wonder if the hundred or more people gathered in Green's patio garden, were all employees of Shawmut soon to take the stage. He did notice several Brooklyn chefs in the mix, and a couple of famous ones from Manhattan. He fanned himself with his program and tried to shield his eyes from the afternoon sun. Carrie and Aaron were beaming, while instructing their waiters how to navigate through the crowd. They passed around an assortment of bites from Green's menu: potato and goat cheese kabobs, pot-stickers on sticks, little mac and cheese biscuits—the most comfortable of comfort foods

Roger was waiting for the signal from Bart to launch his plan into action. He had rented a van to transport his specially made hors d'oeuvres. At the appropriate time, he was going to have Roger and Sherry disseminate his delicacies, as a "gift to Green and wonderful people at Shawmut." Roger questioned the reception of such a ploy, but Bart convinced them it would be good advertisement; he could boost his own brand while upstaging Green at the same time.

A shadow spilled into the corner of his vision, and he noticed a waiter standing next to him with a tray of pot-stickers and a naughty smile. Roger had previously clocked his defined pecs pushing against the fabric of his white shirt, and they'd exchanged a few appraising glances. Now face to face, the waiter spoke first.

"Are you working the party?" He must have been referring to Roger's white shirt and black pants, the collective uniform of indentured server-tude.

"I've another gig after this," Roger said, which was sort of true.

"Want to try one?" The waiter offered up his tray.

Roger shook his head. He estimated a sixty to seventy percent chance of spilling dumpling grease on his shirt and didn't like the odds. "Do you work for Green?"

"Naw. I'm at Brooklyn Events. They called me in for this."

"Good thing. I hear Carrie and Aaron can be tough."

"No kidding." He bowed his head and lowered his voice. "They caught me eating one of the kabobs and told me they would take it out of my pay." He pushed through the crowd, giving Roger another naughty smile, this time exposing a metal tongue ring.

Across the patio, against the wooden fence, Sherry and Bart were whispering. She was nodding and touching his arm with little taps. Her attitude toward Bart and James seemed to have grown in inverse proportion to her attitude toward him. She'd spent the week moving her things to her new apartment, acting all sullen and bad-tempered about it, as if Roger should have forsaken his play rehearsals to help her. Yet still, his medicine cabinet overflowed with her elixirs and potions, which she kept promising to collect. Every time he went to brush his teeth, he had to move aside bottles of eucalyptus oil and tubs of beeswax. Though she'd only come with a few bags of clothes, over the course of her stay, Sherry had bought pillows and dish towels and various healing crystals. He was still finding chakra stones in his couch cushions, and the odd Mala bead stuck in the cracks of the floorboards.

Finally, things looked to be winding down. Carrie and Aaron took the stage in matching striped chef's uniforms. Carrie commandeered the mic while Aaron stood one foot behind and to the left. "We feel so grateful to be hosting this event. We're proud to be a small part of the great Brooklyn restaurant renaissance." She waxed gracious for several minutes, humble-bragging her way through a list of people and events. At the end, she received ample applause, mostly because people were glad for the speeches to be over. As she was stepping down, Bart hopped up on the stage and gave the signal to Roger and Sherry.

He grabbed the mic and announced: "I just want to say thank you to The Shawmut Guide and Carrie and Aaron for hosting this wonderful event. In appreciation, I have some food coming out from my restaurant, Bartholomew. It's my gift to Shawmut and the community…"

That's all Roger heard as he and Sherry rushed outside to the van, where James was waiting with two trays of food. He took a tray of foie gras on crostini with blueberry compote. Sherry's tray held duck meatballs on skewers. There were more trays waiting, with even more extravagant delicacies: white truffle mushrooms, Kobe beef, miniature lobster rolls, Serrano ham and watermelon, blue crab bisque in paper cups. All designed to make Green's comfort food look like a drive-thru happy meal.

James followed behind Roger and Sherry, carrying more trays. When he got to the patio, Bart, Carrie, and Aaron were in a heated conversation, trying to keep civil in front of the Shawmut officials. Aaron kept glancing around, scowling at the people gobbling up Bart's food. James handed off two more trays to Roger and Sherry and ran back to get more. Excitement filled the air. This would go down in New York restaurant lore as one of the most brazen rivalries since the lesbian lovers of Camellia Bakery split up to form competing cupcake companies.

James handed off two more trays and heard Carrie and Aaron in the kitchen.

"No one's going to remember our food," Carrie yelled. "You have to get something out there from us."

"I don't have anything prepared."

"Find something."

"Besides," said Aaron, "anything we put out now they'll think is from Bartholomew."

As James was coming back with more trays, Carrie stormed out of the kitchen and accosted him. "Stop right there. You can't bring that into my restaurant."

James raised the trays over Carrie's head and handed them off to Bart, who gave them to Roger and Sherry. "Carrie. Dear sweet Carrie." Bart fixed her with his biggest, most condescending smile. "This is my gift to you. I want to you to receive it in the spirit in which it was intended."

"I know the spirit in which it was intended, you oversized moron. You're intending to humiliate us."

"Look." Bart pointed to people eating his hors d'oeuvres. "They love the food. Everyone is happy. It's a win/win. Have a white truffle mushroom and relax." He went back out to shake hands and received more pats on the back.

When James came back, Carrie had her waitstaff in the kitchen and was confabbing with Aaron. "Hand me a tin of sardines."

"What are you doing?"

"If they think it's Bart's food. We'll give them Bart's food." She started cubing a brick of cheese and put the cubes on crackers with pieces of sardine. "Sandy. Take these out to our guests"

"You can't serve that." Aaron said. "It's disgusting."

Carrie pointed to the patio and instructed her waiter to go.

James handed off the last of his trays, but kept his eyes on Sandy. She held her head away from the smell of sardines and tried to manufacture a smile. After truffle and foie gras, people were eager to try more, but the expressions on their faces ranged from deep puzzlement to shear disgust. Soon, more waiters were coming out with butter balls covered in grape jelly, dried penne stuffed with peanut butter, and whatever disgusting pairings Carrie could find in her cupboard.

Bart came striding back to James. "What's going on? Who's sending out that shit?"

"Carrie. She's trying to sabotage everything."

Just then a waiter walked by carrying what looked to be chocolate covered raw onions.

"We have to do something."

"Those are our last two trays of food." James pointed to Roger and Sherry.

Bart strode into the crowd, walked up to one of Carrie's waiters, lifted her tray and flung it over the fence. There were a few gasps, but not everyone noticed. When he tried to fling another tray, some pieces of peanut butter covered pasta landed in the hair of a few guests who shrieked in disgust. Carrie saw what was happening and went after Bart's trays. She took a tray from Sherry and tried to fling it over the fence, but it hit a patron in the head, and foie gras went flying into the faces of the surrounding guests. Meanwhile, Bart threw another tray, and chocolate covered onions hit another group of patrons in the eye. Soon, people were shrieking and rushing the door. In the melee, the remaining trays were felled, the dais toppled, and the Shawmut guides pummeled to the pavement, covered with Kobe beef and crab bisque.

Roger found a loose part of the wooden fence and pried it open to escape. The waiter with the tongue ring was standing nearby, visibly trembling and breathing heavily. He held the fence and motioned for him to come through. On the other side, the paved yard of the cell phone store next door provided refuge; it was littered with cardboard boxes and the odd bit of foie gras. The waiter collapsed against the fence. He seemed to be hyperventilating. Roger had seen enough movies where people were told to breathe into a paper bag, and found a small cell phone box and told him to breathe into it. After a few minutes, he calmed down. Roger brought him to a set of cinder block steps and helped him to sit.

"I think you might have saved my life," the waiter said.

"At least, I saved you from a foie gras in the face."

"I panic sometimes in crowds. I'm a bit claustrophobic."

"Not a good look for a cater waiter."

"As long as people aren't throwing trays at me, I'm usually fine." He gestured to the fence, and they listened to the rumblings on the other side. Aaron was saying, "Everybody remain calm." Carrie was quietly muttering, "You don't have to go" over and over. James texted that they were in the van, and Roger told him to leave without him.

"I'm Jordan, by the way."

Roger introduced himself, and Jordan told him about the time he had another panic attack. He was auditioning for the national tour of *Hairspray*. While the choreographer was taking his group through their steps, he started shaking so badly he accidentally hit one of the dancers in the face.

"I guess you didn't get the part."

"Not only that. The casting director didn't bring me in for another audition for over a year." He gazed at a spindly tree in the next yard and let his leg fall into Roger's. They shared more audition horror stories: forgotten lines, inappropriate roles, hyperbolic rejections—Roger had a ton. Occasionally, Jordan would laugh and press his leg into Roger's, and then take it back when Roger didn't respond. Eventually, they ran out of stories. Roger noticed the patio next door had become quiet. He peered through the slats of the fence and confirmed that everyone had gone.

"I've really enjoy talking," said Jordan.

"Me too." Roger held open the loose board so Jordan could enter the yard, but Jordan touched his shoulder and moved in for a kiss, which Roger deflected by pushing him through the opening.

The patio was trashed: tables upset and pots of herbs knocked over. They tiptoed past the kitchen where Aaron rocked a sobbing Carrie in his arms, and ran out the front door. They kept running until they stopped in front of a Pilates studio, where they exchanged numbers. Roger was content to have made a friend and didn't want to turn Jordan, however attractive, into a trick. He was tired of the endless cycle of flirt, sex, and forget. Was this a newfound maturity? Or just old age reducing his sex drive? He couldn't tell.

The next day, Sherry came to collect the remainder of her "potions." She and Roger were standing in the bathroom while she uncluttered his medicine cabinet, confiscating her tinctures and essential oils.

"Are you sure you don't want these?" She held up a baggie of brown stringy things. "It's orchid root. You grind it up and put it in someone's drink and they fall in love with whoever they see first."

"Is that what you gave to James?" He was trying to resist the urge to go back to his office and finish writing the press release, or any of the dozen necessary things he needed to do before his show opened next week.

"I didn't have to. But maybe you need it." She dropped them in the sink and continued stuffing the rest of her jars and bottles into a plastic grocery sack.

Friendships typically ran their course, and between Sherry and him, something had changed. Though sad to see their friendship end, he was also relieved. He'd seen it happen many times. A person doesn't give you what you expect, so you move on. Sherry had moved on. He'd done the same over an imagined slight, a slight disappointment, an unkind word. In this Internet age when friendship was just a click away, people moved through your life as a constant stream of information to be digested, discarded, or ignored. We curated our lives so we never have to face conflict or adversity. And no one person had any more value than the next one to come along. We lived in a perpetual cycle of being unsatisfied and waiting for the next best thing.

He leaned on the doorknob at a loss for words. Ever since their sexual encounter, things had been difficult between them. He thought it was temporary, and they would eventually laugh it off and go back to being friends, but she perceived it differently. At the time, he was too involved with his play to notice. How can we know what others are projecting onto us? And even if we know, what can we do about it?

"I have no one I want to coerce into love," he said.

She cocked her head. "Not even James?"

"I'm fine just being his friend."

She expanded her face in mock shock.

"Why make everything about sex?" He rubbed a spot of soap scum from the tile. "I can be just as close to him as his friend as I was as his lover."

She screwed open a jar and daubed some waxy substance on her lips. "Can you?"

They were practicing being casual while underneath bombs exploded and kittens were drowned.

"I'm tired of sex," Roger said. "Pursuing it. Writing about it. Everything. My next play is going to be about nuclear disarmament or Marxist ecology—there won't be a stiff prick in the house."

She held his glance in the mirror. "That's quite a change."

"People change." He gave a defensive smile.

"Good. Because I was worried about telling you." She casually examined the jar. "James and I have been seeing each other."

He put a hand on the door frame to brace himself for this news. "Seeing as in fucking?"

"Among other things."

"I figured something was going on." He wasn't going to give her the satisfaction of seeing him upset.

"He didn't mention anything about it?" She turned around and leveled him with a glance. "As a friend?"

"We don't just talk about you, Sherry." He folded his arms and kicked the wall with his toe.

"Well, I hope you're not angry with me." She was looking in the mirror, unclumping her mascara with her pinkie.

"That depends." He took a few steps into the hallway to create some space between them. "What are your intentions?"

"With James?"

"With James."

"What are you—his father?" She grabbed her sack and went to the kitchen.

He followed and watched her rummaging through the cupboards, searching for something. Probably ingredients to put into her cauldron. He fully imagined she would find a desiccated bat and hurl it at his feet.

"You're jealous, Roger. Do us both a favor and just admit it."

"I'm actually confused. Only a few weeks ago, you thought he was rather disgusting."

She gave him a big, defensive smile. "People change."

"Maybe not enough."

She continued to peruse the foodstuffs. "It was only a few weeks ago you thought he was a raving homosexual."

"Isn't he?" He straightened his spine, daring her to prove it.

She held up a bag of cookies. "Do you want these Chips Ahoy?"

"Take them out of my house. Please."

She gazed at Roger's dying ivy in the window. "You should water this." She filled a glass and watched the water pour into the plant. "I have to say, he's a very generous and attentive lover."

Roger flinched. He couldn't exactly claim the same experience. "And are you enjoying his lovemaking? His hairy legs and prolific sweat?"

"He's never going to be attracted to you, Roger. I'm telling you 'as a friend.' I wish you could just face the facts."

"I don't care who he's attracted to, so long as they don't hurt him."

She broke open the bag and took out a cookie, smiling silently to herself. "That was so mean what you did. Having him listen in on our conversation."

"I wanted him to hear the truth."

"Oh." She bit into a cookie. "What makes you think I would tell you the truth?"

"I don't know. I thought *we* were friends." He sat down, as this was turning out to be more exhausting than a badly acted Shakespeare. It seemed they were now at war over James, and the issue could never be resolved until one of them was declared the victor, and the other was writhing on the ground impaled on a sword.

She studied her cookie. "I like James. And he likes me. He really does like me." She looked deep into a chocolate chip as if James were in there smiling back at her. "And after Sean ... after you told me to leave Sean ... that's something I appreciate right now."

He ignored her little guilt bomb and stuck to the subject. "So, he's just a band-aid. And as soon as your wounds are healed, you'll be moving along."

"I'm sorry if you're jealous, Roger. But I'm into James. I wasn't before but that was because ..." She stopped herself and bunched up the cookie bag and threw it in her sack. "I don't know where it's going or what will happen, but he's introducing me to his parents on Sunday. I'm sorry if that's difficult for you to hear, but I thought you should know."

Roger gripped the sides of the table and let this news wash over him like the radioactive fallout from a nuclear blast. "I hope it works out for you."

"I like him. I really like him."

"I hope you do. For his sake."

"I'm going to go now." She twisted her sack and walked to the door. "Thanks for letting me stay. I appreciate all you've done. I hope we can still be okay at work."

Roger sat still and listened to her feet stomp down the hallway and the crinkling of her plastic sack. She said one last "goodbye" and then shut the door.

The edges of his table were sharp and surprisingly cold. Sherry had obviously made up a whole story about him: how he led her on, played with her emotions, used, deceived her. He wondered if she was making up another one about James: how much he loved her, was devoted to her, found her irresistibly attractive. Or was Roger the one making up a story? Just as Sherry was trying to surreptitiously coerce him into a romance under the guise of friendship, he was doing the same to James. He rested his chin on his fists. Whatever his feelings for James, he would have to put them aside. Sherry had won. Biology had won. He regretted ever thinking he had a choice in the matter.

After work that night, Roger took James to The Roxy, ostensibly to wish him well on his new adventures with Sherry, and release him from whatever romantic ties bound them together. Manhattans sat in front of them like amber soldiers ready to battle the demons of the night. After a few sips, James confessed the whole Sherry saga, including their disappointing domination sex. And though this presented a new light at the end of the tunnel of love, Roger was reluctant to follow it.

"What d'you think I should do?" James said.

The bartender was cleaning the soda gun, squirting little streams of Sprite over the bar mat. Roger took a sip of Manhattan and surveyed the empty barroom. He knew exactly what James should do, but wanted him to come to that conclusion on his own. "I don't know if I should be advising you on Sherry. We got into a little tussle when she was packing up her things."

"Oh yeah. What about?"

"What do you think?" Roger studied their reflection on the bar mirror. "You."

"Ah. What did she say?"

"She said she likes you. She really really likes you."

"And do you believe her?"

"It doesn't matter what I believe. What do you believe?"

"I wish I knew."

"Well, how do you feel? When you're with her."

James made his big Y-arms and shook his head. He didn't want to say out loud what he felt for fear it would become real.

"Did you enjoy the sex?"

"She's beautiful. The most beautiful woman I've ever been with."

"Yes, but was it enjoyable?"

"Touching her was like touching a goddess."

"And, did you like the sex with the goddess?"

"It was weird because I was so attracted to her, and yet I just felt ..." He let out a long stream of air.

Roger wiped a wet spot with his Bar Nap. "I had the same thing with Diego. The sex was empty, but he was so full of beauty."

"And you guys broke up."

"We break up, then get back together, then break up again." He twirled the liquid in his glass. He had recently found himself back in Diego's bed for a single night of sexual healing. Just a therapeutic to get him over James. And even though Diego had kept his drawer of dildos closed, it wasn't satisfying or restorative. "A person forgets. Emptiness becomes aloofness. Selfishness becomes introspection. Stupidity becomes naiveté. You make excuses. Invent scenarios in your head and you ..." he shrugged, "succumb to them."

James put both hands on the bar and peered into the wood grain. "You make a good couple. You have a lot in common."

"But we don't have anything in common. Not the important things. I kept thinking maybe there was some unexplored depth. Some hidden side. Some way to connect. But there wasn't."

"Uh huh." He didn't want to think about Roger and Diego. He figured they would continue their love/hate courtship for the rest of their days.

"It was foolish of me to think it could be different."

"Uh huh."

"Sex is the oracle. It tells you everything you need to know about a person. What they're capable of—their depths and desperations—their will and their willingness." He drained his glass dramatically and signaled for two more. "I know we're supposed to discount sex as something secondary, but it tells you all kinds of things about a person. It reveals what beauty hides. Listen to your body. If your body isn't feeling it, it's not right."

James was gripping his glass with both hands. "I guess."

"How does Sherry make you feel? When you're with her?"

"I don't know."

"Think. Not here." He pointed a finger at James's head. "Here." He touched his chest. "Does she make you feel loved? Protected? Valued? Seen? Desired? Expansive?"

"I don't know." He pushed his hand away. "Why don't you tell me how she made you feel."

"What are you talking about?"

"When you fucked her. How did she make you feel?" James wasn't planning on mentioning it but Roger's superior attitude provoked him.

The bartender brought their drinks, and Roger picked up his carefully and brought it to his lips. "Oh. She told you about that?"

James regarded their reflection in the bar mirror. "I wish *you* had."

"It happened after your fight with Sean." Roger gave a long, protracted sigh and set down his glass. "We were both drunk and ended up sleeping in the same bed. Sometime in the night, things happened." He slapped his hands on the bar. "It was just sex. I know you breeders get all worked up about it, but it wasn't that big of a deal."

"Did you tell *her* that?"

"Obviously, it meant more to her than it did to me." He looked at James. "I should've told you. I guess I didn't want to rub it in."

"So you have sex with people and it doesn't mean anything?"

"Sometimes."

"I can't do that. I have to have feelings for a person."

"You've only slept with four people, Isaac Newton. Talk to me in ten years."

"I don't want to sleep with a bunch of people. Not if it's empty."

Roger held his glass to his chest and sloshed around the amber liquid. "So every time you've had sex with someone, it was because you had feelings for them?"

"Yeah."

"Interesting. And which one was the best?"

"I don't rate my sexual experiences."

"Okay. Fair enough." Roger swiveled on his seat. "Which one made you feel the best? In here." He touched his own chest.

"I told you. I don't think like that."

"Maybe you should."

James stood up. "I'm tired. I'm going home."

"You haven't finished your drink."

He started walking to the door and then turned around and came back. He rested a hand on the bar. "Hey. Do you want to meet my parents on Sunday? I know you must be busy with your play and all, but I have reserved the chef's table at Fu Bar. I'm sure they could fit in one more."

"Fu Bar? Wow. How did you manage that?"

"Bart got me in."

"That's the hottest ticket in town. How could I refuse?"

"I have to warn you, Sherry's coming too."

"Ah. Well." Roger flourished his hand in a noblesse oblige gesture. "I will be on my best behavior then." He smiled.

"Okay. See you there. 7pm."

James left the bar and walked briskly down the street. The stagnant night air wrapped him in its humid cloak. No matter what time, New York always smelled to him like car exhaust and roasted peanuts. A mix of incongruities and contradictions—a soup his stomach couldn't digest.

17: Fu Bar

James and his parents were walking down Bedford Avenue, in the most hipster-y-hip section of Brooklyn. With all the flannel, work boots, and facial hair, it seemed like a dystopian version of the Wild West. Instead of ten-gallon hats, everyone wore big headphones; instead of moseying to the local saloon, everyone had a microbrewery in their closet. They passed young people with blankets spread on the sidewalk, selling everything from artwork to old cameras and vinyl records. An old-fashioned barbershop advertised straight razor shaves and mustache waxing. At several vintage clothing stores, outdoor racks displayed plaid shirts and pink Chuck Taylors. One would think he'd feel more comfortable surrounded by all the young people and their playful innovations, but he was an old soul at heart. Instead of stately brownstones with wrought iron fences and carved wooden mantels, Williamsburg contained a hodgepodge of asbestos-clad townhouses with aluminum awnings and air conditioners in their windows. Instead of double-decker baby carriages, people navigated with skateboards and ape-handled bicycles. Occasionally, one even spotted a unicycle. And everyone seemed to be wearing big plastic glasses. He adjusted his wire rims defiantly.

His parents kept a few paces ahead, discussing *Momma Mia*, the show he had taken them to last night. He knew they were more into Dylan and Joni Mitchell, but he thought they would appreciate music from relatively the same era. He was soon informed that the greatest American songwriters could not compare to Euro bubblegum pop. They hated the songs and laughed at the bourgeois marriage plot. It seemed he couldn't win with them.

His father now wore a yarmulke all the time, a black velvet one with a gold star of David emblazoned on its crown. It was the silk top hat of yarmulkes, and betrayed his working-class ideology. He'd stopped trimming his salt and pepper beard and let it grow long. He now resembled a friendlier version of Karl Marx, which, as a philosophy professor, was probably appropriate. He often talked about writing a layperson's book on Marx, which he would call *Communism for the Soul.* In spite of his fancy kippah and Tommy Bahama silk shirt, James was grateful that he hadn't abandoned his leftist leanings and turned into a Republican. Instead, he'd taken to making ambiguous jokes and obvious puns. A Shecky Greene cyborg had taken over his body. The man who taught him to sit cross-legged and meditate, the pacifist who put him on his shoulders at peace rallies, the professor who organized benefits to free Tibet, was now advocating for a religion that supported air raids and occupying lands with armed police, while at the same time making jokes about his wife's cooking. James felt he had lost a parent.

His mother also looked different. She dressed more extravagantly, something she attributed to keeping up with the women at the synagogue they now attended. Today she was wearing a fuchsia print blouse with clunky wooden jewelry. She also had started painting her nails a deep purple color. They walked arm in arm and James followed behind in his black wool pants and white shirt, a pale shadow compared to their colorful exuberance.

His father turned around. "So is this Fu Bar place meant to be a reference to the acronym?"

"Yes, but it also refers to the chef—Alex Fujiyama, whom everyone calls Fu."

"That's reassuring." His mother took his father's arm.

"I guess if you call your restaurant F.U.B.A.R., it lowers expectations."

"He was voted one of the best chefs in the country by Food and Wine," James said. He wondered if he was making another mistake by bringing them to such a trendy restaurant.

"So who are these people we're meeting?" his mother asked.

"Just people I work with. Friends."

"It's nice you have friends, Jamie."

His father leaned down and lowered his voice. "Why he wants to inflict them on us is another matter."

"I can hear you, you know," James said.

When they arrived at the restaurant, Roger was outside waiting. James was relieved to see he looked respectable in long pants and a button-down shirt. Sherry had texted that she would be late.

James's father offered his hand to Roger. "I'm Barry and this is my wife Barbara."

"Please to meet you," Roger said, just like a normal person.

Inside, the restaurant was a white box. The walls, tile, and tablecloths blended into each other and seemed to disappear. It was kind of like dining in a cloud. Plastic chairs in a slightly less glaring white were positioned in front of tables set with ivory bread plates and linen napkins. Against this backdrop, the colorful clothes of the patrons popped. In their bright colors, his mother and father resembled middle-aged anime characters. The host led them back to the kitchen where a chef's table had been prepared.

"We're eating in the kitchen?" His mother twisted her mouth.

"It's very exclusive," Roger said. "This way you get to see how they make everything."

"And watch if anyone spits in your food," said Barry.

The kitchen was another white space augmented with stainless steel appliances and metal racks. White-coated line cooks and sous-chefs worked at various stations chopping, sautéing, and grilling. The heat was cloying and fragrant with onions. They sat at a high table with a cloth, where a waiter wearing a long white apron was waiting. Due to his black pants underneath his apron, he looked to be hovering above the floor. "Hello. Welcome to Fu Bar. I'm Judson. Chef Fu will be joining momentarily to explain the menu for tonight. In the meantime, can I bring you sparkling or still?"

"Oh, I think still," Barry looked around the table and everyone nodded.

"Does the menu need explaining?" asked Barbara.

"From what I understand," said Roger, "it's different every night."

"Yes," said James. "The chef makes whatever he feels like cooking."

Barbara clapped her hands together. "Oh. That's exciting."

"But what if I don't feel like eating whatever he feels like cooking?" said Barry.

"Don't be a baby, Barry." Barbara straightened her necklace of geometric shapes. "It's an experience."

While the waiter poured the water, James noticed his knuckle tattoos. One set of fingers said: fist, the other: bump. He told him that one more person would be joining them soon.

"No worries. I'll tell Chef Fu."

After the waiter left, Barry said, "No worries. That's such an odd phrase. Who's worried? I'm not worried. Are you worried?"

"Not particularly," said Barbara. "But just in case you were, he's telling you not to."

"It's a bit condescending, if you ask me," said Roger. "Like someone telling you to calm down, as if you're freaking out."

"Exactly right," said Barry. "I don't need anyone telling me how I feel. That's why I have a wife." He smiled at Barbara, who rolled her eyes and sighed.

"So Roger. How long have you been in New York?"

"Let's see. I came for college, so almost twenty years now."

"I guess you've seen some changes."

"It's a completely different city. James and I were just walking in Times Square and I was pointing out all the porn theatres that used to be there."

James made his big Y-arm gesture. "Apparently, I missed a golden age."

"And what did you study?" said Barry.

"Acting. But I gave all that up. Now I write plays."

"Roger has a play opening in Brooklyn in a few days," said James.

"Oh. It's too bad we're leaving tomorrow. I'd love to see it."

A man in a pristine chef's coat and a white du-rag came to the table. "Hello. Welcome to Fu Bar. I'm Chef Fu." They had surmised that he was the chef since they had seen him walking around the kitchen dipping spoons into pots, offering instruction to sauciers, and examining every plate before it went out. He already had the allure of a minor celebrity, and his appearance at their table made them all the more giddy for it. "The theme for tonight's menu is…" He took a breath and stretched out his arms crucifixion style. "This is my body; I give unto you."

Barry whispered to his wife, "Did he say bounty?"

"I think he said body."

Chef Fu clasped his hands. He was a strongly built man in his early thirties with a thick ponytail protruding from underneath his du-rag. "If I'm a bit out of sorts tonight, you must forgive me. My girlfriend just left me." He paused, presumably for them to contemplate the sacrifice he was making just by being there.

"I'm sorry, dear," Barbara said. "How long were you together?"

"Fifteen months."

"That's heartbreaking."

"She said I didn't give enough of myself. So. I'm going to try … No. I'm doing it." He made a fist. "Tonight, I'm going to give to you what I couldn't give to her." He scrunched up his face and brought a hand to his mouth. James didn't know if he was going to cry or scream.

"That's all right, dear," said Barbara. "Go easy on yourself."

"No. I'm going to do it. Tonight's meal is dedicated to Baby Ganoush." He gazed into the distance longingly, as if Baby Ganoush was hovering somewhere over the table. Then he turned, hurried to one of his cooks, and whispered in his ear. The cook immediately stopped work and started bringing the chef ingredients from the shelves. Fu frantically mixed things in bowls, while they watched, mesmerized by the performance until Sherry walked in.

"Sorry I'm late. The guy came to install my Internet and I couldn't leave."

James stood up and pulled out her chair. She was wearing the same yellow dress with red peppers as at their lunch date. She looked at Roger and then shot daggers back at James. He made the introductions while Sherry slowly seethed in her chair.

"I'm so glad Jamie made friends in the city," Barbara said. "We were worried when he moved here that he'd be all alone."

"We take good care of him." Roger patted James's arm, staring directly at Sherry.

From the head of the table, Sherry scowled and looked around for the waiter. "Did they take a drink order yet?"

"I forgot to mention," James fingered the tablecloth. "They don't have their liquor license yet, so only non-alcoholic beverages."

"Now you tell us." Barry blew out air.

"I didn't think it mattered since you don't drink."

"Your father and I started having wine with dinner."

This was yet another change in his parents that James would have to accommodate. He was starting to wonder if he was sitting across from total strangers.

"James has been known to imbibe himself." Roger gave James's arm another pat. "We've spent many a night after work at the local bar, discussing the troubles of the world."

His father gave him a stern glace. His mother a smile.

Sherry stood up. "Excuse me. I have to find the restroom."

A few moments later, James felt his phone vibrate; Sherry was texting him to meet her outside. He told the table it was a text from Bart and that he had to call him. He left the kitchen and made his way through the restaurant past all the animated people.

Outside, the sun was diminishing into a gray twilight, unable to decide between night and day. Sherry was pacing the sidewalk, rubbing basil oil on her wrists. When she saw him, she stormed over.

"What's he doing here?"

"It was spur of the moment. We were drinking last night after work, and I just invited him."

"You know how I feel about him. You know what he did to me. Now I have to sit through an entire meal with him?"

"I'm sorry. I thought you two might make up."

"I will never make up with that user." Her cheeks were turning red and little pink blotches formed on her clavicle. "Why do you want him to meet your parents? I don't understand."

"They think I have no friends. I wanted to show them…"

"Is this some competition? Are you trying to pit Roger and me against each other? I'm telling you, I'm not competing with that gay narcissist."

"No. No. It's not like that. Roger and I are just friends now. I'm with you. You're the woman of my dreams." He put his arm around her and kissed the side of her head, glad for this new expression of jealousy. "Now, let's go back and have dinner. No pressure." He started to escort her to the door, but she stopped him.

"We can't go back together—they'll know I called you out."

"Okay. You go first. I'll wait a few minutes."

Sherry went back inside and James walked a few paces up the block. Some of the gates were already down for the night and he studied the graffiti: "Queen Andrea" in neon letters. "Boom" inside a cat's claw. He wished he had brought his cigarettes with him, but he didn't want his parents to know he smoked. What Sherry had said troubled him. Was he holding a competition? Putting Roger and Sherry together with his parents to see who was the better fit? Things weren't perfect with Sherry, but he wasn't looking for a way out.

When he got back to the table, the chef was serving the first course. "This is what I call Frozen Tears. Clear gelatin infused with twenty-four karet gold leaf. Enjoy."

Chef Fu bowed and walked away. Everyone studied the three tear-shaped dots placed in front of them. At certain angles on the white doily, they disappeared completely. On closer inspection, James could discern a single speck of gold in each. They dissolved in his mouth instantly.

"So that's what tears taste like," said Barbara. "I always wanted to know."

Barry regarded his empty plate. "Doesn't taste like much of anything, if you ask me."

Roger shrugged. "Maybe they taste like whatever we imagine them to taste like."

Barry pushed his plate to the side "Sherry. Tell us what you do outside of waitressing." She shot James a confused look. "Are you an actress? Artist? Electrical engineer?"

"Well, I make my own cosmetics."

"Sherry makes these amazing essential oils," James said.

"And don't forget soap," Roger interjected.

"I want to branch out into lipsticks and blush, but the recipes are difficult to master."

"That's wonderful," said Barbara. "Do you have a website? I love fancy soaps."

Sherry crossed her legs. "Everybody says I should get one, but I'm not up to speed on the tech."

"You have to hire someone," said Barry. "A colleague of mine did it for tutoring and he's raking in the cash."

Barbara clicked her purple nails on the table. "You'll have to tell us where we can find your products."

"Oh. I'm not at that stage yet. I'm mostly experimenting. You know, in my kitchen."

"She has a basil oil that's so calming. Show 'em." James fluttered his hands on her arm. "I know you have some in your purse."

"I'm sure they don't…"

"No. It's great." He turned to his parents. "You're going to love it. After I put some on, I felt a change right away. It's calming."

Sherry rummaged in her purse and handed Barbara a little blue bottle. "Smells delightful."

"Put some on your wrists," James ordered, and his mother tentatively daubed the oil.

"I feel calmer already." She held up her arms as if at gun point.

"If this means you can't raise your voice or get mad at me," said Barry, "let's order a gallon."

Sherry put the bottle back in her purse. "It's just something I do for myself, right now. Maybe one day, I'll ramp up production."

"Of course," said Barbara. "These things take time. But it seems you have a talent. Did you study chemistry in college?"

"Oh. I never went to college. I took a class in graphic design but that was just because my boyfriend at the time was doing it."

The parental faces froze, nodding in unison as they absorbed this information. There were probably worse things one could say to two college professors, but in the moment, James would have preferred Sherry to have confessed to grand larceny or a heroin addiction.

Sherry started to shred her doily into little bits. "When I first came to New York, I took some instruction in Wicca."

"WICCA?" said Barbara. "Is that a computer language?"

"No, dear." Barry put a hand on her shoulder. "The pagan religions."

"I was part of a coven. They were the ones who taught me about potions and elixirs. How to read Tarot and make astrological charts. Some of them study for decades to become high priestesses."

"It's a complex religion, for sure," Barry said. "A few years ago, there was a petition at Michigan to create a class. But nobody wanted to teach it."

"That was because one of the petitioners nailed a possum to the provost's door," Barbara said.

"Sherry's also studying for her real estate license," James interjected.

She looked at him askance and took a big drink of water. He realized his mistake, but before he could signal an apology, Chef Fu and Judson came waltzing in carrying trays, on which were several organically shaped bowls.

"This. I call Bitter Kisses." The chef set a bowl in front of each of them. "Peach and honey foam, infused with a hint of cardamom. First you get the sweetness of the fruit and then the sour aftertaste of rejection."

"Interesting bowls," Barbara said, looking around for silverware.

"They're hollowed-out plaster casts of the inside of my mouth. You bring it to your lips and drink." He demonstrates with an imaginary bowl. "Bon appétit."

Everyone gazed at their bowls, which, after the chef's explanation, now appeared decidedly mouth-shaped, rimmed with lips, featuring visible teeth and the vague outline of a tongue.

"Bottoms up." Roger kissed the bowl and the others followed.

Chef Fu hovered over them, beaming and excited. "You like?"

"That's some kiss," said Barbara.

"You can really taste the cardamom at the end," said James.

"Best kiss I've had all day," said Barry. "No offense, Barbara."

"Watch it. Or that may be the only kiss you'll have all night."

"You can buy these bowls in the gift shop on the way out." Fu hugged his tray. "They make great stocking stuffers for Christmas." He left and walked over to the massive stove and started pouring oil into a pot.

"I know what I'm getting everyone for Christmas." James smiled and executed his big Y gesture.

"That reminds me, Jamie," his mother said. "I suppose I should tell you now. I'm planning on converting."

"What? Your old VHS tapes?"

"To Judaism."

He pulled his napkin across his lap. "But you're an atheist." It always bothered him that his mother succumbed so readily to his father's whims and beliefs. She acclimated to Buddhism, faithfully followed baseball, and even sat through the socialist films of Ken Loach, all to please his father.

"It's more of a cultural thing."

"You can't convert to a culture."

His father stuck his finger into the mouth-bowl and scooped out a last dollop of foam. "It's more about the desire to connect to a community than a belief in a supernatural being."

"Your father wants to celebrate the Sabbath and needs a Jewess to light the candles. It's just easier if I convert. Either that or we ask Mrs. Bettelheim down the street to come live with us."

"Maybe then she'll stop complaining about our lawn." His father picked up the mouth-bowl and imitated Mrs. Bettelheim. "You gonna cut that grass soon?"

His parents exchanged a private laugh that reflected all of their hostile encounters with Mrs. Bettelheim.

"Isn't the bare minimum for acceptance into any religion a belief in its God?" James said.

"We go to a Reconstructionist temple. They're like the Unitarians." His mother flourished a painted hand. "Anything goes."

"So that's it? Throw away The Four Noble Truths? The Eightfold Path? The zendo and meditation?"

"We're not throwing anything away," his father said. "I still meditate and believe in the Buddha's teachings. Buddhist practices complement Jewish traditions."

"We're Bu-Jews." His mother made namaste hands.

"We're adding to our spiritual experience, not taking anything away."

His mother brushed imaginary crumbs from the table. "It's a new circle of friends for us. After thirty years, you have to change things up. And the potluck suppers at Temple Beth Zion are quite lively."

James pushed away his mouth-bowl. "You don't have to do everything to please him."

"I'm not doing it for him. I'm doing it so we'll have something to do together."

His father leaned back in his chair. "When you've been married for thirty years then you can talk."

"Well, I'm not converting."

"Honey, we don't expect you to." His mother reached across the table into the empty space in front of him. "We're proud that you still follow the Buddha's teachings. And our expanding beliefs shouldn't change that."

He rested his hand on hers for a moment. They'd always had a vocabulary of touch that could resolve disagreements much faster than words.

His father scratched his beard. "Maybe he can make a cartoon about it."

"Barry. Don't start."

An image flashed in his mind of a Buddhist monk wearing a black fur hat, ochre robes wrapped in a tallit. It would make a good animation. He was starting to see how traditions could be combined and melded. Things didn't have to be one thing or the other—they could be both—amalgamated—a little of each.

Judson came to the table and started placing spoons beside each person.

A palpable excitement rose at the prospect of food that wasn't gelatin or foam.

"And just to be clear," his mother said. "I'm not keeping kosher or any of that foolishness."

"I told you a dozen times no one is asking you to keep kosher."

"Or wearing wigs, or headscarves, or those ugly denim skirts with black stockings."

"Have you seen the women at Temple Beth Zion? The only denim they wear is two hundred-dollar skinny jeans."

"They're a very colorful group," his mother said to James.

Chef Fu appeared. This time with a bowl as large as a wash basin. Judson and another waiter followed with identical bowls, and set them in front of each person. If it wasn't for a few murky clouds floating in the broth, James would've thought it was water.

"This is called: I work so hard for you," said Chef Fu. "A reduction of onions, leeks, celery, and garlic. Enjoy." He and the other waiters walked off.

Roger peered into his bowl. "Is this supposed to be what I think it's supposed to be?"

"I'm guessing sweat," said James.

"Oh my." Barbara touched her face.

"Not his actual sweat. But figurative."

"Nothing like figurative sweat in a bowl to get my appetite going," said Barry.

He noticed that Sherry wasn't eating. He didn't know if she was seething over his lie about her real estate course or his parents' skepticism about her makeup line. He puckered his lips and gave her his best, I'm sorry face. She ignored him and picked up her spoon.

"It's actually quite good," said Roger. "He got a lot of flavor out of such a clear broth.

"I'm just hoping for solid food soon," Barry said.

"So, Roger," Barbara leaned across the table. "Tell us what your play's about."

"It's about the limits we place on ourselves. In love. Sex. Relationships." He stole a glance at James. "Whether through society or biology."

"You think biology plays a role in love?"

"I think sometimes we tell ourselves that biology made us a certain way—we're meant to love this kind of person, or be attracted to that kind of person—when in actuality, we're much more flexible."

Barry twirled his spoon. "Aren't we all just falling in love with our fathers and mothers as Freud said? After all, they're the people who taught us how to love."

"God, I hope not," said Barbara. "If Jamie's past girlfriends are any measure, I'm certain to be a castrating lunatic."

"Mom."

"No offense, Sherry."

"None taken." Sherry gave a devilish smile to Roger.

This was the first indication that his parents had assumed anything about his relationship with Sherry, and James was unsure about encouraging it.

"I used to believe we were hardwired in certain ways," Roger said. "That parents make the mold. Genetics runs the game. But now I think those strictures can be broken."

Sherry pointed a finger. "And you think you yourself have broken those … strictures?"

His parents exchanged a look, picking up on the undertones of hostility between Roger and Sherry.

"For instance," Roger said, addressing everyone at the table but Sherry. "I used to only be attracted to a certain type of guy. Someone with more muscles than brain cells. But then a certain person came along who wasn't muscular or conventionally handsome, but was so compelling that it changed everything for me."

"Sounds like your taste matured," Barbara said.

"Or deteriorated," Sherry said.

James registered the insult but just kept smiling. The waiters came to clear the plates.

"It's different for women," Barbara dabbed her mouth with a napkin. "We're not so focused on the physical. We look for something more substantial."

"Like a large bank account." Barry scanned the table for appreciation of his joke.

"Men are fixated on appearance," Roger said, handing his bowl to Judson. "That's our hardwiring. But sometimes we can overcome it. Don't you think so, James?"

There was an implicit threat in the question. Roger's next words might be: You didn't feel hardwired when you were sucking my dick. He assumed Roger and he had settled on friendship, but who knows what could happen if Sherry provoked him. For the sake of peace at the table, he attempted a neutral tone. "Sure. People overcome it. At certain times."

"Are *you* looking for something more substantial? Or do you think you'll settle for," Roger glanced at Sherry, "the conventional comfort of the status quo?"

He bristled at Roger's implication and looked to Sherry for guidance. She pulled on the shoulder strap of her dress and glanced at the floor, articulating her long neck. "I'm a pretty conventional guy," he finally said.

Roger nodded imperceptibly, his jawline becoming a triangular anvil. Sherry smoothed her dress and he felt blood rushing to his cheeks.

Chef Fu came to the table followed by his waiters. They set down plates with tiny slices of meat. "This I call ..." He leveled his palm in the air as if talking to his ex. "Shut Up and Listen to Me. Crispy beef tongue with ginger paste and red onion streusel. Enjoy."

Everyone regarded their plates. The tongue was sliced into strips and arranged in a small tongue-shaped oval. The ginger snaked through the strips with a smear of streusel on the side.

"What's the matter?" said Barry. "Cow got your tongue?"

Barbara held her knife and fork aloft. "I've never had a cow's tongue before."

"At this point, I'm so hungry, I'd eat a cow's anus."

Barbara took a small bite and made a face. "So tell us, Roger. What happened to this compelling person who changed everything?"

"Yes. What happened?" Sherry swirled a piece of tongue in her sauce. "I remember you telling me he was such an awkward, ugly loser that you couldn't believe you hooked up with him."

Roger wiped his mouth and returned his napkin to his lap. He leveled Sherry with a ferocious smile. "It's hard to explain." He rubbed his hands together and studied the length of the table. James followed his gaze to the sous chefs in the kitchen, stirring pots and grilling meats. The room was getting humid and sticky with cooking smells.

"It's like you're rummaging through your attic," Roger continued, "and you find a seashell necklace in an old box. It's just a plain shell on a chain, something you might find on any beach, but it belonged to your grandfather, who carried it over from Normandy. His good luck charm. He gave it to your grandmother as an engagement present, and she put it on a chain and wore it faithfully. You remember sitting on her lap and playing with that shell, and you have all these connections: breathing on it when she rocked you to sleep, its ridged surface wrinkling your face when you cried in her arms. And, all of a sudden, something quite mundane becomes full of meaning. It has nothing to do with what the shell looks like or its uniqueness, but it's because of the experiences the shell evokes. And those experiences transform the ordinary into something beautiful. And that beauty is created through emotions and inner connections."

James had never heard his secret wishes articulated so elegantly. Roger had captured exactly how he felt about beauty and how he'd always wanted a girlfriend to view him. He looked at Sherry, who was subtly shaking her blonde locks and narrowing her eyes.

She leaned forward. "You didn't change your hardwiring though. You're still attracted to men."

"True."

"If you had that experience with a woman, it would've been a change. But you didn't."

Roger folded his arms on the table and looked Sherry in the eye. "No. I didn't."

James felt like he was watching a car crash from the other side of the highway, with no way to stop the impending collision.

Chef Fu appeared with his waiters, each carrying dishes covered with silver cloches. "And for the main course." The waiters removed the cloches and a rich umami scent wafted up. "Take it. Take Another Little Piece of My Heart. Beef heart stew braised in a cabernet sauce with alphabet pasta." He brought his hands to his chest. "It's been my pleasure to serve you tonight. This meal has been painful but also extremely cathartic for me. Thank you for giving me the opportunity to process my grief."

"You'll love again, sweetheart," said Barbara. "Don't worry."

They all thanked Chef Fu; he bowed and left the kitchen. James wondered when his mother had started calling people sweetheart.

"Is there something spelled out in the bowl?" asked Roger.

James peered at the stew. "I think it says Alex + Baby G."

"Oh, that's sweet," said Barbara.

Barry forked a morsel of food. "I guess we can't deny that his cooking has a lot of heart."

The table erupted in varying groans, and everyone started to spoon their stew.

"Tell us what happened with the guy, Roger?" asked Barbara.

"Oh. Well. He moved on to someone else."

"I can't believe it. Why would he do that?"

"You'll have to ask him." Roger glanced at James. "I can be rather difficult, I'm told."

James released an acid bubble of relief. A spiral of gratitude went out to Roger for not revealing their sordid history to his parents.

"Difficult people are often the most compelling," said his father. "I have to keep reminding Barbara of that."

"Yes," said Barbara. "Often the difficult ones are the ones worth the trouble." She smiled at Barry.

Sherry sawed her heart into tiny bits. "In my experience, the difficult ones fuck you and then forget you."

His father raised an eyebrow and squinted. "Sounds like someone had a bad heartbreak."

"Let's not talk about heartbreak while we're eating hearts," said Barbara. "It's macabre."

They all chewed thoughtfully, trying to decide if what they were eating was good or just unusual.

"This particular heart," said Roger, "must have suffered a lot of heartbreak because it's exceptionally tough."

"Mine," said James, "must have suffered the breakup of the century. It's hard as a rock."

They both started laughing.

"Mine has been sued for alimony," said Barry. "It's lost all its flavor."

"Okay, boys. You don't have to eat it if you don't want to."

"Oh, I'm eating it," said Barry. "I'm starving."

"I've never been so glad for small portions," said Roger.

"Jamie. How's your film coming?"

"Good. Roger helped me find some deals on equipment and I've started filming scenes."

"That's wonderful."

"I couldn't have done it without his help. He's been working with me on the script too."

"Maybe he's the muse you need."

Sherry threw down her napkin and stood up. "You know what? I'm done. Why don't you two just keep sucking each other's dicks if you're so perfect together? I'm sick of bouncing between the both of you." She turned to James. "If you're bi or gay or whatever—just own it. It's 2006. Nobody cares. Certainly they sure don't." She gestured at his parents. "I'm tired of being your beard. Your ego boost. Or whatever you think you need from a woman because you're too scared to get it from a man. And you." She pointed at Roger. "Stop sticking your dick in women if you're really into men. We don't want to be your friend. Or your dress-up doll. Find another plaything. I'm done with the both of you."

She marched away. All of the sous chefs and line cooks stopped their stirring and grilling to watch her walk out.

"Excuse me," James said. "I have to take care of this." He placed his napkin on the table as an offer of apology and left.

Roger stared deep into his beef heart, afraid to face James's parents. It took a while before the kitchen clatter of knives chopping and spoons clanging finally resumed. When it did, Barry said, "See. I told you she had some heartbreak."

"She had something all right," said Barbara.

Roger blew a long stream of air over his plate. For once, he was too stunned to speak.

Barbara clapped her hands and rubbed them together. "It doesn't matter. Whatever's going on between the three of you, it's none of our business. I don't care if my son is gay, straight or bisexual, I just want him to be happy."

"Of course. And I feel the same." Barry scooped up a last bite of stew and looked longingly at Barbara's half-eaten hearts, then he turned to Roger. "But how much of what she said is true?"

"Barry!"

"A father shouldn't know what's going on in his son's life?"

Roger handed his plate to Judson, who was tentatively clearing the table, being extra careful not to intervene, yet still taking his time. "James should be the one to tell you." He waited until Judson left before giving them the shortest version of events he could muster. "James and I had a brief romantic relationship. He was more interested in Sherry than me. She and I spent one drunken night together, which she took to mean more than it was, and which I did not encourage or foster in any way. As far as I know now, he's trying to work things out with her."

"That does sound complicated," said Barbara.

"You wanted your son to come to New York."

'It was no different in Ann Arbor. He was still picking the crazy ones. No offense, Roger."

"None taken. He didn't pick me."

James came back to the table, looking sheepish and tired. He leaned his weight on the back of a chair. "I'm going to take Sherry home. She's very upset. Dinner's all paid for. There's still dessert coming, so ..."

"Oh no," said Barry. "You don't have to do that."

Roger bit his tongue but not hard enough to stop him from speaking. "You're a glutton for punishment."

Between the heads of Barbara and Barry, Roger watched him go. It seemed he spent a lot of time watching James leave him and maybe it was time to just let him exit for good. He was trying to think of something funny to say to break the tension when Judson came with a tray of desserts in small parfait glasses.

"This is vanilla pudding with a strudel wafer." He set two servings at James and Sherry's empty places and padded away without further explanation.

Barry stirred his pudding. "Did Fu give up his theme?"

"I don't think so." Roger picked up the wafer, drizzled with a rope of viscous icing. "Look at the strudel."

"I'd say the pudding was also part of it." Barbara scooped up the runny mixture, more watery than pudding. "You don't think he actually..."

"No. Of course not. It's imitation." Roger lifted a spoonful to his mouth. "Definitely the best cum I've ever tasted."

"No. I can't." Barbara pushed her glass away.

Barry lifted his spoon. "Come on, honey. It wouldn't be the first time."

"Barry. Can we please leave our sex life out of the dinner conversation?"

"I don't see why. We've talked about everybody else's." He finished his pudding and grabbed James's serving. "This stuff is pretty good."

"Imitation often improves on the original," Roger said.

"So James said you've been working with him on his ... films." Barry scraped the bottom of his second glass of pudding. "Are they any good?"

"They really are. His puppets, I'm sure you've seen them, are exceptional. Lifelike, but also a bit weird, exaggerated, and hyper-real."

"I've always said his puppets were special," said Barbara.

"And to see them animated would be remarkable. If he can get the story right, the film he's working on will be as good as anything out there. Believe me, we've watched dozens of animated shorts in the last two months."

"So you think he can really make something of this?"

"Depends on what you mean by make." Roger dropped his spoon in his glass. "Grad. School? Sure. Money? Probably not. Hardly anyone makes money with art these days. I should know."

"But he could get a job at Pixar or one of the animated TV shows?" said Barbara.

"He might, if he improved his drawing skills. But that's a long shot."

"So he's going to be poor for the rest of his life?" said Barry.

"It's not so bad. I mean, it sucks, but it doesn't mean you can't be happy. It just means you can't do a lot of the middle-class things people take for granted. But a lot of middle-class people are miserable." Roger held up his hands in what he realized was James's big Y gesture. "Money is no guarantee of happiness. Which would you prefer your son to be?"

"Ideally both," said Barry.

Roger looked around the kitchen, at all the workers in white, busy making precocious meals for elevated palates with large pocketbooks. It was someone's version of an ideal world, but it wasn't his. After he walked James's parents to the subway and sent them on their way to Manhattan, he boarded his train in the opposite direction. He had things to think about other than James. His show was opening in a few days. There were props to acquire, and costumes to finalize, and he still had to talk Garrick out of a net of black babies for the drag ball. He sat down and let the gentle rocking of the train shake James out of his system.

18: Emotional Dildos

It was an hour before curtain and Warren was still unsure of his monologue. He slumped in his pink Polo shirt and gazed at the dressing room floor as if the lines were written in linoleum. Roger held the script in one hand and his heart in another. Phillip was reading over his shoulder, and was about to shout the answer.

"Don't tell me," Warren raised his hand. "And so it goes. Ease on down the road."

"*On* down the road," Phillip interjected. "No 'ease.' We're not doing *The Wiz*."

"Damn it." Warren pounded the makeup table.

"It doesn't matter," Roger said. "You know the beats. Play the objectives. You don't have to get every word right."

"But I want to get it right. They're your words."

"You've only had a short time to study. Think of this as a dress rehearsal with an audience."

"Come on," said Philip. "Let's do an Italian."

"Okay. But don't correct me. You barely know your own lines."

"I'm going to leave you two." Roger rolled his script in his hand and pointed at Philip. "I love the shirt. Where on earth did you find it?"

"In my own closet, of course." He modeled his orange silk shirt, printed with hula girls. "I used to give the most outrageous Hawaiian parties."

Erin was onstage with her headset and clipboard, taping off the beach lounger for act one.

"Did we get the new Leko?" Roger asked.

"It's coming tomorrow. Upstage right is going to be a little dark tonight."

"What about the sound guy?" Their soundboard operator had unexpectedly quit during dry tech and they'd been searching for a replacement ever since.

"I'm going to run sound tonight and show Kyle the ropes." She pointed to a skinny guy in the wings reading over a script.

"Any word on Garrick?"

"He's on his way. His rehearsal in Soho went over."

"You'd think it wouldn't be too much to ask a director to show up for his opening night."

Erin shrugged her unflappable shoulders. "Soho Rep. is a paying gig." She broke off a piece of tape from the roll on her wrist and taped the edge of the lounge chair. "Oh. Diego wants to see you."

Diego was the last person he wanted to see. Ever since their night of sexual healing, he had been making relationship-y overtures, hoping to reignite their toxic flame. But a playwright's job on opening night was to offer solace and assurance, so he went looking for the actor. He found him in the second dressing room, wearing a belted 1970s bathing suit and admiring himself in the mirror.

"What you think, Ruggero? Is better than Speedo, no?"

Roger examined the emerald green suit with its gold buckle. His eyes passing over Diego's flawless skin and eloquent muscles.

"I was thinking Luka would be worried about his bichito and so would wear something bigger. Like granny panties, but from the seventies."

"Good idea," Roger said. "Just clear it with Erin. But it works for me."

Diego put a palm on Roger's chest. "Last night, I was thinking about us: the playwright—the actor. All this time I am speaking your words. You know what effect they have? Your words in my mouth? Is like your words are inside me."

Roger puts both hands on Diego's shoulders and felt his cold marble beauty. "Let's talk about this later. After the show."

"Si. Si. The show must go on." He took another look in the mirror and stripped off the bathing suit. He stood naked and checked his ass for pimples. "We have this connection, Papi. The playwright and the actor: I am pregnant with your words." He put a hand on his stomach, presumably where Roger's words were waiting to be birthed—at least it wasn't his ass. Then he put on a jockstrap, and changed into his act one costume of stretchy shorts and a sleeveless tee. He turned around and let Roger absorb his no-panty line beauty. "What you think? Are we ready to make theatre babies?"

Hal and Vik came sauntering into the dressing room, trailing an odor that suggested they had either been outside smoking pot or a skunk was spraying pedestrians on Fourth Avenue. They regarded Diego in the mirror and fell into peals of barely smothered giggles.

"Come on, guys. We have forty minutes," Roger said. "Get dressed."

Hal sheepishly approached him, rolling his hands in his shirttail. "Are there any comps left for tonight? Some friends from my acting class want to come."

Roger knew the house wasn't full and so agreed. But he made sure to say loud enough for everyone to hear, "Remember. There are no comps for Friday and Saturday. We're sold out." He hoped this was true, though suspected it wasn't.

In the lobby, a few early birds milled about but no one he recognized. He went to the box office, which was just a table staffed by an intern with a metal cashbox, and gave her the names of Hal's friends. Outside, through the glass door, he saw James smoking on the sidewalk. A bubble of excitement rose in his chest. He'd taken the last three days off of work for tech and dress rehearsals, and hadn't seen James since the dinner at Fu Bar.

When he stepped outside, the hot air clung to his limbs like wet cement. He pushed through the humidity to the bottom of the steps. Traffic on Fourth Avenue roared by in rhythmic waves, and there was James, leaning on a mailbox, peering into the distance like some urban pioneer waiting for his delivery of organic kale. Beads of sweat dotted his t-shirt.

He stepped into James's line of vision. "So you're smoking now?"

"My one a day." He crushed the cigarette under his foot.

"I'm glad you came. I wasn't sure you would."

"I got Melissa to cover for me."

"So how's work?" Roger came a few steps closer and touched the hot metal of the mailbox.

"Slow. The regulars have all gone on vacation."

"And what have you been up to?"

It's been ..." James wanted to tell him that he was right about Sherry. That she didn't make him feel good, or special, or anything but insecure and filled with anxiety. And he wanted to say that in spite of that he was still in love with her, and ask his advice about what to do. But a chasm had opened up between them that seemed impossible to cross. "It's been ... weird."

"That's sometimes the best life has to offer."

James looked at the dirty wads of gum stuck to the pavement. "Yep."

"I thought you'd bring Sherry. She said she would come."

"Melissa wouldn't let her off. She said she'd come on the weekend."

"I guess that's one situation she couldn't manipulate to her advantage."

Roger's presence had altered the molecules in the air, burning through his fog of confusion. He always forced James to see the world in all its ruthless machinations. As much as he wanted to return to his state of innocent optimism, Roger had given him a cold electric eye: recording everything, mitigating nothing. He felt like a turtle with its belly exposed to the searing rays of the sun. After the disastrous night at Fu Bar, he took Sherry home and listened to her rail against Roger, and then Sean, and then lament her dead grandmother, all while he was troubleshooting her modem and hanging her Venetian blinds. He tried to support and validate, but he didn't exist in any real way for her. "She doesn't really like me," he admitted.

"Well, I didn't like you at first either but you have a way of growing on people."

"Like a staph infection."

"Hey. Staph infections are hard to get rid of."

James smiled and Roger moved aside to let three girls pass, who were laughing and drinking smoothies. A slight breeze danced in his hair and scattered it across his forehead. James could feel the difference—something tangible between them, a root connecting something. He could feel it tugging on him now, pulling him in. With Sherry, he only felt his own desire casting about for a place to land.

"Am I so hard to get rid of?"

Roger put his hands in his pockets. "You were for me."

James felt Roger's x-ray beams scanning him. Did this mean that Roger was no longer interested? Or was it a declaration that he still held hope? Either alternative gave James a flutter of apprehension in the pit of his stomach. In some way, it was easier to hide in Sherry's indifference. Roger illuminated the shadowed corners and forgotten crevices. He had expectations. He wanted things from James. It was much simpler to love someone who didn't see you—who didn't understand your hopes and desires. Even someone who regarded you with scorn. Consequently, you could hide behind that scorn and never be touched. You were the one touching them, adoring them, and their own indifference kept your authentic self at bay. To allow yourself to be loved was to be exposed—obligated.

Roger looked at the theatre door with his show's poster tacked to the front: Syd and Diego, Vik and Hal in bathing suits, frolicking on the beach—The United Colors of Gay Abandon. "I have to get back. I'll see you in the audience. Save me a seat on the aisle."

"Sure. Um, break a leg."

He hustled up the steps and entered the chilled theatre. The change in temperature sent goosebumps down his spine. Or maybe it was the effect of James: his raw insecurities in need of mending; his vulnerable ego seeking confirmation. He'd never had the desire to nurture someone before, and this new inclination put him off balance. Even more so since James was a nurturer who clearly wanted to nurture Sherry. Or some other needy, emotionally unstable woman. The surprising thing was that Roger was willing to accept second place. He could be the supporting actor in *The Story of James* if only James would let him have the part.

The lobby was starting to fill. A few acquaintances waved to Roger, and he gave them the hand signal for 'I'll see you after.' Over by the bio board, Garrick was inspecting his photo, wearing cargo shorts and a hooded sweatshirt.

Roger went over to him. "Glad to see you dressed for the occasion."

Garrick continued staring at the board. "They left out my credit at Second Stage."

"You want me to get the actors together for pre-show notes?"

"Sorry I'm so dowdy." He picked at his clothes. "I rushed right over from rehearsal. If it makes a difference, this is actually my dress hoodie. Pure Egyptian cotton." He held out an arm for Roger to feel.

Roger waited for Garrick to acknowledge his question, but he was too preoccupied with his bio.

"Did I tell you? Soho Rep. is letting me do Madame Ranyevskaya as Barbara Bush. A white wig and three strands of pearls."

"Sounds topical."

"Why don't I give notes after the show. I don't want to spook them."

Roger went into the auditorium, where the vertically challenged Noah was sweeping the stage with a push broom—the broom almost as tall as he. Erin was in the lighting booth running cues, casting patterns of sun-drenched light on the blue backdrop. She called down to him, "I'm opening the house in five minutes." He gave her a thumbs up. It was Garrick's idea to suggest a beach rather than recreate it: the sparse stage and stark blue vista evoking an emptiness that needed to be filled. The actors, with their beach towels and coolers, sunglasses and water bottles, would make the space come alive. Bringing with them lust and jealousy, despair and insecurity—the carry-on baggage of gay men everywhere.

Always, before an opening, a wave of exhaustion crashed over him, as if he would never again write another play. This one had been particularly difficult, and he could now let it go. Over the next couple of days, there would be tweaks and adjustments, but for the most part, his job was done. He was fully dilated, and the final push had come.

Backstage, Syd, Hal, and Vik were in costumes, doing vocal warm-ups: Syd mouthing "mother-butter" in rapid-fire succession, Hal and Vik panting on their diaphragms. In the first dressing room, Warren and Philip ran lines. Roger retrieved some envelopes from his satchel and placed them at each actor's station. The envelopes contained cards with personal notes of thanks and encouragement.

"This is my last show," Warren said. "Just so you know. I'm moving to Myrtle Beach."

"I told him he's a fool," said Philip.

Warren periodically made threats to leave New York, but the matter-of-fact dullness in his voice told Roger that this time it might be true. He picked up a tube of eyeliner from the floor. "There's no theatre in Myrtle Beach."

"I'm through with theatre." Warren swatted at the air. "I'm taking up miniature golf."

"You've been acting for over thirty years."

"And look what it's got me." He raised his hands to indicate the cinder blocks in the dressing room.

"No offense," said Philip.

Roger sighed. "We're making theatre."

Warren looked in the mirror and lifted his heavy jowls with his fingers. "My face used to have some distinction. Now it's just a blob of flesh. I've surpassed my face."

Roger recalled Warren's previous roles in his plays: a celibate watchmaker, an aphasic voyeur, a letch. It was hard to imagine not being able to go out for drinks and hear him rail at the Bush administration, or describe his latest unrequited go-go boy romance. "Let's see how you feel after the run." He put a hand on Warren's shoulder. "Break a leg. Not a hip."

The second dressing room was empty and he placed envelopes at Diego, Hal, and Vik's stations. He'd been in many dressing rooms over the years. At college, the dressing rooms for the theatre had melamine counters with pull-out drawers and a full display of bulbs around the mirrors. Some off-off-Broadway theatres didn't even have dressing rooms; the actors put on make-up in the restrooms and changed in dark hallways. Others had small rooms with wooden dressers attached with mirrors and rickety garment racks for clothes. This room wasn't the worst. He rubbed a finger across the particle board folding tables and walked around the metal chairs, their backs threatening to topple over with the shirts and pants of the actors. The mirrors were stuck to the cinder blocks with some kind of adhesive that leaked out the sides. This was enough. For now. But in another twenty years, would he too be ready to give it all up for sunshine and miniature golf?

Diego came rushing in, walking funny, with his shorts unbuttoned. "Oh. Ruggero. Thank God is you. I cannot go on the stage." He took Roger's hand and pulled him into the bathroom. He closed and locked the door, and turned to him with a grave expression. "You must promise me not to laugh."

"What are you talking about?"

"This is no joke, Papi." He stooped slightly and winced.

"Are you getting nervous?" Roger put both hands on his shoulders. "Don't worry. You're an exceptional actor. You're fantastic in this part."

"I need you to help with something." Diego looked at the rusty sink, the toilet with the cracked lid, the walls with their smattering of dirty words and crude penises. "I lose something."

Roger backed himself against a paper towel dispenser to gain a few inches of distance. "We go on in ten minutes. Whatever it is, it can wait."

"A chingar su madre." He pressed his hand against the wall. "I told you.

I cannot go on the stage like this."

"Okay. Okay. What is it?"

"Is ... is ... embarrassing." Diego took a deep breath and regarded Roger through the shielded safety of his dark lashes. "A dildo."

"For Christsakes. I'm not looking for one of your sex toys ten minutes before curtain."

Diego tugged down his shorts and gave a sheepish smile.

"Oh my God. You didn't?"

"I need something to calm down. Is better than taking Valium, no?"

"Valium doesn't get stuck in your throat."

"Is my ritual before a show. Only this time, I put my leg up on the toilet ... and then I made a sneeze and schoop—is gone. I did not know my culo could do that. And now I cannot reach to get it out." Diego looked at him like a helpless baby with a full diaper. An analogy more apt than Roger wanted to admit.

"All right, let me have a look."

Diego peeled off his shorts and bent over. At least his jockstrap kept some level of modesty between them. It wasn't as if Roger had never put his fingers inside Diego before, but seeing his tender pinkness exposed under the harsh fluorescent light stirred something. He would have to proceed with strict professionalism.

Diego pointed to a small bag on the back of the toilet that contained a bottle of lubricant. His ass looked smooth as a baby's bum, if the baby had been doing a hundred squats a day and was on a low-carb, high-protein diet. A few stray hairs marred its pristine bronze surface, and, for the first time, Roger noticed a trace of a tan line below his lower back. It was odd how a body could be an inspiration at one time and a mere bag of meat at another.

Diego bounced on his legs. "Get it out, Papi. Please."

He lubed up and went inside but only bumped the dildo and pushed it further in. "Try to relax." He circled his fingers and moved them around. He felt the object but couldn't get a purchase on it. Diego braced himself against the toilet tank and rotated his hips, making little humming sounds.

"This is a medical procedure. You're not supposed to be enjoying it."

"Si, doctor. Si."

Roger couldn't deny an inadvertent thrill himself, and started feeling a bit tender toward Diego. He wondered if pleasant stimuli always came with emotional attachment. Humans felt something good and immediately associated it with an emotion. We see a beautiful ass and want to fuck it; if the experience is pleasurable, we tell ourselves we're in love. But in reality, our bodies are just finding a way to continue the pleasure. We call it love, but it's just nerve endings and synapses encouraging pleasure, which is nature's way of securing procreation.

He heard Erin down the hall giving the five-minute call and asking about Diego. Then a pounding on the door. "Come on. Open up. I have to pee." It was Syd.

"We're busy," Roger called out. "Use the bathroom in the lobby."

Syd pounded again. "This is unprofessional. I'm going to report you to Actors' Equity."

Roger leaned in and whispered in Diego's ear, "Maybe he can help. He's a nurse."

"That cabrón? Don't let him in."

Syd pounded harder. "I'm going to sue you for urinary tract obstruction."

"Just a minute." Roger reached over and unlocked the door.

Syd threw open the door. He took one look at Roger's greasy fingers hovering over Diego's bare butt and said, "When you said we'd be receiving digital notes, I had no idea."

"Mamabicho."

"He has something stuck ..."

"I don't want to hear it. I've been holding it in for half an hour." He pushed them aside and peed a loud stream into the toilet. Afterward, he shook his member, dangerously close to Diego's face.

"Puñeta! Watch your piss."

"Nectar of the Gods, honey."

"Syd. Can you help?" Roger spread Diego's cheek. "It's a dildo."

"You open up that can of worms and half the dicks in Puerto Rico will come spilling out."

"Vete a la mierda."

"Come on. You must have had experience with this."

Syd rubbed his bald head and sighed. "You need to lube him up good, and then have him squat down and press on his stomach."

They got Diego into a half squat, bracing his hands on the toilet. Syd reached under Diego's shirt and started rubbing his stomach. "Okay, now squat down, Casanova." He turned to Roger. "Give me some of that lube."

"No," cried Diego. "Let Ruggero do it."

Roger put a hand on Diego's back. "He's the professional. Maybe we should let him."

"No. Only you. Only you can touch me there."

"This is no time to play hard to get," said Syd. "You've had more fingers inside you than the bowling balls at Melody Lanes."

"Puta negra."

"Okay. Okay. I'll do it," Roger said. He put more lube on his fingers and made slow circular motions. It was uncomfortable doing this in front of Syd, but they worked like a team of doctors with a critical patient. Syd palpated the stomach and Roger stretched the anus, while Diego panted and groaned like a dumb animal.

"Now bear down," Syd said.

Diego put his hands on his knees and squatted lower. "Is not coming. My legs are getting tired."

"Pretend you're Julianne Moore in *Nine Months*," said Roger. "And you'll never win the love of Hugh Grant if you don't push out this baby and change Hugh's playboy ways."

Diego squinched up his face and pushed some more, then finally stood and shook out his legs. "I can't do this. We have to cancel the show. I go to emergency room."

"We are not canceling the show," said Syd. "All my friends from the hospital are coming. If I have to operate on you myself, that thing is coming out." He pushed Diego back into a squatting position and started rubbing his stomach. "Roger, get in there. And this time twist with your hand." Roger reinserted his fingers and pretended he was Queen Elizabeth, waving to the crowd.

"Oh, my." Philip came to the door. "No one told me there was going to be an orgy in the bathroom. I would've brought my carnival mask."

Hal followed behind. "Is this one of those new trust exercises?"

Diego yelled. "Iros todos a la mierda!"

"Guys, please," Roger said. "Give us some privacy. I'll explain later."

"Stop looking at my culo, pervertidos."

"What's going on?" Warren called from the hallway. "Why's everyone standing in the bathroom?"

"Roger is finger-banging Diego while Syd holds him down," Hal explained.

Philip turned to Warren. "And you wanted to quit the theatre."

Erin came down the hallway talking on her headset. "We're holding for five. Has anybody found Diego?" When she got to the bathroom, she pushed past Hal and Philip and confronted Diego's bare ass with Roger's fingers inside it. "Ah, Diego. There you are."

Roger tried to explain what was happening but she held up her hand. "I don't want to know. Just tell me when you're ready to go on." She spoke into the headset. "We're holding for ten." She hurried from the bathroom, her face much redder than when she came in.

"Push," Syd yelled, and pressed his palm into Diego's stomach.

Diego bore down and grunted.

"It's crowning," said Roger. "I can almost get it." He made an attempt, but it slipped through his fingers.

"Push. Push. Push," cried the animated crowd.

"This is like a gay nativity," said Hal.

"What do you think will come out?" said Warren. "A Cher doll?

"I'm hoping for a golden egg," said Philip.

"Let's just hope it's not a brown speckled one."

"I got it," cried Roger. He pulled out a slender purple tube.

Syd flourished his hand and made a bow. "And unto us a dildo was born."

Warren rolled his eyes. "I've seen bigger dildos at cocktail parties attached to cubes of cheese."

Diego rose on wobbly legs and did some standing quad stretches, as if he had accomplished nothing more unusual than running a sprint.

"Okay, everybody," Roger said. "Let's get ready. We have a show to do."

"After that," said Philip, "any other drama will be a letdown."

The cast dispersed, wandering back to their dressing rooms, full of mirth and conjecture, leaving Roger and Diego alone.

"Thank you, Baby." Diego rubbed Roger's arm. "That was wild. You see how they all look at my culo?"

"You all right?"

"Me? Oh yes. I am very relax." He took some toilet paper and wiped off the excess lube, then stumbled over to Roger and laid his head on his shoulder. Roger couldn't help but wrap his arms around him. He stroked the musculature of Diego's back. Ran his fingers down the hollow of his spine. He felt a distant stirring, but at the same time he knew that this was just nerve endings and synapses firing. He didn't need to make it into anything more. Roger kissed him gently on the cheek, like a stranger, like a friend. Like someone who knew what he wanted.

"Fix your makeup and get ready. The show must go on." He swatted his ass.

Diego peered at him through his thick lashes. "The playwright and the actor." He gave Roger's crotch a playful squeeze, and then picked up his shorts and sauntered into the hall naked.

"Take a good look, pervertidos. You won't see a better ass in your lives."

Roger went to the sink to wash up. The cold water turned his hands pink. The liquid soap smelled like chemical roses, and he breathed in its sterile scent. He lathered and rinsed until the water ran clear of bubbles, and his hands went numb from the cold. He rinsed the dildo as well, which was surprisingly clean considering all it had been through. In spite of the fuss, it was just a plastic tube, several inches long and not very thick. It held no answers and made no avowals. He found it disconcerting that this thing could replace human interaction. People wanted sensation without emotion. But for Roger, sex without emotion always felt empty. And yet, he spent a good deal of time pursuing men like Diego, and James, who couldn't return his affection. Men who allowed him to love without any of the risks. They were, in effect, emotional dildos.

He ran wet hands through his hair and blotted his face with a paper towel. As he was leaving, he noticed the dildo defiantly standing on the sink, damp and glistening in the blue fluorescent light, unscathed by the tribulations of man. He picked it up and tossed it into the garbage.

At a quarter past eight, James wondered if something had gone wrong backstage. The audience was chatting happily, some even standing in the aisle; he figured tardiness must be protocol for small theatres. Roger himself was always late, so why should his plays be any different? The house was mostly full and he couldn't help feeling excited. Roger had carved out a space for himself. People were going to experience his vision. He managed to make his art and get people interested in viewing it. No small accomplishment when there were so many other entertainments competing for people's time. James was curious to immerse himself in Roger's mind, and witness the progress from rehearsal to production. At least, he hoped it was progress. If the show was awful, he needed to think of something comforting to say.

No sooner had this thought come into his head than Roger plopped down next to him with a heavy sigh.

"Is everything okay?" he asked.

"Long story."

He felt the weight of Roger in the next seat, the vibrations of his movements: fingers tapping, legs jouncing, his shoulders brushing against him. He gave him a supportive smile. He wanted to let Roger know that he cared. Roger had made *his* feelings known, and James didn't want to be withholding. It was a comfort to know that someone cared about you. Even someone as cynical and judgmental as Roger. Especially someone as accomplished and talented as Roger. He recalled his tomcat scent. The way he kissed his stretch marks. And rubbed his head. And made him laugh. And discussed his film. He made him feel seen. And he was grateful.

"I wanted to tell you that I missed you," James said. "These past few days."

Roger smiled and concentrated on the stage.

The lights started to dim, and James surged with excitement. Perhaps this was what kept Roger interested in theatre—this chance every night to recreate experience. This going into the darkness and waking up some place else. Was it a dream? An imagination? An alternate reality? It happened fast and continued to happen. The world changes in the blink of an eye. Every time we closed our eyes, the lights dimmed. And when we opened them again, we could be someone else. In a different place. Transformed. Every blink was an opportunity to start again. Our own personal theatre happening every second of our lives.

He reached over and grabbed Roger's hand. "Your hand is wet," he whispered.

"Sorry." Roger tried to remove it, but James held on, giving him a little squeeze.

Music began to play.

As the lights came down, their fingers entwined, creating sparks of electricity and warmth. Their blood pumped. Their skin tingled. Their palms sweated. They were held hostage by a battery of sensations and desires beyond their control. So they sat. In the dark. Joined together. Waiting for the show to begin.

Acknowledgements

For me, this means acknowledging the good and the bad. So with that in mind, I want to acknowledge my mother, who was so bewildered by my writing that she maintained until the day she died that she didn't understand what I was doing with my life. My father, who, on the few occasions I saw him, accused me of being a sissy and threatened to beat my ass. My grandmother and extended family who repeatedly said, "Why you always have your nose in a book? You're missing out on your childhood." I want to acknowledge my ex boyfriend, who after ten years of watching my writing receive little recognition and scant remuneration said, "When are you going to give up this pipe dream?" I want to acknowledge the members of my writing group, who told me after two years of working on this novel, "Better put this away. It's not working." I want to acknowledge Agent #1 who said, "Your characters are too unlikable and the tone is too ironic and distant." I want to acknowledge Agent #2 who said, "There's no moment of grace and your worldview is too bleak." I want to acknowledge Agent #3 who said, "You have three strikes against you: you're middle-aged, your writing is niche, and you don't have enough new material in the pipeline." And I have to acknowledge the 335 agents who passed on or never responded to my queries. And the twenty small presses that also rejected this novel.

This only makes acknowledging the good all the more sweet. At the top of the list is my editor, Naomi Rosenblatt. She understood my humor, appreciated my worldview, and wasn't afraid to take a risk.

I have to acknowledge the editors of the literary journals who accepted my stories, five of which eventually evolved into sections of this novel. Their encouragement and recognition kept me going over the years; sometimes it was all that I had. If you're an editor at a literary journal, please know that you are making a difference. With much gratitude and many thanks to: Luis Valadez, Jeff Brewer, Dave Clapper, J.T. Barbarse, Thom Bassett, Robert Owen Butler, Eric Primm, Vivian Dorsel, R.T. Smith, Leslie Pietrzyk, Richard Mathews, Noah Milligan, Chris Boucher, Anthony Varallo, Christina Thompson, Steve Campbell, Frances Badgett, Robert Paul Cesaretti, Anil Menon, and Jonathan Bull.

I have to acknowledge my teachers: Joshua Henkin, Andre Dubus III, Antonya Nelson, Steve Almond, Josh Weil, Jenny Offill, Joy Williams, and Ellen Tremper. Writing might not be able to be taught but it can certainly be improved. Through their guidance, I learned a lot and improved a lot.

I want to acknowledge my faithful readers and friends, who suffered through my many drafts and sundry anxieties: Edmund White, Jessamyn Hope, Douglas Silver, Stefani Nellen, Ann Amodeo, George Blecher, Leigh Feldman, and Genevieve Gagne-Hawes.

And, a big thank you to my partner Ken, who is steadfast and loving, and one of the best copy editors around.

www.ingramcontent.com/pod-product-compliance
Lightning Source LLC
Chambersburg PA
CBHW030645020726
47493CB00006B/1886